STOCKTON-ON-TEES BOROUGH LIBRARIES

A FINE WILL BE CHARGED IF THE BOOK IS
RETURNED AFTER THE DATE ON WHICH IT IS DUE

This book should be returned on or before the latest date
stamped. It may, if not required by another reader, be
renewed on request for a further loan period.

Welcome to the world of St Piran's Hospital

Next to the rugged shores of Penhally Bay
lies the picturesque Cornish town of St Piran, where
you'll find a bustling hospital famed for the dedication,
talent and passion of its staff—on and off the wards!

Under the warmth of the Cornish sun Italian doctors,
heart surgeons, and playboy princes discover that
romance blossoms in the most unlikely of places...

You'll also meet the devilishly handsome
Dr Josh O'Hara and the beautiful, fragile
Megan Phillips…and discover the secret
that tore these star-crossed lovers apart.

Turn the page to step into St Piran's
—where every drama has a dreamy doctor…
and a happy ending.

ST PIRAN'S: THE WEDDING OF THE YEAR

BY
CAROLINE ANDERSON

First published in Great Britain 2010
Harlequin Mills & Boon Limited,
Eton House, 18-24 Paradise Road, Richmond, Surrey TW9 1SR

© Harlequin Books S.A. 2010

Special thanks and acknowledgement are given to Caroline Anderson for her contribution to the *St Piran's Hospital* series

ISBN: 978 0 263 87932 2

Harlequin Mills & Boon policy is to use papers that are natural, renewable and recyclable products and made from wood grown in sustainable forests. The logging and manufacturing process conform to the legal environmental regulations of the country of origin.

Printed and bound in Spain
by Litografia Rosés, S.A., Barcelona

Dear Reader

When my editor initially approached me about writing some of the books in the *Penhally* series, I said that if Nick and Kate were to have their own story, *I wanted it*! Well, you know the saying: be careful what you wish for... And here it is, right at the beginning of a stunning new continuity series based in Penhally's nearest hospital, *St Piran's*.

Kate was easy. Lovely, straightforward woman, with great compassion, devotion to her child, and the guilt that all women feel about keeping the peace at any price. Nick, on the other hand—well, Nick was Nick. Stubborn, obdurate, opinionated, demanding, contrary, dogmatic and passionate. And tortured. Tortured by his guilt, tortured by the past, unable to see a future with the woman he'd loved all his life.

Add into the mix his children—three of them all past heroes or heroines of the series, and the youngest, Jem, as yet unacknowledged—and it all gets a whole lot more complicated! But Kate loves Nick, has always loved him, and she sees the good in him, the decent, hard-working and still deeply attractive man who is struggling to find the way forward with the boy he now has to acknowledge is his own, and the woman who has his heart. And between them they find the way.

It's been a long and hard journey for them, and I hope it gives you the reader as much joy to see their resolution as it gave me to write it.

With love

Caroline

CHAPTER ONE

'OH, DR TREMAYNE, Kate left this for you.'

Nick stopped by the reception desk and took the sealed envelope from Sue, glancing at it in puzzlement. How odd...

'Is she still here?'

'Yes, I think so, but she's about to go. She has to pick Jem up from holiday club. Do you want me to find her?'

'No, it's OK.' He gave the envelope another glance, and with a curt nod to his patients as he passed them, he went into his room, closed the door and slit the flap open with his forefinger as he dropped into his chair behind the desk.

He drew out a single sheet, handwritten in her elegant, decisive script, and as he smoothed it out with the flat of his hand he stared at it in disbelief.

Monday 12 April

Dear Nick,

I've written to the PCT, and will tell Chloe and all my other colleagues and friends over the next few days, but I wanted you to know first that I've decided to leave Penhally and my post here as midwife. I'm putting my house on the market and Jem and I will move away from here over the summer, in time for him to start secondary school in September. It's the right time to go, as far as his education is concerned, and I thought we could move closer to my mother in Bristol.

I'll miss the practice and all the people in it, but it's time for us to move on. There's nothing here for me any more.

I would just like to thank you for all the support and kindness you've shown to me over the years.

Yours,

Kate

Stunned, Nick scanned the letter again. She couldn't leave. Where the hell did she think she was going? And taking Jem away...

He pushed back his chair and crossed to the window, pressing his hand against the cold glass and staring out numbly at the sudden squall that had sprung up. The rain was streaming down the pane in torrents, bouncing off the roofs of the cars outside, and people were running for cover.

Including Kate. She wrenched open her car door, and as she got in her head lifted and she met his eyes, holding them for a moment through the lashing rain, then with a tiny shake of her head she slammed the door, started the engine and drove away, leaving him staring after her.

He sucked in a harsh, juddering breath and turned

on his heel, moving away from the window before he put his fist through it in frustration. The letter was lying there on the desk, taunting him, and he crumpled it up and hurled it at the bin. It missed, and he picked it up, crushing it tighter in his fist.

Why? Why now, of all times, when he'd begun to feel there might be a chance…?

There was a tap on the door and old Doris Trefussis popped her head round and came in with a smile.

'Cup of tea for you, Dr T., before you start,' she said brightly, 'and a couple of Hazel's fairings. I saved them for you.'

'Thank you, Doris,' he said tightly, and held his breath until she'd shut the door. The last thing he could do was eat, it would choke him, but there was no way he could tell Doris that. She'd kill him if he didn't eat Hazel's biscuits, he thought, dropping down into his chair and dragging his hands over his face before flattening out the crumpled page and reading the letter again.

It didn't make any more sense the second time. Or the third.

Maybe the tea would help.

He cradled the mug in his hand and stared blankly out of the window. It was slack water, the boats in the harbour swinging every which way in the squalling wind. He knew the feeling. He'd been swinging at anchor himself ever since Annabel had died five years ago, unsure of what the future held, of which way the tide would turn.

For a time he'd thought Kate was getting married, but then he'd heard on the grapevine that it was over now, and with Rob out of the way, he'd thought that maybe now, with both of them widowed—but then this, out of the blue. He'd never expected this. Never expected that she'd go...

She couldn't leave. She couldn't. She'd lived in Penhally for ever, her entire life. He'd known her since she was twelve, dated her when she was fifteen and he was seventeen, left her at eighteen to go to university, intending to come back for her—but then he'd met Annabel, and everything had changed.

Except Kate. She'd stayed the same—sweet, funny, kind—but those soft brown eyes had held reproach and disappointment ever since. Or maybe he'd imagined it, but all he knew was that every time she looked at him, he felt guilt.

He shut his eyes and sighed. God knows, there was enough to feel guilty about in the past thirty-odd years.

He folded the crumpled letter and put it in his pocket. He could go round there this evening, see if there wasn't a way he could convince her to stay—but there was no point, he thought grimly. She'd made up her mind, and maybe it really was for the best.

He'd miss them both, but especially Kate—Kate he'd depended on for her kindness and common sense when he'd been in turmoil, Kate who'd managed the practice for years before she'd returned to midwifery and become a firm favourite with the mums.

Kate he'd loved, all those years ago.

Had loved, and lost, because of his own stupid fault. His chest felt tight just thinking about it, and he stared out of the window again, trying to imagine the practice without her. His life, without her. She couldn't go. He couldn't let her.

There's nothing here for me any more.

Particularly not an emotionally bankrupt old fool like him. He had no choice but to let her go. No power to do anything else. The least he could do was do it with dignity.

He pushed the tea aside, strode to the door and yanked it open. 'Mr Pengelly, would you come in, please?'

He tried to concentrate, tried to give the man his attention while he described his symptoms, but the letter was burning a hole in his pocket and judging by the feel of it the acid was doing the same thing to his stomach.

'Sump'n's goin' on out there,' Mr Pengelly said, jerking his head at the window.

'Hmm?' Nick dragged his mind back into the room and listened, and then he heard it over the rain and his clamouring thoughts. The sirens wailing, the rapid footsteps as Oliver Fawkner ran to his car outside Nick's window and shot off up the road. He was on call today, acting as First Responder in the event of a serious accident as part of those duties, and he'd obviously been called out to the emergency.

'The sirens,' Mr Pengelly said unnecessarily.

'Yes,' Nick said, blanking it out of his mind as he examined him, weighed him, checked his blood pressure, listened to his chest. He was a heart attack waiting to happen, and if he had one, it wouldn't be Nick's fault. He'd given him sage advice for years, and it was time to lay it on the line.

More sirens. It was a big one, he thought, and eyed his patient firmly. 'Right, Mr Pengelly, I think we need to have another look at your lifestyle. You're overweight, you're unfit, you don't take your drugs regularly, and then you come in and tell me you have chest pain, but you don't seem to be prepared to do anything about it and if you go on like this you'll kill yourself. We need to check your cholesterol level again. It was high last time, and you're still smoking, aren't you?'

'Ah, but I've cut down, Doc.'

'To what?'

He hesitated, then under Nick's uncompromising stare he sighed and came clean. 'Only twenty a day now.'

Only? 'That's twenty too many. Make an appointment on your way out for a fasting cholesterol test first thing one morning, as soon as possible, and then we'll review it, but you need to start exercising and attend the stop smoking clinic—'

'Must be a big'un. There's the chopper coming now,' he said, gesturing at the window again, just as the phone rang, and Nick frowned and reached for it, irritated that the man didn't seem to be paying any attention.

'Excuse me a moment—Tremayne.'

'It's Sue. I'm sorry to disturb you, but Oliver rang. Kate's had an accident, and they're airlifting Jem to hospital. He said you'd better get over to St Piran's.'

He felt the blood drain from his head, and sucked in a breath. 'What's wrong—? How bad is he—is he—?'

'Head and pelvis, he said, but he was quite insistent that you should go, Nick. Kate's going to need you. And he said to tell her not to worry about the dog, he'll sort it.'

The dog? He mumbled something and cradled the phone with a clatter. 'Um—Mr Pengelly, I have to go. I'm sorry. Make the appointment, if you wouldn't mind, and we'll talk again when we get the results.'

'So—do you want those biscuits?'

The man was a lost cause. 'Help yourself,' he growled,

and got to his feet and went out to Reception, his legs moving automatically. 'Right, Mr Pengelly needs a fasting cholesterol ASAP with a follow-up appointment,' he told Sue. 'I'm going to St Piran's—can you get Sam to cover my surgery for me?'

And without waiting for her reply, without even pausing to pick up his coat, he strode briskly out of the doors into the lashing rain.

The drive to St Piran nearly killed him.

His stomach was in knots, adrenaline pouring through his veins, and with no one to distract him his thoughts were free to run over all the things that could be wrong, and all the things that could go wrong as a consequence.

The list was hideous, and just thinking it all through made him want to retch.

He called Ben's mobile from his hands-free. His son-in-law would be there today, in A and E, and he'd give him advance warning. He drummed his fingers on the steering-wheel, waiting impatiently for Ben to answer, and when he did, Ben got there before he did.

'It's OK, Nick, we're on it. I can hear the helicopter now, we're going out to meet it. Just drive carefully and meet us in Resus. I'll get someone to look out for you.'

'OK. Ben—check Kate over, could you? Or get someone to? She was in the car with Jem and I don't know if she's hurt. And tell her I'm coming.'

'Sure. Got to go. See you soon.'

The phone went dead, and he sliced through the traffic and in through the hospital gates, abandoned the car on the kerb and ran in. It would probably be clamped but he'd worry about that later.

He was met at the door and ushered straight through to Resus, and as the door swung open he froze for a second. He was assailed by memories, his emotions suddenly in turmoil. He couldn't do this. Not here, not this room, of all the places.

He had to. On autopilot, he looked around at a scene of organised chaos, Ben snapping out orders and the team anticipating him like a well-oiled machine. A machine that held the boy's life in its hands?

The same machine—and the same man—that had held Annabel's—and lost it?

Dear God.

They were cutting Jem's clothes off, slicing through the sodden fabric, peeling it away so they could get a proper look at him, talking reassuringly to him all the time, and it could have been any of his boys lying there, all skinny limbs and ribcage with only the pelvic binder left to hold his pelvis stable.

Don't let him die. Please, God, don't let him die…

'OK, let's cross-match for ten units and get five units of O-neg to start with, and some packed cells, and let's get some X-rays—a full trauma series, starting with head, spine and pelvis. What about pain relief?' Ben asked. 'What's he had already?'

'Three milligrams of morphine IV, but his blood pressure's dropping. Want to try—?'

The voices washed around Nick, only two things really registering. One was the bruised little face scarcely visible under the mask, most of Jem's head concealed by the padding of the neck brace; the other was Kate, sodden and bedraggled, standing a few feet away watching as they worked on her little son, her eyes wide with fear, her lips moving soundlessly.

Praying?

Probably. There was little else to do. He crossed over to her, and she gripped his hand and gave a tiny sob.

He squeezed back. He wanted to hug her, to say, 'It's OK, it's going to be all right,' but he wasn't sure it was, wasn't sure she'd want him to hold her, wasn't sure she'd believe him—and anyway his tongue was glued to the roof of his mouth.

He freed it with effort and concentrated on the facts. 'Have you done a FAST exam?' he asked, sticking to something safe, and Ben shook his head.

'No, we're just about to.'

'Fast?' Kate murmured.

'Ultrasound, basically,' Ben said. 'It might show what's going on.'

Such as free fluid in the abdomen. Blood, most particularly, from torn arteries, sheered bone ends...

Nick felt the bile welling again, and dragged his free hand over his face.

The radiographer was setting up the X-ray machine as Ben quickly ran the head of the ultrasound wand over Jeremiah's thin, slightly distended abdomen, and Nick watched the screen, wincing at the image. Free fluid. Lots of it. Damn.

They were handed lead aprons. Ben must have realised they wouldn't leave, and as the X-rays appeared on the computer screen a few moments later, Nick sucked in a breath.

Even across the room, he could see the fractures on the left side of Jeremiah's pelvis, the bony ends displaced, the damage they'd caused all too easily imaginable.

'OK, this needs fixation before he goes anywhere,' Ben was saying. 'Are the orthos free?'

'No. They're just finishing off so they're ready for him,' the charge nurse said. 'Want me to get Josh?'

'Please—and fast-bleep the anaesthetist, we need to get on with this.'

'Who's Josh?' Kate asked, her face white.

'New guy,' Ben said. 'He's good—don't worry, I've known him for years. He's done a lot of this—he's a bit of a trauma specialist. But we need to get this pelvis rigid before we move Jem and he needs to go straight up to Theatre if we can't stop the bleeding here. You need to sign a consent form for that. Why don't you do that and then get a cup of tea—?'

'His pressure's dropping.'

Ben frowned and bent over the boy. 'OK, Jem, stay with us, come on, you're doing really well. Let's give him a 250-mil bolus of O-neg and we'll see if he stabilises. Kate, I don't suppose you know his blood group, do you?'

She shook her head, her face terrified. 'No. No idea. I'm O-positive, if that helps.'

'Cross-match results are up,' someone said. 'He's B-negative.'

B-negative? Through the roaring in his head, Nick heard Ben sigh harshly. 'Damn. We used all our stock this morning. I don't know if it's been replaced yet.' Ben's eyes flicked questioningly to Nick's, and he swallowed.

'I'm B-negative,' he confirmed, the last traces of doubt obliterated from his mind with this one small fact. 'So's Jack. We're both regular donors.'

Ben didn't miss a beat. 'OK. Nick, contact Jack

and ask him if he's able to donate today, then we'll get Haematology to sort it. That'll give us two units, and we'll salvage his own in Theatre and recycle it and give it back to him, and we can use O-neg if necessary until we get more, but if we get the ex-fix on, the bleeding may well stop anyway.'

Or it might not. 'You can take two units from me,' Nick said, and he saw Kate turn towards him, heard the hitch in her breath as she waited for what he was going to say. Not that. Not out loud, but he met his son-in-law's eyes squarely, and Ben gave a brief, imperceptible nod of understanding.

A door flapped shut behind him, and Nick turned and looked straight into Jack's eyes.

'Kate, Dad—hi. What's going on?' he asked. 'I was out in cubicles—they said Jem was in here.'

'He is,' Nick said, and Jack looked at the X-rays, winced and glanced down at the child on the trolley.

'Hell,' he said softly. 'Poor little chap. What's the damage?' he asked Ben.

'Pelvis, for sure, and maybe abdominal and head injuries. We were about to contact you,' Ben told him. 'We're short of B-negative. Have you given blood recently?'

'Um—about three months ago? No—just before Christmas, so nearly four.' Jack sighed harshly and glanced at the clock. 'I've got a meeting I should be at and I'm already late. Can you call me if you definitely need me?'

'We definitely need you,' Nick said, his voice deliberately low so that only Jack could hear. 'He's your brother, Jack,' he added, and watched the disbelief like a shockwave on his firstborn son's face.

'Jeremiah? Kate's son? He's—?'

'My son,' Nick said softly, voicing the words in public for the first time, and beside him he felt Kate squeeze his hand. His words hung in the air between them for a moment, and Jack's face was suddenly expressionless.

'Well, we'd better roll our sleeves up, then, hadn't we?' he said after a long pause, and Nick let out his breath on a shuddering little sigh.

'Thanks,' he said, but Jack turned to him, his blue eyes like chips of ice.

'Don't thank me,' he said, his voice deadly quiet. 'I'm not doing it for you.' He turned back to Ben. 'Give me five minutes. I just want to make a couple of calls.'

'That's fine, we're using O-neg for now. You've got a little while. We'll save cross-matched blood until he's stable.'

He nodded curtly and walked out, slapping the door out of the way with his hand, and Nick closed his eyes and swallowed. He'd known it would come out at some time, he'd known it would be hard, but like this, with Jeremiah's life hanging in the balance—

'OK, what have we got?' a new voice asked, and a man strode in, a man they'd never seen before, with a soft, lilting Irish brogue and that dangerous blend of rakish charm and lethal good looks that would leave trouble in his wake.

Nick knew all about that. He'd been like that in his youth; it had gone to his head, and look where it had got him. He almost felt sorry for Josh O'Hara, the new A and E consultant, but maybe this man wouldn't make the same mistakes he had. He'd have to try hard to do worse.

He was bending over Jeremiah now, smiling at him. 'Hello, Jem, I'm Josh. I'm just going to have a quick look at your X-rays, and then we're going to send you to sleep and fix you, OK? That'll take away a lot of the pain for when you wake up.'

Jem made a feeble sound of assent, and beside him Nick heard Kate give a little sob.

Nick tightened his grip on her fingers. 'It's all right,' he said, reassuring himself as much as her. 'He'll be all right,' he repeated, and hoped to God it wasn't a lie.

Josh looked up and met their eyes. 'Are you the parents?'

They nodded, the irony of it striking Nick like a hammer blow. Of all the ways—

'OK. You need to sign a consent form, and then I think someone needs to take you to the relatives' room and give you a cup of tea.'

'I don't want a cup of tea, I want to be here with my son!' Kate said adamantly. 'I'm a midwife, you don't need to mollycoddle me.'

'We don't need to scrape you off the floor, either, and it's a sterile procedure. You can stay till he's out, then you go.'

Nick put an arm round her rigid shoulders, squeezing them gently. 'He's right,' he said, fighting his instinct to argue, to stay. 'You shouldn't be here. Not for that. And someone needs to take a look at you.'

'I'm fine.'

'We don't know that. Nick's right, you need your neck checked, Kate,' Ben said gently, lifting his head to meet her eyes. 'And your feet. I gather they were trapped. Let us sort Jem out, and then while he's in Theatre I'll come and have a look at you, hmm? And in the meantime, go and have something hot to drink, and some biscuits or something. You're in shock.'

She'd signed the form by the time the anaesthetist arrived a minute later, and Kate clung to her son's hand, pressing it to her heart and murmuring softly to him as he drifted off, then Nick ushered her away, leading her out of the room and down the corridor to the relatives' room, his reluctant feet tracing the familiar path.

'You can wait in here—I'll bring you both some tea,' a nurse said with a kind smile. 'How do you take it?'

'Hot and sweet, isn't it?' Kate said shakily, trying to smile back, but Nick couldn't say anything, because the last time he'd been in this room had been in the horrendous minutes after Annabel had died, almost exactly five years ago.

It came flooding back the shock, the horror, the guilt. He should have realised she was ill, should have done something, but he'd been so tied up in the practice he'd scarcely noticed she was alive. And then, suddenly, she wasn't. She'd had a ruptured appendix, and Ben hadn't been able to save her.

And yet again the guilt and the senseless futility of it threatened to swamp him.

CHAPTER TWO

KATE cradled the tea in her hands and tried to force herself to drink it.

'I hate sugar in tea,' she said, and looked up at Nick, trying to smile, trying to be brave, but his face was shut down, expressionless, devoid of colour and emotion, and she felt the fear escalate.

'Nick? He'll be OK.' He had to be, she thought desperately, his stark expression clawing at her control and threatening to destroy it, but Ben had seemed confident, Josh also, and there was no talk of ifs or buts or maybes, so he would be OK. Wouldn't he?

'Nick?'

He sucked in a breath, almost as if he'd forgotten to breathe for a while, and turned his head to meet her eyes. 'Sorry, I was miles away.'

Miles away? When his son was under anaesthetic, having his pelvis stabilised with an external frame so they could try and stop the bleeding that was draining the life out of him? Where on earth had he been, miles away? And with that look in his eyes...

He scanned the room, his face bleak. 'I haven't been in here for years. It hasn't changed. Still got the same awful curtains.'

And then she realised. Realised what he was seeing, what this must cost him, to be here with her, and her heart went out to him.

'Oh, Nick, I'm sorry,' she murmured, and he tried to smile.

'Don't be, I'm all right. It was five years ago.' And then he frowned. 'More to the point, how are you? Were you hurt? What was Ben saying about your feet? I didn't realise you'd been trapped in the car.'

'It was nothing—just a pedal. I'm fine.' Her smile was no more successful than his, she supposed, because he came over and sat beside her, searching her eyes with his.

'So what happened?' he asked.

She shrugged. 'I was picking him up from outside the high school. It was my fault—I parked on the right, hitched up on the kerb and rang him, and he ran up and got in, and I pulled back out onto the road. I couldn't see a thing—the rain was sheeting down, but there were no lights coming, and I remember thinking only a fool would be out in this without lights, so it must be clear, and I pulled out, and there was an almighty thump and the car slammed sideways into the car I was pulling out around, and the airbags went off and—'

She broke off.

It had been over in an instant.

There had been nothing she could have done at that point, no way she could have changed it, but for the rest of her life, with the stunning clarity of slow motion, she knew she would hear the sliding, grinding crash, the scream of her child, and the thump as the airbag inflated in her face...

'Ah, Kate,' he murmured, and she looked up, into

dark, fathomless brown eyes that normally hid his feelings all too well. But not now. Now, they were filled with sympathy and something else she couldn't quite read. 'I'm sorry. It must have been horrendous.'

She nodded, looking away because if she didn't she'd lose her grip on her emotions, and she couldn't afford to do that, couldn't afford to succumb to the sympathy in his eyes.

'I can't believe I didn't see him coming.'

'You said there were no lights.'

'I didn't see any, and I was looking, but—'

'Then it's not your fault.'

She gave a soft snort. 'Tell it to the fairies, Nick. I pulled out in front of a big, heavy off-roader when I couldn't see, and Jem could have been killed. How is that not my fault?'

His mouth firmed into a grim line.

'He must have been speeding, Kate.'

'Very likely. It doesn't absolve me of blame.'

'Don't,' he warned, his voice strained. 'Believe me, don't take on the blame for this. It'll destroy you.'

As his guilt over Annabel's death had nearly destroyed him? She bit her lip, trapped the words, looked at the clock. It had hardly moved, and yet they seemed to have been in there for ever.

'He'll be all right, Kate. He's in good hands.'

'I know.'

She gave him another little smile, and reached up to touch his cheek fleetingly in comfort. The day's growth of stubble was rough against her fingers, ruggedly male and oddly reassuring, and somehow his strength centred her. She had to stop herself from stroking her thumb over his cheek, backwards and forwards in a tender caress, the way she would with Jem. With anyone she loved. She dropped her hand hastily back into her lap. 'Are you OK?'

His smile was crooked. 'I'm the last person you should be worried about,' he said gruffly, but it wasn't true. She always worried about him—always had, always would, and running away wouldn't change that, she realised. And even though it was tearing him apart, he was here for her now, when she needed him the most, just as he had been on the night her husband James had died. And he needed her now, too, every bit as much as he had then. So, yes, she was worried about him. She could never rely on him, not in the long term, but she worried about him.

'Don't be silly,' she said with a little catch in her voice. 'I'm really grateful to you for coming. I know it's really hard for you, being here. All those memories. It was such a dreadful time for you, and I'm sorry to have to put you through it again.'

'It just caught me by surprise, coming in here again, that's all. All a bit too familiar.' His smile was crooked and didn't quite reach his eyes, and he rested his hand over hers. 'He'll be all right, Kate,' he murmured, his eyes reassuring, his touch steadying her tumbling emotions.

The unexpected tenderness brought a lump to her throat, and gently she eased her hand away before she crumbled. 'I'm sorry about Jack.'

He shrugged slightly. 'I knew he'd hate me for it, but it's not a problem. He's hated me before, I can live with it.'

It was a lie, even if he was trying to make himself believe it, and she felt herself frown. 'He's a good man,

Nick. He'll come round. And he'll be good to Jem. They all will.'

He nodded, sighed, and stood up, thrusting his hands into his pockets as he crossed to the window and stood staring out into the rain. 'Oh, they will. They'll close ranks round him and take him into their hearts, all three of them. They're like that. They take after Annabel.' He glanced down at the table, at the mugs sitting there, the tea growing cold.

'You haven't touched your tea,' he said, and she let him change the subject and picked up the mug, giving him room, not crowding him. He hated emotion, and he was awash with it today, trying hard to hang together through all the horror of it. It was all right for her, she thought, her eyes welling. She could cry her eyes out and everyone would sympathise, but Nick—Nick had to stay aloof and distant, hold himself back, because for him, today was judgement day.

And, boy, would they be judging, and talking, and there would be plenty to say. Nick had been well and truly married twelve years ago, at the time of Jem's conception, and the good people of Penhally held no truck with infidelity. When they found out...

Not that it mattered now. The only thing that mattered now was that her son—their son, she corrected herself—survived this, and lived long enough for Nick to build a relationship with him. She wondered what they were doing to him at this precise instant, and decided she'd rather not know. Midwife or not, there were things one didn't need to see.

She pressed her hand against her heart, and realised it hurt. It was tender where the seat belt had tugged tight in the accident, pulling on her lumpectomy scar and the still fragile skin where the radiotherapy had burned it, and she suddenly felt very uncertain. Dr Bower had given her the all-clear from her breast cancer in January, but it was very much an 'it's OK for now' result, and there were no guarantees for the future.

And if anything happened to her, Jem would need Nick. Assuming he survived—

'Nick, drink your tea,' she said, slamming the brakes on that thought, and he sat down beside her again and picked up the mug and took a mouthful, toying with the biscuits, crushing them to dust between his fingers, crumbling them all over the table.

'Josh O'Hara's a friend of Jack's from London,' he said out of the blue. 'I gather he's red hot. Ben used to work with him as well. That's why he sounded him out about the vacancy. And Ben won't let anything happen to Jeremiah—'

The door opened and Ben came in, and she dropped her mug onto the table with a clatter, fear suddenly closing her throat.

'How is he?' she asked, barely able to find the words. 'Is he—?'

'He's stable, his blood pressure's low but holding, so Josh and the anaesthetist have taken him to CT now to rule out any other injuries, then he'll be going straight up to Theatre. And we need to check you over. Come on.'

She tried to stand, and suddenly realised how weak she felt, how uncooperative her legs were, how very long she'd been holding her breath. She wasn't really listening any longer. All she'd heard was 'He's stable', and her mind had gone blank, unable to take in any more than this one, most important, fact.

Relief was crashing through her, scattering the last shreds of her control; she sucked in some air, but it wouldn't come, not smoothly, not sensibly, just in little jerky sobs, faster and faster, until at last the dam burst and she felt Nick's arms close around her, holding her firmly against a broad, solid chest that felt so good, so safe that she wanted to stay there for ever, because if she leant on him, if she stayed there, then surely it would be all right...

Nick stood there for a second—scarcely that, but it felt like an age before he came to life again and his hands gentled, cradling her head against his shoulder, holding her against his heart as he rocked and shushed her.

She must be going through hell, he thought, and then it hit him that this wasn't just her son, but his, too. Emotions slammed through him one after the other, but he crushed them down. There'd be time for them later. For now, he just had to be here for Kate, for as long as she needed him.

'Why don't you go and let them take the blood?' Ben suggested, once Kate had stopped crying and been mopped up and taken through to X-Ray. 'I'll keep an eye on her.'

'Isn't Lucy expecting you home?'

He smiled again. 'She was—two hours ago. Don't worry, I've told her what's going on.'

'All of it?' he asked, his heart jerking against his ribs, but Ben shook his head.

'No. I thought I'd let you or Jack do that.'

'She'll be disappointed in me.'

'I don't know,' Ben said thoughtfully. 'Maybe a little,

at first, but she's said before how well you and Kate get on, and she knows you went out with her before you met Annabel, so I don't think she'll be exactly surprised to know you had an affair. In fact, she said only the other week that you ought to get together, now you were both free.'

His laugh sounded hollow to his ears. 'I hope she's not holding her breath for that. Kate's going. She's handed in her notice—she's leaving Penhally.'

'Wow.' Ben frowned. 'That's a big step.'

He shrugged. 'She told me today—well, she left a letter for me.'

She hadn't even told him to his face. That hurt, but he put it on one side, like all the other feelings that were swamping him.

'I'm sorry,' Ben said, and Nick blinked in surprise and met his eyes.

'Why should you be sorry?'

'You tell me,' Ben said softly, and Nick looked away from eyes that saw too much.

'She's blaming herself. She said she didn't see any lights, and she pulled out.'

Ben accepted the change of subject without a murmur. 'Visibility was awful, apparently, and I gather the other guy not only didn't have his lights on but he was speeding significantly, according to witnesses. He wasn't wearing a seat belt, either, and the car wasn't taxed. He's in overnight for observation, and the police have been in to talk to him already. It definitely wasn't Kate's fault. I need to check her out. You go down to Haematology and I'll see you when you come back.'

He nodded, and walked quickly down to Haematology to give the blood they would process and give to

Jeremiah later, after his surgery, after he was stable. God willing. Jack was standing at the reception desk waiting, and turned to him, his eyes raking over Nick's face.

'Are you OK?' he asked, and Nick nodded.

'Yes. Ben's taking a look at Kate.'

'Have you eaten recently?'

Nick nearly laughed. For a moment there, he'd thought his son was enquiring after his emotional well-being, but, no, he was checking that he was OK to donate.

'Lunch,' he said, trying to remember and recalling a sandwich of some sort. He'd left half of it, and it seemed a long time ago. It had been a long time ago. He should have eaten Hazel's fairings instead of leaving them for Mr Pengelly. 'They gave us tea and biscuits in A and E, but I didn't have them.'

'Here.' Jack handed him a small packet of biscuits from his pocket. 'Eat those, and get a drink from that water cooler, otherwise you'll pass out when they take the blood from you.'

And without another word Jack turned back to the desk and spoke to the haematology technician who'd just come to find him. Nick followed them, grabbing a cup of water on the way, and then lay in the next cubicle to his son, the curtain between them firmly closed, while the technician set up the intravenous line and started collecting his blood.

'Can you be quick? I need to get back,' he said, and she smiled.

'It's a good job you're a regular donor, Dr Tremayne,' she said tolerantly. 'Saves all the screening. I take it nothing's changed since the last time?'

'No, nothing.' Nothing except his youngest son nearly

dying and Kate deciding to leave the county. 'Take two units,' he insisted.

She tried to argue, but Jack's voice cut across them both.

'Just do it. It might keep him quiet. You can take two from me as well.'

'Are you sure? I don't like to, but our B-neg donors in the hospital have all been called on recently and there isn't any available until tomorrow. Stocks are really low at the moment; we've got O-neg but obviously this is better. You're not still working this evening, Mr Tremayne?'

'No. I've finished for the day and I've got a light day tomorrow. My registrar can cover me if necessary,' Jack answered.

'And you, Dr Tremayne?'

'I'm not leaving the hospital until I know Jem's all right.' Nick replied.

If he was all right. Hell, he had to be all right. There was so much to say to him, so much lost time to make up for. It would be the bitterest irony if now, when he was finally beginning to accept that Jem really was his son and realise what he meant to him, he lost him before he could tell him.

Nick rested his head back, closed his eyes and prayed as he hadn't prayed since the night Annabel had died.

He couldn't lose another member of his family, and neither could Kate. It just wasn't an option. He pumped his hand to speed up the flow, so he could get back to her side as quickly as possible…

'She hasn't got any fractures, but she's sore,' Ben said softly, taking Nick to one side when he returned to A and E. 'Her right ankle's got a nasty bruise, and she's whiplashed her neck slightly, and her chest is a bit tender where the seat belt cut in. The skin's still a bit fragile anyway, after the surgery and radiotherapy last year.'

He realised he didn't even know if it had been the left or right breast, and asked—not that it made any difference, or was anything to do with him, but he just wanted everything straight in his head, trying to make order of the chaos of the day, and this was another brick in the wall he could straighten.

'Left,' Ben said, not even questioning his need to know that stupidly irrelevant fact. 'I wanted to keep her here for a bit, let her rest, but she won't hear of it. She's very shocked, though. I've given her some pain relief, but she wouldn't let me give her a sedative.'

'No. She wouldn't. Stubborn woman.'

Ben smiled tolerantly, and Nick gave a short, ironic laugh.

'Pot and kettle?' he said, and Ben chuckled.

'Go in and see her, she's waiting for you. And give me your car keys, I'll get it moved. It's obstructing the entrance and the ambos are getting cross.'

He handed over the keys, thanked Ben and went to see Kate.

How long could he be?

Ben had insisted she should lie there for a while and wait for Nick, and frankly she didn't have the strength to argue. Anyway, there was nothing she could do for Jem now except will him to be alive, and she could do that lying down in A and E as well as she could hovering outside the scanner room in Radiology.

Once Nick was back, she'd get up and go and sit there,

waiting for news, but for now, she was lying wide-eyed, alert, her adrenaline running flat out, her pulse rapid, her throat dry.

'You're a mess, Kate Althorp,' she told herself, and closed her eyes. She wouldn't sleep. No way. But she could shut out the light.

She'd dozed off.

Or so he thought, but as Nick stepped into the cubicle, her eyes flew open.

'Is there any news?' she asked, her face worried, and he shook his head.

'No. I've just spoken to Ben, but they haven't heard anything. Josh is with him in CT. Are you OK to go down there now?'

She gave a humourless little laugh that cut him to the bone, and tried to smile. 'Sure. My right ankle hurts, but I've got some arnica gel in my bag, I'll put it on later. Let's go.'

'Want me to do it now?' he asked, wondering how he'd cope with touching her, smoothing his hand over her skin, feeling her warmth beneath his fingers and knowing she wasn't his to touch, to hold—to love?

Would never be.

'Not now. Later, maybe. I need to be with Jem.'

'I'll get a wheelchair,' he told her. 'Stay there.'

'Don't be ridiculous, Nick,' she said, swinging her legs down and wriggling her feet into her damp shoes with a grimace. 'I'm perfectly capable of walking. I'm fine.'

She wasn't. She wasn't fine at all, but she had guts. He tried to smile, but his own guts were strung tight. He tucked her hand in his arm so she could lean on him, and walked with her to Radiology, glad they were moving fairly slowly. He was feeling a little light-headed and wondering if his stubborn insistence on giving two units had been such a good idea after all. It was a quarter of his circulating blood volume—enough to crash his blood pressure into his boots. He ought to get something to eat and drink, but now wasn't the time.

'He'll be out in a minute, he's nearly done,' the receptionist told them, and they sat and waited, Kate suddenly even more nervous because of what the CT might show up.

She thought her stomach was going to turn inside out it was churning so hard, and the painkillers Ben had given her didn't seem to be helping. Well, they were helping, but not enough. She rolled her neck slightly to ease it, but it didn't work. It was because she was tense, coiled like a spring, poised for bad news.

'I can't sit here, I'm going to have to walk around,' she told Nick, pushing herself to her feet just as the doors opened and Jem was wheeled out by Josh and the anaesthetist. The radiologist came over to them, nodded to Nick and then turned to her.

'Mrs Althorp?'

'Yes,' Kate said, trying not to fall down and feeling Nick's firm hand on her waist holding her in place. She dragged her eyes from Jem and the gap in the blankets showing the frame holding his pelvis rigid, and leaned against Nick, grateful for the support, both physical and emotional, wondering what was coming, hardly daring to ask. 'How is he?' she managed, her throat tight.

'Stable. No damage apart from the fracture—he's been lucky, and there's no sign of a bleed from the head injury, so they're taking him straight up to Theatre now.

You'll need to go up with him and sign the consent forms, if you haven't already done it, and I imagine you'll want to wait up there for news?'

She nodded and looked at Jem. She wanted to talk to him—touch him, just touch him so she could reassure herself he was still alive, but he was unconscious, still under anaesthetic. She leant over the trolley anyway, and rested her hand on his cheek briefly, reassured by his warmth but frowning at the bruises as they walked towards the lift.

'Jem? It's Mum,' she said softly. 'You're all right, my darling. You're going to be OK, can you hear me? I'll be waiting for you, OK? I'll be here, all the time. I love you—'

She cracked, and Nick hugged her to his side as they followed the trolley to the lift and went up with him. They watched him go through into Theatre, and then Nick guided her to the chair-lined recess, and the long wait began...

'So that's your father-in-law?'

Ben grunted in confirmation, and Josh watched him. 'Interesting undercurrents between him and the woman. I thought he was the kid's father at first. It took me a minute to work it out. He seems OK—bit distant, but supportive. I take it they're friends?'

Ben sighed and put down his pen, and Josh propped his hips on the back of the other chair and raised an eyebrow.

'She's a colleague as well. He's known her for years.'

Josh nodded. 'I know you didn't always get on with him. Jack mentioned that he could be...'

'Difficult?' Ben supplied, his smile wry, and Josh grinned.

'He probably wasn't quite as polite as that.'

Ben gave a grunt of grudging laughter. 'Yeah. But that's all behind us now.'

'Is it? I passed Jack on the way into Resus, and he was steaming down the corridor with a face like the Grim Reaper. I take it they'd had words?' Josh waited, but Ben obviously wasn't being drawn. He capped his pen and pushed his chair back, changing the subject.

'Nice job, Josh,' he said. 'The ex-fix. Very neat. You're going to be an asset to the department.'

He took the hint. 'Thanks. Let's hope I can convince them all.'

'Giving you a hard time?'

He shrugged. 'Some of them. Not all. I'm the new boy. They're suspicious.'

'Well, they don't need to be. I'll have a word.'

'No, leave it. I'll win them round—I'll bring in doughnuts and smile a lot, work a bit late, you know the routine. A little of the blarney thrown in for good measure...'

'Well, don't expect it to impress me, I know you better than that, and they won't be fooled by it. Stick to what you're good at. Save a few lives—that'll win them round.'

'I'll do that for an encore,' Josh said with a lazy grin, happy that Ben, at least, seemed pleased to have him there. Shrugging away from the desk and putting the Tremayne family out of his mind, he went off to conquer some of the sceptics.

How could the time pass so slowly?

Kate watched the hands crawl round the clock face—a

minute, two. She shifted yet again on one of the padded plastic armchairs, resting her head back against the wall with a fractured sigh.

'He'll be all right, Kate,' Nick said, for the hundredth time, and she just nodded slightly and flexed her ankle.

It was enough to make her wince, and she felt him shift beside her.

'Give me the arnica gel.'

She handed it to him and pulled up her trouser leg a little, kicking off her shoe, and he squeezed a blob onto his fingers and crouched in front of her, so she could rest her foot against his lean, hard-muscled thigh. That was all the running and walking he did, mile after mile over the moors, trying to outrun his demons. She could feel the muscles flex beneath her sole as he shifted his position slightly, and the open neck of his shirt gaped so she could see the pulse beating in the hollow of his throat, hard and fast, driven by the adrenaline that must be coursing through his body as it was through hers.

She lifted a hand and laid it against his shoulder, and he went still. 'Thank you, Nick,' she murmured. 'For everything.'

'Don't be ridiculous.'

'I'm not. Nick, we need to talk.'

He squeezed more arnica gel onto his fingers and smoothed it gently over the top of her other foot where a small bruise was starting to show.

'About?'

'Did you get my letter?'

He said nothing for a moment, just kept rubbing her foot, round and round until the skin was all but dry, then he stood up again and washed his hands in the sink in the corner.

She wriggled her feet back into her shoes, wondering how long the leather would take to dry, how she could have got so wet. Standing in the rain, of course, watching while they'd cut Jem out.

'Nick?'

He dried his hands, then like a caged lion he started pacing, from one side of the small waiting room to the other, then back again, ramming his hand through his hair and rumpling it further. It suited him, she thought randomly. The steel grey threading through it made him look distinguished, setting off his strong features—the features Jem had inherited from him. He was going to be a good-looking man, her son—their son.

Nick's son.

Finally he stopped pacing, sucked in a long, slow breath and turned back to her, scanning her face for clues, but there were none. Her warm, golden-brown eyes met his calmly, giving nothing away, as usual. She never gave anything away unless she meant to, and then it was usually disappointment in him. 'May I ask why you're going?' he asked, his voice carefully expressionless.

'Why? I would have thought it was obvious, Nick. I can't just be here for ever waiting for you to sort yourself out. Did you think I would? That I'd stay, to let you see your son a few times a year, in carefully arranged, apparently casual circumstances, so you can keep in touch without having to tell him you're his real father? Or, more to the point, so you didn't have to rock the boat and tell your other kids that we made love while their mother was still alive?'

'Once,' he said flatly. 'Just once. It's not as if we had an affair, Kate.'

'No, you're right. It was nothing so premeditated, was it?' she acknowledged gently, as if he needed reminding about anything that had happened that hellish night. 'We just reached out, to someone we could trust, someone who could trust us. But we were married—well, I suppose technically I was probably widowed at that point, but you weren't. And we did make love.'

And they'd made a child. Until Ben had told him about the blood group, there had still been an element of doubt in his mind, of disbelief. But not now. Not any more.

He looked away from the shrewd, understanding eyes that saw too much. 'Neither of us was thinking that night.'

'And you've done your level best to avoid thinking about it ever since,' she murmured. 'So I'm going to make it easier for you. Easier for all of us. I'm taking Jem away, and we're starting a new life.'

'With Rob?' he made himself ask, even though he'd heard it was off, but maybe it was back on, maybe that was why. 'Is he going, too?'

A flicker of distress crossed her face. 'No,' she said quietly. 'He deserves better than me. I'm like you, Nick. Scarred, broken, emotionally bankrupt. I'm no good to anyone. He's a good man. He was very kind to me, and to Jem.'

He said nothing. After all, she was right. Rob Werrick was a good man, a decent man, who'd stood by her last year during her treatment for breast cancer, who'd supported her through the most dreadful days of fear and uncertainty, a role Nick had sorely wanted to play, but all he had been able to do was sit, isolated from her, and pray for her. And Rob was the man who'd taken Nick's son to his heart and made room there for him, when the man who was his father had found he was unable to do so.

'So was it you or him who called it off?' he asked in spite of himself.

'Me. He asked me to marry him, and I said no. I don't love him—I can't love him, not in the way he deserves to be loved.' Her brown eyes were reproachful, her voice tinged with sadness. 'So I'm going, and we'll start again, and we'll be fine.'

His heart felt as if it was being crushed in a giant fist, but if this was what she wanted, to go, to leave, then maybe she was right. Maybe it was for the best. Easier all round. And away from the shadow of this guilt they both carried, perhaps she'd find happiness with another man.

He ignored the little twist in his chest and nodded. 'You're right. If that's what you want, then go, Kate. I won't stop you—'

'You can't stop me, Nick.'

'True. What about Jem? Will I ever see him?'

She gave a mocking little laugh that gave his heart another little wrench. 'What about him? He'll be fine. He doesn't know you're his father, it hasn't done him any harm not to know, so it won't in the future. I'll tell him when he's eighteen. I can't stay here so you can ignore him at close range. Anyway, you don't see him now—why would this make any difference?'

'Don't be ridiculous—of course I see him,' he denied. 'I see him a lot.'

'Only if you can't avoid it. Seeing him reminds you of your human frailty, and you don't like that.'

He didn't. He hated the constant reminder of what they'd done that night, of how he'd betrayed Annabel, tarnished the memory of James. But that didn't mean he didn't want to watch the child grow up, make sure he was all right—

'How the hell am I going to explain it to my children? They won't understand.'

'You could tell them you're human?' she suggested softly, her eyes so wise, so—so damn knowing.

He gave a quiet snort. 'Oh, they know that.'

'And this is about what they think of you?' she said, her voice heavy with reproach. 'What about what Jem will think of you when he finds out that he doesn't matter as much as your other children—your proper children, all respectably born in wedlock? They're no different, Nick' she reminded him, her words still soft and yet flaying his skin off with their accuracy. 'Conceived in haste, every single one of them. Story of your life. Well, I don't want to be a part of it any more, of the carefully constructed illusion of reality you fool yourself with every day,' she said wearily. 'I'll work my notice, once Jem's better, but then I'm off, Nick, and you won't hear from me again. It's better that way.'

Was it? He wasn't sure. He was suddenly filled with a cold, nameless fear for the future—a future without Kate, and without the boy, this last, unacknowledged and yet still infinitely precious child who, it seemed, he'd managed to love in spite of everything.

He sat beside her, the chairs so close he could feel the warmth radiating from her body, feel the air move with every shallow breath as her chest rose and fell.

'I thought you wanted me to be in his life?'

'I do—but not like this, giving him fragments of yourself from time to time. He deserves more from you.' Her eyes suddenly filled with tears. 'I can't do this any more, Nick. I'm leaving, and that's an end to it. Please. Just let me go.'

Let me go…

He held her eyes, watched the threatening tears well, watched in despair as one slipped down her cheek and fell to the floor. She never cried. Before today, the last time he'd seen her cry had been the night he'd taken her into his arms and held her. The night Jeremiah had been conceived.

Swallowing the bitter taste of regret, he stood up and turned away.

How could he let her go?

He couldn't—but how could he make her stay?

CHAPTER THREE

HE SAT down again a while later, but not for long, pacing restlessly, ramming his hand through his hair again and again until she thought he'd tear it out.

And then the doors swung open and Lucy and Jack came down the short corridor towards them.

'How is he?' Lucy asked, looking at Kate, avoiding Nick's eyes as if she wasn't sure how to do this.

None of them, in truth, knew how to do this. They'd just have to feel their way through.

'Still in there. They stopped the bleeding, they're just plating his pelvis. He's been lucky, apparently—'

She broke off, wondering how on earth what had happened to her son could in any way be considered lucky, but then she felt Nick move closer, his hand on her shoulder, warm and reassuring despite their earlier words. Unable to resist the pull of that warmth, she dropped her head against his side, listening to the steady thud of his heart, and above it, the tension coming off them in waves, she could hear their quiet, fraught conversation.

'I'm glad you came,' Nick said, and she saw Lucy tense.

'I had to, Ben asked me to give you back your car

keys. It's in the staff car park.' She dropped them in his hand, then shook her head. 'I'm not here for you, anyway, I'm here for a little boy who's apparently my brother. I don't know what to say to you. All that fuss when Mum died, but all the time you'd been carrying on behind her back—'

'Lucy, it wasn't like that. It was just once, right after the storm. Kate was distraught, I was distraught. It just—'

'Happened?' she said, her voice a little hard, unlike her usual self, but then she would be, Kate thought. None of them were themselves.

Nick let Kate go and moved away a fraction, and she lifted her head and looked up at Jack and Lucy.

'It wasn't just his fault. It takes two, remember. I was as much to blame. And just as married, really. James had only just died. There was no decent interval, believe me. It was inexcusable, but it never happened again.'

'Not with you, maybe, but were there others?'

Jack's question made Nick suck in a sharp breath.

'No,' he said firmly. 'There were no others. Apart from that one occasion when we were both beside ourselves with grief and I didn't really know what I was doing, I was never unfaithful to your mother. I loved her.'

Jack snorted. 'Strange way of showing it.'

'Jack, leave it,' Lucy said. 'It's irrelevant to this. But what I can't understand,' she went on after a slight pause, 'is why you've never told us he's our brother— why you've kept it a secret for, what, eleven years or more?'

'Two. I didn't know about Jem until two years ago,' Nick said, and their eyes swivelled to Kate.

'So, did you know?' Lucy asked incredulously. 'Before then, did you know? I mean, you are sure about this? That James wasn't his father? Have you had a DNA test?'

'James isn't his father. You've only got to look at him, Lucy. Look at his eyes. Look at his mouth. He was just like Jack's little Freddie when he was three or four, just like Jack and Edward at his age now. And, anyway, James and I had been having fertility investigations. We were talking about adoption. Why would I need a DNA test? Besides,' she added, 'if I needed any other proof, I have it now. James was A-positive.'

Lucy sat down hard, her eyes accusing and filled with tears. 'So—for eleven and a half years you've been convinced he was Dad's child, and you didn't tell him until two years ago?'

Kate reached out a hand, but Lucy snatched hers away, and she gave a fractured sigh and dropped her hand back in her lap. 'How could I? He was happily married, he had three other children—who was I to throw all that into chaos?'

Jack gave a short, hard laugh. 'The mother of his child?'

She met his accusing eyes. 'Exactly. I wasn't Nick's lover, I wasn't his wife—I was the mother of a child. And I did what I could to protect my child, and you, his other children, and his marriage. There was no point in upsetting all of that. Two wrongs don't make a right. And we've been fine. Jem's had a good life, settled, and I've given him all the love he could ever need.' Her voice cracked. 'And now he could be dying...'

She felt Nick sit down beside her again and slide his arm around her, there for her, giving her his strength and support—at least for now. 'It's OK,' he said softly, turning her head into his shoulder and cradling it gently. 'Don't cry, Kate. He'll be all right. It's going to be OK.'

Was it? She hoped so, but she couldn't for the life of her think how she'd cope if it wasn't.

She felt Lucy sit beside her, felt the gentle touch of her hand. 'Kate, I'm so sorry, I didn't mean to upset you, I'm just— It's a bit of a shock, that's all. And I'm so worried about him.'

'I know,' she whispered, patting Lucy's hand reassuringly. She loved Nick's daughter, she'd delivered her babies—she hated it that Lucy thought less of her now because of this, but it was only what she deserved. She'd given Lucy's father the means to commit adultery, and it was every bit as much her fault as his.

But for now her guilt was directed towards her son, lying there on the operating table, his life hanging in the balance, hoping that when they opened him up they didn't find anything unexpected.

She concentrated her mind on him, focused all her thoughts, willing him to pull through, to make it, to be all right. And then the door opened, and her heart stopped in her chest, eyes locked on the surgeon as he approached.

Nick got slowly to his feet, and Kate held her breath, unable to move until she knew he was all right, but he was, she could see that from the surgeon's smile as he pulled off his mask, and with a leap her heart started to beat again, the slow, dull thud threatening to deafen her.

He acknowledged Jack with a nod, then crossed to her, his hand extended.

'Mrs Althorp—I'm Martin Bradley. I've just finished operating on your son.'

She shook his hand on autopilot. 'How is he?'

'He's OK.' He perched on the chair beside her, taking Nick's place. 'I'm sorry I didn't have time to talk to you before we started, but I was already scrubbing in and I'm sure Ben Carter will have explained what we were going to do. Under the circumstances I didn't want to make him wait. Anyway, he's fine, he's come through the operation well, we've managed to fix the fractures and I think he'll get a very good result. He's broken the two bones at the front of his pelvis on the left, hence all the bleeding, but the pubic symphysis, the cartilage joint between the two halves at the front, wasn't disrupted so he'll be back on his feet quite quickly. We've sorted out the vascular damage, plated the fractures, and in fact it's all come together very neatly. It shouldn't give him any problems once it's healed in a few weeks.'

'So—he'll be all right? He hasn't got any nerve damage?'

'Not that we know of. His left sacroiliac joint might be sore for a while, but it wasn't displaced and I'm confident he should make a complete recovery. We'll know more later, but it's looking good at the moment. We're running whole cross-matched blood into him now, and we salvaged the free blood in his abdomen— that's gone off to the lab to be cleaned up so it can be returned to him if necessary, and then we'll do some tests and balance the blood components over the next twenty-four hours, but that's all pretty routine stuff. Any questions?'

'No. I just want to see him.'

'That's fine. If you think of anything, don't be afraid

to ask. I'll be around for the next couple of hours, just in case there are any problems. Jem's in Recovery now, so you can come and talk to him. He's very drowsy, but he's come round and he's fine. I'm sure he'll be pleased to see you.'

Kate nodded, her body suddenly turning to jelly, and she was glad she was sitting down. Nick helped her up, his arm around her as they went through into Recovery, and it tightened as she stood by Jem's side, sucking in her breath at her first sight of him.

He was linked up to a mass of tubes and wires and drips, a monitor blinking on the wall behind him, and his poor bruised little face was so chalk-white against the pillow he almost disappeared on it.

She took his hand in hers, wondering at how small and fragile he looked—somehow so much more vulnerable, with his eyes shut and all the tubes and wires. Where was her lively, vibrant boy, his gangly limbs and eager enthusiasm carrying him through life at a hundred miles an hour? Where had he gone? She stroked his hair back from his bruised forehead with a shaking hand and bent to kiss it.

'Jem? It's Mum. I'm here, my darling, right next to you. You're going to be all right. You sleep now, OK?'

There was a small sound that could have been acknowledgement, and his fingers flickered in her hand. She squeezed them back, and he seemed to sigh and go off to sleep again, and she felt her legs start to buckle with relief.

But Nick was there, holding her up, giving her moral and physical support. She didn't want to rely on him, but there was something about him, like a rock, an anchor in a world that had gone mad, and she leant against him and let him hold her. Just for now, just while she stared at her son and let herself believe he might live.

'You won't get much out of him,' Martin Bradley murmured. 'He's heavily sedated, and we've given him some pretty hefty pain relief, but he should be more comfortable now his pelvis is stable.'

'So what happens now?' Nick asked, staring down at the injured child who looked so fragile amidst the plethora of tubes and wires and technology, and he shrugged.

'He'll stay here for a while—an hour or two? Just until we're quite happy that he's stable and we don't have to take him back into Theatre. Then he'll be in PICU—Paediatric Intensive Care—for the night. He doesn't really need to be there, but they've got the bed available and they'll be able to monitor him more closely overnight while we balance his bloods, so we might as well take advantage of it. He'll probably move to the ward tomorrow, and then he'll be there for a couple of weeks, I expect, while we get him up on his feet again, and then it's just a case of getting slowly stronger. We'll have to see. The plates and screws will have to come out at some point, as he's still got a lot of growing to do, but we'll worry about that in a few weeks or months. Anyway, I'll be around, so we'll talk again tomorrow if I don't see you later. And try not to worry. He's going to be all right, you just have to give it time.'

Kate wanted to smile, but her muscles didn't seem to work. She realised she was still leaning on Nick, and she straightened up, moving away a fraction, distancing herself. 'Thank you,' she murmured, and held out her hand. 'You've been very kind.'

He shook it firmly. 'My pleasure. I'm glad to see

you've got someone with you—the whole Tremayne clan, no less, including Lucy. I haven't seen you for a while. Are you well?'

'Yes, very,' she said with a smile, but Kate could see it didn't reach her eyes. 'Busy. I've got two children now.'

'Yes, so Ben tells me. Well, it's good to see you again, and it's nice that Kate's got so many friends around her supporting her.'

Nobody contradicted him, and he left them alone, nothing to break the silence but the soft beeps and hisses from the instruments, and the distant ringing of a telephone in another room.

Lucy broke the silence first.

'Um—I ought to go. I've left Ben with the children, and Annabel's had a cold, so she's a bit fractious, and Josh is teething, but keep in touch.'

'Yes, make sure you do that,' Jack agreed. 'I should go, too, I haven't seen the kids at all today, and I've only seen Alison under the edge of the duvet, so I'd better go home before they can't remember who I am. I'll come up tomorrow and see Jem, but if there's any change in the meantime, Kate, give us a ring, OK? Or if there's anything we can do?'

'Of course I will,' she promised, and they walked out, shoulder to shoulder, Jack putting his hand against Lucy's back to escort her through the door. And then it swung shut behind them and Nick let go of some of the tension that had held him for the last few hours and looked down at Kate with a fleeting smile.

'I told you he'd be OK.'

She dredged up a smile. 'Of course you did. I just didn't dare believe you.'

'Do you believe me now?'

'I might be starting to,' she admitted, and looked back down at Jem, her face drawn and fraught. 'You don't have to stay, Nick.'

Was she mad? 'Of course I'm staying. You can't believe I'd leave you alone now.'

'Why not? You heard the surgeon, he's out of danger. You don't need to be here, you've got to work tomorrow.'

'No. I'm not leaving you, Kate. I'm here for you, for both of you, for as long as you need me.'

She met his eyes, and they seemed sincere, but she'd thought that thirty-something years ago, and he'd left her. Left her and married Annabel when she'd become pregnant with the twins. 'I can't lean on you, Nick. I won't let myself. Every time I do, every time I think I dare, you let me down.'

'I won't let you down. I promise you, Kate, I won't walk away from this.'

She stared at him, at the serious expression on his face, the conviction in his eyes, in his voice. Dare she trust him? 'You always walk away,' she said at last.

'I didn't the night James died.'

She gave a soft huff of laughter and shook her head. 'No, you didn't, did you? Maybe it would have been better if you had.' But then she wouldn't have had Jem, and her life would have been empty and pointless. And she needed him now.

'I know I've let you down,' he said softly. 'I know I've let Jem down. But I'm here now, and I'll stay here for as long as you need me, and I'll do whatever I can to help you. Just give me a chance.'

She shrugged and looked away. 'I can't stop you. But I can't lean on you, either. I have to do this on my own.'

'No, you don't,' he said, trying to inject something into his voice that she could believe in. 'And I'll prove that to you.' Even if it took years. A lifetime.

Her shoulders were drooping, and his heart went out to her. Poor Kate. She was exhausted, he thought, exhausted and shocked and traumatised, and it was late. 'You ought to eat,' he coaxed gently. 'Keep your strength up.'

She shook her head. 'I can't eat. Not when he's like this. Maybe later. I could murder a drink, though. I wonder when they'll move him to PICU?'

'An hour or so? Shall I go and get you something? Tea, coffee?'

'Tea would be lovely. Do you mind? I really don't want to leave him.'

'On one condition—you sit down beside him and rest, and you eat something if I bring it back.'

'You're a bully, do you know that?' she said, but she was smiling, an exhausted, rather watery smile that in a heartbeat could have morphed into tears, and she sat obediently in the chair he put there for her.

'I'm looking after you is what I am,' he said, and headed for the door. 'Any special requests?'

'Tea. And a sandwich, if I must, but no cheese. I'm going to have nightmares as it is.'

'OK. Back in five.'

He went through the door and down the stairs, pausing halfway because he felt suddenly light-headed. Damn. That was giving two units of blood, not drinking anything like enough to replace the lost fluid or taking in any food—apart from Jack's biscuits, he'd had half a cup of tea, a cup of water and whatever he'd had in A and E in the relatives' room, and that was all since his miserable half-sandwich and instant coffee at lunchtime. And it was—good grief—a quarter past midnight.

And the café, when he got there, was shut, with a sign directing him to the main canteen some distance away.

There was a vending machine, and he pulled some coins out of his pocket with fingers that were starting to shake violently, and put them into the machine, pressed the button for a bottle of sports drink to boost his fluids and blood sugar, and twisted the cap to loosen it. And it sprayed him.

He swore, twisting it shut again, and suddenly it was all too much. He dropped his head forwards against the vending machine and resisted the urge to slam it into the gaudy metal case. Head-banging wouldn't cure anything.

'Is it broken again?'

The voice was soft and feminine, and he lifted his head and stared vaguely at the woman.

'Um—no. Sorry. Did you want the machine?'

'No, it's OK.' She tilted her head on one side, looking at him keenly. 'Are you all right?'

He opened his mouth to say yes, and then stopped. The woman was slender and delicate, but curvy in all the right places. She was probably younger than Lucy, her dark hair twisted up into a clip, and there was compassion and understanding in her emerald-green eyes.

'A friend's little boy's just been admitted,' he said, gagging on the half-truth. 'They had a car accident. His pelvis is fractured. I was getting us something to eat, but…'

She frowned. 'I'm so sorry. Has he been to Theatre?'

'Yes—yes, he's had an op to plate it, and he's OK, he's in Recovery at the moment and then he's going to PICU, but he shares my blood group, and it's B-negative, and stocks were very low, so they took two units from me, and...'

'And you haven't eaten or drunk anything because you've been too stressed, and the café's shut, and now the bottle's got its own back on you.'

He smiled. 'Something like that.' He held out his hand, then looked at it ruefully and smiled again as he withdrew it. 'Sorry—it's a bit sticky. I'm Nick Tremayne.'

She flashed him an answering smile. 'Jack's father— of course. You look just like him. I'm Megan Phillips. I'm a paediatrician, so I'll be looking after your friend's son. What's his name?'

'Jeremiah Althorp. Jem.'

'I'll keep an eye out for him.'

'Thanks.' He tried to unscrew the drink again, but his fingers were shaking so much now he fumbled the lid and it fell to the floor. She picked it up and handed it back to him.

'Come on, you need to sit down. Let me go and get you something to eat.'

'No, I couldn't.'

'Well, I'd rather you did, otherwise I'll have to pick you off the floor on the way to the canteen. I'm going to buy myself some sandwiches. Why don't I get you some? I can bring them up to you, I'm going that way.'

'I couldn't ask you to do that.'

'You didn't ask, I offered.' Her smile was gentle.

'Chicken salad? Ham and cheese? Tuna? There isn't a fabulous choice, I'm afraid.'

'Anything. One without cheese for Kate, and I don't care what I have, whatever's going. And two teas, if you've got enough hands. You're a star. Here, take some money.' He pulled a twenty-pound note out of his wallet and handed it to her.

She took the note out of his hands and smiled. 'I'll come up in a minute. Drink some of that before you go back up there, and I'll come and find you.'

He took her advice, downing half the cloyingly sweet drink, and after a moment he began to feel better. Less shaky and light-headed. He made his way slowly back upstairs, and when he pressed the buzzer a young woman let him back in, waving goodbye to Kate as she left the room.

'Oh—were they shut?' Kate asked, eyeing his all but empty hands in surprise.

'Yes. I was going to the main canteen, but I met someone. A paediatrician, of all things. She's gone to get something for us. She said she was heading that way anyway, so I gave her a twenty-pound note. At least I hope she was a paediatrician.'

Kate chuckled softly. 'Nick, you're so cynical.'

He gave a weary smile and offered her the bottle.

'Do you want some of this? I saved you some.'

Kate eyed him thoughtfully. 'No, I loathe it, thanks, you have it. What was her name?'

'Megan Phillips. Who was that, by the way, who let me in?'

'Jess Carmichael. She's a counsellor. She heard I was here and she's been working late so she popped in. I saw her for a while after my lumpectomy. She was lovely.

Really kind to me. She gave me a lot of support when I needed it the most.'

He felt a little stab of pain to accompany the familiar guilt. 'I'm glad.'

Kate met his eyes, her own holding that particular brand of gentle reproach that she reserved for him. 'I could have done with your support then, too, Nick.'

He looked away, swamped with regret, but what could he have done? 'You had Rob,' he reminded her.

'That didn't exclude you.'

Oh, it did. 'I didn't want to get in the way,' he said. 'He seemed genuinely decent, very fond of you—I thought you might stand a chance of happiness, a future for you and Jeremiah with a man you loved. A man who could love you back. I didn't want to get in the way of that.'

'You wouldn't have done,' she reasoned, remembering how it had felt when he'd kept his distance—Nick, the only man she'd ever really loved, keeping her at arm's length when all she'd really wanted was for him to hold her and tell her it would be all right. Tell her that if it wouldn't, he'd be there for their son. 'You wouldn't have been in the way,' she told him, realising, even as she said it, that of course he would have been.

'You know that's not true,' he said gently, and she shook her head.

'Nick, I needed you—even if you weren't with me, I needed to know that you cared, but you never said a thing.' She laughed, but it came out slightly bitterly with the remembered hurt. 'I thought you'd brought me flowers, but they were from everyone at the practice, you were just the messenger.'

He gave her a wintry smile. 'Would you have accepted them if they'd been from me?'

And then she knew—realised, with sudden insight, that they had been from him—been his idea, his choice, probably even paid for himself. And him bringing them had been the nearest he could get to telling her that he was thinking of her, worrying about her.

That he cared.

He hadn't let her down, he'd just given her space, stepped back out of Rob's way. And she'd misunderstood.

Her eyes filled, and she nodded, just once. 'Yes,' she said. 'Yes, I would have accepted them. Thank you.'

'Don't thank me,' he said gruffly. 'I did nothing—just as I always do nothing. If I'd acknowledged Jeremiah sooner, if I'd done what I should have done, then I would have been supporting you financially, making sure you had a safer car, a car with side impact protection instead of a little tin box that crushed like an eggshell—'

'No!' she said, reaching for his hand, clutching hold of it so he couldn't avoid her, her voice no more than an urgent whisper in the quiet room. 'I won't let you do that! This is not your fault. This is my fault, my guilt, and I'm damned if I'll let you have it and add it to the endless layers that you hide behind! I had the crash, I bought the car—'

'Because of me,' he returned stubbornly. 'Because I didn't accept that he was my son. Because I was letting you down again, hiding from the truth, hoping it would go away, but it won't, will it? But you are, and you're taking my son with you.'

And he didn't want her to, he realised. He really, really didn't want her to.

He turned his back on her, and saw Megan Phillips at the door, beckoning to him. 'Looks like our food's here,' he said curtly, and went out.

Kate followed him, and the woman smiled at her.

'You must be Nick's friend. I'm Megan Phillips, one of the paediatric registrars,' she said. 'I'll be looking after Jem when he's in PICU and on the ward later. How's he doing?'

'He's all right. He's going to be all right. Mr Bradley said it's just routine now,' she said, trying to inject some conviction into her voice, and as she did so she realised that for the first time she believed that he might be all right, that he might turn the corner, might actually make it, and the relief nearly took her legs out from under her.

Megan handed over the food she'd brought up for them, gave Nick his change and then left them to it. Nick opened Kate's sandwich and handed it to her, pushing her into a chair.

'Eat that before you collapse,' he ordered gruffly, ripping open another packet and demolishing the contents, then he drained his tea and dropped his head back, rolling it towards her with a sigh. 'You're not eating, Kate. Come on. You need to keep your strength up.'

'I can't eat.'

'Come on, you promised.'

She nodded. She had, and he wouldn't give up until she'd eaten the darned sandwich, she knew that, so she took a bite, and he stopped watching her like a hawk and glanced at his watch.

'I need to make a call.'

'A call?' she asked, realising she hadn't told her mother yet. Or Chloe, or Rob. She ought to tell them

Jem was all right—but not now. Not in the middle of the night. She'd call them tomorrow—except…

'Oh, Nick, the dog. I need to make arrangements. I hadn't even thought about it.'

'It's OK. Oliver said not to worry, they'll sort it.'

'Bless them. They're so kind.' She sighed with relief, then looked at her watch. 'Nick, it's awfully late. Who are you ringing?'

'Edward.'

His other son, currently in South America and still, presumably, unaware. 'Oh. Oh, Nick.' She reached for his hand and he squeezed hers reassuringly.

'Hey, I'm fine. I'll be back in a minute. Eat, and have some tea. It's just the right temperature.'

She nodded, and forced herself to finish the sandwich and drink some of the tea before going back into Recovery to sit by Jem's bedside.

They'd been monitoring him constantly, checking him every few minutes, and as she went back in, they told her he was ready to go through to PICU.

'We'll find you a bed if you like—are you staying?' the nurse who was moving him asked her, and she nodded.

'Yes—if I can. I'll sit in the chair beside him, though. I don't need a bed.'

'We'll see. Let's take him and get him settled, and you can decide then, but he's stable now and he'll sleep all night; if you take my advice, you'll get your head down, because he'll need you when he wakes up and being the parent of a sick child is very wearing. You'll need your rest if you're going to be any good to him.'

Sensible advice, but she wasn't happy to take it. She

wanted to be beside Jem, couldn't bear to leave his side, and even if she did, she didn't think she'd sleep.

'Kate, you were in the accident, too, you need to rest,' Nick said firmly when she continued to protest to the PICU nurse after he was settled. 'I'll sit with him. Go and have an hour, at least.'

'Half an hour,' she conceded, giving in because she knew it made sense and she was at the end of her tether. And the nurse was right—if she was going to be any use to Jem, she needed some sleep. 'I could do with lying down. What about you? Are you feeling better? Less shaky since you ate?'

'I'm fine,' he said, telling her nothing, as usual.

'Did you get hold of Edward?'

He shook his head. 'Go on, go and lie down. I'll get you if there's the slightest change.'

'Promise.'

'I promise,' he said, and she didn't know why, but she believed him. Maybe because she had no choice. Or maybe because this time, at least, she knew she could trust him?

So she went, escorted to a tiny room nearby just big enough for a chair, a little bedside locker and a bed made up with crisp white hospital linen. She'd never been more pleased to see a bed in her life. Her neck was a little sore, she had a killer headache, probably from the stress, her ankle was aching where the pedal had been squashed into it and she was emotionally exhausted.

She took some of the painkillers Ben had given her, then crept under the covers with a shaky sigh. Oh, that was better. Half an hour of this and she'd be able to cope again. Rolling to her side, she closed her eyes and lay there in the quiet room, and as the tension drained

out of her, the only thing that had held her together up
to now, she gave a tiny sob and tears leaked silently out
of the corners of her eyes and dribbled down onto the
pillow as she lay there.

Jem was all right. He'd be all right. He would.

She told herself the same thing, over and over again
like a mantra, and gradually she fell into a shallow,
restless sleep.

CHAPTER FOUR

NICK closed the door softly and stood looking down at her.

He didn't want to wake her, but he'd promised her he would, and she'd had over three hours, not just the half hour she'd agreed to.

But she was sleeping so deeply, curled on her side with one hand tucked under her cheek, and she looked defenceless and vulnerable. He perched on the hard plastic chair by the bed and watched her sleep for a moment, then with a quiet sigh he leant forwards and stroked her hair. She didn't stir, and he let his hand fall to the pillow.

And frowned. It was wet, and in the soft glow from the bedside light he could see a damp stain under the edge of her cheek, below her eye. Salt trails had dried across her temple, and down over her nose from the other eye, and he realised she'd been crying in her sleep. He closed his eyes and took a slow, steadying breath, then touched her again.

'Kate?'

Her eyes flew open, and she started to sit up. 'What is it? What's wrong?'

'Nothing,' he said hastily, kicking himself for scaring

her. 'It's all right, he's fine. He's asleep, but you asked me to wake you.'

She let her breath out on a shaky little sigh, and dropped back against the pillows. 'Oh. Sorry. I must have dozed off— What time is it?'

'Twenty to five.'

'Five!'

She sat up again, pushed back the covers and slid to her feet, swaying slightly. 'Steady,' he murmured, standing up and putting his arms around her to support her, and she rested her head against his shoulder with a sigh.

'How's your neck?' he asked, and she gave a little shrug.

'OK.'

He was pretty sure it wasn't. A bang hard enough to do that to Jem must have shaken her up, and he slid his hand carefully around the back of her neck and massaged the taut, tired muscles under the soft waterfall of dark hair. She shifted so her forehead was propped against his chest, just above his heart, and if he'd bent his head a fraction he could have dropped a kiss on her hair.

But he wouldn't. Of course he wouldn't. She wouldn't want it, and he wouldn't embarrass her by doing anything so stupid, but he held her head, his hand curved protectively round it, steadying her as his fingers worked slowly, gently on the muscles.

'Better?' he asked, and she nodded slightly, so he eased back and let her straighten before he moved away. 'Go and sit with him and I'll get us a coffee. Do you want anything else?'

'Tea. Tea would be lovely, and maybe a pastry or something. Thanks, Nick.'

'Any time,' he said, and backed away, leaving her to straighten her clothes and freshen up while he made the round trip to the canteen. He could do with stretching his legs, and a change of scene wouldn't hurt after hours of staring at his son's bruised and swollen face and wondering how the hell to tell him he was his father.

More to the point, wondering what Jeremiah would make of the news. He suspected not a lot. All in all, it was probably shaping up to be another thoroughly bloody day...

She sent Nick to lie down when he got back with the hot drinks and pastries, and he nodded and went without a word. He looked exhausted, she thought. Drained and stressed and emotionally threadbare.

She'd never seen him like this, even when he'd lost Annabel. He desperately needed a shave, and for a man who usually dressed so fastidiously, he was falling apart. His shirt was creased and open at the neck, the tie long gone, and his usually immaculate suit was crumpled and weary.

And despite it all, he was still the best-looking man she'd ever seen, the only man she'd ever really wanted. Apart from necessity he hadn't left her side since he'd arrived in Resus, and she didn't know how she would have got through it without him.

Although, of course, even though the biggest hurdle had been overcome in that Jeremiah was still alive, there was still the next obstacle to deal with, the one they'd been avoiding now for years, and she had no idea how Nick would be when the time came. One thing she knew for sure, he couldn't bottle out now, and maybe it wasn't the right time to go away. Her letter to the PCT was still in her bag, waiting for her to post it after she'd picked Jem up, only of course that had never happened, and now...

Oh, what on earth should she do? It had been complicated enough before this, but now...

She sipped her tea, hands cradling the paper cup, fingers tracing the ribbed cardboard holder round it, chafing it rhythmically as she sat with glazed eyes fixed on her sleeping son, watching the slow rise and fall of his chest, the occasional flutter of his eyelids, the trace of his heartbeat on the monitor, and prayed that when the time came, he could forgive them both for what they'd done to him.

They woke Jem at six, when they came to check his obs, and he smiled at her a little wanly. She'd never been so pleased to see his smile in her life.

'Mum,' he croaked, and she felt her eyes well with tears.

'Hello, darling. Good morning.' She leant forwards and took his free hand, the one that wasn't wired up to the drip, and kissed his bruised cheek gently. She'd studied his notes, and he'd had several units of blood overnight. She wondered if any of them had been Nick's, if his father's blood was now circulating in his veins. Or Jack's.

Like blood brothers cutting themselves and swapping blood, but on a grander scale and one-way. Would it bring them all closer? She hoped so. Apart from her mother in Bristol, and James's brother, the man Jem called Uncle John, there was no other family. It would be nice for him to have the family he should have had all along, but she wasn't going to make assumptions. Maybe they wouldn't want that level of involvement. She couldn't blame them. And there was still that hurdle to overcome, of course.

She stroked her thumb lightly over the back of his hand, and his fingers tightened a little. 'What time is it?'

'Six in the morning.'

'Oh.' He thought about that for a moment, then gave a tiny sigh. 'Can I have a drink? My throat's sore and my mouth's really dry.'

She glanced up. He was still nil by mouth, but she could give him a mouthwash. She spoke to the nurse, and a minute later she was swabbing his lips with the cool liquid, wiping away the dried secretions so he'd be more comfortable. 'Better?' she asked, and he smiled and nodded.

'Mmm. I'm sore all over, Mum.'

Her heart contracted. 'I bet you are, my love. You've been through the wringer. Do you remember what happened yesterday?' she asked him softly.

He shook his head. 'No. The last thing I remember was making you a pot.' He frowned. 'Did I tell you I'd made you a pot?'

She nodded, thinking it might have been the last thing he'd done, the last thing he'd said to her, and she struggled not to cry. 'Yes, you did. A yellow one. I'm looking forward to seeing it. Do you remember me picking you up? Or the helicopter?'

He shook his head. 'Helicopter? No. I don't remember anything after making the pot. Did I go in a helicopter?'

'Yes. The air ambulance brought you here.'

'And I don't remember,' he mumbled, looking disgusted. 'I've always wanted to go in a helicopter. So what happened to me? Why am I so sore? Did we have a car accident?'

'Yes. I pulled out, and—'

She broke off, just as Nick appeared on the other side of the bed. 'Someone was going too fast,' he said firmly, 'and ran into the side of the car. It was his fault.'

'Oh,' he said, but she could see he was flagging. 'I can't believe I don't remember the helicopter,' he mumbled drowsily, and then looked at Nick and his brows clumped together in a little frown. 'Uncle Nick, why haven't you shaved today?'

She heard the quiet rasp as he scrubbed his hand over his jaw. Emotions chased across his face, and he pressed his lips together briefly. 'I haven't had a chance, I've been here all night,' he said. 'We both have.'

'Really? Why?'

Because you were sick. Because we thought you were going to die—

Kate met his eyes, and Nick reached out and brushed his knuckles over his son's thin, pale cheek and tried to smile. 'We were worried about you. You've been pretty sick. You had to have an operation.'

'Why did I need an operation? I don't really understand. I'm just really sore all over and I can't move, it hurts too much.'

Her fingers tightened involuntarily. 'I know. The surgeon will come and see you later—he'll explain. You had some broken bones, and they had to fix the ends together, to keep them still so they can heal and stop them hurting.'

He frowned. 'I can remember it hurting,' he said

slowly. 'Much worse than this. And Ben—was Ben there?'

'Ben was there,' Nick confirmed. 'Don't worry about it, it's all over now and you're on the mend. You just need to rest and get well again, and then you'll be able to go home.'

'When?'

Kate swallowed. 'Not for a little while.'

His face fell. 'I'm going to miss the rest of holiday club, aren't I?' he said, looking worried, and she nodded.

'I'm afraid so. You could be in here for a few weeks.'

'Oh. Can Matt get my pot for you? Will you ask him?'

'You can ask him yourself. I'm sure he'll come and visit you soon.'

She saw Nick stiffen, but she couldn't pander to his feelings. Rob and his son Matt were an important part of Jem's life, and although she wasn't going to marry Rob, she wasn't going to avoid him, either, or his son. For Jem's sake, he needed to keep some continuity in his life.

Nick would just have to get over it.

Martin Bradley came to see Jem just before eight, and decided he could be moved into a side room on the paediatric ward just down the corridor as soon as it was cleared.

'You're doing really well, we're very pleased, so you can have a nice room to yourself for a few days so you can rest quietly until you're feeling a bit brighter, then we'll move you down into the other ward with kids of your own age, to give you some company. I'm going to increase your pain relief, because you're obviously quite sore, and once you're a bit more comfortable you'll feel a lot better.'

'Thanks,' Jem murmured, and his eyes flicked past Kate to the door, and he grinned weakly. 'Hey, Ben,' he said, and Ben came into the room and perched on the end of the bed.

'Hi, tiger. So, how is he, Martin? Will he live?'

'Oh, I reckon. Nice work, that pelvic fixator, made my job a lot easier. Did you do it?'

'No, that was Josh O'Hara. He's going to be a real asset. I had a look at the X-rays—it's looking good.'

'Mmm. It went back nicely. I'm pleased. Well, I'll leave you all to it. I'll catch up with you later, Jem.'

'So, how's it feeling, young'un?' Ben asked, and the boy shrugged.

'Sore.'

'Yeah, I'll bet. Still, you'll soon be up and about. Look on the bright side, you won't have to go to school for a few weeks.'

Kate frowned. Of course he wouldn't. And that meant she wouldn't be able to go to work, because there was no way she was leaving him with anyone else until he was better.

'Kate, don't worry, they'll get cover,' Nick said softly, reading her mind. 'I'm going to have to go in and sort it all out shortly, but you're not to worry, it'll be fine.'

She nodded. Of course it would be, but there were so many patients she wanted to be there for—Gemma was a few days overdue now and she didn't want to hand her over at this stage; she was one of their own, a practice nurse who was married to one of their GPs,

Sam Cavendish, and Kate hated the fact that she'd have to bail on them at this stage. And there was a woman she'd seen—heavens, only yesterday—who she'd been a bit worried about. She couldn't even remember her name, but Chloe would sort it for her. As the only other midwife based in the practice, she'd have to.

'Nick, I need to speak to Chloe. There's a patient—'

'I'll get her to come and see you. She'll want to, anyway. They all will.'

Of course they would. They were a fabulous bunch of people, and she didn't know how she would have got through the last year without their support. She nodded, and turned back to Ben, who was making Jem laugh weakly with a dreadful joke. She smiled at him, and he winked and stood up.

'I need to get back to work, but I just thought I'd come and touch base. And Lucy'll be in later. She's going to leave the kids with me at lunchtime and slip up for a minute. You might want to shave by then.'

His teasing eyes met Nick's, and Kate thought she could read reassurance and support in them. Had Lucy come round? Maybe Ben had been able to listen to her and let her talk it all through last night, and maybe she'd softened her stance a little. Goodness, she hoped so. She didn't care if Lucy never forgave her for her part in it, but that she shouldn't forgive Nick—that was unthinkable.

She was his little girl, the apple of his eye, and he adored her. He'd be gutted if there was a permanent rift between them.

And then, when Ben had hardly left the room, Jack came in and grinned at Jem and perched on the end of the bed where Ben had sat.

'Hi there, kiddo. How're you doing?'

'OK. Bit sore.'

'I'll bet.' Jack glanced up at his father, and winced at the state of him. 'Dad, you look like a tramp. I think you need a shower and a shave. I've got a clean shirt here—do you want it?'

'No, it's OK, I'm going to go shortly and sort some stuff out at the surgery, so I'll have a shower then. Thanks, anyway.'

'Don't thank me, I just didn't want you scaring the children,' he said, but this time his voice was kinder, less condemnatory than the last time he'd told his father not to thank him, over the blood donating issue, and Nick gave a wry smile.

After a few moments of banter, Jack, too, left them alone, and it wasn't long before the nurses came to move Jem through to the paediatric ward.

'All ready to go?' the staff nurse asked cheerfully, and he nodded as they kicked the brakes off the bed and wheeled it through the door, down a corridor and then into a bright, sunny room off the children's ward that looked out over the gardens below.

'There are ducks down there,' Kate told him, peering out of the window and trying to find something normal to talk about as they sorted out his oxygen and monitoring equipment and pushed his locker back into place. 'A mother duck and some ducklings. You'll be able to see them when you can move around a bit more.'

'How many ducklings?' he asked, but she couldn't really tell.

'At least five. Not sure. We'll count them together later. They can't go anywhere, they're in a courtyard.'

'What, trapped?'

'Until they can fly. I expect someone's looking after them, but they'll be safe from any cats and foxes, at least.'

'Mmm.'

His eyelids were wilting, and it was obvious he was still very far from well. The move from PICU to the little side room had been more than enough for him, and Nick glanced at his watch. Ten-fifteen, give or take.

'I need to go to the surgery, sort a few things out, and if you're staying, you could do with some clothes and wash things, and some stuff for Jeremiah. Give me your keys, I'll sort it.'

She stared at him blankly. 'I haven't got my keys,' she said slowly. 'They must be in the car still.'

'Has anyone else got a key?'

She nodded. 'Yes. Chloe. Take her with you, she'll know what to get. And tell her I'm sorry about Bruno. If she can't manage, then I'll have to—'

'I'm sure they can manage the dog between them,' he said reassuringly. 'They said you weren't to worry. I'll be as quick as possible, ring me if you need to or if you think of anything specific you need.'

'Thanks.'

He found his car in the staff car park, and drove straight to the surgery, even though he was desperate for a shower and a change of clothes. There was a tie in his jacket pocket, and for a moment he contemplated it, but he was in a hurry now. He probably should have gone home, but for some reason he just needed to be here, amongst his friends, and it was nearly eleven, so with any luck the patients would have gone by now so they didn't have to see him looking like this. He walked in, straight up the stairs past a couple of waiting patients and the startled receptionist, ignoring their concerned questions, and into the staffroom.

It was crowded, and they all turned and stared at him, Sam Cavendish getting to his feet and breaking the silence first.

'Nick! How is he?'

'He's…' He couldn't finish, couldn't find the words, and Chloe gasped and covered her mouth with her hand. 'No! He can't be—'

He shook his head. 'No. He's all right,' he said hastily, and there was a collective sigh of relief. 'He's stable now and out of Intensive Care. It's been…um…'

He didn't know what to say, but they were clustered around him, gathered there as if they'd been waiting, and he lifted his head and met their eyes, seeing the love and concern and support there for him, for Kate, and for Jeremiah. And there was only one thing that mattered, one thing he needed to tell them, these people who were his friends, first and foremost, although they might well not be when they knew.

'It's been a bit of a worry, but it looks like he's going to be all right,' he said, and then he added, 'Actually, we're both going to need some help in the next few weeks with cover. There's something you should know, something I'd rather didn't leave this room. Jeremiah's my son.'

If he'd expected a shocked reaction, he didn't get one.

There was no condemnation, no gasps of horror, just acceptance and support.

It turned out that most of them had worked it out— some, like old Doris Trefussis, cleaner, tea-lady and general all-round good egg, years ago. Sam Cavendish knew, certainly, and when everyone had dispersed and left them alone, Sam put a mug of coffee in his hand and sat down at right angles to him, his bad leg stretched out and propped on the other ankle, a mug cradled in his hands and his eyes thoughtful.

'You can do it, you know,' he said, surprising Nick. He frowned. 'Do what?'

'Be a good father to him. You were more of a father to me in my teens than my own father had ever been, and I know you've been good to my brother in the ten years I was away. And you love the boy. That means more than anything else.'

Nick gave a soft huff of laughter, and smiled tiredly at Sam. He'd been fond of him since he'd been a boy, and he'd been more than happy to take him on at the surgery when he'd come home wounded after a run-in with insurgents in Africa. And he was glad he had, because Sam had ended up back with Gemma, one of their nurses and his childhood sweetheart, and their baby was due any day. 'When did you get to be so wise, Sam?' he asked softly, but Sam just smiled back and ignored his remark.

'We need to sort the rota out, because Gemma can't go on much longer. She's been having contractions off and on for days and every morning I wake up and think, How can she still be pregnant? So it won't be long, and we'll need another locum if you aren't going to be here.'

'Why not? I can still work most of the time.'

'No—because you'll be at your son's bedside,' he offered gently. 'Does he even know yet?'

Nick felt emotion well in his chest and cleared his throat. 'No. We're going to tell him when he's a bit stronger. To be honest, I'm dreading it and I'm happy to put it off as long as possible.'

'Don't leave it too long,' Sam advised, as if he hadn't already done that very thing, then he tilted his head on one side and raised a brow. 'You look like hell, by the way,' he said conversationally, and Nick growled softly under his breath.

'If one more person tells me that today I'm going to—'

'What? Go home and shower? Good idea, Nick. You could do with a seriously close shave, a shirt that's seen an iron in living memory and trousers that haven't got more wrinkles than an elephant's hide.'

He looked down at himself and remembered what he'd looked like less than twenty-four hours ago. How could that be? It seemed a lifetime ago. Nearly had been...

'We'll sort out the rota,' Sam was saying. 'I'm booking myself off now for a fortnight, because Gemma was looking iffy this morning, and I'll make sure they book you off, too, and we'd better have open-ended cover for Kate. I think Chloe might already have organised that, but I'll check. Kate's dog is being looked after, so all you need to worry about is your family. Go on, go and sort yourself out and get back to them. Have you had any sleep at all?'

'I had an hour this morning.'

'You might want to get your head down as well, then.'

He shook his head. 'No time. I can't leave Kate without back-up. Oh, and I'll need Chloe to find some stuff for them both. She's got a key to Kate's place. Kate's house keys were on her car keys, and they got left in it.

I expect the police have taken them. I need to follow that up.'

He got to his feet with a sigh, put his mug on the draining board and paused at the door. 'Sam—thanks.'

'What for? I owe you more than I can ever repay, Nick. You go and look after your son, and leave the practice to us. We can manage.'

He laughed. 'Easy for you to say, you're booking yourself out on paternity leave as of now!'

'The others can cope. They love a challenge. Go on, shove off.'

He shoved. Half an hour later, after a rapid shower and a desperately-needed shave, dressed in clean trousers and an open-necked casual shirt and feeling a little more human, he headed back to the hospital, armed with Chloe's love for Kate and Jeremiah, the spare key to her cottage and a bag of toiletries and clothes for each of them, which Chloe had kindly picked up while he had been sorting himself out.

He got back at a little after one-thirty, and found Kate sitting by Jem's bed, her face exhausted.

'How is he?' he asked, putting the bags down by the chair, and she shrugged.

'The same, really. He's in a lot of pain—they've just given him more painkillers, and he's gone to sleep at last. Jess came and sat with me for a while, she's very kind. Oh, and Lucy popped in a little while ago—she's going to come back later when you're here. She sends her love. And Jack's been up again.'

He nodded, his eyes welling up. Lucy had sent her love. And Jack had been back, too, giving up his time to a brother he hadn't known he had. It didn't surprise him. His twins were both kind and generous to a fault, and he was immensely proud of them.

'Have you had lunch?'

She shook her head. 'I didn't like to leave him. Have you?'

'No—but he's asleep now, so why don't we pop down to the café and grab something while the going's good?'

She nodded, and got stiffly to her feet, easing out the kinks and giving him a wry smile. They told the nurses where they were going, then she fell into step beside him as they headed for the café.

'Oh, it's nice to move. I've been so afraid to make a noise in case I disturbed him.'

He smiled ruefully. 'I'm sorry I was so long, but I had to sort out the fallout at the surgery, and I got sick of everyone telling me I needed a shower. So, do I look better?'

She smiled up at him. 'Just a bit.' Actually, she'd quite liked him with the roguish stubbled look, but it was better to have him back with her—much better. She'd missed him. He'd been gone what felt like ages, and it had been a bit of an emotional roller coaster watching Jem in pain. It was good to step off the ride for a moment now he was comfortably asleep.

Nick looked up at the menu, then glanced at her. 'What are you having?'

'Oh, I don't know. Vegetables! All I've had in the last twenty-four hours is sandwiches. I'm sick of bread.'

'They've got salads.'

'Perfect.'

'I'll get you one. Go and sit down over there by the

window and relax,' he ordered, so she went, and a few moments later he set a laden tray down in front of her.

She tried to summon up some enthusiasm. 'That looks nice,' she lied. 'What do I owe you?'

'Owe me?'

'For my lunch.'

He scowled at her. 'Don't be ridiculous. I got you a fruit smoothie as well as the salad because I know you like them and I thought you were probably sick of tea and coffee, too.'

'I am.' She gave him a tired little smile, all she could manage. 'Thank you, Nick.'

He scowled again. 'Don't keep thanking me. I've made a complete fist of everything I've ever done for you. It's high time I started balancing the books.'

If only. She gave a quiet sigh and picked up her knife and fork, wondering how long she was going to be based at the hospital and when she'd be able to go home and lie down in her own bed, just for an hour or two. She was so tired, so very, very tired...

'Kate?'

She pushed her plate away. 'I'm sorry. I'm not really hungry.'

'You're exhausted. You should be in bed.'

'I can't, Nick. I have to be here for him. Tomorrow. I'll go home tomorrow—maybe in the morning, once we've seen Martin Bradley and we know if he's happy with him. I could go home then and have a rest.'

'OK. But if you're doing that, you're eating your salad now. Come on, you can do it.'

And so, with him coaxing and cajoling her, she finished most of it, drank the smoothie and then realised she was feeling more human. 'You're so sickeningly right always, aren't you?' she said with a smile, and a fleeting frown crossed his face.

'Now I know you need sleep,' he said gruffly, and stabbed his fork into the last slice of tomato on his plate and put it in his mouth.

She laughed at him. 'That's better,' she said softly. 'You sound more like the old Nick.'

He pushed his plate away and thought about it, realising she was right. 'I feel better. It's amazing what a shower and a square meal can do. I've brought you some things, by the way. Chloe sorted them out—she sends her love. Well, everyone at the practice sends their love,' he amended with a smile that felt distinctly crooked. 'I told them he's my son,' he added, his voice low. 'I hope you don't mind. I asked them to keep it quiet.'

'How did they take it?'

He shrugged. 'It was odd. They didn't seem at all surprised. In fact, they were incredibly supportive. Chloe had arranged cover for you for the rest of this week already, but I've told her I'm writing you off sick for four weeks—'

'Four? Why?'

He smiled again, this time a little wryly. 'Because you've got whiplash,' he reminded her.

'No, I haven't.'

'I'm sure you have. You're having four weeks to get over it, whatever,' he told her, and, actually, she found she didn't mind his high-handed approach this time, because she needed the time to devote to Jem, and it wasn't entirely false. Her neck was a little sore.

She rolled it, wincing slightly, and he found himself aching to ease it for her, to massage it gently until it relaxed so she could get some relief. 'Sam's signing off on paternity leave—and, no, Gemma's not in labour, as far as I know, but he wasn't quite sure if she was on the verge this morning so he's booked a locum anyway.'

'She's a week overdue,' Kate said, biting her lip. 'I should be there for her.'

'Don't worry. Chloe's there, she'll look after her. And Sam is a doctor. They should be able to cope without you. And Sam's getting a locum to cover me for the next week at least, unless they really can't manage without me. I want to be here for you both,' he added, when she started to protest.

She said nothing for a moment, then sighed softly. 'Thank you. I don't know how I would have coped without you yesterday and last night.'

'I would have been here anyway, Kate,' he told her quietly. 'Even if he wasn't my son, I would have been here for you.'

She nodded. 'Yes, I know you would. That's the funny thing about you, you're so generous, so kind, so helpful, but if anybody dares to realise it, you get so uncomfortable —look, you're doing it now.'

She shook her head slowly, carefully folding her paper napkin for something to do with her hands, because it would have been so easy to reach out to him, to take the hand lying on the table, fiddling with the little sugar packets.

'We ought to tell Jem, I suppose,' he murmured. 'Nobody in the hospital apart from Jack and Ben knows, so it shouldn't leak out, which means we can tell him when the time's right.'

He carried on fiddling, piling up the sugar packets and pushing them into straight lines with his fingertip. 'I'd just like to do it when I've had a chance to build a relationship with him—made friends with him, got to know him a bit better. You're right, I haven't ever really talked to him, or spent meaningful time with him, and it's time I did. Time I gave him a chance to get to know me, too. And it'll give you a bit of a break as well, if we're sharing the visiting. It's going to be a long haul.'

She nodded. 'Yes. Yes, I know. It should be better once he's on the mend, though. They have lessons and activities and he'll be doing physio, and there will be other kids for him to talk to. And his friends'll be able to visit in a few days' time, so that'll take the heat off us, too.'

And who knew? They might even find some time to be together themselves. That was a novel thought, but probably not one that would lead to anything. She'd do well to keep reminding herself of that fact, because it would be all too easy to fall into the habit of relying on him only to find he wasn't there when it came to the crunch.

She was sure he meant well, and maybe this time he really thought he could do it, but she wasn't holding her breath.

CHAPTER FIVE

MEGAN PHILLIPS, the pretty young paediatric registrar who'd been on call overnight, was waiting for them at the nursing station.

'We've got his blood results,' she began, and Nick felt his heart stall.

Don't let him have a problem. Not thrombocytopenia, he thought. Please don't let it be that, don't let him have DIC.

'He's OK now, but the biochemistry was a bit skewed. We needed to tweak some of the components, but it probably explains why he was feeling a bit rough. We've started an infusion and he should be fine now. We'll check it again in a while, OK?'

Relief hit him like a wall, and he smiled and thanked her, wishing, as a doctor, he didn't know so much. Ignorance would be bliss, he thought as he ushered Kate back into the side room where Jem was still sleeping. She stopped in the doorway and put her hand over her mouth for a second, sucking in air, and he squeezed her shoulder.

'He's all right,' he murmured.

'I know, but he looks so vulnerable, so fragile lying there like that,' she murmured.

'He'll be fine. You heard Megan,' he said firmly, and watched as she perched on the edge of the armchair by the bed.

It was upholstered in a hideous pink—wipe-clean vinyl, of course—and he found himself wondering how many parents had sat on it and watched their children.

He sat on the arm, laid his hand on Kate's shoulder and watched his son sleeping…

Megan reached out her hand to pick up the phone, and it fell back to her lap, nerveless with shock.

No!

It couldn't be him! She'd heard there was an O'Hara starting in A and E, but it had never occurred to her it was him, that he'd be here in Cornwall, of all places! She'd thought she'd be safe here, never have to see him again, never have to be reminded…

Her heart raced, and she shrank back into the chair, trying to get away, retreating from the sight of him. She must be mistaken, she told herself. It wasn't Josh. It couldn't be.

But it was him—tall, lean, more attractive even than he'd been eight years ago. He was the most good-looking man she'd ever seen, so sure of himself, so at home in his own skin that he exuded an almost tangible aura of confident masculinity. Alpha man. A man that women couldn't resist. A man who only had to crook his little finger and stupid, senseless little girls would abandon all their brains and follow him to the end of the earth.

He glanced over and caught sight of her, his body arresting momentarily, then excusing himself he walked towards her, resting a hand on the top of the counter and looking down at her with those extraordinary indigo-blue eyes, and she couldn't look away, for all she wanted to.

'Megan?'

His voice was shocked, his eyes dark with a host of emotions she couldn't even guess at, but it wasn't his emotions she was worried about, it was her own, tumbling in free-fall as she stared back at him, mesmerised, horrified, memory after memory crashing through her and robbing her of speech.

She unglued her tongue from the roof of her mouth and tried to remain professional.

'Hello, Josh.'

Just the two words. It was all she could manage, all she could force out through lips that were stiff with shock.

His hair fell over his forehead, and he threaded his fingers through the glossy black strands and raked it out of the way, making her suck in her breath. She could still remember the soft, silky feel of it between her fingers. 'I didn't know you worked here,' he said, that soft Irish brogue rippling over her nerve-endings like little tongues of flame. 'How are you?'

He looked vaguely stunned, his eyes wary now, concerned. As well they might be after what he'd done...

'I'm—I'm fine. Busy. Excuse me, I need to make a call.'

'That's OK, you can do it in a moment. I'm looking for a patient who's had surgery for a fractured pelvis— Jem Althorp? I put on the ex-fix in A and E.'

'He's fine. There's a minor problem with his bloods, that's all. He's in that room there. Now, I need to deal with this, Josh, and I don't need to deal with you. Excuse me.'

And picking the phone up again with shaking hands, she rang the haematology department, conscious all the while of Josh standing there, until with a quiet sigh he turned on his heel and walked away.

She nearly wept with relief.

The rest of the day dragged for Kate and Nick.

Josh O'Hara had popped in briefly, but he'd seemed distracted and hadn't stayed long. Just long enough for them to thank him for the procedure that might well have saved their son's life.

Jem's blood was quickly sorted, as Megan had promised, and he was feeling better, but by the evening Kate was at the end of her tether, and Nick sent her off to bed at nine, when Jem had drifted off to sleep again.

'I'll sit up with him.'

'But you haven't had any sleep either,' she protested. 'I've had more than you.'

'I haven't been in a car accident,' he said firmly. 'Go on. I'll get you if there's the slightest thing to worry about, but there won't be.'

'But how will you know?' she asked, fretting. 'You don't know him—you don't know how he sleeps, and what's normal—'

'Kate, he's just a child, like any other,' he said gently. 'If he's sick, I'll know. He'll be fine. Go to bed before you drop to pieces.'

So she went, reluctantly, and he settled down in the hateful pink chair and watched the monitor blinking steadily, watched the nice, even trace of Jem's heartbeat through the night, while the staff came in and did hourly obs and brought him endless cups of tea.

And then at three Kate came and took over, sending

Nick off to grab some sleep, and he went into the little room where she'd been sleeping and lay down on the still-warm bed, her scent all around him and the residual heat of her body seeping into him like a soothing balm, sending him into a deep, restful sleep.

Jem woke shortly before six, and Kate could see at once that he was stronger.

'Morning, soldier,' she murmured, and, leaning forwards, she stroked his hair back off his forehead and smiled at him. 'How are you?'

'I feel better,' he said. 'I don't hurt so much, and I don't feel so sick. I'm hungry, though.'

He'd graduated from nil by mouth to sips of water, and so Kate poured a little into the beaker and held it to his lips. 'Maybe they'll let you eat something light later on. I've got some wash things for you. You'll feel better after we clean your teeth and wash your face with nice hot water,' she said soothingly. 'Grandma sends her love, and so does Chloe and everyone at the practice.'

'Where's Uncle Nick?' he asked.

She stroked his hair. 'He's here. He spent the night next to you in this chair, and then I got up and swapped over. I expect he's still sleeping. Why?'

He shrugged his skinny shoulders. 'Just wondered. I thought he might have gone home.'

She shook her head. 'No. He wouldn't leave you,' she told him, and she watched something terrifyingly like hero-worship dawn in his eyes.

But all he said was, 'Oh,' and then his eyes drifted shut again and he lay quietly for a while.

Behind her the door opened and closed, and she knew it was Nick without turning round.

'How is he?'

'Awake. Better. He was asking where you were.'

'I'm right here, son,' he said softly, the irony of it catching her in mid-chest as he perched on the foot of the bed and laid his hand lightly on Jem's ankle 'How are you?'

Jem opened his eyes. 'OK.'

'Good.'

Kate saw Nick's shoulders drop a fraction, and knew he'd been worried. 'He's hungry.'

'That's a good sign,' he said, and his shoulders dropped a little further.

'My bruises hurt,' Jem mumbled from the bed. 'My leg's really sore, and my side hurts, and my elbow's sore, but it's not like it was yesterday.'

'It'll feel better soon.'

There was a tap on the door, and a nurse popped her head round. 'We were going to give Jem a bit of a wash, if you two want to get some breakfast,' she said, and so they went down to the café that was fast becoming their second home, and had bacon rolls and pastries and lashings of coffee.

'One day I'll get home and start eating proper food,' she said, pushing the last crumbs around the plate. 'I never have anything like this for breakfast. I have yogurt and fruit.'

'You could have had yogurt and fruit,' Nick said with a frown, but she just smiled.

'I know, but I wanted a bacon roll, and I couldn't resist the pastries.'

He laughed, and, reaching out his hand, he covered hers and enfolded it in his warm, gentle grasp. 'Crazy woman,' he said, his thumb stroking slow circles over the back of her hand, and she felt the ice inside her starting to thaw, replaced by a strange heat that warmed her from deep inside, somewhere in the region of her heart.

'You need to go home this morning,' he went on gently. 'You're exhausted, and you need a shower and just to get out of here. Once the doctors have been round and they're happy, I'm going to take you home—and don't argue.'

She smiled a little unsteadily. 'I won't. It sounds wonderful. I could really do with a change of scenery, just for a little while. I ought to sort my car out, too, really. I need the keys.'

'We can phone the police, get that organised,' he said. 'I'll contact them. And you'll need another car.'

She rolled her eyes. 'I have no idea how long that'll take.'

'We'll get you one today,' he said. 'What do you want?'

She frowned at him. 'Why should you do that?'

'Because he's my son? Because you need it to transport him? I'll get you a bigger one, a stronger one.'

'No! I'll get it, and, besides, it can't be big, I have to be able to park in tight spaces.'

'So I'll get you a small stronger one.'

She sighed. 'Nick, that other driver must have been going at well over forty. Nothing's that strong. And I need it to do my job as well. Maybe I'll have to get a contract one through the PCT after all.'

'They can't do it that quickly. I can get you a car today—or at least organise it.'

She sighed again. 'Nick, it's very kind of you, but I

don't really need it in a tearing hurry if I'm going to be stuck here for days.'

He shrugged. 'So you can have one in days. Just tell me what you want.'

She gave up. Sort of. 'I'll think about it,' she told him, and changed the subject.

The doctors were pleased with him. The blood setback seemed to have been resolved—routine, as Martin Bradley had said—his wound was healing well, and he was happy for them to leave the hospital—for a short while.

'Don't be too long,' Jem said, having a little wobble just as they left, and she hesitated, but Nick's hand on her arm was firm, and she promised they wouldn't be long and let him lead her out.

They went via the police station to pick up her keys and the items that had been in her car, and Nick put the bag in his boot and drove her home. It was the first time she'd been back since the accident, and it felt like for ever. She walked inside, picking up the post as she went, and then looked around.

The place was littered with Jem's things. A book on the stairs, his sports bag in the hall, a jumper dropped on the floor in the sitting room.

It caught her totally unawares, and she stared at the things numbly. What on earth would it have been like to come back to this if he'd died?

'I need a shower—put the kettle on and make yourself a drink,' she said, and hurried upstairs, needing to get away from Nick, to hide herself away in the shower where the sound of water might drown the threatening sobs that were rising in her throat.

She stripped her clothes off, the sobs starting to break free, and stepped into the shower, turning her face to the wall and slumping on it, her hands pressed over her mouth to hold in the pain that had been bottled up for days, the pain she couldn't hold inside any longer.

She could so easily have lost him. Just another couple of miles an hour...

A wrenching sob ripped through her, and she folded over, propping herself up under the pounding spray.

She was crying.

He'd heard the sound before. She'd done the same thing when James had died, and he'd brought her home from the headland and sent her to shower and warm up.

He couldn't go there again—not in the shower with her, holding her—but how could he leave her? How could he have left her then, torn apart by grief?

He went up.

She hadn't locked the bathroom door, and he opened the shower cubicle and turned off the water. She was huddled in the corner, and he reached for a towel and crouched down, draping it round her as he lifted her out, sitting down on the floor with her curled into his lap, her tears giving way slowly to fractured sobs that tore at his heart.

'He could have died,' she said at last, her voice fragmented by emotion. 'I came in and saw all his things, and I thought, What if I'd come back here, like I did when James died, and his things were everywhere—and...'

She broke off, fisting her hands in his shirt, and he held her closer, rocking her gently, hot tears scalding his eyes again as she clung to him, sobbing. 'Shh. He's all right, Kate, he's getting better now. He's going to be all right, sweetheart, he really is. You have to believe that.'

She nodded and sniffed, the sobs dying away to random hiccups. Every now and then there was another little bout, but he just held her close and let her cry, let her get it out of her system until at last she lifted her head and let go of his shirt, then swiped the tears from her face with shaking fingers.

'I'm sorry.'

'Don't be.'

'I always do this, don't I? Hide in the shower to cry.'

He shushed her again, smoothing the damp strands of hair back from her face and pressing his lips softly to her tear-stained cheek.

'All right now?'

She nodded slowly, and he eased her out of her arms, rescuing the towel as it slid down and tucking it back round her.

'I'll leave you to wash. I'll be downstairs,' he told her, and, standing up, he pulled her to her feet and kissed her cheek again. 'I'll make you a cup of tea.'

'Thanks.'

She came down a few minutes later just as the kettle boiled, dressed in clean clothes, her hair still damp and combed out over her shoulders and her smile wry.

'Sorry about that,' she said, looking a little sheepish. 'I just lost it.'

'Don't apologise, you've had a hell of a couple of days. You needed to get it off your chest. And talking of which, I'm a little underdressed. There's a bag of clean clothes in my car that I keep there for emergencies—could you do the honours while I shower? Since I'm already drenched?'

He'd taken off his sodden, crumpled shirt, but the trousers clung to his legs and her eyes scanned his body. Comparing him to Rob? He wouldn't come off well. He took care of himself, but Rob was a fitness fanatic and a PE teacher. And an ex, he reminded himself, and took small comfort from that.

'Sure,' she said, and took the keys, and he went upstairs to the bathroom. When he emerged from the shower a few moments later, the bag was there, just inside the door, with a clean, dry towel. She'd come in, and he hadn't noticed. Just as well, he decided, because when that towel had slipped he'd had a whole plethora of inappropriate thoughts and frankly he wouldn't trust himself with her at the moment.

He went back downstairs and found her sitting at the kitchen table with a cup of tea, and she ran her eyes over him again and smiled.

'It's a good job you keep spare clothes in your car,' she said, pushing a mug of tea towards him, and he gave a rueful laugh and sat down.

'Well, more or less. Trousers and shirt, at least, for predictable accidents. I don't tend to carry underwear.'

She chuckled, then sat back and eyed him thoughtfully. 'Are you telling me you're going commando, Dr T.?' she asked softly, raising an eyebrow and trying to stop her mouth from twitching, and the inappropriate thoughts leapt into his head again.

'That depends who wants to know,' he murmured, feeling the smile tug his own mouth, and the twitch got worse.

'Are you flirting with me?'

He felt his smile fade and searched her beautiful, teasing brown eyes. 'Would that be such a bad thing?' he asked softly.

The teasing look vanished, and there was a moment of breathless silence. 'I don't know—would it?'

'I'm not sure. It might be fun. It would make a change—we haven't had fun like that since our teens.' He glanced down at the mug, lined the handle up carefully exactly at right angles and then met her eyes. 'How about it?'

'How about what?' she asked carefully, and he thought she was holding her breath.

'Us.'

'I'm not sure that would be a good idea,' she said, after a seemingly endless pause. 'Maybe we'd just better concentrate on Jem for now.'

She'd hesitated, and in that time he'd held his own breath. He let it out now and gave a little shrug. 'If you want.'

'I want. Things are complicated enough.'

He nodded, and she gave a quiet sigh of relief. She didn't want to rush into anything. There was, however, another worry that was playing on her mind, a more immediate problem, and she raised it now.

'Nick, how am I going to manage when he comes out of hospital? I don't have a downstairs bathroom, or even a cloakroom, and stairs could be really difficult at first.'

'You could come to mine.'

She shook her head instantly. 'No. Not to Annabel's house,' she said softly, and watched the guilt flash across his eyes before he looked away.

'No. You're right, it wouldn't feel appropriate and,

anyway, it's not exactly off the beaten track. So—perhaps we could rent somewhere? A bungalow or something, neutral ground. Just for a while, until he can manage the stairs again. I'm sure there are things out there. It's only April. It might be harder in August with the tourists, but I'm sure we could find something now and it needn't be for long. A few weeks, maybe.'

A rental property? 'It's worth a try,' she said, feeling the weight of that worry lifting from her shoulders with relief. 'I would never have thought of that.'

His smile was a little crooked. 'You see? I can have my uses, slight though they might be. I'll call the agents now.'

He made a couple of calls while she dried her hair, and when she came down he was fizzing with suppressed excitement.

'There's a single-storey barn conversion. They've been trying to sell it, but it hasn't gone because it's quite pricy and the owners have been unrealistic, but they've now decided to let it, but only to people who don't want a long lease, which we don't.'

She nodded slowly. 'OK. Where is it?'

'On the way to Ben and Lucy's, so only about three miles out of the village. It's got a distant sea view, apparently—it's U-shaped, two-storey in the central section, with a courtyard garden and surrounded by farmland. Worth a look?'

'Definitely,' she said, then hesitated, not sure how to ask but just knowing that she had to, that this needed to be set out in black and white. 'Nick—is this just for me to stay in, or were you thinking of being there, too?'

He gave an enigmatic shrug, his eyes veiled. 'That depends.'

'On?'

'You, Jem? I don't know. If you want me there, I'd like to be there, but I don't want to confuse him or pre-empt any decision you might make in the future. I know Rob lived with you, but—'

'No,' she corrected hastily. 'Rob didn't live with us. He and Matt came to stay after I came out of hospital, but the boys shared Jem's room and Rob was on the sofa bed downstairs. We didn't share a room. It didn't feel right, when it came to it.'

He wasn't sure why, but that made him feel better. Not much. He knew they'd had an intimate relationship, because he'd gone to talk to her one night about a year ago and seen them through the window. He could still picture Rob bending his head to kiss her in the kitchen, and then the lights going off and coming on upstairs. Not that there was any reason why they shouldn't, but that had been before her surgery. Maybe that had changed things. Was that what she had meant about it not feeling right?

'I don't have any ulterior motive, Kate,' he told her. 'There are four bedrooms there. Two upstairs, each with en suite, and an en suite guest room, another bedroom or snug and a study downstairs in one of the sides. It's got a big open living space with a sitting room one end, a kitchen at the other and an open vaulted dining hall in the middle, with the stairs off it, and the third side is utility, workshop and garaging, apparently. We'd have plenty of space.'

She blinked. 'It sounds amazing.'

'That's what I thought. I've asked the agent to meet us there in twenty minutes.'

Her eyes widened. 'Wow. OK. You don't hang around, do you?'

'Is that a problem?'

'No. No, no problem, it's been worrying me to bits. It would be great if it was any good. The only thing is, how much is the rent, because I can't afford a fortune.'

'You let me worry about that.'

'Nick, I can't—'

'You can. It's not for you, it's for our son, and God knows I've done precious little for him in the last eleven years. Just let it go, Kate. Please. Don't argue.'

She opened her mouth, thought for a moment and then gave in. 'OK. But don't get in the habit of doing this.'

'What? Caring for my son? Why the hell not?'

There was a look in his eyes she hadn't seen for years, a purpose, a passion, and it was as if this whole course of events had brought him back to life.

She smiled. 'Shall we go and look?' she said, and he grinned and tossed his car keys in the air.

'After we've been via mine and I've got some underwear on,' he said with a mischievous twinkle that gave her heart an unexpected lurch, and he ushered her out, closing the door firmly behind them.

It was fantastic. Perfect.

Built of granite, it was solid, tucked down in a fold of the land to shelter it from the prevailing south-westerly wind, and he couldn't find a single thing wrong with it.

It was to let fully furnished with every necessity and equipped to a very high standard, with king-size beds in the main bedrooms, lovely battered leather sofas in the sitting room and invitingly luxurious bathrooms with showerheads like dustbin lids.

He hadn't felt so excited about anything for years. He'd made his mind up after the most cursory walk-through and an exchanged glance with Kate, who was looking slightly stunned. It was wonderful, and he couldn't imagine why it hadn't sold instantly.

He said as much to the agent, who just shrugged. 'I don't know, either. It's been a second home and their circumstances have changed and they want to sell it, but they want a lot for it. The only thing I can assume is that it's too expensive for a holiday cottage and there aren't enough people living around here who can afford to buy it. As far as I can see, there isn't a single catch apart from the price, but the market's been a little odd recently. Maybe that's it.'

Maybe. And it was expensive, but Nick was doing some quick calculations. He wasn't a big spender. He'd been careful over the years, he was sitting on the cash he'd got for his parents' house when Ben had bought it at auction for Lucy, and if he sold his own house, he'd have enough to buy it.

Not that he was going to do anything rash just yet, but it might be worth having a word with the agent to see if he could have the option on it as they were renting. And maybe, if things went well...

'What do you think, Kate?'

Her smile was enigmatic. 'I think we need to talk.'

He frowned, as if he couldn't see what on earth they might need to talk about, and then with a slight shrug he turned to the agent.

'Can we have another wander around for a few

minutes, talk this through?' he asked, and the agent nodded.

'Sure. Take your time. I've got a few calls to make, I'll be in the car.'

He left them, and Nick turned to Kate.

'Well? Come on, let's hear it, you've obviously got something you want to say.'

She smiled at his impatience, but she wasn't going to be railroaded, no matter what she thought of the house. 'I think it's wonderful,' she told him honestly. 'Absolutely gorgeous. I also think it'd be impossible going from this back to my house when he's better.'

He gave her a level look. 'Maybe you won't have to.'

'Because I'll sell up and move away?'

'I wasn't thinking of that. I was thinking you might stay on, live here.'

'Nick...' She gave a little, despairing laugh and shook her head. 'We can't just live here for ever.'

'Why not?'

She felt her eyes widen. 'Why not? Because it's outrageously expensive! I can't even afford to rent it, let alone buy it—'

'But I can. I could buy it, and you could stay here.'

'No.' She backed away from him a step, shaking her head again but in denial this time. 'Nick, no. Don't try and buy me, please. Or Jem. Especially not him. I'd rather carry him up and downstairs or put his bed in the sitting room with a commode beside it than let you do that. Please. I mean it.'

He sighed and rammed his hand through his hair. 'Kate, I'm not trying to buy you, don't be silly. I'm just talking through the possibilities.'

'Well, how about possibly finding a simple, small bungalow somewhere with three bedrooms while he recovers?' she suggested bluntly, not sure she could picture him in that setting but pushing him just to see if he'd go for it, for his son's sake. For hers.

He stabbed his hand through his hair again and gave an exasperated sigh. 'Look, forget the money, forget the value, because it's not about that, it's not about impressing you, or Jem. It's about giving us somewhere to get to know each other, all of us, somewhere calm and safe, tranquil, somewhere we can all heal, because I'm under no illusions about it. When we tell him I'm his father there will be some wounds that need healing, Kate, and we'll need somewhere to do that in peace.'

He was so right—of course. He took her hands, meeting her searching gaze with troubled eyes, eyes that were filled with sincerity and pain. 'That's why I've held back, Kate, why I haven't involved myself with Jem, not because I didn't want to rock the boat with my other kids, but because of what it would do to him. I thought, when there was a possibility that you'd marry Rob, that he might not ever need to know, that he could have a stepfather who'd love him and keep him safe, and the knowledge that his father had died a hero. But now you aren't going to marry Rob, and it was only with the blood group thing that I realised there was no question that he was mine, and that he had to know.'

He dropped her hands and turned to the window, gesturing at the courtyard garden. 'Look at it, Kate. It's warm, sheltered, with flat paths where he can walk safely while he heals. Your garden's terraced at the back, your drive slopes up to the house and there are steps to the front door. My garden's the same, and it's so public there—so many people who'd make it their business to have an opinion and to express it. If I'm ten minutes late taking the milk in, there's someone there with it in their hand, ringing the bell and checking up on me.'

'And you don't want people to see us together? Is that it?' she asked, a hideous sinking feeling in her chest. 'Are you ashamed of him, Nick? Because if you are, this stops now. I'm not having my son thinking you're ashamed of him—'

'Kate, no!' he exclaimed, his face horrified, and she knew instantly that he wasn't lying. 'Of course I'm not ashamed of him! I think he's a great kid—and I'm really proud to be his father. I just dread the impact it'll have on him when it gets out, and if there was anything I could do to protect him from that, to prevent it happening, I would do it, believe me, but I can't. I can just be there for him, to fend off the gossips, and the easiest way to do that is to avoid them. At least here we'd be free to explore our relationship in peace, and can you think of a better place to do it?'

He was right, of course, but even though she was reassured about his motives, she still had doubts.

'I don't want him to know you're thinking of buying it, Nick,' she said slowly. 'Not at first.'

He lifted his hands in a shrug. 'Why not? I'm still his father, I still intend to be part of his life, and maybe it's time to move on from the home I shared with Annabel. He can come and stay here with me. And if you move away, he'll be staying for longer—weekends, weeks…' He broke off and rammed his hands in his pockets.

'I don't know if I am,' she said slowly. 'Moving away.'

His eyes narrowed. 'I thought you'd handed in your notice to the PCT?'

'Not yet. I didn't get round to posting it. And now—well, now, maybe I should stay. That depends on you, on your relationship with Jem, on how you get on once he knows you're his father. We'll have to see.'

'But—'

'Nick, don't push it,' she warned, too emotionally fraught to make sensible decisions about their future right then. 'I need time to think this through, and I don't want to feel under pressure.'

'I know. And I want to give you that time. Please don't feel pressured, Kate. I don't want to do that. I'm just trying to give you all the options, and this might be one of them, if you think you'd like it to be.'

'You obviously would,' she murmured, watching his face, and he turned and gave her a crooked little smile.

'I would. I love it here. The moment I stepped inside, I felt it wrap itself around me. I know it sounds crazy, Kate, but I felt as if I'd come home, for the first time in my adult life. And I want it—the whole package. All of it.'

The whole package? Did he mean them, too? Or was she reading things into his words that didn't exist? Whatever he meant, when she searched his eyes she found nothing but a burning sincerity. For all his flaws, Nick Tremayne was nothing if not honest and honourable, and she knew he was only telling her the truth. If he said he'd give her time and not pressure her, he meant it. Whatever his ulterior motives.

And so she nodded. 'OK. We'll try. We'll tell Jem it's just rented, that it's only till he's better, so there are no carrots dangling in front of him, nothing to influence him in any way, and we'll see how it goes. All right?'

His mouth quirked into a wry smile, and he nodded.

'Sure. Sounds good. Let's go and tell the agent he's got a deal,' he said, and she followed him, wondering if it would work, hoping that it would and that it wouldn't all turn out to be the most hideous mistake...

CHAPTER SIX

THEY shook hands on the deal, agreed they could take possession of it as early as the next day and went back to the hospital, Nick still with that air of suppressed excitement about him, Kate assailed by doubts.

Their track record wasn't great. What if this was just another disaster in the making?

Think positive! she told herself, and walked with him up to the ward.

They found Lucy at her new-found brother's bedside, Jem propped up a little, a games console in his hand and an intent expression on his face. Lucy looked up at them with a smile. 'Hi.'

'Hi. Everything all right?'

'Fine.'

'OK, I'll see you in a few minutes, I've got some calls to make,' Nick said, and headed for the door. 'I won't be long.'

Kate perched on the chair by the bed and leant over towards Jem. 'So what's this?'

He grinned at her. 'Lucy's lent it to me—it's Ben's, and it's really cool. And I made her cry.'

Lucy looked a little sheepish. 'He was so sweet—he said he'd wanted one for ages, and it just got to me.'

'Oh, Lucy.'

She shrugged, smiled and carried on watching him as he got to grips with it, and moments later Nick came back in and sat on the chair beside her, perching on the arm with his hip against her side and the subtle scent of his cologne drifting over her, carried on the warmth of his body.

She thought of sharing the barn with him, and a little shiver of anticipation swept over her skin.

'So what's that?' he asked, and she looked up at him and smiled.

'Lucy brought him in a games console,' she said softly. 'He was so thrilled, he made her cry. He's wanted one for ages and we just haven't been able to afford it.'

Jem caught sight of Nick then and grinned excitedly. 'Hey, look what Lucy's lent me, Uncle Nick,' he said.

'I'm looking,' he said, deeply touched that his son wanted to share his excitement, but—Uncle Nick? 'That looks cool.'

'It's not just cool—it's awesome,' he said, stretching the word and making Nick's lips twitch. 'Absolutely epic! Lucy's lent it to me. You can do all sorts of things with it.'

'That's kind of you, Lucy,' Nick said, feeling a little choked and also inadequate because he'd been in such a hurry to get back yesterday he hadn't brought him in anything, and today he'd been so preoccupied with the barn that a simple thing like a present for his child hadn't even entered his head.

Lucy tutted. 'Don't be silly, Dad—it was lying around at home and we hardly ever use it, but don't imagine you're keeping it, half-pint, because it won't happen.'

She ruffled his hair gently, and he grinned and ducked

slightly out of her way as she bent to kiss him, but she followed him and blew a raspberry on his forehead and made him laugh and grimace.

'You be good, and no giving the nurses trouble, or I'll set Ben on you, OK?'

'OK,' he agreed, and smiled at her a little shyly. 'Thank you for bringing it in. It's really nice of you.'

'My pleasure. You take care. I'll see you soon.' She hesitated by Nick, and then, going up on tiptoe, she kissed his cheek. 'Bye, Dad. I'll see you later. We need to talk,' she added, and he gave a brief nod.

'Yes, we do. Soon. Bye, Lucy. And thank you.'

'I want to try the face thing later,' Jem said as she went out. 'It's got a really cool thing where you can take pictures of people and it shows how they're the same, like eyes and stuff. And Lucy says you look like Jack, so we're going to try it when he comes to see me again.'

Nick swallowed. It wasn't only he and Jack that looked alike, he realised now that he was able to admit it, and Lucy had obviously thought of that, too. 'That sounds really interesting, I'll have to have a look at it some time. You seem much better,' he added, quickly changing the subject and relieved that he was sounding so much perkier, even though he could see he was beginning to flag now Lucy had gone.

'It doesn't hurt so much any more. They gave me some stronger painkillers just before Lucy came. My leg still aches a lot, though.'

'I'm not surprised. It got thumped pretty hard.'

'Is the car completely trashed?' he asked Nick.

'I don't know. I haven't seen it.'

Kate thought of the state it had been in by the

time they'd cut the roof and the doors and the front wing off.

'Completely,' she said, shuddering inwardly. 'The boot was full of stuff, and it all got wet when they cut the roof off.' She laughed and felt herself colour. 'The boot's always full of stuff, but I'd sorted out all kinds of things for the charity shop, and I hadn't got round to dropping them off. And it'll be getting mouldy, it's still in the back of your car in a bag, Nick. I ought to deal with it.'

'Don't worry,' he told her, wondering how she could get worked up about something so incredibly trivial in the face of her son's injuries. Or maybe it was because it was trivial that it was safe to worry about it. Safer than thinking about Jem? 'We can sort it out tomorrow.'

She smiled at him and agreed, and then looked at her watch.

'Have you had lunch, Jem?'

'Yes, there was shepherd's pie and peas and jelly and ice cream, but I could only have toast and jelly and ice cream, but I'm having pasta bake tomorrow 'cos I can eat properly then, they said. The jelly and ice cream was nice, though.'

'Good, I'm glad. And it's good news you can eat properly tomorrow, but you should be resting now. Why don't we leave you to sleep, and Uncle Nick and I—'

She broke off, hesitating over the Uncle Nick thing, and looked at him in mute distress, but he just smiled and said, 'We'll go and grab some food while you have a bit of a zizz, and we'll be back. OK, Jem?'

'OK,' he said, and he held the game out to Kate, his eyelids drooping. 'Can you stick that in my locker so it's safe? I don't want it to fall on the floor. I promised Lucy I'd look after it.'

'Sure. Sleep well,' she murmured, and bent over and brushed her lips over his forehead, her stumble over Nick's name reminding her all too forcibly of the conversation that was to come.

'I don't care if you both still call me Uncle Nick,' he said quietly as they walked down to the cafe. 'I don't care what he calls me. It's not what matters.'

Kate felt a little stab of pain for him. 'I know. I'm sorry, it's just—you've been Uncle Nick for years, and—'

'Kate, it's all right,' he said, squeezing her fingers with his free hand. 'I don't need to be anything else. I was happy being a surrogate uncle, and if that's what he wants when we've told him, I'll carry on. All I ask is the chance to be part of his life.'

'You are part of his life, Nick. You always have been, I've made sure of it. And you always will be.'

She heard him sigh softly, and paused on the stairs, her hand on his arm. 'Nick, it'll be all right. We'll get there.'

'Will we?' he asked doubtfully. 'I hope you're right, Kate, because I've suddenly realised how much I want it, and the thought of losing it all now is untenable.'

The day dragged slowly by.

Jem slept for most of it, still not allowed any visitors apart from family, and Jack and Ben came in turn during the afternoon, when they had a moment.

He was sleeping when Jack arrived, and Kate excused herself for a moment and left the men to talk.

God knows, they had enough to say to each other, she thought.

'I'll be back in a few minutes, I just want to make a few phone calls,' she said, and slipped out of the door, pulling it ßbehind her.

Jack met his father's eyes, his own guarded, and Nick sighed quietly. It had taken him a while to rebuild his relationship with Jack once he'd returned to Cornwall, and he was desperately sad that it now seemed in peril again.

'Jack, I—'

'I'm not stopping. I've just come to tell you we want to see you. Tonight, Lucy's house, eight o'clock. Be there—and no excuses.'

And without giving him a chance to argue, he walked out, and Nick sat down heavily on the awful pink vinyl armchair beside the bed and stared unseeingly at his son's face until Kate camc back.

'He didn't stay long.'

'Long enough to say what he came for. I've been summoned,' he told Kate softly, standing up again and giving her the chair. 'Eight o'clock tonight, Lucy's. Will you be all right if I leave you to go there?'

She smiled sadly. 'Of course I'll be all right. I've just heard Gemma's been admitted. I might take a walk up there and see how she's doing. You go and see them, Nick, and try and build some bridges.'

He nodded, wondering how he could be in two places at once and only really wanting to be here, by this injured child he was beginning to realise he loved more than life itself...

* * *

Ben came by on his way home after his shift finished, by which time Jem had woken up in pain again.

'I've got the most amazing bruises,' he told Ben, but although he was trying to sound as if he was showing off, Kate could tell he was frightened by them, and she wasn't surprised. When he turned back the blankets and showed his side to Ben, she winced yet again, the sight making her curl up inside.

'That's impressive. I'm not surprised you're hurting. I'll go and find someone.'

He went out, coming back a few moments later with Megan Phillips. They consulted the chart together, and she chatted to Jem about his pain, and then she turned to Kate.

'We want to get the pain under control because we don't like him hurting, but also because we'd like to get him up soon. We might start sitting him up on the side of the bed tomorrow and see how it goes, and if he tolerates that we'll move to the chair, and so on. It'll be slow, but you'll be in control of what you can manage, Jem. We'll let you guide us. And Mr Bradley wants your physio to start properly from tomorrow, so all your muscles don't forget how to work, but very gently at first, so nothing to worry about. Anyway, I'll talk to you in the morning, and I'm on all night if you're worried about anything, Mrs Althorp. Just get them to call me.'

'Thank you,' she said, smiling at the lovely young woman, her dark hair held back in a clip out of the way, the thick curls trying hard to escape. She was kindness itself, but there was something lurking in the back of her eyes today, Kate thought, that hadn't been there yesterday. Something sad and desperate and a little lost. Her heart went out to her.

'I'll go and update your notes right now, Jem, and get someone to come and give you the extra pain relief shortly, OK? And if you're still really uncomfortable, press the bell and they'll get me and we'll have another look at things.'

'Thanks,' he said, looking relieved, and after she'd gone out he looked up at Ben again. 'Thanks for asking her, Ben.'

'Any time. Right, I'd better go home. Apparently I'm cooking tonight. I'll see you later, Nick?'

'Yes. I'll be there.'

Ben gave him a fleeting smile, murmured, 'Don't worry,' and left them alone with their son.

'Here you go, my gorgeous—jelly and ice cream,' a nurse said, putting it down on his bed table with a smile and helping him sit up a little.

Nick glanced at his watch, and realised it was suppertime. He looked at Kate. 'Why don't you go and have a rest for an hour or so while I sit here with Jem?' he suggested gently. 'Or you could go and get something to eat, as I'm eating at Lucy's.'

For a moment he thought she was going to argue, but then she smiled slightly and went out, and he settled himself on the edge of the pink chair and looked at the instructions for the games console while Jem ate the jelly and ice cream and told him how to work it.

'I don't know how you guys work these things out,' Nick said, frowning at it, and Jem laughed and took it from him.

'It's easy, Uncle Nick, but don't worry, Rob couldn't work out how to use Matt's, either. It's because you're too old for this kind of thing,' he explained innocently.

'Is that right?' he asked, taking the machine back and

having another go. So Rob couldn't work it? He ignored the voice that mocked him for his childish urge to be better than the other man, and got Jem to show him once again. And finally, finally, he cracked it.

After that, dealing with Lucy and Jack didn't seem nearly so daunting...

He left Jem's bedside at seven-thirty, just after Kate came back to sit with him. She'd had a rest, and something to eat, and she looked more like herself.

'I'll come back later and update you,' he promised. 'And I could stay, if you like—take turns, like we did last night.'

'We'll see. Have a lovely time,' she said, but her eyes were saying, Good luck, and he gave her a fleeting smile and left.

It took fifteen minutes to get there, and he parked the car outside and went in through the kitchen door, the way he'd always gone into his family home. He braced himself for the reception committee, but it was only Ben in the kitchen and he greeted him with a smile and a glass of wine. 'Here—I thought you might need this.'

'I'm driving.'

'Not for a while, and it's only a small glass. They're in the sitting room, go on through. And, Nick? Don't worry. They aren't going to skin you, they just want to understand.'

He nodded, and, taking the wine with him, he walked through the familiar house, feeling like a condemned man going to the gallows. Crazy, because in many ways this was none of their business, it was between him and Kate and Jem, and the only other person he owed an explanation to was Annabel, and she was dead.

But he supposed they felt they were acting as her representatives, and of course there were financial implications. Jeremiah, as his son, was entitled to an equal share of his estate, so each of them would lose a percentage of their stake. Maybe that was what they wanted to discuss. Although he doubted it. His children weren't like that.

Shaking his head slowly, he straightened his shoulders and went through into the sitting room, and the conversation stopped dead.

'Well, don't mind me,' he murmured, and Lucy coloured.

Not Jack. He stood up, looked his father in the eye and said, 'You'd better sit down. We've got Ed on the webcam.'

He nodded, glad that he'd be able to talk to his other son at last, and sat down opposite the laptop on the coffee table, with Jack and Lucy across from him, visible over the top. So he could see them all, and they could all see him. It was like an interview panel, he thought. Or a jury.

I swear by Almighty God...

'Dad.'

He glanced down at Edward, his face moving a little jerkily but still very recognisable.

'I've been trying to ring you,' Nick told him.

'I know. I didn't answer because I don't know what to say to you,' Ed told him, his voice puzzled and hurt. 'I can't believe it—what the hell were you thinking of?'

Nick sighed and ran a hand through his hair. 'There's nothing I can say or do to change what happened, and I'm not going to make excuses,' he told them all, 'but I meant my vows to your mother, Edward, and I swear it was the only time.'

I swear by Almighty God…

'It's not that. That's between the two of you. I just hope she never knew. It's him I'm thinking about, a boy who thought for years that his father was dead when you could have been taking an active role in his life. Sure, it would have hurt Mum, but we were grown up, it was none of our business, and we could have spent time with him and made him feel wanted. That's what's so gutting, that he didn't have any brothers or sisters there for him when we could have been, so easily.'

Nick shook his head. 'I didn't know. It was Kate's decision not to tell me, and she made it for good reasons. Wrong ones, maybe, but still out of consideration for everyone involved, and there weren't any right ones—'

'Don't palm it off on Kate. You've known for two years,' Jack retorted, cutting in. 'That's two lost years he could have had a father. You should have said something sooner, Dad.'

'How?' he asked. 'And when? She was with someone all last year, and she's been ill. You know that. She's had breast cancer. We could hardly tell him then, could we, with his life in turmoil and another man there ready and willing to act as his father? And before then, well, I guess I was still coming to terms with it—still in denial. I'm sorry you're so angry with us, but the only person I can worry about at the moment is your little brother, and I'm afraid he's taking all my time and thoughts right now.'

Edward frowned. 'How did he take it?'

'He doesn't know yet. He's still in a lot of pain. We're going to tell him later, when he's stronger, and when we've had some time to get to know each other. I'm hoping that with time we'll be able to get to know each other better and he'll learn to forgive us both, but I'm going to be part of his life now, come hell or high water, so I'm glad you've all accepted that, at least.'

'Don't worry about us. We're big enough and ugly enough to take care of ourselves. It's Jem we're all worried about.'

He pinched the bridge of his nose, pressing his thumb and forefinger against his eyes before dragging his hand down his face. 'Who the hell do you think I'm worried about?' he asked hoarsely, scanning all their faces. 'At the end of the day, I've done my bit for you lot. I haven't even started with him. I owe him so much I don't know where to begin—'

'That's what we want to talk to you about. You need to change your will, to make provision for him,' Lucy said, and he glanced across at her and wondered if this had been her idea, his little girl, his peacemaker.

'I already have,' he said quietly. 'I did it yesterday, as soon as I found out—as soon as I was sure. The amendment to the will is with my solicitors in St Piran waiting for my signature.'

'And what about his schooling? We all went to private school. Where will he go?'

'Wherever he wants, Jack. I would think the high school in Penhally, with his friends. I don't want to change his life, I don't have the right to interfere.'

Jack snorted, and he met the condemnation in his eyes with new understanding.

'Is that how you saw my involvement in your lives? As interference?'

'Somewhat,' Edward said bluntly. 'It was "My way or

the highway". No middle line, no grey areas, just black or white.'

Nick frowned. 'That's not how I see it at all. I did my best to be a good husband and father. I gave you guidelines. I thought that was what being a father was, but this—I don't know how to deal with this, how to be a father to him now.'

'Is that why you haven't?'

He looked at her and let his breath out on a long, ragged sigh. 'Yes. Yes, that's exactly why. I want to be a good father to him, to all of you, but I just—I can't seem to do it right, apparently. And with Jem—I didn't even get the chance until recently, and it was so nearly too late…'

He broke off, squeezing his eyes shut, pinching the bridge of his nose again, determined to hold it all together in front of them, but it was all still so raw, the image of Jem lying there in Resus while they cut his clothes away and poured fluids into him etched on his memory in acid.

'I still don't understand how you ended up sleeping with Kate when you were married,' Jack said, sounding so like him that at any other time it might have been funny. 'All the morals you rammed down our throats as kids, and yet you could do that—and you ended up with a child you won't even acknowledge! It's just so damned unfair. At least we knew you loved us—and we thought you loved our mother.'

'I did—and I love Jeremiah,' he told them earnestly. 'Don't imagine for a moment that I don't, and I fully intend to show him that, given a chance.'

'You're changing the subject,' Jack said. 'I want to

know how the hell you came to have a random one-night stand with another woman totally out of the blue!'

'I don't think that's any of your business,' he began, but then he sighed and sat back, giving up the unequal struggle. If he ever hoped to make them understand, he had to explain at least some of it. He looked up and scanned their faces in turn.

'You want to know? All right, I'll tell you.'

'Dad, you don't have to,' Lucy protested, but he shook his head.

'I think I do—because it wasn't totally out of the blue at all. Kate and I go back thirty-five years.'

'We know you dated her.'

He smiled gently at Lucy. 'It was rather more than that. I'd know her since I was fourteen, but I was seventeen when I first really became aware of her; she was only fifteen, though, so we took things slowly—walks up on the moors, swimming, surfing, going for picnics. We went to the cinema, I took her to a rock concert—all pretty innocent stuff. And we fell in love.'

He hesitated, remembering those halcyon days, and then he sucked in a breath and carried on. 'I was in my last year at school, and I'd got into med school in London. We talked about me going away, and I promised I'd come back for her. She was sixteen by then, I was eighteen, and although we still weren't sleeping together, that was pretty much a technicality. By the end of that last summer, I knew Kate's body as well as I knew my own, and I cherished it. But I was going away, and people change, and I didn't want to do anything that might hurt her later, so we held back from that last step. And then I met a girl during Freshers' Week, a beautiful girl with stunning blonde hair and the most incredible blue eyes, while we were being dragged round on some crazy pub crawl in fancy dress, and somehow we ended up in her room. I woke up in the morning feeling sick and ashamed and appalled at what I'd done, but it was too late. She came to me a few weeks later in floods of tears and told me she was pregnant, and I didn't know what to do. I just knew I had no choice but to ask her to marry me, and to make it work.'

'And Kate?' Lucy asked softly. 'What happened about Kate?'

'I came down and saw her, and for the first time ever I lied to her. I told her I'd met someone else and fallen in love, and I was going to marry her. I told her she was pregnant—and Kate was devastated. So was I, because I loved her so much—I never had to explain anything to her, I still don't. She still understands me as no one else ever has, anticipates me, and somehow forgives me. She actually sent us a card, saying she hoped we'd be very happy together. And I did everything I could to be fair to Annabel, to be good to her, because it wasn't her fault I'd got her in that mess, and she was lovely. It was no hardship being married to her, and if I didn't think about Kate, it was OK. But even though I did everything I could to make it feel right, I couldn't, not entirely, because my heart was with Kate and always has been. And even though I was with your mother, I always knew what was going on in Kate's life—we went to her wedding to James, we saw them socially from time to time, and I managed to convince myself that we'd both moved on. Only I never really did, of course, and I don't think she did.'

He tried to smile at them, but his mouth felt frozen. 'I don't know that I can explain what happened that night—the night of the storm. It was a few hours after my father and your Uncle Phil had died, and Kate's husband had been washed out to sea.'

He filled in the details of the day, the rescue that had gone wrong and led to the death of three men, the horror of it. 'Later that night your mother told me to find Kate, to see if he'd been found, and he hadn't. She was still on the clifftop, so I took her home and tried to look after her, but she was falling apart, devastated, and so was I, and we just reached out to each other. We've never needed words, and we didn't need them that night. We just hung on while the storm raged all around us, and afterwards I put her to bed and left her, and went back to your mother and tried to carry on.

'And that's what I've done for the past twelve years,' he said, 'tried to carry on, to keep going, keep putting one foot in front of the other and not hurt too many people along the way. And then I find I have another child, a son, and we're going to have to tell him, and yet again I'm going to hurt someone I love.'

He stopped, unsure what else, if anything, he could tell them, but there was nothing more of any relevance, so with a long, deep breath, he sat back and waited.

He'd told them things he'd never told anyone, not even Kate, and there was a long silence until Lucy knelt up beside him, put her arms round him and rested her head on his shoulder. 'Dad, I'm so sorry,' she whispered, and he could feel a wet patch forming on his shirt from her soundless tears.

He hugged her back, and she dragged in a shuddering breath and sat up. 'Ed, are you OK?' she asked.

Nick looked at Edward, clearly moved even on the jerky picture.

'I'm sorry,' he said. 'We had no right to make you go through that. You were right, it was none of our damn business. Look, I'm going to go. Just—look after him, could you, and send him my love? I'll write to him. You can give him the letter when you think he's ready.'

'Thanks.'

The screen went blank, and Lucy shut the laptop and leant back with a sigh, and he glanced across and saw Jack, stony-faced and silent, but he was far from unmoved, however tight his control.

'Well—I suppose we ought to eat,' Lucy said at last, and, unfolding her legs, she got off the sofa and went out. Seconds later, they heard her crying, and Ben's voice murmuring quietly as he soothed her.

'I'm sorry, I probably shouldn't have told you all of that,' Nick said softly, but Jack made a dismissive noise and shook his head.

'No, I'm sorry. I owe you an apology. I thought—'

'That it was some dirty little affair? That we'd gone out and got drunk? Believe me, that would have been easier to deal with.'

'I'm sure. How's Jem doing?'

'Oh, he's all right, I suppose. Still sore, still got the drain and the catheter, and I don't think that pleases him, but maybe he'll have them out tomorrow.'

'Probably,' Jack agreed. 'Are they going to get him up?'

How odd, Nick thought, that Lucy could hug him and then go and cry, but Jack was here talking about his treatment, hanging onto normality. So like him, so ready to push his emotions aside if they became inconvenient or embarrassing.

But this business with Jem was teaching him a lot about his emotions, most of it uncomfortable, and he was learning to deal with them.

Ben appeared in the doorway. 'Supper's ready when you are. There's no rush.'

'It's OK, we're ready,' Nick lied, because his guts were so knotted with tension he didn't think he could possibly eat again.

'So—what happens now?' Lucy asked, and he shrugged.

'I don't know. We're taking it a day at a time. I've found a converted barn to rent—it's near here, you probably know it. St Adwen's. It's been for sale, but they haven't managed to shift it, so they're letting it, and it's mostly single storey, with two bedrooms upstairs and two down, so when he comes out of hospital we're going to stay there for a while until he recovers. It'll give us a bit of privacy and time to be together as a family, without the pressure of having to buy anywhere.'

'What about your house?' Jack suggested. 'That's got a room downstairs he could use as a bedroom, and a shower room next to it.'

'Neither of us would feel comfortable there, under the circumstances. It's very much your mother's house, but maybe it's time I moved on.'

'Meaning?' Lucy asked, looking at him keenly.

He set his fork down, very precisely, and met her eyes.

'I'm thinking of asking Kate to give me another chance. We're going to see how it goes with Jem, but if I think we could make a go of it, I might ask her to marry me.'

Her eyes flooded again, and she got up and came and hugged him. 'Oh, Dad. I'm so pleased. I've been so worried about you on your own, and Kate's so lovely, and now we know how much you love her—'

'Hey, hey, don't jump the gun, I haven't asked her yet and she certainly hasn't said yes. It could all fall apart if Jem throws a hissy fit at the idea of us living together.'

She sat down again and propped her chin on her hand. 'Do you think he will?'

He shrugged. 'I really have no idea. He doesn't know I'm his father yet, we still have to cross that hurdle, and I have no idea how he'll react.' He sighed. 'Although with my track record maybe he'd be better off not knowing—'

His children both chipped in then, contradicting him, telling him he was a good father, the best...

'What about "My way or the highway"?' he quoted back at them from one of their recent conversations. 'What about all the morals I stuffed down your throats?'

'Well, at least you had principles, even if you weren't always strong enough to stick to them,' Jack said reasonably.

'And you've always loved us, even if you were a bit tough and uncompromising, and we've always known that,' Lucy said, reaching out and squeezing his hand. 'Don't worry. Just give him time. And we'll be there, too. Once he's better I'll take the kids in to visit. They love him, and he's their uncle, of course. I think he may find that a bit of a shock when he works it out.'

'I hadn't even thought of that,' Nick said, and picked his fork up again, suddenly hungry. 'This is good chilli, Ben. Thanks.'

'My pleasure,' Ben said, giving him a wry smile. 'There's plenty more.'

'D'you know, I don't mind if I do,' he said with a grin, and handed Ben his plate.

Kate waited for him, lying awake on the top of the bed they'd given her at the hospital, and when he called her, shortly before midnight, she told him to come up. He tapped on the door and came in and perched beside her, and she reached for his hand and held it.

'How was it?'

'Oh, pretty much as expected. They were angry at first, worried about Jem, about the impact this would have on him—you were right about them, they've taken him to their hearts, he's part of the family now whether he likes it or not. Curiously it wasn't that much about the fact that I was unfaithful to their mother, although that didn't thrill them. They seemed more concerned for him—about my provision for him in my will, about his education and what I intend to do to take care of him, and about you.'

He hesitated, then went on, 'I told them about us, about how we met, and a bit about that night—not all of it, but enough. I know you didn't want me to, but they didn't understand, and how could they, without being there, without understanding how devastated we were that night, how bonded together by our grief we were. So I tried to explain.'

'And did they understand, in the end?'

He gave a low laugh. 'I think so. I was pretty graphic.

Not about us, but the rest. They apologised for making me dredge it all up—they were pretty shocked. They hadn't realised what it had been like that day, and I didn't pull any punches. I even told them about their Uncle Phil and how he died.'

'Oh, Nick,' she said, squeezing his hand tighter. 'I'm sorry you had to go through it all again.'

'It's all right. It was important that they understood, and I think they do now. I also thought they should know that Annabel sent me to make sure you were all right.'

She stared at him. 'Annabel sent you?'

'Yes. I thought you knew that?'

'How would I know, Nick? We've never talked about it—never discussed the night of the storm. I'm not sure I even know fully what happened. Will you tell me?'

'Really?'

'If you can bear to go over it all again.'

He shrugged. 'Sure. If you really want to know.'

'I do,' she said, and then, because he was still clearly running it over in his head, still chock-full of emotion, she patted the bed and shuffled over. 'Come here. You need a hug.'

For a moment he did nothing, but then with a tired sigh he lay down beside her and drew her into his arms. She put her head on his shoulder, and wrapped her arms round him and held him.

'So tell me,' she urged softly. 'Tell me how it happened.'

'Well, you know the school kids were stranded down on the rocks at the foot of the headland—that's where James was, of course, and my father was on the top of the headland, helping with the children that had been brought up the cliff while my brother was abseiling

down the face and rescuing the ones still stranded. The
last child's helmet had fallen off on the way up, and
so Phil took his off and gave it to her, and then a huge
wave—the same wave that swept James off the rocks—
picked them up and threw them against the cliff and
shattered his skull. My father helped pull them up, and
failed to tell anyone he'd had a heart attack three weeks
earlier.

'I hadn't been there at first, I was in my surgery over
in Wadebridge, but I was called to help and I arrived
to find my father collapsing with another heart attack,
and my brother lying on the grass in the lashing rain
with the back of his skull caved in. There was nothing I
could do for Phil, he'd died instantly. My mother was at
home, unaware of what was going on, but Annabel was
in the church hall, making tea for everyone, so I told her
to pick my mother up and meet us at the hospital, and
I went in the ambulance with my father, trying to keep
him alive when he arrested. And by the time we set off,
we knew that James had been washed off the rocks by
the same wave.

'I managed to keep my father going until we got to
the hospital, and my mother was with him when he died,
although he never recovered consciousness, and after
she'd said goodbye to her husband, I had to take her
down to the chapel of rest to say goodbye to her son.'

He broke off for a moment, reliving it, and beside
him he heard Kate suck in a shaky breath. 'Nick, you
don't have to do this.'

'It's OK,' he said softly, taking her hand and squeezing it. 'It's time we talked about it, because otherwise it's
too damned easy to say we should have known better.
Anyway, I took them back to the house, Annabel and

my mother, and we had tea.' He gave a shaky laugh. 'It's funny how tea always seems to come into this equation. I can't tell you how much tea and coffee I've drunk in the last couple of days. Anyway, after a while Mum started to cry—that terrible sound of grief.'

'Oh, Nick. Poor, poor woman. How on earth did she cope, losing both of them on the same day?'

'She didn't. It broke her. And on that night of course we couldn't leave her, but I couldn't stop thinking about James, and neither could Annabel. She told me to go and find you and see if there was any news of him. I think we both knew he was dead, and afterwards I wondered if she knew what she was doing when she sent me. I suspect she did. She wasn't stupid.'

It had been a bizarre conversation, most of the words unsaid, he remembered. And he could remember, too, the look in her eyes. The understanding, the quiet resignation. The blessing. He gave a quiet sigh and went on.

'The rest you know. I found you on the headland, with the wind and rain lashing your clothes, and you were so cold—chilled to the bone.'

'I was waiting for you. I knew you'd come.'

'I don't know how. I just knew I had to.'

He'd undressed her and put her in the shower, and put the kettle on, just like the other day. And just like the other day, he'd heard her crying, like his mother, with inconsolable grief, and he'd gone to her. The woman he loved, the girl he'd fallen for. The woman, he realised, he still loved with all his heart. He closed his eyes and swallowed.

He paused, remembering that he'd already stripped off his saturated, blood-stained shirt, and he'd taken off the rest and gone into the shower and put his arms around her and held her, and she'd clung to him, just as she'd clung to him that morning, and they'd cried together. He had no idea how long for. Ten minutes? An hour?

He wasn't really sure what had happened then. He hadn't understood it at the time and he still didn't understand it now, but they'd needed each other in a way so deep, so elemental that there had been no denying it. They were both angry, furious that something so crazy had happened to kill two young, healthy men with years ahead of them and an old man who should have lived to enjoy his retirement and instead had been snuffed out like a candle.

Maybe it was just defiance, and the fact that people they'd loved had died so senselessly, and it was almost as if they'd had to prove to themselves that they were still alive, but there had been no stopping it, no reasoning, just a soul-deep need that had driven them half-crazed into each other's arms.

Afterwards he'd turned off the water and dried her and put her to bed and then he'd gone home and showered and changed and gone back to his wife. They'd never spoken of it again, but after that, nothing had been quite the same...

'Nick?'

He started a little and stared at Kate, then shook his head to clear it of the unwanted, haunting images.

'I'm sorry that night was so awful for you all,' she whispered. 'Thank you for telling me. And I'm sorry the kids were hard on you.'

'It's OK. It's over now, and I'm glad it's out in the open. I think they realise now that it wasn't a premeditated decision to betray their mother, or that Jem was conceived as a drunken result of some sordid little date, just two people, who had always cared about each other, on the edge of despair and reaching out to each other that night.'

'We weren't ourselves. No wonder we didn't think about contraception, not then and not afterwards.'

'I did, but not till weeks later, when you told me you were pregnant, and I asked you if it was my child, and you said no. And I accepted it without question, with relief, even, because I didn't ever want to have to think of that night again. But you knew, didn't you? You knew he was mine because of the fertility problems.'

'Yes. Yes, I knew. James's notes had gone back to the PCT when he died, so I'd had to ring the clinic and ask them for the results, and they'd told me that James was sterile. But I couldn't tell you. Not then. It wouldn't have achieved anything and so many more people would have been hurt. But maybe now we can move on.'

'Maybe.'

He turned his head, and she lifted her face and their lips met in a gentle, tender kiss that made her heart skip a beat. He shifted, turning towards her, and their legs tangled, their bodies hard against each other.

'Nick, we can't,' she whispered, and he sighed, his breath soft against her cheek.

'I know. I just need to hold you.'

But he kept on kissing her, his lips tracing soft circles over her cheeks, her eyes, her throat.

'Nick…'

'Shh. It's all right,' he murmured, drawing her closer again and settling her head on his shoulder once more. 'I'm going in a minute.'

* * *

Except he didn't. He was asleep in seconds, emotionally exhausted, and although her arm had gone to sleep, she didn't have the heart to wake him. So she lay there for an hour, until he stirred and gave a sleepy grunt, and she murmured his name.

'Sorry—I didn't mean to doze off. Are you all right?' he asked, sitting up and shifting out of her way.

'I'm fine. My arm's dead, though.'

He tutted and took it in his hands, rubbing it briskly until the pins and needles had gone and she sighed with relief, and then he stood up. 'I ought to go home. How's Jem been? Did he go to sleep all right?'

'Yes, he's fine. And Sam and Gemma have a baby boy. They're calling him Archie—Archie Nicholas, for you.'

She heard him suck in his breath, and then let it out again, obviously touched by the gesture. 'That's great. How are they?'

'Well. Fine. The baby's beautiful, and Gemma's OK, it was a nice, straightforward delivery. It was lovely to see them. A bit of normality, really. They send their love.'

'I'll pop up tomorrow, take them something. And I ought to bring Jem in something, but I have no idea what. I don't want to look as if I'm trying to buy him,' he said with a wry grin, and she laughed.

'So bring him grapes. He adores grapes, and he needs fruit on all these opiates.'

'Grapes? Lucy gives him a games console that probably cost well over a hundred pounds, and you suggest I bring him grapes?' he said, laughing softly.

'Or you could look as if you're trying to buy him,' she said reasonably, and he sighed.

'OK. Grapes it is. And I suppose the games console's only on loan.'

It was, although of course he could always buy him his own, she thought, but she didn't suggest it. Time enough later for extravagant gestures, and she'd rather he didn't get into the habit of playing on a games machine as a regular thing.

He bent and kissed her cheek, then lifted his head slightly, stared into her eyes and slowly lowered his head again, touching his lips to hers once more. Just briefly, very lightly, but it was like being stroked with fire.

'Sleep tight. I'll see you in the morning,' he murmured, and he went out and closed the door softly behind him, leaving her lying there with her fingers on her lips, and her body tingling with anticipation.

CHAPTER SEVEN

NICK didn't arrive until ten the next day, to her surprise.

By the time he came in, Martin Bradley had been round, and as Jem seemed comfortable, the surgeon said he could try sitting up a little in bed, instead of just having his head and shoulders being propped up.

It ached a bit, Jem said, but Kate could tell he was happier. He was getting so bored lying down, and sitting up properly he was able to play with the games console to his heart's content while she sat beside him with a magazine and let it all go on around her.

Her presence was less essential now than it had been. He was no longer in danger, and he was used to the staff, familiar with his surroundings and happier about being left.

She'd already decided the night before that it would be the last time she stayed, and she was getting desperate for her own bed.

Or at least one that didn't have a plastic mattress.

If Nick would only arrive, she thought, she could talk to him about the barn. She hadn't told Jem yet what their plans were, she wanted to do that with Nick, preferably before he signed on the dotted line at the letting agent's, but when he arrived he dangled a bunch of keys in front of her with a smug grin, like a magician pulling a rabbit out of a hat.

'Your keys, ma'am,' he said, dropping them into her hand. 'You can move in whenever you like.'

She was at the nurses' station, out in the ward, talking to the ward sister and Megan Phillips about what was to happen next, and she stared at the keys in slight consternation.

'What's the matter?' he said, his voice dropping. 'I thought that was what you wanted?'

'It is,' she said. 'But—I thought we were going to talk to Jem first? What if he says no?'

'What if he does? He's ten years old, Kate. There are some decisions that aren't his to make. This is a temporary fix, for a few weeks initially, to cover his convalescence. His friends can come and visit, he can treat it as a holiday—and if it doesn't work out, if he doesn't want me around, then I can go home. It doesn't change anything. It's just for now.'

He was right, of course—he was always right, she thought, except when he was wrong, and then it tended to be on an epic scale. But this—this was just common sense, and she let her breath out on a little huff of laughter and tried to smile.

'You're right. I'm sorry, it's not as if it's a permanent thing. I'm being silly.'

And she'd been letting herself get carried away with all the possibilities. A temporary fix, she reminded herself. Just that, nothing more, for a few weeks, and it might be a total disaster on several counts.

'This might be more long term,' he said then, pulling

another set of keys from his pocket, and dropping them in her hand too.

She glanced down, and blinked. 'Car keys?'

'Mmm. I wasn't sure what you wanted, so I asked Chloe if you'd said anything. She mentioned a model you liked.'

She stared at the keys, confused. 'You've got me a car on the PCT contract this quickly?' she said. Surely she had to sign something…

'No. I've bought you a Golf—a nice economical little diesel. They're delivering it to the barn this afternoon.'

She stared at him as if he'd gone mad. 'You bought me a new car?'

'No. It's not new. It's two years old. I thought you'd shout at me if I got you a new one.'

She opened her mouth to shout at him anyway, and to her horror a little sob came out instead.

'Kate?'

'Sorry,' she said, flapping her hand and blinking hard. 'I— It's just— Oh, Nick, you didn't have to do that. I could have got myself another car. Renting the house is one thing, this is quite another. You're doing too much, going too fast.'

'No, I'm not.' This one's got a much better NCAP crash rating. I'm not trying to bribe you,' he said grimly, 'I'm trying—too late—to make sure my son stays safe.'

She swallowed, unable to argue, filled with guilt that her car had contributed to his injuries, but he misunderstood her silence and sighed.

'I'm sorry. I know I interfere. It doesn't matter, you can use it for the moment and once you get yourself the car you want, I'll give it to Lucy or something, make it a pool car for the practice maybe.'

'No!' She closed her hand around the keys, reached up and kissed his cheek. 'Thank you. I was just stunned, that's all. I've had to rely on myself for so long, and— Oh, damn.'

Her eyes were welling up, and she rummaged for a tissue in her pocket. He got there first, plucking one off the top of the nurses' station and handing it to her, and she blew her nose and sniffed hard. 'Sorry. It's been a bit of a roller-coaster.'

'I know. How is he?'

She filled him in on the day's events, and he went in to see Jem while she packed her things in the little room she'd been using and gave herself a thorough talking to. She handed the key back to the staff nurse and thanked her, and went into Jem's room to find Nick perched beside him on the bed, leaning up against the backrest and watching him with the games console while he ate grapes.

'You could put that down for five minutes, you know,' she pointed out, but Jem just grinned.

'Uncle Nick wanted to see how I was doing. I was just showing him. I've been teaching him how to use it.'

She stared at him, realising how easily these two had slipped into an easy relationship, almost as if Jem knew Nick was his father. He must have been so desperate for a father all these years, she thought, and he'd never said a word about it; perhaps he didn't realise it, even now. She'd thought he was all right, that they were fine on their own, but maybe she'd been deluding herself and all the time there'd been a void.

A void that should have been filled by Nick.

'We've got something to talk to you about,' she said, determined to get the barn out into the open. 'Could you put that down and listen, please?'

He looked up at her, his eyes wary, and then looked down again. 'Oh, no, it killed me!' he wailed, and put the console down on the locker, then looked up at her again a little worriedly. 'What did you want to talk about?'

'You. When you come out of here, you might not be able to walk up and down stairs for a while, and we've got no bathroom downstairs.'

'Oh. Does that mean I'll have to stay in here longer, till I can go upstairs?' he asked miserably. 'I don't want to. I want to go home as soon as I can. It's not the same here.'

'I know. And, no, it doesn't mean that. It means we'll have to stay somewhere else for a little while. Uncle N—' She broke off, met Nick's eyes ruefully and went on, 'Uncle Nick's found somewhere for us, somewhere he can stay, too, just outside Penhally, near Ben and Lucy. It's a barn, and it's got a downstairs bedroom with doors out to the garden, and an en suite wetroom—'

'What's a non-sweet wetroom?'

'En suite—it's French. It means it's a bathroom attached just to one bedroom. And a wetroom means it's got a tiled floor and you just walk into it and shower, so you wouldn't even have to step up to a shower tray.'

'Wow. And we can stay there?'

'Yes.'

'And you're coming?' he asked, swivelling his head round to look at Nick, and he nodded.

'Yes—so I can help out, and I can do stuff for you

that you might not want your mum doing, like help you shower and so on, if you need help at first.'

He nodded. 'Can the dog come?'

'Yes.'

'OK. So was that all you want to talk about?'

She met Nick's eyes and they were full of relief and wry humour. She smiled. 'Nothing else. Just that.'

'Oh. Well, can I try and get to the next level, then? I was nearly there and then it killed me.'

'Kids.'

'Don't. I can't believe he took it so well.'

'Of course he did,' Nick said as if it was obvious, and put the tray down on the table. 'He trusts you to take care of him. You've done it—made it possible for him to be discharged as soon as it's practicable. Why should he take it any other way?'

'Because we always talk everything through. Before I do anything, we talk it through. We're not impulsive like you.'

He looked at her as if she had two heads, and she thought of Lucy and Jack pointing out to him that he interfered, and stifled a smile.

'Don't laugh at me. I'm not impulsive, I'm decisive. It's different,' he protested.

'Actually, you're both,' she pointed out gently, reaching for her coffee. 'Nick, you're going to have to get used to him. Jem likes to see all sides of a thing before he'll commit to it. If I say jump, he doesn't ask how high, he asks why. And I know it's an alien concept to you, but it's the way I've brought him up.'

'It's not an alien concept,' he disagreed, stirring his coffee with huge concentration. 'It's just that some things are as they are. He has to know that there isn't always an answer, that sometimes you have to take some things and some people on trust.'

'And you know what he'd say to that?'

'"Why?"' they said together, and then laughed, reaching out and linking their fingers on the table.

'Did you get anything for Gemma's baby?' she asked, and he nodded.

'Yes. I found a lovely pop-up book of farm animals. It's not for now, obviously, but I thought he might like it later.'

'That's a lovely idea, and it goes really well with my present. I've knitted him a little jumper with fluffy sheep on the front.'

He frowned quizzically. 'Really? You can knit?'

She laughed. 'Of course I can knit! All women can knit.'

'Annabel couldn't knit.'

She felt her smile die. 'Nick, I'm not Annabel,' she reminded him gently. 'And that's not a criticism of her, it's just a fact.'

He closed his eyes for a second and sighed. 'I know you're not Annabel. I'm only too aware of who you are. I just didn't know you could knit. It's one of the very many things I don't know about you, that I've never had the chance to find out. I didn't mean to offend you by comparing you to Annabel.'

'I'm not offended,' she said quickly. 'Not at all. But we are—were—different. You need to realise that if we're going to live together.'

'Well, then, isn't it a good job that I've already noticed?' he said softly, and, draining his coffee, he got to his feet. 'There's Lucy—she said she'd try and pop in. Come on, we'll go up with her.'

He held out his hand to help Kate up, and then tucked her hand in the crook of his arm. 'Hello, darling,' he said, kissing his daughter's cheek, and she took his other arm and walked with them to the ward.

'I've got something for you, from Ben. His chilli recipe. He says you can look after Kate, spoil her a little. Here.'

He grinned and tucked it in his pocket, and vowed to make it for her soon.

They left Jem with Lucy, telling him they were going to see the barn and would be back later, and twenty minutes later they'd pulled up outside and unlocked the door.

'Welcome home,' he said softly, pushing the door open, and she stepped inside, a little bit of her disappointed that he hadn't carried her over the threshold. But how stupid was that? They weren't married—far from it, and they might never be. This was just about Jem, and if she'd expected more because of his tenderness with her last night, she was deluded.

The entrance was in the single-story section on the left-hand side, between the living space and the bedrooms, and they walked through to the sitting room with its low beamed ceiling and comfortable furniture grouped around the log burner, and into the central section where a battered old oak refectory table sat in pride of place.

It would be the perfect setting for family get-togethers, she thought—all Nick's children with their spouses and families gathered around, the air filled with their laughter. She could hear it now, as she looked around her at the great vaulted space of the dining hall. Its huge, soaring window faced the courtyard, with its flat, winding paths and low shrubs giving structure to the sheltered little garden, the wings of the house wrapped round it like arms, protecting it from the elements, and then beyond it were the fields and then the sea.

And like Nick had the first time he'd stepped inside, she felt the house welcome her, as if those arms had folded round her and gathered her to its heart.

Romantic nonsense, she thought, and yet...

'You were right, it is calm and tranquil here,' she said softly, feeling the tension drain out of her. 'It'll be so good for him. Thank you, Nick.'

And going up on tiptoe, she kissed his cheek.

For a long moment he stared at her, their eyes locked, and then he seemed to pull himself together and looked away, and they walked around the rest of the house slowly and had their first real, proper look.

'It's amazing,' she said, standing on the galleried walkway above the dining hall and looking out over the courtyard to the sea in the distance. 'Beautiful. I could stand here all day and look at that view.'

'There are plenty of chairs you could sit on,' Nick pointed out with a smile, and she laughed softly and turned away from the window, looking up at the vaulted ceiling with its heavy beams. The gallery spanned the space, leading to a bedroom at each end, and they were both amazing.

'Which bedroom do you want?'

She glanced at him. 'I don't know. Maybe I should be downstairs with Jem. He could call me then, if he needed me in the night.'

And she'd be further from temptation.

'It doesn't have its own shower.'

'There's a bathroom almost next to it. I'm sure I'll manage.' She went back downstairs and round the corner to the wing with the two bedrooms and the study in it, on the other side of the entrance hall. The bedroom there which she would take was a small room in comparison to the ones upstairs, but big enough for her, and most importantly it was close to Jem's.

'It'll be fine,' she said firmly, and he nodded. She wasn't sure, but she thought he looked a tiny bit relieved. 'What about you?'

He gave a wry smile. 'If there's no competition, I'll have the one with the sea view from the window by the bed.'

It also had a view of her bedroom window, she realised, glancing out of it and looking up at the taller section of the barn. 'We ought to get some food in,' she said, trying to be practical and not think about his bedroom.

'I've done it. I ordered it on line last night. It's being delivered in the morning between seven and nine.'

'Will you be here?'

'Yes. I thought I'd stay here tonight, start moving some things in. I ought to go into the practice tomorrow, too, and catch up on some admin. I can't just bail on them, and Jem seems to be improving steadily. I'll take you over there whenever you like so you can be with him, if you don't feel ready to drive yet. Just tell me when you want to be picked up.'

'After the shopping arrives?'

He nodded. 'Sure. I'll come and get you from your place once it's here.'

'Or I could stay here, too,' she said rashly, and his eyes locked with hers.

'You could.'

But their eyes remained locked, both of them trapped, like rabbits in headlights, transfixed by the prospect of being alone together in this house.

Nick dragged his eyes away. 'Of course you could move in, start getting settled, and I could stay at home. And you could get the dog back from Chloe and Oliver. He must miss you.'

'But I can't really leave him alone here, he's not used to it. He'd be better in our puppy crèche until Jem's out of hospital, at least for the days. And I'm not sure how safe the garden is. I don't want him getting out.'

'There's a fenced area—I had a look at it this morning on my way to the agents. I couldn't get into the house, but I walked all round the garden, and the back of it's entirely enclosed to about four feet in height with sheep netting. He'd be quite safe. He could just run around and let off steam when you're here, and he could go to the puppy crèche when neither of us is around. And I can come over and help you walk him.'

'But you've ordered food. It should be you here, not me.'

'I can eat with you. You have to eat, too, Kate. As Ben said, I can wait on you,' he said with a wry smile, and she chuckled.

'I can just see that.'

'Let me try. You never know, I might be good at it. One of my hidden talents.'

She gave a splutter of laughter. 'Very successfully hidden. You've kept it from me for thirty-four years,' she said drily, and went back to the kitchen to acquaint herself with it.

She heard a quiet sigh behind her, and turned back to him, shocked by the sadness in his eyes. 'Oh, Nick...'

'I'm sorry,' he said, his voice bleak. 'It wasn't the way it was meant to be, was it?'

'What?'

'Life. Our plans.'

'We don't always get what we're expecting in life,' she said gently. 'I always thought you'd come back from university and marry me and I'd have your children. Instead you married Annabel, and I married James, and we couldn't have any, and you ended up with loads.'

'Was that why you gave up midwifery? Because it hurt too much not being able to have your own?'

She smiled. 'That and watching you and Annabel bring the children down here on holiday year after year when they were little. All the children I might have had if I'd been with you, and yet there I was with James, banging our heads against a brick wall. And then you moved back down here close to your family and got a job in Wadebridge and bought the house on Harbour Road, and I was falling over you all the time, a constant reminder of what I'd lost.'

He sighed heavily. 'Kate, don't. We can't turn the clock back.'

'No. But even if we haven't gone home together every night, I've worked with you for years now in the practice. I've seen you every day, spent time with you, so it hasn't all been bad,' she pointed out gently. 'You've still been part of my life. And I have Jem. You can have no idea what that's meant to me, over the years.'

'I can imagine. My children are infinitely precious to

me, even though I haven't always seen eye to eye with them, so you don't have to try and explain.'

She smiled sadly, wishing that Jem had been one of those precious children, that she'd been their mother, but, as he said, they couldn't turn the clock back and if they did, it would all be very different. And so she couldn't wish it undone, no matter how hard it had been at times.

He came over to her, standing just inches away, and with the tip of a long forefinger he tilted her head up so she met his eyes. 'Don't be sad, Kate. We've got a chance now, if we choose to take it. Let's not waste it.'

A chance? For them? So maybe she hadn't misunderstood. 'I still don't know how good you could be at waiting on me,' she said lightly, and he laughed.

'Oh, I'm good,' he said, his eyes twinkling with mischief, and she sucked in a tiny little breath and turned away, before she did something silly, like kiss him. He'd kissed her last night, but that had been in the safety of the hospital, where anyone could have come in. They were alone here, and awareness of that and of him made her tingle with nerves.

'I'm looking forward to finding out,' she said lightly. 'So, are you moving in here tonight, or am I?'

'Do you want to?'

'Not alone. It makes me feel a bit nervous,' she admitted. She held her breath for a second, then said, 'We could always be grown up about it and share.'

His mouth twisted into something that could have been a smile if it hadn't been so touched with sadness.

'Grown-ups sleep together, Kate,' he said softly. 'And I'm not sure you're ready for that yet.'

Her heart hammered against her ribcage. 'Can't we have a little restraint?'

'Oh, yes. We can have a little. I just think it might take rather more than that.'

She looked away, his eyes too revealing suddenly, full of feelings that had been locked away for very many years. Her tongue flicked out and moistened her lips, and he groaned.

'Kate, don't,' he whispered, his voice almost inaudible.

The air was vibrating with tension, almost solid, as if she could cut it with a knife, and it seemed to have set all around them, holding them in place, their eyes locked again.

The sound of the doorbell was shocking, dissolving the air so they could move again, and Nick walked to the door as if he was in a trance.

He opened it and looked past the man standing on the broad flagstone path. There were three cars outside. His, and two others.

Of course. Kate's new car.

'Delivery for Mrs Althorp?' the man said, brandishing a clipboard and some keys, and he gave himself a mental shake and breathed in.

'Yes—thank you. Kate?'

'I'm here,' she said, coming to stand beside him. 'Is that it?'

'The metallic grey one,' he said, his voice sounding strained. 'You have to sign for it.'

'You'd better check it over,' the man said.

It could have had square wheels, for all the attention they gave it. Kate could see nothing but the look in

Nick's eyes, he could see nothing but her tongue flicking out to lick her lips.

'It's fine,' he said, and she signed the sheet with trembling fingers and the delivery driver handed her the keys.

'Enjoy your car, then,' he said, and drove away in the other vehicle, leaving them standing there.

'So, will it be all right? The car?' he asked, trying desperately for normality, and she nodded.

Not that she was really able to concentrate on it, but it was exactly what she'd wanted, top of her wish list, and she was thrilled with it. She would be thrilled with it, just the moment she could get that look in his eyes out of her head.

'It's wonderful. Thank you, Nick. I'll look after it, I promise.'

'No. I'll look after it. I've bought a service package with it. It's got the next three years of servicing paid for. All you have to do is book it in.'

Her eyes filled. He seemed to have thought of everything, and she ought to pay a bit more attention to it after all his trouble and expense. She sat in the driver's seat, and rested her head back with a sigh.

'All right?'

'Lovely. Really good seat. Gosh, it's nice to rest my head. My neck's still a bit achy.'

He gave a short sigh and held the door for her. 'Come on, you need to lie down, and I'm going to massage it for you,' he said firmly, and, locking the car, he ushered her back inside and down the corridor to her bedroom.

'We'll need to bring bed linen,' she said, clutching at normality.

'Yes. What have you got on under that top?' he asked, and she swallowed.

'A vest top and a bra.'

'Right. Take the top off, leave the vest top on and lie down on your back with your head at the foot of the bed,' he instructed in a businesslike doctor's voice, and then he covered her with her top so only her shoulders were exposed, put a pillow under her knees, knelt down on the floor by her head and slid his warm, hard hands under her shoulders, running his fingers gently but firmly up the columns of muscle each side of her spine and up into her neck.

'Oh, that's amazing,' she groaned, and he said nothing, just kept on with the gentle, rhythmic movement until the tension had eased out of her neck and shoulders and she was utterly relaxed. Then he got to his feet and stood looking down at her, an odd expression in his eyes.

'Stay there for a while, have a rest. I won't be long.'

'What are you going to do?'

'Get us some milk from the Trevellyans' farm shop, and something for supper. I'll only be a few minutes, it's just up the road. Try and have a sleep.'

She heard the front door close behind him, and then the sound of a car driving away, crunching on the gravel. Odd, how they hadn't heard the other two arrive, but, then, she'd not been able to hear anything over the pounding of her heart.

She got up and pulled her top back on, lay down the right way up with a pillow under her head, and curled on her side, staring unseeingly out of the French doors at the courtyard beyond.

There. They'd managed it—been in a bedroom, had their hands on each other, even, and survived it.

They could do this. Behave like grown-ups.

Grown-ups sleep together, Kate.

'Not if they choose not to,' she said out loud, and closed her eyes determinedly. Before she knew it, she'd drifted off to sleep.

He wasn't long—just long enough to give himself some much-needed sea air and take Kate's new car out for a spin. He drove to the Trevellyans' with the windows open and the wind in his hair, and by the time he'd returned with the shopping, he was almost back under control.

He pottered round the kitchen, putting everything away while the kettle boiled and investigating the contents of the cupboards. It was such a blessing that the place was furnished as a holiday cottage and equipped with everything. It meant they only had to bring clothes and bedding, and they could pick them up later. Or whoever was staying would. He still wasn't sure who it would be.

The kettle boiled, and he made a pot of tea, left it to brew and tapped on her door.

There was no reply, and when he opened the door he saw she was fast asleep on her side, her hand lying open, relaxed, the fingers loosely curled. He stood there for a few moments, watching the slow rise and fall of her chest, and as if she'd become aware of him she opened her eyes and looked up.

'Oh. You're back,' she said softly.

'I've made tea. It's in the kitchen. And Mike Trevellyan sends his love.'

'Oh, you saw him.'

'Yes. And he'd heard a rumour about me and Jem. I told him it was true. He won't spread it further, but I thought he ought to know. And, anyway, they're Ben and Lucy's neighbours.'

'Yes, of course. So it's out, is it?'

She sat up on the edge of the bed and ran her hands through her hair, lifting it away from her neck and letting it fall, and he felt heat slam through him.

'It seems that way.' He walked away, heading back to the kitchen before he did something he'd regret. 'I've poured the tea,' he called over his shoulder, 'and I bought one of Fran's lemon drizzle cakes.'

She followed him, tugging her top straight and reminding him of what was underneath it. Not that he needed reminding, after kneeling by her head and staring down her cleavage for ten minutes. 'That's my favourite,' she said with a smile.

'I know. That's why I bought it.'

He slid a plate towards her with a generous slice on it, and followed it with a cup of tea, and she sat down at the table overlooking the courtyard and the sea and smiled again.

'I could learn to love it here,' she said.

He sat down beside her, propped his elbows on the table and looked out at the view while he bit into the cake.

'Good. Me, too. So, who's moving in when?'

'Both of us. Tonight,' she said firmly, and he nearly choked. He couldn't blow it, he reminded himself. It was too important, there was far too much at stake.

He could do this. He could.

Even if it killed him.

CHAPTER EIGHT

WATCHING Jem slowly recover his strength was both a joy and a relief, but unbelievably draining.

Every hour brought further progress—sitting up in bed, then sitting out, then standing for a moment on his right leg as he swivelled onto the chair for himself. It was like watching a time-lapse sequence of a baby turning into a toddler, but Kate was more than happy to sit through it. She was looking forward to seeing him walk again, to seeing him run, but for now, she was just glad he was alive and making progress.

And to know she'd be going home to the barn every night with Nick. She felt that if she pinched herself, she'd wake up and find it was all a dream, and the thought was frightening.

They'd moved in last night, collecting just enough clothes and linen to see them over the next few days, and then he'd cooked for her—not Ben's chilli, but a cold chicken and ham pie from the farm shop, with a lovely fresh salad and boiled new potatoes, followed by some utterly delectable honey and ginger ice cream made on the farm.

And they'd talked about telling Jem. Today. Later, after Nick arrived. He was at the surgery now, doing a clinic and seeing a few patients, and then he was coming over and they were going to tell him.

Somehow. She still had no idea how.

She went for a walk up the corridor to see Gemma and her baby while they took out Jem's catheter, to his relief, and then they moved him to the ward downstairs, which was for the children who were on the mend; it had access on one side to a courtyard with seats and toys and lots of things to look at, and on the other side, right near his bed, was the courtyard with the ducklings.

Five of them, they finally concluded, watching them peck about amongst the moss and bark chips, brown and yellow and fluffy and very cute. They watched them for ages, until at last the mother tucked them back under her wings for a rest, and he went back to his games console.

He was allowed other visitors now, and the first people to come in the afternoon were Rob and Matthew.

The boys had plenty to talk about and they left them to it. Rob took her hand and squeezed it fleetingly. 'How are you? It must have been hell—have you coped OK?'

She nodded. 'Yes. It's been pretty awful, but Nick's been great. Rob—there's something you need to know.'

He shook his head and smiled. 'I know already—I can see it in your eyes, and I'm really pleased for you. You go for it. I know how you feel. Your heart will never really belong to anybody else, just as mine won't, but at least you've now got that chance, and you have to take it.' He glanced at Jem, his head close to Matt's, bent over the games console. 'Does Jem know yet?' he asked softly.

'The paternity thing?' she murmured. 'No. Or about Nick and me. That's so new I'm not sure I know about it, really.'

He smiled. 'I think Jem will be fine with it once he's used to the idea. Is there anything I can do, anything I can get you?'

She shook her head. 'No. Just bring Matt to see him sometimes. He's going to be horribly bored. Oh, and we've taken a rented barn up near the Trevellyans' farm, with some bedrooms and a shower room on the ground floor, in case he can't manage stairs for a while. I'll give you the directions. Matt can come and stay later on, if you like. It'll give Jem something to look forward to when he comes out.'

'That would be really nice. Look, is Nick all right about this? He does realise I'm just bringing Matt to see Jem?'

'Yes, he does. And he's fine with it. He likes you.'

Rob laughed softly. 'That's good of him. I'm not sure I'd be so generous in his shoes. I hope you can make this work.'

So did she, but they still had the hurdle of the great reveal, as she was beginning to call it in her head, and she couldn't really think past that.

They didn't stay long, and Nick appeared soon afterwards. She wondered if he'd been lurking somewhere, waiting until the coast was clear, giving them space.

She didn't know. He'd been a little odd with her that morning, maybe because of the barn and being there alone together. She'd gone to bed early, closing her door quite firmly, and he'd gone up a short while later. She'd seen his light come on, seen it go off shortly afterwards, and she wondered if he'd slept as well as her. They were both tired, both drained, and he'd looked better at breakfast, but he'd been quiet, a little distracted.

'So, how's it going?' he asked Jem. 'Worked your way up another level yet?'

'My battery's flat again,' he said. 'I had to ask the nurses upstairs to charge it, but I don't know any of the nurses down here so I don't know who to ask.'

'I can charge it for you,' he said. 'We've got to go soon—we're going to pick Bruno up from Chloe and take him back to the barn and settle him in, so it can be charging while we do that and we can bring it back this evening.'

'Great—and then can we do the face thing on it, Uncle Nick?'

'Yes, I'm sure we can,' he said, and there was a flicker of emotion in his eyes, just as there always was when Jem called him that. And Kate got a stupid lump in her throat, just as she always did. But maybe not for much longer. She felt a shiver of dread, and stifled it. It would be fine. It would.

He found the charger in the locker, and packed it up with the console and put it in her bag, and they went back to the barn, put it on charge and collected Bruno. He was so excited to see her, she thought the young dog was going to wag his tail right off, and her eyes filled with tears.

'Oh, sweetheart, have you missed me? I'm so sorry,' she said, getting down on the floor with him and hugging him, but he was too excited, and bounced around barking, and Chloe laughed and let him out into the garden so he could race round like a lunatic and have a mad five minutes with Chloe and Oliver's little bitch from the same litter of flat-coated retriever puppies.

'It's been a bit hectic on the puppy-sitting front this last week,' Chloe admitted when Kate thanked her yet again for her kindness. 'I haven't even had time to see Gemma yet—how's the baby?'

Kate smiled. 'Gorgeous. He's absolutely gorgeous. I had the nicest cuddle yesterday morning. One of the advantages of being a midwife—I can pull rank and sneak in outside visiting hours! But they were coming home today, so you should be able to pop over there anytime over the weekend.'

'Oh, I will, don't worry!' Chloe laughed. 'I'll give her ten minutes to settle in, and I'll be there. Right, young man, back inside and settle down, and then I think you're going to go to your new home. That'll be a bit exciting, won't it?'

Bruno wagged and leant up against her leg, tongue lolling and a big smile on his face, and Kate clipped his lead on.

'Come on, you big hussy. That's enough flirting,' Nick said, and put him in his crate in the back of his estate car—much, much easier to transport him in—and they drove back to the barn and introduced him to the house.

'It's a good job they don't mind pets here,' she said, wondering how much damage he would do, but he hadn't wrecked anything at home yet, and she hoped if he settled here quickly, there wouldn't be a problem.

'Can you put him in the crate, if necessary?' Nick asked, reading her mind, and she nodded.

'Yes, but I hardly ever use it, he's been so good. And

I've got him a new rope toy to play with. That might keep him occupied.'

They took him out and let him run around in the garden, and he christened a few of the bushes and came back inside, flopping down in a patch of sunshine on the wooden floor of the dining room and watching them from under his eyebrows as they made a pot of tea.

'We mustn't forget to take this back,' Kate said, checking the charge on the games console while Nick poured the tea, and while she waited for it to cool and stared at the view, he cut them thick slices of the lemon drizzle cake and put one down in front of her.

'I'll be like a house,' she protested, but he just smiled.

'You haven't put an ounce on in years,' he told her. 'You work too hard.'

'Well, I'm not working now.'

'No, but you haven't been eating in the hospital.'

'That's rubbish, I've been eating junk food! Except for the pie last night, and that was hardly low calorie.'

'It was good, though, and let's face it, a little weight on you won't hurt. You'll just get curvier, and there's nothing wrong with that. You've got a beautiful body, Kate. Be proud of it.'

She met his eyes and saw the heat flicker in them before he banked it, and she felt tears clog her throat. He didn't know what he was talking about. Maybe once, but not any more. Not since her surgery.

She looked away. 'I'd rather not gain if I can avoid it,' she said, 'so I hope you're planning something low calorie for supper.'

'Not tonight,' he said with a wry laugh. 'Tonight is Ben's chilli, but I'll cut down on the oil and it's extra-lean steak mince. And kidney beans are good for you. Anyway, you'll love it, it's a great recipe—assuming I can pull it off.'

She raised an eyebrow. 'Isn't it a bit ambitious for you?' she asked, glad to get off the topic of her body. 'I mean, I know you're trying to spoil me, but we all know you're the king of the ready meals aisle.'

He laughed and picked up his cake. 'I don't know. We'll see, won't we?' He took a bite of the cake and put it down, then stared back out of the window, his smile fading. A quiet sigh eased from his body, and he turned to her, his eyes troubled.

'How are we going to tell him, Kate?' he asked softly.

She gave a helpless little shrug. 'I have absolutely no idea.'

In the end, it was easy.

Jem was sitting up in his bed when they arrived, waiting for them. They gave him the games console and settled themselves down, Kate on the armchair by the bed where he sat during the day when he was allowed out, and Nick on a hard plastic chair facing them, so they could both see him.

There was a child in a bed near Jem who was having a blood transfusion, and he looked around, his eyes tracking to his drip and up to the bag of blood running slowly into him. He watched it drip for a moment, then said thoughtfully, 'I wonder who my blood came from?'

She saw Nick stiffen slightly, and their eyes met. Was this it? The time? She felt her heart thump against her ribs, and he gave her an imperceptible nod.

'It could have been Uncle Nick,' she said quietly.

'Or Jack. They took some from both of them. You're B-negative—it's a fairly rare blood group and they'd run out, and you have to have the same otherwise it makes you very ill.'

'And you're the same as me?' he asked, looking straight at Nick.

She saw his jaw clench. 'Yes.'

'That was lucky. Are you the same, Mum?'

She shook her head. 'No.' His head swivelled back to Nick. 'So how did they know we were the same?'

'They tested you. I know mine, because I give blood regularly. So does Jack.' He hesitated, then said carefully, 'You inherit the genes that determine your blood group from one or other of your parents,' he said, and then waited.

Jem frowned. 'So—my dad must have been B-negative, too, then?'

'Yes.'

It wasn't strictly true. His father could have been AB, but they both knew he wasn't, and thankfully Nick didn't complicate it any more than it already was. Because the essence of it was already registering, Kate could see.

'And it's rare?' Jem was saying, a little frown pleating his brow, and she saw the muscle in Nick's jaw flicker again.

'Yes. Yes, it's rare. Less than three in a hundred people.'

The frown deepened, and his eyes swivelled to Kate's. 'That's weird.'

'Not really.' She could feel her heart pounding, and she swallowed before continuing, 'Jem, there's something you need to know, something I should have told you before.'

She saw the light dawn in his eyes, and he turned his head slowly back to Nick and stared at him hard. 'Are you my father?' he asked, his voice flat.

She saw Nick's throat work, and he nodded slightly. 'Yes,' he said, his voice gruff. 'Yes, I am.'

For an endless moment he just stared at Nick in silence, and Kate could see the pulse beating in his throat.

'But—how? I thought— Why didn't you tell me? Why did you tell me my dad was dead?' he asked, turning back to Kate and spearing her with accusing eyes. 'I thought I didn't have a father, but if Uncle Nick's my father, I could have had a dad all my life! Why didn't you tell me?'

Her stomach knotted into a ball at the look in his eyes. 'I couldn't. Nick was married, he had a family, and I didn't think making them all sad would make us any happier, and it wouldn't have helped us. We had each other, Jem. We were all right—'

'No, we weren't! I didn't have a dad. I wanted a dad— I've always wanted a dad. But I thought he was dead, and all the time he was alive and you didn't tell me! If I hadn't had the accident, if I hadn't needed his blood, would you have told me? Ever?'

She swallowed down the tears. 'Of course I would. I always knew I'd have to tell you one day when the time was right, I just didn't know when that would be. We've been trying to work out how to do it without hurting you.'

He stared reproachfully at her, then at Nick again, and asked him a question she'd asked herself over and over. 'Why don't you want to be my dad?'

Nick flinched as if he'd been kicked in the gut. 'I do.'

'You don't,' Jem said firmly. 'When we were on the beach flying the kite, ages ago, after Christmas last year, that American lady said I was like my father, and I laughed, and you said you couldn't do this and stormed off. I didn't understand, but that was it, wasn't it? She realised you were my dad, and you didn't want me to know, so you walked away, because you don't want to be my father.'

'I do.'

'No, you don't!' he said, his voice rising, a catch in it. 'If you did want to, you would have stayed, you would have told me then. But you didn't want me.'

'I did want you, Jeremiah,' Nick said hoarsely. 'I do want you—more than you can ever imagine. But I didn't think you'd want me. The man you've always thought was your father was a hero, a brave man. How could I be as good as that?'

He stopped abruptly, turning to the window and propping his hand on the frame, staring out into the courtyard. Kate could see the muscles working in his jaw, see the tears tracking down his cheek, and she reached out a hand and laid it against his side in comfort. He closed his eyes and swallowed, and she dropped her hand and turned back to her son.

'Don't blame him, Jem,' she said softly. 'It was me who lied to you, me who let you believe my husband was your father. And Nick didn't know. I didn't tell him for ages, because of Auntie Annabel. It wouldn't have been fair to her. He's only known for two years.'

'So why didn't you tell him before? After Auntie

Annabel died, why didn't you tell him then? You could have told him then,' he said, his voice accusing.

'I didn't know how,' she said softly. 'He was very sad and angry when she died, and he was very busy at work sorting out the practice. It wouldn't have been a good time. There was never a good time. I thought there would be, I kept waiting, but then—when he did know—'

'I tried,' Nick said, turning back from the window again, his face taut. 'It may not seem like it, but I did try. But James was a hard act to follow. I thought maybe you'd be happier with things as they were, with me just as Uncle Nick, just as I've always been. And I tried to spend more time with you, quality time, to get to know you and let you get to know me, and I thought we might be getting somewhere, but then that woman commented on us looking alike, and I panicked. I wasn't sure the time was right, and I was so worried I'd make it worse. And just when I thought we ought to try again, your mother met Rob, and they seemed to be getting on so well. He's a good man, and I thought he'd make you a good father, a much better father than I would. You all seemed to be so happy together, and I didn't feel I had the right to destroy that. What good would it have done, Jem? I could have ruined it for you, for all of you. I didn't want to do that. I didn't have the right—'

'But you're my real father,' Jem sobbed, his bruised face anguished. 'You should have told me! I should have known.' I don't care if you're complete rubbish. It's better than being dead!' And he turned his face into the pillow and sobbed brokenly.

Kate leant forwards, resting a hand on his shoulder, but he shrugged her off, and she bit her lip and tried to stop the tears, but they fell anyway, coursing down her cheeks and dripping off her chin, and then she felt Nick's arms round her, cradling her gently against his side as he perched on the arm of the chair.

'Shh. Come on, he'll be all right,' he murmured, his voice ragged. 'He'll come round.'

'No, I won't,' Jem sobbed from the depths of the pillow. 'I won't be all right. Leave me alone! I hate you both! Go away!'

And then she felt Nick shudder, felt the pain tearing through him, and she slid her arms around his waist and hung on.

'Come on, let's give him some space,' he muttered after a few seconds, but she wouldn't leave him.

'I can't go. Not now. You go, leave me with him. I'll talk to him.'

'Will you be all right?'

She lifted her tear-stained face to him and tried to smile. 'I'll have to be, won't I? I have to do this, Nick. He's my son.'

A tremor ran through him, and he stood up. 'I'll see you later—I'll give you an hour. Call me if you need me to come back,' he said, and, closing the curtains around the bed, he walked swiftly away.

She watched him go, listened to the sound of his foot-steps retreating, and then she turned back to Jem, biting her lip and wondering how on earth she could unravel this sorry mess of hurt and lies and broken trust that they'd created.

She had no idea. She just knew she had to find a way.

Tentatively, with nothing but love on her side, she reached out her hand and touched him.

'I'm sorry. I'm so, so sorry,' she said unsteadily, and after a moment he opened his eyes and turned his head to look at her.

'Why?' he asked, his voice breaking. 'Why didn't you tell me? I could have kept a secret. All these years, I thought I didn't have a dad, that I'd never have a dad. And then you met Rob, and I thought maybe he could be my stepdad, but all the time I had a real father, and I didn't know!'

'I know. But you do at least know him, even if you didn't realise he was your father. I've made sure you see him regularly, and he knows you, and all about you. I did everything I could under the circumstances. Don't blame him, Jem. It was my fault, too, and he didn't have any choice. I kept it from him too. And I'm so sorry we've hurt you.'

He sniffed, but the tears still welled, and, unable to bear it, she got up and leant over, taking him gently into her arms, and he burrowed his face into the side of her neck.

Nick held it together just long enough to get out of St Piran, and then he pulled over on the coast road into a parking area, got out of the car and sucked in a lungful of the fresh, salt air.

If he'd been that sort of man, he could have wept bitter, anguished tears for the son he'd let down and all the years that had been lost. Years he couldn't give him back, years that were gone for ever. But he wasn't, and so he shoved it all aside and concentrated his efforts on the future.

If it took him till the end of his life, he vowed, he'd do his best to build a relationship with this child.

He got back in the car and drove to his house. There were some things he needed to pick up, and he could be alone there, think things through.

Except he wasn't alone. Sam Cavendish was there, just coming out of his mother's house next door, and he propped himself against the fence and frowned at Nick.

'You look like hell. Fancy a drink?'

'No, I'm going back to the hospital. We just told him.'

Sam winced sympathetically. 'Ouch. How did it go?'

'Pretty much as expected. Why don't you come in? I don't really want to talk about it here.'

So Sam followed him into the house and propped himself up on the worktop while Nick put the kettle on, for something to do as much as anything.

'So—what happened?' Sam prompted.

Nick sighed and rammed a hand through his hair. 'There was a kid in there having a blood transfusion, and Jem was asking about where his own blood transfusion had come from, and it sort of followed from there. He's the same blood group as me.'

'Yeah, Jack told me,' Sam said. 'And how did he take it?'

'Badly. He's angry. He said he'd spent nearly eleven years thinking he didn't have a father, and all the time he did, and he said...' His voice cracked, and he coughed again and flexed his fingers. 'He said he didn't care if I was complete rubbish, it was better than being dead.'

Sam snorted. 'Well, I'd agree with him if my own

wasn't so useless he might as well be dead, but what made him think you'd be rubbish?'

'I did. I told him James was a hard act to follow, that he might have preferred a hero. Apparently not. I didn't realise Jack had told you about the blood group thing.'

'Mmm. He was angry, but he's not really surprised.'

Nick's head snapped up and he stared at Sam, stunned. 'What makes you say that?'

Sam laughed softly. 'Oh, come on, Nick, everyone knows you've always loved Kate.'

They did? Well, why the hell hadn't they all reminded him of that in Freshers' Week when he'd been busy drinking himself senseless and making love to the first pretty girl who'd had enough alcohol to make her forget her common sense and sleep with him—the pretty girl who'd told him four weeks later that she was pregnant, and nine months later had presented him with twins, and then a year later with another son, while he'd worked his way through university supported by their parents and tried not to think about the girl he'd left behind. Had Annabel known she wasn't his first choice? Had she known he'd only done the decent thing and made the best marriage he could with the hand fate had dealt him? He sincerely hoped not, but if his feelings had been so obvious to everyone else, then why not to her?

And she'd sent him into Kate's arms, the night of the storm, almost as if she'd known that only Kate could comfort him.

'I tried to love her,' he murmured, as much to himself as to Sam, then he lifted his head and met Sam's eyes. 'I did love her, and I tried to be a good husband, and I think we had a good marriage, but maybe I was deluding myself.'

'I don't think so. I remember her—I grew up next door, don't forget. I spent a lot of time in this house. It was like a second home to me at one point. And she always seemed very happy, contented. At peace. She had a good life with you and a lovely family. I don't think you let her down, Nick. And she's been gone five years now. I think if anything you let yourself down, cheated yourself, and Kate, for too long. And maybe now it's time to do something positive about that.'

Sam shrugged away from the worktop, clapped Nick on the shoulder and headed for the front door. 'I'm going home to my wife and child. And tomorrow we're going house-hunting.'

Nick followed him through to the hall.

'Why?'

Sam laughed. 'Because my ankle doesn't like the hill and Gemma can't lift the buggy up the steps into the house. And we need to be nearer my mother.'

'How much nearer?' he asked, an idea dawning. 'Like—next door?'

Sam's eyes narrowed and he tilted his head on one side. 'Next door? As in, here?'

He nodded. 'There's a barn. I've just moved into it with Kate, so that when Jem comes out of the hospital in a few days he can live on the flat for a bit until he's got his mobility back—assuming he's speaking to us by then. And it's for sale. We're renting it at the moment, but I think it's time to move on, time to lay Annabel's ghost to rest, whatever happens with me and Kate and Jeremiah. So I'm going to sell this house, and buy the barn, and then if it works out...'

Sam's jaw sagged slightly, and then he laughed. 'Really? You're selling? How much?'

He shrugged. 'I have no idea. It's the least of my worries. I won't cheat you, Sam.'

Sam grinned. 'I'll make sure of it. Talk to the agents—let me know. And I'll go and sound Gemma out, but I know what she'll say. She loves this house, and so do I.'

Nick felt himself smile as the weight lifted a little. 'I know you do,' he said. 'And it needs another family.'

And if Sam and Gemma bought it from him, it would bring his dream a little closer...

CHAPTER NINE

HE FOUND Kate in the deserted café, sitting nursing a stale cup of coffee and looking like death.

He sat down opposite her and took the cup out of her hands. It was stone cold, and he tutted softly and wrapped her hands in his to warm them. 'How is he?'

She shrugged. 'They had to give him some more morphine and something to help him sleep. I think it was all the upset...'

She trailed off, and he sighed, stroking his thumb over the back of her hand. 'What did he say? After I left.'

She shrugged again, a helpless little gesture that made his heart ache for her. 'He's just really shocked, I think. It's a lot for him to take in. I explained to the staff—the night sister and Megan Phillips. They were really nice to him. Megan, especially, was really lovely. She's such a nice girl. And I rang Jess Carmichael, and she came up and talked to me for a minute while he was asleep, and she makes so much sense. She's going to come and see him when he's feeling a little better and let him talk it through with her.'

'Do you think he will?' Nick asked, not sure about the idea of unburdening to a counsellor, but Kate nodded.

'I think so. He likes her. He talked to her before, when I was ill.' She sighed. 'Nick, I'm really tired, can you take me home?' she asked, and his heart contracted.

'Sure,' he said softly, and, helping her to her feet, he wrapped an arm round her shoulders and led her out to the car.

'So much for Ben's chilli,' she said as they went into the house, and he just pulled her into his arms and held her while the dog sniffed and wagged around their feet. She was exhausted, and she had to be hungry. He was—or his body was. His heart wasn't in the least bit interested in anything as trivial as food, but for her sake, he'd fix them something to eat and make sure she ate it.

'I'll cook us something quick,' he said, giving her a last little hug and letting her go. 'We can have more of the cold pie, or toast, or anything you want.'

'Toast,' she said. 'Toast and a nice, hot cup of tea. And it's cold—I know it's April, but do you think it would be possible to put the heating on?'

'Want me to light the fire?'

She glanced at the big woodburner and sighed longingly. 'Oh, that would be lovely. Is there any wood?'

He nodded. 'There's a pile out in the cart lodge, I'll get some while I'm taking the dog out. I'll put the kettle on, you go and sit down. You look done in.'

'Do you think we could have done things any differently?' she asked later, as they lay side by side with their legs stretched out towards the fire and its living hearthrug.

Nick stared at the dog and wondered what it must be like to have no responsibilities. 'In what way?' he asked. 'Do you mean the way we told him now, or if we should have told him years ago? Either way, I don't know. I don't think there was a right way, under the circumstances, but I wish you'd told me sooner, Kate. I wish I'd known, right back at the beginning. I would have made sure I saw more of him.'

'How?' she asked, turning her head to face him, searching his eyes and finding only confusion that mirrored her own. 'You were working in Wadebridge, living in Penhally, and I can see your house from mine—I could look across sometimes and see Annabel hanging the washing out! How were you going to spend time with him, under those circumstances, without arousing suspicion? And I didn't want to do that to you, to put you under that sort of pressure for something that hadn't been your fault.'

'Of course it was my fault!' he said. 'I heard you crying and I walked in when I knew you were naked, when I'd seen you, I'd undressed you—dammit, Kate, I knew what was going to happen if I opened that door.'

'Nick, I was falling apart, and so were you.' She lifted her hand and cradled his jaw, feeling the muscles clench beneath her palm. 'You needed me, every bit as much as I needed you. We were on autopilot—we didn't set out to make love, and if I hadn't got pregnant, nobody would ever have known.'

'I would have known. I never forgot, Kate. It haunted me—it still haunts me. And things with Annabel were never quite the same after that. I don't really know why, if it was because I'd changed, or because she sensed what happened between us that night. Maybe she even knew Jem was mine. I'll never know. But I knew when

I walked through that door how dangerous it was, and I should have stopped myself.'

'And left me there alone, in that state? How was that right?' She leant over, closing the gap and touching her lips lightly to his cheek, then rested her head on his shoulder. 'I needed you, Nick, and you needed me, more than we'd ever needed anyone before. It wasn't your fault, it was just one of those things—part of being human. And you can't take all the responsibility for the fact that I got pregnant.'

'Why not? I know how the system works, Kate, and God knows I'd had enough object lessons in it!'

She eased back so she could look at him. 'Was Annabel on the Pill?'

'Yes.'

'So it wasn't unreasonable that you didn't think about contraception, because it wasn't a normal part of your sex life at the time. Nor was it mine. I didn't even think about it. James and I had been trying for three years, and we'd finally admitted that there might be something wrong and gone for tests, just a week before. We were still waiting for the results when he died, and maybe I should have told you, but how? Who would have gained?'

He sighed, and his arm around her back tightened a fraction and eased her closer.

'You're right,' he murmured as she rested her head back on his shoulder. 'It was an impossible decision, a no-win situation. There was no right way to deal with it, we've just got to make sure we do it right now. Maybe you'd better give me a script.'

'You don't need a script. Just rely on your instincts, Nick.'

'My instincts are fatally flawed,' he said drily. 'If we rely on them, it's a sure-fire recipe for disaster. And talking of my instincts, before I do anything else I'll regret, I'm going to take the dog out, and then I'm going to bed.'

She tilted her head and stared up into his eyes, held motionless by the sensual message in their rich chocolate depths, and with a ragged sigh he eased her closer and touched his mouth to hers.

She parted her lips, and he growled low in his throat and took instant advantage, the hot, silken sweep of his tongue plundering her mouth, sliding one hand around the back of her neck and threading his fingers through her hair to steady her as the other hand curled around her bottom and hauled her closer. Her legs parted at the pressure from his knee, and one hard thigh lodged between them, sending need shooting through her, turning her body to fire.

'Nick,' she moaned, but the sound of her voice seemed to stop him in his tracks, and he pulled back, lifting his head and staring down at her, his chest rising and falling rapidly. She could see the hammer of his heartbeat in the hollow of his throat, and after an endless moment he got to his feet and walked away, calling the dog.

'Nick?'

'Leave it, Kate. For the love of God, just leave it,' he said rawly, and she heard the door shut behind him, the lights coming on automatically as he walked out of the back door from the utility room into the garden, the dog at his heels.

For an age she sat there, staring after him, her eyes fixed blindly on the closed door, and then with a fractured little sigh she got to her feet, put their glasses in the kitchen and went to bed.

They were supposed to be being grown up about this, she reminded herself, and so far it was only Nick who was sticking to the plot. How long that would last, she had no idea, but as she lay down in her bed, her mind went back to Jem.

How on earth had she forgotten about him? He was lying there in hospital, distressed and heartbroken, and all she could think about was making love with Nick, which was what had got them all in this mess in the first place!

It was a long, long time before she went to sleep.

The next day was very hard.

Jem refused to talk to Kate at first, and he refused to let Nick visit. After he'd got over his crying spell the night before, he'd withdrawn into himself, and the only thing he showed any interest in was Lucy's games console. It took him out of himself, she thought, gave him something to concentrate on, something to hide behind while his subconscious sorted out the wood from the trees.

So she just sat beside him, reading a magazine and waiting, and finally he cracked.

'Why did you lie to me?' he asked suddenly, and she put her magazine down and made herself meet his hurt, accusing eyes.

'I didn't—well, not really. I tried very hard not to, and I never actually told you that James was your father, because I knew it was a lie, and it was more a case of letting you believe something than telling you something wrong. So when you asked about your father, I told you

that if he'd known he had a son, he would have been
very proud of you, and that, at least, is true. He is proud
of you, and he loves you. He always has.'

'But you let me think that James was my father. That
was a sort of lie.'

It was. A lie of omission, and she nodded. 'Yes, it
was. But it seemed like the best of some not very good
choices, and I wanted to do the best I could for everyone.
I didn't really know what else to do without hurting innocent people.'

'I'm innocent,' he said, and her eyes filled.

'I know. I'm sorry. It's a mess, and it's my fault, not
your father's. You shouldn't blame him, he had no say
in it.'

'Where is Uncle N—?' he asked, and then frowned.
'Mum, what do I call him now?' he asked fretfully.

She stroked his hair. 'I don't know. You'll have to
ask him that. Whatever feels right. What do you want
to call him?'

He shrugged. 'Dunno. I mean, he's my dad, isn't
he?'

She nodded, blinking back the ever-ready tears. 'Yes.
Yes, he is, but you must do what feels right for you both.
I can't tell you that, darling, it's up to you. And he's
here—I expect he's in the café. Why? Do you want to
see him now?'

He shrugged his skinny shoulders again. 'Just wondered if he'd gone. He went home yesterday.'

'Because you told him to.'

'But I didn't think he'd go,' he said perversely. 'Not
if he really cared.'

'Oh, he cares, Jem,' she said softly. 'He was really
upset. He went because you asked him to, not because

he wanted to, and that's why he's not here now, but he is in the hospital, in case you want to see him. And he'll be here, waiting, until you're ready.'

'Really?'

She nodded. 'Really. However long it takes. He wants to see you,' she told him, and she watched that sink in, watched the realisation that Nick did care, that he wanted Jem. Was here for him, any time he asked.

He didn't ask, not then, but later, when he'd obviously been thinking about it for a while, he lifted his head and said, 'This face-merging thing. Do you think it would work with him and me?'

She took a second to realise he was talking about the games console, and lifted her shoulders. 'I don't know. Probably. Do you want to try?'

'Maybe. If he's still here.'

She felt a great weight lift off her chest, and smiled. 'I'll find him.'

He was in the café, in a litter of torn sugar and salt packets, pushing a pile of white crystals around on the tabletop.

She sat down next to him, and he lifted his head and gave her a weary smile. 'Hi. How is he?'

'He's OK. He wants to see you.'

His eyes widened, and she could see hope flickering in them. 'Really?'

'Really. He was talking about the photo-merging thing. I think he wants to try with your faces.'

'Ah. That might need Jack or Lucy.'

'It might not. You might be able to work it out. You've got the instructions.'

He nodded slowly. 'I could try. Any tips or hints? For him, not the game.'

'Give him time. He's still angry with us, but more than that, he's confused and he needs time to adjust to the new reality of having a father. We all need time to adjust to it, but we'll get there.'

'Will we?' he asked doubtfully, as they left the café and walked along to the ward. 'I hope you're right.'

She sent him in on his own, and Jem looked up and gave him a wary smile.

He smiled back just as warily and sat down on the chair. 'Hiya. Your mum says you want to try the face-merging thing.'

'Mmm.' Jem fiddled with the games console for a moment, then mumbled, 'Uncle Nick? Can I call you Dad? 'Cos that's what you are, really, and it's what Jack and Lucy call you. But I'm still mad with you, though, for walking off and not explaining,' he added hastily, just in case he wasn't aware of it.

No chance of that. Nick's throat closed, and he swallowed hard. 'That's fine, I deserve it. You can call me whatever you want. And if you want to call me Dad—well, that would be awesome.'

His son rolled his eyes and grinned, looking so like Jack that Nick couldn't believe he'd never seen it. 'You can't say that, Dad, you're too old, you sound silly. And I am still mad with you.'

He gave him a wry smile. 'That's OK. We can talk about that,' he agreed, and blinked hard. He'd called him Dad—as if he'd been practising it in his head all day, and finally felt brave enough to try it out. Brave enough, and trusting enough.

He sucked in a deep breath, and picked up the games console. 'Right. Instructions?'

'They're here. Where's Mum?'

'I think she's having a drink and a bit of fresh air. Why?'

He shrugged. 'Just wondered. I thought she'd like to see this.'

'We can show her later when she comes back, if we can work it out. Or I can go outside and phone her,' Nick suggested, realising Jem was still scared. Still scared, and still needing his mother, but the man who'd been Uncle Nick all his life didn't have the power to fill that gap, and maybe never would. He realised that he was jealous of her relationship with him. So stupid. Of course he needed his mother, he was a little boy, still not quite eleven years old, for all his courage.

'Want me to call her? She could come now, I'm sure. She's not far away.'

Jem shook his head. 'No, it's OK. We can show her later, like you said,' he agreed, and Nick felt himself relax a little. One step at a time...

'We did it, Mum, it was amazing,' their son said by way of greeting, and she felt the tension ease out of her.

'Did you make it work, then?' she asked him, and he nodded.

'Yeah—come here, let me show you. And I'm going to look so like him when I'm older. It's awesome, isn't it, Dad?' he said, and Kate's eyes widened slightly and then filled with tears.

'Yes, you will be like him,' she said, looking at the games console as Jem switched from one face to another, the similarities striking. Her voice wobbled slightly, and she swallowed hard and avoided Nick's eyes. But he'd seen, and his hand came out and squeezed hers in support.

'Lucy sent me a text. She's invited us for supper. Want to go?'

She shook her head. 'No. I ought to let the dog out and I could do with putting some washing on before I come back here this evening, but you can go, if you like.'

'No. That's fine. I'll drop in and have a cup of tea with her after I take you home, and I could go and pick up my post—yours, too.'

'You can go now, Dad, if you like,' Jem said. 'Mum and me'll be all right.'

'Mum and I,' she corrected automatically, and turned in time to see the flicker of pain on Nick's face.

'Sure. I'll do the dog and the post and have tea with Lucy, and I'll come back this evening and take you home after visiting, then, if you're both sure?' Nick said gruffly, and then, after a fractional hesitation, he bent over the bed and dropped a kiss on his son's bruised forehead. Just a fleeting one, the sort of kiss he'd given his other boys in their youth, but he wasn't sure of his reception and when Jem slid his arms round him and gave him a quick hug, he felt the love swell in his chest and threaten to choke him.

'You take care,' he said gruffly, ruffling his hair with a gentle hand, and because he didn't want to leave her out, he stooped and kissed Kate's cheek, as well, in passing, and he was rewarded by her smile.

At least supper was sorted out, he thought as he headed back to Lucy's—fresh sea bass from one of the fishermen in the harbour. He'd been spotted turning into his drive when he'd collected his post, and Toby Penhaligan had pulled in behind him and given him two beautiful, plump fish straight from the sea.

'How's the lad?' he'd asked, and Nick wondered if he'd heard the rumour, too.

'Doing well, thanks,' he'd told him. 'He should be out of hospital by the end of next week.'

'I hear you've taken the barn for the summer.'

So the jungle drums were working overtime. No surprises there, then. 'For a while, anyway. I'm giving Kate a hand to look after Jem—he can't manage the stairs, so it seemed to make sense.'

He'd felt Toby's eyes track to the more-than-adequate family house behind him, and was hugely grateful that the barn was out of the way and might afford them a little much-needed privacy.

He'd gone straight there, put the fish in the fridge and walked the dog, then gone to Lucy's.

'So, how is he?' she asked.

'OK,' he told them. 'Good. He called me Dad today…'

His voice cracked a bit, and he cleared his throat and gave them a wry smile. They were gathered round the kitchen table, his two eldest children and Ben, drinking tea and talking through Jem's progress, and Lucy reached out a hand and squeezed his shoulder. 'Sorry,' he muttered, patting her hand. 'It got to me. But he says he's still mad with me. He thinks I don't want to be his father.'

'Do you?' Jack asked. 'Because I could understand if you didn't. I was appalled when India died and I was told Freddie was mine—talk about hurled in at the deep end.

It really wasn't easy, but you've got to give it a go, Dad, because—well, he's the best thing that's ever happened to me, him and Alison and our growing family. But it was Freddie that turned me around, and he's given me so much.'

'I'm sure you're the best thing that's ever happened to him, as well. And I do want to be his father. I just hope I can do him justice.'

'Of course you can! It's not about being perfect, it's about being there,' Lucy told him. 'And listening. You could maybe do a bit more of that. But we were never short of love, and that's what he needs most of all. To know you love him.'

'I do.' He swallowed and tried to smile. 'He hugged me. When I said goodbye. He's never hugged me before.'

Lucy tutted again, and got up and came round and snuggled onto his lap. 'You soft old thing,' she said kindly, and he laughed and tapped her on the bottom.

'Less of the old,' he told her, and hugged her back, then frowned and looked down at her slightly rounded abdomen. 'Are you pregnant again?'

She blushed. 'Um—I might be.'

'I think you might. Congratulations. I take it this is planned?'

Ben's lips twitched. 'Sort of. She caught me in a weak moment. I think it's a ploy to be on permanent maternity leave.'

Nick laughed again. 'Come on, let me up. I have to go and see your little brother.'

Jem was tired—exhausted, really, after a busy day with two lots of visitors and all the upset of the previous day—and he was still getting used to being out in an open ward with six-bed bays, rather than his own quiet little side room, so Kate and Nick didn't stay late, and were home by quarter to eight.

Home, he thought, turning into the drive, and wondered how, in just a little over forty-eight hours, it could possibly feel like home.

Because Kate was there.

There was no other possible reason, and he ushered her in, poured her a glass of wine while she let the dog out and fussed over him, then scrubbed the new potatoes while she sat and sipped the wine and watched the last pink streaks of the sunset fade over the sea.

'Anything I can do?' she asked him, feeling guilty for sitting there, but he just smiled at her and carried on scraping and scrubbing.

'No. You stay there and enjoy being waited on. You heard the doctor—I have to spoil you.'

She chuckled. 'If you insist. So how was Lucy?'

'Ah, Lucy. Pregnant again.'

Kate smiled indulgently. 'Have you only just realised?' she said.

He rolled his eyes. 'Of course, you're a midwife. You notice these things.'

'That's right,' she said smugly. 'So, what are you feeding me for supper?' she asked, and he grinned.

'Sea bass, courtesy of Toby Penhaligan.'

'Sea bass? Really? Are you going to make the house smell of fish?' she queried, and he laughed.

'I shouldn't think so, the extractor fan's like a jet engine, I'll be surprised if it doesn't suck the fish out of the pan. I tell you what, while I do this, why don't you go and have a shower?'

'Do you mind?'

'Not at all. Consider it all part of your pampering,' he said, and his eyes raked slowly over her and he smiled. 'You could even wear something pretty.'

Pretty? Her heart thudded, and she felt a sudden flutter of nerves. He was looking at her as if…

Oh, lord. She wasn't ready for this. Last night she had been, but tonight, just like that, without the benefit of cuddling up to him and getting in the mood, she felt a shiver of ice slide down her spine. Nick wasn't coy, and he wouldn't be a shy lover. He'd want the lights on and access to every part of her, and she wasn't sure she could do this. Not now, and maybe not ever.

'I'll see what I've got. It might just be jumper and jeans,' she said, and headed for her bedroom, panic clawing at her throat.

He put the potatoes in the pan and glanced at his watch. She might be half an hour in the shower and then getting ready, so he had time to light the fire to give it time to warm up the room.

He brought some wood in, and while he was laying the fire, he heard a noise coming from the area of her bedroom.

'Kate?'

He walked down the corridor towards her room, and heard the shower running, and then a muffled sob.

He rested his head against the door. Not again. He couldn't do this again.

So he went into her room and stood by the window, staring out into the courtyard and listening in agony as she wept just feet away from him. There was nothing he could do—nothing he would let himself do—but wait until the crying stopped, and a minute later she turned off the water, then he heard the door open and she walked into the room, closing the door and then dropping her towel.

And then she saw him, and gasped, scrabbling for the towel, her eyes red-rimmed and wild with some unfathomable emotion.

He reached for her, shocked at the ravaged look on her face, the pain in her eyes, desperate to comfort her, but she wouldn't let him.

'Nick, no,' she said, pushing him away and trying to turn her back to him, the towel twisted somehow round her now. 'Please!'

'Don't be silly, I've seen you cry umpteen times in the last few days,' he said gently, his hands cupping her shoulders, but she shook her head.

'No—it's not that. Please, Nick, just go—'

She broke off, the smothered sobs returning, and he felt swamped by her pain, the light slowly dawning as he realised belatedly why she'd turned away.

'Oh, my love, my darling girl, come here,' he said tenderly, turning her back into his arms and folding her against his chest once more, his hands stroking her back rhythmically through the damp towel. 'After all we've been through, do you really think a few scars are going to make any difference to me?'

'They make a difference to me,' she sobbed, pushing him away again, but he wouldn't let her go this time, he couldn't, because the pain and fear for her, suppressed for nearly a year now, were rising up and choking him, and he cradled her tenderly against his heart and rocked her. Rocked them both.

'I thought you were going to die,' he said unevenly. 'I thought I was going to lose you, lose everything that kept me sane. You're my best friend, Kate, the one person who really understands me; the only thing that's kept me going is working with you, having you there near me, even if you weren't with me. I prayed so hard that you'd make it, even if you ended up with Rob—that didn't matter, just so long as you were alive, just so long as I knew you were somewhere in the world. Why the hell should I care about a scar?'

'Oh, Nick,' she whispered tearfully, and, resting her head against his shoulder, she slid her arms round him and held him. 'I'm sorry. I didn't even think about how you might have felt, just that you hadn't been there for me, but nobody was there for you. I'm so, so sorry.'

She breathed deeply, then looked at him again. 'It's just— Nobody's seen it, and when you said wear something pretty, I felt ridiculously shy all of a sudden, and I thought, what if it turned you off?'

'Kate!' he chided softly, gutted that she thought so little of him. 'How shallow do you think I am?'

'I don't. It's how shallow I am.'

He gave a ragged sigh and cradled her head against his shoulder. 'Can we start again? Wear something that makes you feel good. Something that makes you feel all woman, because you are, Kate. You're a beautiful woman, and I want to show you that, but only when you're ready. There's no pressure. I don't care if it takes months. Years. I want you, and I'll wait for you.'

She sucked in a breath and took a little step back. 'I'll see what I can find. Why don't you go and start cooking?'

CHAPTER TEN

'ANYTHING I can do?'

He lifted his head and smiled at her, but he didn't comment on her clothes, and she felt perversely irritated. 'You could top and tail the mangetout, if you're bored. And you look lovely, by the way. Beautiful.'

The irritation dissolved in an instant, replaced by a rush of heat and affection for this complicated and loveable man. He brought her the packet of peas, a pan and a small knife, dropped a tender, lingering kiss on her lips, and she sat at the table with a silly smile and trimmed the peas and sipped another glass of wine while he put the fish on to cook and prodded the potatoes. Music was playing in the background, something soft and smoky and sensual, and between that and the wine and the last streaks of the sunset fading into the night, it was the perfect romantic setting.

All she needed was her son back home, safe and sound, and her happiness would be complete. Once she'd found the courage to make love to Nick, at least.

Did he feel the same way about it? She glanced across at him, and saw he was humming softly as he worked. He looked happy enough. It was lovely to be able to sit there and enjoy all of the house without moving, she thought, and told herself it could be permanent, that they could stay there and make it their home.

'Right, let's have those peas. How's your wine?'

'It's fine. I don't need any more. I'm still on the occasional anti-inflammatory and I don't like to mix drugs and alcohol.'

'I thought that was what the modern youth did.'

'It is. I'm not the modern youth.'

'I'm thankful for that.'

They shared a smile, and then with a shake of his head, as if he was collecting himself, he turned back to his cooking and the moment was gone.

'That was gorgeous, Nick. Thank you.'

'My pleasure. It was worth being grilled by Toby Penhaligan to get those sea bass. They were gorgeous.'

'Did he give you a very hard time?'

Nick shrugged. 'The jungle drums are obviously working, but I suppose we should expect that. I think we need to present a united front, for Jem's sake, and if the gossip gets too much—well, who knows what the future might hold?'

His words hung in the air, and Kate met his eyes and saw a hope in them that must surely be reflected in her own. She wanted him. She wanted to be with him, to spend her life with him, and their son did, too.

And to do that, she had to find the courage to do what she had to do next.

'Nick? Will you do something for me?'

'Sure. What is it?'

'Will you make love to me?'

He froze, his glass suspended above the table, and

after what seemed like for ever he set it back down very, very carefully and uncurled his fingers from the stem.

'Are you sure?' he asked hoarsely.

'Yes. Yes, I'm sure, but I'm scared.'

'Oh, Kate...'

He stood up and came round to her side, taking her hands in his. 'You don't have to be scared. This is me. Why on earth are you scared?'

'Because—I just am. It's been a long time, Nick. And—well, I don't look the same.'

'You know what I feel about that,' he said.

'But it's not only about what you feel, it's about what I feel, and I feel—I know it's stupid, I know it's irrational, I've seen lots of women who've had breast surgery, but they weren't me. This is me, my body, and that makes it different. And illogical,' she explained, and he frowned slightly and squeezed her hand.

'I can understand that, but, Kate, I could have lost you, but I didn't. You're here with me, now, and that, at the end, is the only thing that matters. That you're alive and well.'

'And then there's the competition,' she went on, ignoring him. 'I'm not Annabel,' she said, pointing out the obvious. 'Or any one of the other glamorous women you've been seen with.'

He sighed and shifted to the chair beside her, lifting her hand and pressing it to his cheek. 'I know you're not Annabel,' he said gently. 'You don't have to live up to her, Kate. I loved her, just not the way I've always loved you. You were always my soul mate. You were the one I should have been with all this time. She was a lovely girl, and she turned into a kind, sensitive and generous woman; as a mother, I couldn't fault her. As a wife, she was perfect. We were good friends in many ways, but there was no great passion there, no desperate yearning. And as for the other women—there's only really been one since Annabel, and she has no expectations. I've seen her from time to time. Her name's Louise. We've had dinner, gone to the cinema.'

'Made love?'

'I'm not a monk, Kate. Neither am I promiscuous. The others have just been passing distractions, but I haven't slept with them. And I'm not going to beat you up about Rob.'

'What makes you think I slept with him?'

He shook his head and gave a wry smile. 'I saw you. I came to see you, last summer. I wanted to talk to you, and I pulled up outside. And Rob was kissing you, in the kitchen, right in front of the window. And then you walked away, and a light came on upstairs, and you shut the bedroom curtains. It wasn't rocket science, Kate.'

She felt sick. 'Nick, you weren't meant to see that.'

'Of course not. But you're adults, so why not? After all, we weren't going anywhere, were we, at the time, and he's a good guy. So—why not? It's what people do. I know that. And I can understand it, but it's all very well in theory, but in practice, I realised I was jealous.'

'Because even though you didn't want me, you didn't want anyone else to?'

'But I did want you. I just didn't know how to ask. I went to see Louise, after I drove away that night. I thought—what was sauce for the goose, I suppose. But, well, let's just say I think I was a bit of a disappointment to her. I couldn't get you out of my head, couldn't stop seeing you kissing him, and I didn't want to be with her. I didn't want to be with anyone if I couldn't be with you, and obviously I couldn't. So I went home, picked up a bottle of Scotch from the kitchen, walked down to the beach and drank half of it. I haven't seen her since.'

'So who was the woman at Ben and Lucy's barbecue last summer?' she asked.

'An old friend from London. She's divorced, she was down here on holiday, and she was lonely.'

Kate smiled indulgently. 'I think she was probably more than lonely, the way she was looking at you.'

He shrugged. 'I'm a good-looking guy—what can I say?' he murmured, and she laughed, as he'd meant her to. But then his smile faded, and he lifted his hand and touched her cheek. 'She was nothing, Kate. Nothing happened with her, I promise. I can't dismiss Annabel, she was my wife, the mother of three of my children, a very important person in our lives, and I loved her. But there truly has been no one else who matters at all, no one who's ever claimed my heart or made me want to behave like an irrational teenager or a romantic fool. No one else who's been such a good friend to me no matter how badly I've behaved. No one else that I've loved the way I love you. The way I've always loved you.'

'Oh, Nick. What happened to us?' she asked softly, and he stood up slowly and drew her to her feet.

'I don't know. I just know that now we seem to have a chance, and I want to take that chance with you, Kate. Let me try again,' he murmured softly. 'I know I don't deserve it, but give me a chance to prove that I can be a good husband and father. We're stuck with each other for good now, anyway, as Jem's parents—why not do it properly? There's so much at stake here now—so much that's infinitely precious that I really don't think I can bear to lose.'

Her mouth dropped open slightly, and she stared at him in confusion. 'Are you—? Did I imagine it, or did you just ask me to marry you?'

He felt emotion choke him, and swallowed. 'I'm not sure. I think I might have done, but not just because of Jem. I can be a father to him whatever, if I get the chance, and that's down to him. And if he hates me, if he wants me out of his life…'

'He doesn't. He won't.'

'Then give me a chance, Kate. Let's wind back the clock and start again, only as adults with hopefully a bit more judgement and common sense and compassion. See if we can make it work this time.'

She studied him doubtfully. 'Do you think we can do that?'

'I think we can try.'

'Maybe.'

'Is that a maybe maybe, or a definite maybe?' he asked, sure his smile didn't reach his eyes because her answer was so important to him.

'I think that's a definite maybe,' she said, her smile slow, and he felt the tension drain out of him. And then ratchet up again another gear. He lifted his hand and grazed his knuckles gently against her cheek.

'I want to make love to you,' he murmured, 'but I want you to be sure that you're ready for this, because if you're going to change your mind, I'd rather you did it now.'

She gave a quiet sigh. 'The only thing that would change my mind is Jem, and he seems to love you. He's always been very fond of you, and now, knowing you're his father just seems to be strengthening that bond. So, no, I'm not going to change my mind, Nick. But I am still scared.'

He drew her into his arms and cradled her against his heart. 'Don't be scared, my love. I'll take care of you. I'll always take care of you.'

He let her go, then took her hand and led her slowly and carefully up the stairs to his room, closing the door behind them just in case Bruno decided to follow them, but he was lying on a rug chasing rabbits in his sleep, and she didn't think he'd worry.

'Do you want the lights off?' he asked, and she swallowed.

She had to do this. She had to be brave enough to show herself to him, to open up all her physical and emotional scars to him and trust him to heal them. But the lights...

'How about the bathroom light? We could leave the door open,' he suggested, and she nodded, ridiculously nervous now.

He turned back the bed, stripped off his clothes down to his boxers—jersey boxers that fitted snugly over his firm, muscular buttocks and thighs and did heart-stopping things in other areas—and then held out his hand to her.

She went to his side, and he stared down at her, his eyes sombre. 'Are you sure, Kate?' he said softly. 'We've had years to talk this up in our heads, and I don't want to disappoint you.'

'You won't disappoint me.' She knew he wouldn't. She didn't know how, she just knew. She went up on tiptoe and brushed her lips against his, then dropped back onto her heels and waited.

He unbuttoned the silky blouse she'd put on, the sheer

fabric sliding against her skin as he loosened it and slipped it over her shoulders. He laid it carefully on the chair, then his fingers found the zip on her trousers and slid it down, the faint noise loud in the breathless silence. The button was next, and then they joined the blouse on the chair and he stood back and looked at her, standing there in her underwear.

'You're still a really beautiful woman, Kate,' he said softly. 'Come here. I need you.'

He held out his hand, and she put hers in it and went into his arms, closing the gap between them slowly, so that when their bodies touched, it was like coming home.

She rested her head on his shoulder, and he slid his arms round her waist and held her gently against his body, so she could feel the beating of his heart, the rise and fall of his chest as he breathed, the warmth of his skin, and as she lifted her head, his came down and his lips found hers, meshing and melding in a gentle dance that was filled with promise.

She knew he wanted her. She also knew he'd wait for her, give her time for her fears to fade, and it gave her the confidence to step back out of his arms and take off the last of her clothes, so she was standing in front of him naked.

And then she waited.

Her trust was unbearably touching.

He felt his eyes fill with tears, and because he knew she wanted him to, he made himself look down, to study the scar on her left breast, the fine line that ran round underneath it in the crease, the hollow left by the surgery that had saved her life. The skin was a little discoloured from the radiotherapy, but that would fade with time. And it was very neat. The doctor in him admired the surgery. The man wanted her, more than he'd ever wanted any other woman in his life, and if it killed him, he was going to do her justice now.

Her courage humbled him, and he gave her an unsteady smile. 'I feel a little overdressed,' he said gruffly, and skimmed off his boxers, tossing them aside and standing in front of her, wondering how he measured up to Rob and hating himself for caring about something so trivial. Well, at least she could see that he wasn't in the least put off by her appearance. In fact, if she kept him waiting much longer...

'Nick?'

He met her eyes.

'Make love to me.'

He lifted her carefully onto the bed, tutting at the faint bruising on her right foot, touching his lips gently to the little stain. He could imagine her feet trapped in the footwell, knew that if the fuel tank had blown, she would have died.

Don't think about that, he told himself, and moved up, skimming past her thighs, not allowing himself to linger till he reached her waist, then trailing his tongue slowly around her navel, dipping into it, teasing her till she trembled.

Then he moved higher, his hand cupping her left breast, pressing a gentle, healing kiss to the scar. She shuddered a little, and he moved on, his lips sipping and tasting the other breast, reluctant to miss a single inch of her. She moaned and arched up, her body image issues forgotten now, need taking over, the need that had haunted them both for so very many years. The purely sensual need that their one tragic night had never addressed.

He moved up until his face was level with hers, and kissed her as he'd always wanted to kiss her, long and slow and deep—heavy, drugging kisses that cranked up the heat and made his body burn for her.

And hers for him. She plucked at him, her fingers restless, her breathing light and rapid, almost hyperventilating. 'Nick, please…now,' she begged, and doing what he'd failed to do before, taking the time to protect her, he moved over her and thrust slowly, lingeringly home.

She gasped, her body bucking beneath his, and he locked his mouth to hers, plundering it as he drove into her again and again and again, until at last he could hold it no more and he let himself go, joining her in the long freefall into ecstasy.

The next few days were blissful.

The weather was gorgeous, and when they weren't in the hospital visiting Jem, they were at the barn, sitting under a little ornamental tree in the courtyard garden with the dog at their feet and drinking coffee or sipping wine, and every now and then he'd cook them something wonderful.

And his hidden talent for waiting on her was turning into an art form. He ran errands for her, spoiled her rotten, massaged her neck when it ached and then, when she was boneless and utterly relaxed, he'd make love to her.

They were slow, lazy days, days in which they all recovered from what had been a gruelling ordeal, and gradually they relaxed into a quiet, orderly routine.

He went back to work in the mornings, coming home to cook them lunch before driving to the hospital to visit Jem. He'd settled really well in the new ward, made friends, watched the ducklings grow and gradually, bit by bit, he was getting back on his feet.

Jess Carmichael had been to see him, and he was less angry with his parents, more accepting now that there had been valid reasons why his parentage had been kept from him. 'She's a wonderful person,' Kate said. 'I don't know how I would have coped last year without her. She's a miracle.'

She wasn't the only miracle. Lucy had formed a wonderfully close attachment to Jem, and on a day when Nick was there alone because he'd treated Kate to a pamper break, she brought the children in to see him.

'Hey, you've got the monsters,' Jem said with a grin, and Lucy chuckled.

'Annabel, say hello to Uncle Jem,' she said, letting go of her daughter's hand, and his eyes widened.

'Wow—I really am an uncle, aren't I? That's weird—awesome! Hi, Annabel.'

'We bringed you grapes,' Annabel said, handing him the bag shyly.

'That's because Grandad ate the last lot,' Lucy pointed out with a firm look at her father, and he rolled his eyes.

'Naughty G'andad!' Annabel said, and stared at them longingly.

Jem gave her some, and she settled down on the floor by the window and ate the grapes and counted the ducklings, while Lucy hung onto the baby and tried to keep him out of mischief.

'I can't believe he's a year old,' she said.

'I can't believe I'm a grandfather,' Nick said drily.

Lucy grinned. 'Oh, I can. Look at the grey hairs, Dad! But I can't believe Annabel's nearly two and a half. It seems like five minutes. Joshy, no! You can't have the grapes.'

'Gape!' he yelled, his little fist working, and lunged for them, slipping out of Lucy's grasp and cracking his head on the edge of the clipboard hanging on the end of the bed.

'Oh, I don't believe it!' Lucy wailed, lifting him up and hugging him while Nick looked at the little gash on the screaming toddler's temple.

'He'll live, but it needs gluing,' Nick said, pressing a clean tissue to the cut and holding it there.

'Oh, well, at least it's into the hairline,' she said with a sigh. 'Come on, Annabel, we're going to have to take him to see Daddy. Joshy's got a little cut.'

'Leave her here, she'll be fine with me,' Nick said, and she smiled gratefully and hurried along the corridor and out of the ward, Josh's screams fading as she took him further away.

'Joshy's screaming,' Annabel said matter-of-factly. 'He always screams.'

'He's a little boy. They get in trouble a lot, but he'll be fine,' Nick said with a reassuring smile, and sat down on the floor with his granddaughter and watched the ducklings.

'Oh, Megan, brilliant—are you busy?'

She wasn't, but she didn't want to hang around in A and E any longer than she had to. She'd managed to avoid Josh O'Hara so far, but she could hardly refuse to help Ben Carter. She stepped into the cubicle and smiled at the woman. Lucy. She'd seen her on Paeds, visiting Jem, and knew she was Ben's wife. 'Well—no, not really. What's the matter?'

'This is our son,' he said. 'He's managed to cut his head, and we could do with a hand to hold onto him while I glue it, but he's like an eel and the nurses are all busy.'

'I can do eels,' she said, conjuring up a smile, and she took him from Lucy, steeling herself against the warm, sturdy little body writhing against her.

'Shh, shh,' his mother said, holding his hands and kissing them and blowing raspberries on them, and Megan sat down and held the child's head firmly against her shoulder while Ben glued the little laceration.

'Did you make that kid scream loud enough?' a lazy, sexy voice asked as he finished, and Megan felt her blood run hot and cold.

Ben lifted his head and laughed. 'Yes, thank you for your concern. This is my son—Josh, say hello to mini-Josh. We even gave him your name, so don't be too rude about him. I take it you've met Megan Phillips, our paeds registrar?'

Met her? Oh, yes, he'd met her. And seeing her there, comforting the wriggling, unhappy baby, sent a shaft of pain right through him, stealing his breath away.

Megan looked up at him, a desperate pleading in her eyes, but she needn't have bothered. He was in no hurry to have the past dragged out for public consumption.

'We met the other day up on Paeds,' he said, being deliberately noncommittal, and to his relief his pager went off and he was able to walk away.

Away from Megan and the child, but not his memories...

* * *

Nick got back to the barn to find Kate there, home after her spa day relaxed, sleepy and looking utterly irresistible.

So he didn't even try. 'Good day?' he asked, snuggling up to her on the sofa, and she turned into his arms and kissed him.

'Lovely. I've been spoiled to bits. Thank you.'

'My pleasure.' He nuzzled her neck. 'You smell nice. Do you smell nice all over?'

'I don't know. You probably ought to check.'

She did, he discovered, although he got blissfully distracted and forgot what he was supposed to be looking for, and it was almost an hour later before he remembered about little Josh's accident.

He told Kate, lying lazily beside her on the big bed with the view of the sea in the distance and wondering when he was going to wake up and find it was all a dream.

'Poor little mite. You ought to ring and find out how he is.' She trailed her hand over his chest and propped herself up, looking down at him with a slightly bemused smile.

'What?'

'I find it really hard to believe I'm sleeping with a grandfather,' she teased, and he closed his eyes and groaned as she slid her hand down his ribs and kept going.

'I was a very early starter,' he reminded her, and caught her hand. 'Stop. I have to phone Lucy.'

'Mmm. You do. And then we need to go to the hospital. I haven't seen Jem all day, and I miss him.'

She handed him his mobile, and he rang Lucy.

'So how's the little hooligan?' he asked, and she chuckled.

'OK. He's running around as if nothing's happened. There's something funny going on with Josh O'Hara and Megan Phillips, though,' she told him. 'Ben doesn't remember him ever talking about a Megan, but she was helping with holding him and Josh came in and Ben introduced them, and there was a definite atmosphere. He said he'd met her on Paeds, but I'm sure there was more to it. Something in his eyes.'

'Don't go there, Lucy,' he warned. 'Lots of people have a past. Sometimes it's best left where it belongs. Just remember Pandora's box.'

'Oh, don't worry, I'm not going to say anything, but at least Ben's alerted so he can keep an ear open in case of trouble. You never know when Josh might need a friend.'

'You're a good girl,' he told her with quiet pride. 'You've got your mother's kindness. Give the kids a hug from me, and we'll see you tomorrow.'

Kate met his eyes. 'What was that about?' she asked as he put the phone down.

'Nothing, really. They think Josh and Megan might have a past, and not a happy one, judging by the sound of it.'

She frowned. 'Do you know, I was thinking the other day she looked sad and a little lost. Poor girl. Poor both of them, whatever it is.'

She glanced at her watch. 'Come on, Grandad. We need to get a move on.'

'You realise if you marry me they'll be calling you Grannie,' he said slyly, and her eyes widened.

'Well, that's a good reason not to,' she said, but he

just laughed and got out of bed, hauling her up into his arms and kissing her soundly.

'Coming in the shower with me?' he asked, and she chuckled.

'Now, there's an offer I can't refuse,' she said.

They took Bruno in to see Jem the next day, after arranging access to the courtyard off the ward with the help and permission of the ward sister and Sid Evans, the ancient and very co-operative handyman, who was only too happy to let them into the garden through the locked outer gate.

Jem was delighted to see him, and Bruno, far from being over-excitable and boisterous, sniffed him cautiously, licked his hand and, when he leant forwards and brought it in range, his face, and then sat beside him, his head on his knee, gazing adoringly at him and moving not a muscle.

'Do you think Bruno realises he's not well?' Kate murmured to Nick.

'I have no idea, but if you told me that, I'd believe it. He's much livelier with me than he is with you, so maybe he knows I'm stronger. He knows I can take it, so he jumps all over me.'

'Yes, and you shouldn't let him! And am I imagining it or did I see dog hair on the sofa yesterday?'

He looked guilty, and she laughed and told him off.

'He's not allowed on the furniture! Especially when it's not ours!'

'He just wanted a cuddle,' Nick said, revealing more of the sentimental side of him she'd hardly known existed.

But there was lots about him she hadn't known. She'd

expected him to be a skilful lover, for instance, but he was far more than that, he was patient, humorous and teasing and then, when the chips were down, shockingly passionate. She discovered highs she hadn't known existed, and she just hoped she'd never have to discover the lows to balance them.

Or maybe they'd already had their lows. Maybe now it was time for their highs, their time served, and this was their time.

She hoped so, because to walk away from this was going to be far harder than walking away from him before, and she'd thought that would break her.

But Jem wasn't home yet, and that was the acid test, whether he'd accept Nick being part of their lives, whether he'd accept his authority, learn to take his say-so without question instead of debating every issue to death. And Nick might have to learn to compromise, not something that was second nature to him.

Jem came 'home' three days later, to the barn, and Bruno was overjoyed.

He followed him everywhere, sat beside him, and had to be dragged off to go for walks. Long, energetic walks along the cliffs that helped Nick work off some of the unforeseen frustration. Because since Jem had been home, there had been no long, lazy love-making, no romantic dinners, no casual touches, random kisses in the kitchen, unscheduled hugs that had gone on to become something much, much more.

And he was climbing the walls.

Not that he was any stranger to sexual frustration, but having her so close, wanting her so much, needing her for so very, very long and finally having her there—it was eating him alive.

So he walked the dog, and he went to work to try and forget about her, and every time he came home she'd look up and smile, and the need would slam through him and he'd be back to square one.

But Jem was flourishing, growing stronger every day, and with the help of Lauren, the physio, he was doing strengthening exercises that helped to keep his body balanced. Kate was still not working, but she was driving Jem here, there and everywhere, loving her new car, and she brought him down to the surgery to see Lauren three times a week, and sometimes, if they were lucky, they could catch a few minutes alone together.

But even though that time alone was short, Nick had no complaints. The crooked little slab pot Jem had made her on the day of his accident always sat in pride of place in the middle of the dining table, and today she was arranging yellow tulips in it, a troubled look on her face, and he left the cooking and went and hugged her.

'He's all right,' he murmured, knowing the pot served as a reminder of how close she'd come to losing him.

'I know.' And she turned in his arms and kissed him, then rested her head against his shoulder for a moment before easing away. Just in case Jem came in. Just in case he saw them and it upset him.

They were very wary about that. Jem had forgiven his mother, her reasons for not telling him the truth had been understandable, but Nick's initial reluctance to accept Jem as his son had left deep scars, and although he called him Dad and seemed to love him, there was still a certain wariness.

But Nick couldn't wait any more—couldn't go on

like this, living in the barn and playing happy families and hiding his head in the sand. Jem was now strong enough to go up steps, and soon would be able to climb the stairs. Which meant if necessary they could go home to their house, and he could go home to his, and life could carry on as it had been, with a few adjustments.

It would be down to Jem to make that decision, and it was time to ask him to make it.

So when he got home from work that afternoon, he went and found him. It wasn't hard. He just patted the dog when he came to greet him, and then followed him when he ran off again.

They were in the garden, sitting in the courtyard under a tree, Kate reading a book, Jem doing a maths puzzle—in a book, this time, the games console having been returned to Lucy—and he looked up and grinned. 'Hi, Dad,' he said, and carried on.

'Oh, you're back early! I'll go and put the kettle on,' Kate said with a welcoming smile, getting to her feet and squeezing his hand in passing. 'In fact, I need to ring Chloe. Want to keep Jem company?'

'Sure.' It was, after all, why he was there, and this just made it easier. He smiled reassuringly, and she smiled back and went in, and he sat down beside his son and turned towards him, his arm along the back of the bench.

'Jeremiah, can we talk?'

He put the puzzle book down and looked at Nick warily. 'Why do I always get the feeling that when you call me Jeremiah I'm in trouble?' he asked, and Nick chuckled.

'You're not in trouble, son. Far from it. I want to ask

you something—well, several things, really. First of all, and probably most important, are you happy?'

'What, here?'

'Here, with me here, with us as a family—all of it, really.'

'Oh. Well—yeah. The house is great, but I know it's only for now, but us—yeah, it's good. You're a bit stuffy sometimes, and you tell me what to do, but I guess that's just being a dad, and I want a dad, so it's cool.'

Hurdle one, he thought with a sigh of relief. 'What about your mother? Do you think she's happy?'

'Oh, yeah. She's much smilier. She's like she used to be, before she was ill, but more than that, too. Like she's really happy, all the time.'

'And do you think that's anything to do with me?' he asked tentatively, and Jem nodded.

'I guess. She watches you sometimes, and gets a soppy look on her face, a bit like when she looks at Bruno, but sort of more. And I think she likes it that we're all together.'

Nick felt a huge weight lift off his chest, but a sudden attack of nerves took him by surprise and he rubbed his hand over his leg, surreptitiously wiping his palm, flexing the fingers of the other hand.

'Um—there's something else, too. It's sort of a tradition that when a man wants to marry a woman, he asks her father for permission, so he has his blessing first. And your mum hasn't got a father, and her mother lives a long way away, and I was thinking, you're the man in her life, really. So I was wondering, if I wanted to ask your mother to marry me, would you be happy with that?'

Jem stared at him. 'You want to marry Mum?'

He nodded, and Jem frowned thoughtfully. 'So we'll live together always? Like a proper family?'

He nodded. 'If that's what you want, and what your mum wants. But it won't make any difference to you and me, really, because I love you, and you'll always be very precious to me. And I want to be a part of your life, whatever happens, so don't think that if I don't marry your mother, you won't see me whenever you want to, because you will. But we don't want to make you unhappy. We've done enough of that, for one reason or another, and we want to do the right thing now, which for me means spending as much time with you as you feel you'd like, and being with your mother if I can, because I love her, and I always have. I just couldn't be with her before. But if you have a problem with that, then we can talk about it, maybe find another way that I can spend time with her. It's up to you, really.'

'Wow. So if I say yes, we can all be together? For ever? Like a real family?'

He opened his mouth to say yes, but couldn't speak, so he just nodded, and Jem grinned even wider.

'Excellent! Wow, that would be epic! But no yucky stuff when I'm around,' he added firmly, and Nick had to stifle a smile.

Actually, no, he didn't. He grinned back, and said, 'Absolutely no yucky stuff at all. No PDAs whatsoever.'

Jem frowned in confusion. 'They're funny diary things, aren't they? Like phones and stuff all in one?'

'That's personal digital assistants. This PDA means public displays of affection.'

'Oh. Right. That's OK, then. No PDAs.'

'Except at the wedding. I'll be expected to kiss her at the wedding.'

His son's eyes widened. 'Wow—are you going to have a real wedding?'

'I don't know. I haven't asked her yet—not properly.'

'Are you going to go down on one knee? 'Cos she might like that. It was on a film, and she went all pink and blew her nose.'

'I haven't got that far,' he said laughing, 'but I'll bear it in mind.'

'And she'll want a ring.'

'And a house. Yours isn't big enough, mine's—well, it's in a very busy place, and there isn't much garden for the dog. But—how would you feel about living here? If we could buy it?'

His eyes grew even wider. 'Here? For ever?'

He nodded, and to his surprise Jem's eyes filled. 'Mum would love that,' he said unsteadily. 'And so would the dog.'

'And you?'

'And me,' he said, and Nick forgot everything about PDAs and yucky stuff, and, putting his arms round his son, he hugged him firmly to his chest.

'That's settled, then,' he said, releasing him, and cleared his throat. 'I'd better ask her.'

'I'll go and tell her you want to talk to her,' Jem said, getting up and limping hurriedly towards the house.

'Hey, Jem, I wasn't going to do it now—'

He turned. 'What? You want to wait? Why?'

Why, indeed. He smiled. 'OK. Tell her I'd like to speak to her. I'll be down the garden.'

He walked slowly down across the lawn to the fence, and leant on the top rail staring out over the sea in the distance, twisting a blade of grass into a little circle around his finger and plaiting the ends in.

'Nick? What's going on? Jem said you want me.'

He turned and smiled, and held out his hands, taking hers and drawing her closer. 'Clever boy. I do.'

She blushed slightly and laughed. 'Don't be silly. What did you want?'

'You. In my life. For ever.' He glanced towards the house, and saw Jem standing outlined in the window, the dog at his side. He'd had his orders. With a wry smile, he went down on one knee in front of her, looked up into her slightly shocked, welling eyes and, his son forgotten, he said, 'Kate, I love you. I've always loved you, through everything. You've been the one constant in my life, the rock that's always been there. I need you, but more than that, I need you to need me, to want me, to smile every time you see me, to open your arms to me because you want to hold me, to make me feel whole again. I don't want you unless you want to be with me. This isn't for Jem. He's another thing altogether, and I'll always be part of his life. This is about us, you and me, and how we feel.

'I know I'm not much of a catch—and you probably never thought when you fell in love with me that I'd be a grandfather when I got round to doing this—but will you do me the honour of sharing the rest of your life with me? Will you marry me, Kate?'

'Oh, Nick,' she said, biting her lip and pressing her fingers to her lips as the tears cascaded down her cheeks. 'Oh, my darling, of course I'll marry you! I've waited years for you—I'd given up hope. Oh, Nick, of course I'll marry you,' she said again, so he took her hand and slipped the little twisted circle of grass onto her ring finger.

'This is just for now, because Jem said you should have a ring, but we'll go and get you a proper one,' he said, and as he got to his feet and she fell sobbing into his arms, he turned his head and gave Jem a thumbs-up.

There was a cheer from the house, and she lifted her head and looked up at him. 'What are you doing?'

'He's watching us.'

She turned and looked at him, and held out her arms, and he limped down the path to them, meeting them at the edge of the lawn, and their arms wrapped around each other, the three of them together, laughing and crying and holding on, because finally—finally!—it was all going to be all right...

EPILOGUE

HE GAVE Kate away, their son, so proud, so serious,
walking her down the aisle of the crowded church and
standing straight and tall beside her, and, when the time
came, he placed her hand in his father's with the great-
est solemnity and then gave him the biggest grin she'd
ever seen.

And Nick grinned back, and winked at him, and then
they turned back to Jeff Saunders and made their vows,
long overdue but so very heartfelt, and when Jeff said,
'You may kiss the bride,' she saw Nick wink at their son
as he bent his head to kiss her, and a great cheer went
up from the congregation.

Family, friends, patients—there wasn't a soul there
who wasn't cheering this long overdue couple on their
way, and Kate felt her eyes fill as Nick touched his lips
to hers and sealed their vows with a tender, lingering
kiss.

While the choir sang, they signed the register, Jack
and Lucy their witnesses, and then turned and walked
back down the aisle between all the people who'd come
to see them do what should have been done so many
years ago.

Her mother was there, mopping her eyes and smiling,

and Nick's children, of course—Lucy, Kate's very pregnant matron of honour, with Ben and their children; Jack, his best man, with his growing family and of course Jem, fully recovered and fizzing with excitement and pride at his role in the proceedings.

Nick's niece Charlotte was there with her husband James, and Jess Carmichael, the counsellor who'd helped them all so much, with her 'plus one'. And of course the practice was closed, their on-call covered by an agency because everyone was there with an assortment of babies and children.

Showered with love and good wishes, they walked down between the pews, packed so tightly that Health and Safety would have had a fit, dozens more standing outside or crowded into the doorway, listening over a PA link, and as they came out into the glorious September sunshine, everyone cheered and showered them with rose petals.

Cameras were clicking, everyone was hugging them, and Kate thought she'd never been kissed by so many people in her life. All sorts of people. Friends, family, colleagues, but others, patients, neighbours, people she'd known all her life, people who'd taken this little broken family to their hearts and made them whole again with their kindness and acceptance.

Nick stopped and looked around. 'Thank you so much for coming. I'm sorry we can't fit everybody for the reception,' he said, 'but if you go up to the Smugglers' and see Tony, there's a drink there for all of you on the house.'

That raised a cheer, and in a blizzard of rose petals Nick and Kate walked down the path, through the lychgate and to the waiting car.

'You're coming with us,' Kate heard Lucy say to Jem, and they entered the car alone, Jem standing with his sister and brothers. The chauffeur handed them glasses of champagne, and as they linked arms and drank and the cameras were popping, the car pulled slowly away.

'All right?' Nick said softly, and Kate smiled back at him.

'Very all right,' she said, and kissed him again.

'Good party?'

'Fantastic party. It's a good party house.'

He chuckled and slid his arms round her from behind, nuzzling her neck. 'No doubt we'll regret that when he's seventeen,' he said wryly, and she laughed.

'We'll get over it.' She turned in his arms, lifting her face up and kissing him softly in the moonlight. 'I want to be alone with you. It's been utterly fabulous, but I just want them to go now. Is that really selfish of me?'

He laughed quietly. 'No, not at all. I feel just the same. I love them all to bits, but I want them to go now.'

'So how do we get rid of them all?'

'We don't, Jack does. I've bribed him. We're having the kids for them next weekend when they go away. And when the coach turns into a pumpkin, he's kicking them all out. He said we should have gone away, but why would we, when we live here, in this beautiful place? We've waited all our lives for this. I don't want to run away from it.'

'Nor do I, but I wish they would.'

There was a quiet cough, and she looked up to see Jack standing a few feet away, an indulgent smile on his face. 'You need to come for the last dance, and say goodbye,' he told them, and so they went into the marquee on the lawn, swirling round the dance floor one last time before they saw their guests off, closed the front door behind them and turned.

'It's a mess!' Kate wailed, but Nick just scooped her up in his arms and carried her up the stairs.

'It's fine,' he said firmly. 'We're going to Ben and Lucy's for lunch tomorrow with Jack and Alison and all the children, and the catering team's coming back to sort it. You don't have to do a thing. And besides, you're busy.'

'I am?'

'Oh, yes.'

She gave a slow smile.

'I do love it when you're masterful, Dr T.,' she said, and kissed him...

ST PIRAN'S: RESCUING PREGNANT CINDERELLA

BY
CAROL MARINELLI

First published in Great Britain 2010
Harlequin Mills & Boon Limited,
Eton House, 18-24 Paradise Road, Richmond, Surrey TW9 1SR

© Harlequin Books S.A. 2010

Special thanks and acknowledgement are given to Carol Marinelli for her contribution to the *St Piran's Hospital* series

ISBN: 978 0 263 87932 2

Harlequin Mills & Boon policy is to use papers that are natural, renewable and recyclable products and made from wood grown in sustainable forests. The logging and manufacturing process conform to the legal environmental regulations of the country of origin.

Printed and bound in Spain
by Litografia Rosés, S.A., Barcelona

Dear Reader

I am thrilled to be a part of the *St Piran's Hospital* continuity series, and have loved working alongside my favourite authors and being involved in such an exciting series.

My heroine Izzy is going through such a difficult time that my first instinct was to send in a hero that would fix everything for her—and, with a baby on the way, fix things soon! I was delighted to find, though, that Diego had other ideas.

He's my ultimate sort of hero—he lets Izzy find her own solutions, trusts her perhaps more than she trusts herself, and is also incredibly sexy—I mean, *way* too sexy for a heroine who's sworn off men to deal with!

Happy reading!

Carol x

Carol Marinelli recently filled in a form where she was asked for her job title, and was thrilled after all these years to be able to put down her answer as 'writer'. Then it asked what Carol did for relaxation. After chewing her pen for a moment Carol put down the truth—'writing'. The third question asked—'What are your hobbies?' Well, not wanting to look obsessed or, worse still, boring, she crossed the fingers on her free hand and answered 'swimming and tennis'. But, given that the chlorine in the pool does terrible things to her highlights, and the closest she's got to a tennis racket in the last couple of years is watching the Australian Open, I'm sure you can guess the real answer!

Carol also writes for
Mills & Boon® Modern™ Romance

Recent titles by the same author:
Medical™ Romance
KNIGHT ON THE CHILDREN'S WARD
ONE TINY MIRACLE...

Modern™ Romance
WEDLOCKED: BANISHED SHEIKH,
  UNTOUCHED QUEEN
THE LAST KOLOVSKY PLAYBOY

CHAPTER ONE

'I'M READY to come back to St Piran's.'

No words filled the silence, there was no quick response to her statement, so Izzy ploughed on, determined to make a good impression with Jess, the hospital counsellor. 'I'm really looking forward to being back at work.' Izzy's voice was upbeat. 'I know that a few people have suggested that I wait till the baby is born, I mean, given that I can only work for a couple of months, but I really think that this is the right thing for me.'

Still Jess said nothing, still Izzy argued to the silence. 'I'm ready to move on with my life. I've put the house on the market....' She felt as if she were at an interview, effectively she *was* at an interview. After the terrible events of four months ago, Ben Carter, the senior consultant in A and E, had told her to take all the time she needed before she came back to the unit where she worked as an emergency registrar.

It would have been far easier to not come back, and at nearly twenty-eight weeks pregnant she'd had every reason to put it off, but Izzy had finally taken the plunge, and instead of ringing Ben to tell him her decision, she had dropped by unannounced. But to her surprise, instead of welcoming her back with open arms, Ben had gently but firmly informed her that it would be *preferable* if she see one of the hospital counsellors.

'I'm fine!' Izzy had said. 'I don't need to see a counsellor.'

'You are seeing someone, though?' Ben had correctly interpreted the beat of silence.

'I was.' Izzy had swallowed. 'But I'm fine now.'

'Good!' Ben had clipped. 'Then you won't have a problem speaking with someone else.'

'Ben!' Izzy had hardly been able to contain her fury. 'It's been four months! You know me—'

'Izzy!' Ben had interrupted, refusing to be manipulated. 'I worked with you daily, I've been to your home, I got on well with Henry and yet I had no idea what you were going through, so, no, I'm not convinced I do know you or that you'd come to me if you had a problem.'

Izzy had sat with pursed lips. Ben could be so incredibly kind yet so incredibly tough too—he would let nothing jeopardise the safety of his patients or his staff and he was also completely honest and open, so open it actually hurt to hear it sometimes. 'I've spoken with my senior colleagues...'

'You've discussed me?'

'Of course,' Ben had replied. 'And we all agree that coming back to A and E after all you've been through is going to be tough, that we need to look out for you, and rather than us asking every five minutes if you're okay, which I know will drive you crazy, I'm going to insist that you see someone. I can page Jess Carmichael—she's good, all very informal, you can go for a walk, have a coffee...'

'I'm not sitting in the canteen, chatting about my life!' Izzy had bristled. 'I'll see her in her office.'

'Fine,' Ben had responded, and then his voice had softened. 'We want what's best for you Izzy.'

So here she was, on a Friday lunchtime, just before her first shift back, *again* sitting in a counsellor's office, telling the same thing to Jess that she had to Ben, to her mother, to her friends, that she was fine.

Fine!

'It's often suggested,' Jess said, when Izzy had told her that her house was on the market, 'that people wait twelve months after a bereavement before making any major life changes.'

'I'm twenty-eight weeks pregnant!' Izzy gave a tight smile. 'I'd suggest that change is coming whether I'm ready or not. Look...' She relented a touch because Jess was nothing other than nice. 'I don't want to bring the baby home to that house—there are just too many memories. I really want a new home by the time the baby comes.'

'I can understand that,' Jess said. 'Have you people to help you with moving?'

'Plenty,' Izzy said, 'Now I just need someone to make a half-decent offer on the house.'

'How will you feel—' Jess had a lovely soft Scottish accent, but her direct words hit a very raw spot '—when a domestic abuse case comes into the department?'

Izzy paused for a moment to show she was giving the question due thought then gave her carefully prepared answer, because she'd known this would be asked. 'The same as I'll feel if a pregnant woman comes into the department or a widow—I'll have empathy for them, but I'm certainly not going to be relating everything to myself.'

'How can you not? Izzy, you've been through the

most awful experience,' Jess said and even her lilting voice couldn't soften the brutal facts. 'You tried to end a violent, abusive relationship to protect the child you are carrying, and your husband beat you and in his temper drove off and was killed. It's natural to feel—'

'You have no idea how I feel,' Izzy interrupted, doing her best to keep her voice even, a trip down memory lane was the last thing she needed today. 'I don't want the "poor Izzy" line and I don't want your absolution and for you to tell me that none of this was my fault.'

'I'm not trying to.'

'I've dealt with it,' Izzy said firmly. 'Yes, it was awful, yes, it's going to be hard facing everyone, but I'm ready for it. I'm ready to resume my life.'

Only Jess didn't seem so sure, Izzy could tell. She had made such an effort for this day—she was immaculately dressed in a grey shift dress with black leggings and black ballet pumps, her blonde short hair, teased into shape, and large silver earrings adding a sparkle to her complexion. She had been hoping to look every inch a modern professional woman, who just happened to be pregnant. She would not let Jess, let anyone, see behind the wall she had built around herself—it was the only way she knew to survive.

Jess gave her some coping strategies, practised deep breathing with her, told her to reach out a bit more to friends and Izzy ran a hand through her gamine-cut blonde hair that had once been long and lush but which she'd cut in a fit of anger. Just when Izzy thought the session was over, Jess spoke again.

'Izzy, nothing can dictate what comes into Emergency, that's the nature of the job.' Jess paused for a moment before continuing. 'No matter what is going on in your life, no matter how difficult your world is right now, you have to be absolutely ready to face whatever comes through the doors. If you feel that you'd rather—'

'Are you going to recommend that I be sent to Outpatients?' Izzy challenged, her grey eyes glittering with tears that so desperately needed to be shed but had, for so long, been held back. 'Or perhaps I can do a couple of months doing staff immunisations—'

'Izzy—' Jess broke in but Izzy would not be silenced.

'I'm a good doctor. I would never compromise my patients' safety. If I didn't feel ready to face A and E, I wouldn't have come back.' She gave an incredulous laugh. 'Everyone seems to be waiting for me to fall apart.' She picked up her bag and headed for the door. 'Well, I'm sorry to disappoint you all, but I refuse to.'

Izzy was a good doctor, of that Jess had no doubt.

As she wrote her notes, she was confident, more than confident, that Izzy would do the right thing by her patients, that she was more than capable to be working in Emergency. But at what cost to herself? Jess thought, resting back in her chair and closing her eyes for a moment.

Jess wanted to send a memo to the universe to insist only gentle, easy patients graced Izzy's path for a little while.

Only life wasn't like.

Jess clicked on her pen and finished writing up her notes, worried for her client and wishing more progress had been made.

Izzy Bailey, while still fighting the most enormous private battle, was stepping straight back into the front line.

CHAPTER TWO

'OBSTETRIC Team to Emergency.'

Izzy heard the chimes as she tossed her coffee and sandwich wrapper in the bin and did a little dance at the sliding door that refused to acknowledge her, no matter how many times she swiped her card. An impatient nurse behind her took over, swiping her own card, and Izzy tailgated her in.

They'd start her in Section B.

Of that she was sure.

Writing up tetanus shots and suturing, examining ankles and wrists… Despite her assured words to Jess earlier, Izzy was actually hoping for a gentle start back and was quietly confident that Ben would have arranged for one.

'*Obstetric team to Emergency.*'

The chimes sounded again, but Izzy wasn't fazed. It was a fairly familiar call—frenzied fathers-to-be often lost their way and ended up bringing their wives to Emergency rather than Maternity.

Izzy glanced at her watch.

In ten minutes she'd be starting her first shift…

Walking through another set of sliding doors, which

this time opened without the use of her card, Izzy found herself in the inner sanctum of the emergency unit.

She'd timed it well, Izzy thought to herself.

By the time she'd put her bag in her locker, it would be almost time to start, which meant that she could bypass the staffroom, the small talk…

'Izzy!' Beth, an RN she'd worked with over the years, was racing past. 'Cubicle four… Everyone's tied up… She just presented…'

Except Jess *had* been right.

There would be no gentle easing in, Izzy fast realised as Les, the porter, relieved her of her bag. Beth brought her up to speed as best she could in short rapid sentences as they sped across the unit.

'About twenty-three weeks pregnant, though she's vague on dates,' the rapid handover went on. 'She won't make it to Maternity, I've put out a call…'

'Who's seen her?' Izzy asked as she squirted some alcohol rub on her hands.

'You,' came Beth's response

Oh, yes!

She'd forgotten just how unforgiving Emergency could be at times. Just then she saw Ben, wrapping a plastic apron around himself, and Izzy was quite sure he'd take over and usher her off to Section B.

'Have you got this?' Ben said instead, calling over his shoulder as he sped off to Resus.

'Sure!'

'Her name's Nicola,' Beth said as Izzy took one, very quick, deep breath and stepped in.

'Hi, there Nicola. I'm Izzy Bailey, the emergency registrar.' Izzy wasn't sure who looked more petrified, the student nurse who'd been left with the patient while

Beth had dashed for a delivery pack or the mother-to-be who brought Izzy up to date with her rapid progress even before Izzy had time to ask more questions—it was Nicola who pulled back the sheet.

'It's coming.'

'Okay.' Izzy pulled on some gloves as Beth opened the delivery pack, Nicola was in no state to be sped across the floor to Resus. 'Let Resus know to expect the baby,' Izzy said. 'Tell them to get a cot ready.' She took a steadying breath. 'Emergency-page the paediatric team.'

'Vivienne!' Beth instructed the student nurse to carry out Izzy's instructions, and Vivienne sped off.

'There's going to be a lot of overhead chimes,' Izzy explained to Nicola, 'but that's just so we can get the staff we need down here quickly for your baby.'

The membrane was intact, Izzy could see it bulging, and she used those few seconds to question her patient a little more, but there were no straightforward answers.

'I only found out last week. I've got a seven-month-old, I'm breastfeeding…'

'Have you had an ultrasound?' Izzy asked.

'She's just come from there,' Beth said for Nicola, but, as was so often the case in Emergency, a neat list of answers rarely arrived with the patient. They would have to be answered later, because this baby was ready to be born.

He slipped into the world a few seconds later, just as a breathless midwife arrived from Maternity and the overhead speaker chimed its request for the paediatric team to come to Emergency. He was still wrapped in the membrane that should have embraced him for many months more and Izzy parted it, using balloon suction to clear his airway. He was pale and stunned, but stirring into life as Izzy cut the cord. Though outwardly calm, her heart was hammering, because difficult decisions lay ahead for this tiny little man.

'You have a son,' Izzy said, wrapping him up and holding him up briefly for Nicola to see. Though seconds counted in the race for his life, Izzy made one of the many rapid decisions her job entailed and brought the baby up to the mother's head, letting her have a brief glimpse of him. Nicola kissed his little cheek, telling him that she loved him, but those few brief seconds were all there was time for.

Beth had already raced over to Resus, and Izzy left Nicola in the safe hands of the midwife and student nurse as she walked quickly over to Resus holding the infant. A man, dressed in black jeans and a T-shirt, joined her. Walking alongside her, he spoke with a heavy accent.

'What do we know?'

'Mum's dates are hazy,' Izzy said, and though he had no ID on him, there was an air of authority to him that told her this was no nosey relative. 'About twenty-three weeks.'

'Mierda!' Izzy more than understood his curse—she was thinking the same—this tiny baby hovered right on the edge of viability. At this stage of pregnancy every day *in utero* mattered, but now he was in their hands and they could only give the tiny baby their best care and attention.

'Diego.' Beth looked up from the warming cot she was rapidly preparing. 'That was quick.' The chimes had only just stopped summoning the staff, but he answered in that rich accent, and Izzy realised he was Spanish.

'I was just passing on my way for a late shift.' He had taken the baby from Izzy and was already getting to work, skilfully suctioning the airway as Izzy placed red dots on the baby's tiny chest. 'I heard the call and I figured you could use me.'

They certainly could!

His large hands were rubbing the baby, trying to stimulate it, and Izzy was incredibly grateful he was there. His dark hair was wet so he must have stepped straight out of the shower before coming to work. He had gone completely overboard on the cologne, the musky scent of him way too heavy for a hospital setting. Still, she was very glad he was there. As an emergency doctor, Izzy was used to dealing with crises, but such a premature baby required very specific skills and was terrifying to handle—Diego was clearly used to it and it showed.

'Diego's the neonatal…' Beth paused. 'What *is* your title, Diego?'

'They are still deciding! Sorry…' Dark brown eyes met Izzy's and amidst controlled chaos he squeezed in a smile. 'I should have introduced myself. I'm Nurse Manager on the neonatal unit.'

'I guessed you weren't a passing relative,' Izzy said, but he wasn't listening, his concentration back on the baby. He was breathing, but his chest was working hard, bubbles at his nose and lips, and his nostrils were flaring as he struggled to drag in oxygen.

'We need his history,' Diego said as he proceeded to bag the baby, helping him to breathe. He was skilled and deft and even though the team was just starting to arrive he already had this particular scene under control. 'You're late.' Diego managed dry humour as the anaesthetist rushed in along with the on-call obstetrician and then Izzy's colleague and friend Megan.

Her fragile looks defied her status. Megan was a paediatric registrar and was the jewel in the paediatric team—fighting for her charges' lives, completely devoted to her profession. Her gentle demeanour defied her steely determination when a life hung in the balance.

Megan would, Izzy knew, give the baby every benefit of every doubt.

'Ring NICU.' This was Diego, giving orders, even though it wasn't his domain. They urgently needed more equipment. Even the tiniest ET tube was proving too big for this babe and feeling just a touch superfluous as Megan and Diego worked on, it was Izzy who made the call to the neonatal intensive care unit, holding the phone to Diego's ear as he rapidly delivered his orders.

Though Megan's long brown hair was tied back, the run from the children's ward had caused a lock to come loose and she gave a soft curse as she tried to concentrate on getting an umbilical line into the baby.

'Here,' Izzy said, and sorted out her friend's hair.

'*About* twenty-three weeks, Megan.' Diego said it as a warning as the baby's heart rate dipped ominously low, but his warning was vital.

'We don't know anything for sure!' Megan words were almost chanted as she shot a warning at Diego. 'I'll do a proper maturation assessment once he's more stable. Izzy, can you start compressions while I get this line in?'

Diego was pulling up the minuscule drug dosages; the anaesthetist taking over in helping the tiny baby to breathe. The baby was so small Izzy compressed the chest rapidly with two fingers, hearing the rapid rhythm on the monitor.

'Nice work.' Megan was always encouraging. The umbilical line in, she took the drugs from Diego and shot them into the little body as Izzy carried on with compressions for another full minute.

'Let's see what we've got.' Megan put a hand up to halt Izzy and the babe's heart rate was up now close to a hundred. There were more staff arriving and a large incubator had arrived from the neonatal unit along with more specialised equipment, but until the baby was more stable it wouldn't be moved up to the first-floor NICU. 'We're going to be here for a while.' Megan gave Izzy a grim smile. 'Sorry to take up all your space.'

'Go right ahead,' Izzy said.

'How are things?' an unfamiliar face came in. 'Ben asked me check in—I'm Josh, A and E consultant.' She'd heard there was a new consultant, that he was Irish and women everywhere were swooning, but no one was swooning here! Izzy couldn't really explain it, but suddenly the mood in the room changed. Izzy wondered if perhaps if Josh's popularity had plummeted, because there was certainly a chill in the air.

'It's all under control.' It was Izzy who broke the strange silence. 'Though the babe might be here for a while.'

'How many weeks?' Josh's voice was gruff, his navy eyes narrowing as he looked down at the tiny infant.

'We're not sure yet,' Megan responded. 'Mum was in Ultrasound when she went into labour.'

'We need to find out.' Josh's was the voice of reason. Before there were any more heroics, some vital facts needed to be established. 'Do you want me to speak with Mum?'

'I'll be the one who speaks with the mother.' Megan's voice was pure ice. 'But right now I'm a bit tied up.'

'There's a full resuscitation taking place in my department on a baby that may not be viable—we need to find out what the mother wants.'

Megan looked up and Izzy was shocked at the blaze of challenge in them. 'It's not like it was eight years ago. We don't wrap them in a blanket now and say we can't do anything for them.'

'I'll tell you what!' A thick Spanish accent waded into the tense debate and abruptly resolved it. 'While you two sort out your own agenda, why don't you…' he looked over at Izzy '…go and speak with the mother? You have already met her, after all. See if you can clarify the dates a bit better—let her know just how ill the baby is and find out if someone can pull up her ultrasound images.'

'Sure!'

She was more than grateful for Diego's presence, and not just for the baby—Izzy hadn't known what was happening in there. She'd never seen Megan like that! Her response had been a blatant snub to Josh's offer to speak with the mother, but Izzy didn't have time to dwell on it—instead she had a most difficult conversation in front of her.

'I don't know…' Nicola sobbed as Izzy gently questioned her. 'My periods are so irregular and it's my fourth baby, I was breast feeding…'

'The doctors will go through your scans and assess your baby and try to get the closest date we can,' Izzy said gently, 'but I have to tell you that things aren't looking very good for your son.' Izzy suddenly felt guilty talking about this to the mother when she was pregnant herself, and was incredibly grateful when Diego came into the cubicle. He gave her a thin smile and, because he would be more than used to this type of conversation, Izzy allowed him to take over.

'Another one of my staff is in with your baby,' he said, having introduced himself to the mother, and did what Megan had insisted Josh didn't. Izzy felt the sting of tears in her eyes as very skilfully, very gently Diego talked Nicola through all that had happened, all that was now taking place and all that could lie ahead if her baby were to survive.

'Right now,' Diego said, 'we are doing everything we can to save your baby, but he is in a very fragile state. Nicola. Do you understand what I said to you about the risks, about the health problems your baby might face if he does survive?'

'Do everything you can.'

'We will,' Diego said. 'Megan, the paediatrician, will come in and speak at more length with you, but right now she needs to be in with your son.' He was very kind, but also very firm. 'We're going to be moving him up to the NICU shortly, but why don't I get you a wheelchair and we can take you in to see him before we head off?'

To Izzy it was too soon, Resus was still a hive of activity, but she also knew that Diego was right, that maybe Nicola needed to see for herself the lengths to which they were going to save the baby and also that, realistically, this might be Nicola's only chance to see her son alive.

She didn't get to hold him, but Diego did ask for a

camera and took some pictures of Nicola next to her son, and some close-up shots of the baby. And then it was time for him to be moved.

'Nice work,' he said to Izzy as his team moved off with its precious cargo, Diego choosing to stay behind. 'Thank you for everything, and sorry to leave so much mess. I'm going to have a quick run-through of your equipment, if that's okay. There are a few things you ought to order.'

'That would be great,' Izzy said. 'And thank you. You've been marvellous!'

'Marvellous!' He repeated the word as if were the first time he'd heard it and grinned, his teeth were so white, so perfect. If the rest of him hadn't been so divine, she'd have sworn they were capped. 'You were *marvellous* too!' Then his eyes narrowed in closer assessment. 'You're new?' Diego checked, because even though he was rarely in Emergency he was quite sure that he'd have noticed her around the hospital.

'No. I've worked here for ages. I've been on...' She didn't really know what to say so she settled for a very simple version. 'Extended leave.' She gave him a wide smile. 'You're the one who's new.'

'How do you know that?' He raised the most perfectly shaped eyebrow, and if eyes could smile, his were. 'I might have been here for years. Perhaps I did my training here...' He was teasing her, with a question she was less prepared to deal with than a premature birth. 'Why do you think I'm new?'

Because I'd have noticed you.

That was the answer and they both knew it.

Now there was no baby, now there was no emergency to deal with, now it was just the two of them,

Izzy, for the first time in, well, the longest time, looked at a man.

Not saw.

Looked.

And as she did so, the strangest thing happened—the four months of endless chatter in her head was silenced. For a delicious moment the fear abated and all she was was a woman.

A woman whose eyes lingered for a fraction too long on a beautiful man.

His hair had dried now and she noticed it was long enough to be sexy and short enough to scrape in as smart. He was a smudge unshaven, but Izzy guessed that even if he met a razor each morning, that shadow would be back in time for lunch. Even in jeans and a T-shirt, even without the olive skin and deep accent, there was a dash of the European about him—his black jeans just a touch tighter, his T-shirt from no high street store that Izzy frequented. He was professional and he was well groomed, but there was a breath of danger about him, a dizzy, musky air that brought Izzy back to a woman she had once known.

'Well,' he said when the silence had gone on too long, 'it's nice to stand here *chatting*, but I have to get back.'

'Of course.'

'A porter took my bag. Do you know where I can find him?'

'Your bag?' Izzy blinked, because it was the sort of thing she would say, but rather than work that one out, she went and called the porter over the Tannoy.

'Come up and see him later,' Diego suggested.

'I will,' Izzy said, consoling herself that he would

have extended that invitation to any doctor, that the invitation wasn't actually for her, that it had nothing to do with him.

Except Diego corrected her racing thoughts.

'I'm on till ten.'

What on earth was that?

She'd never been on a horse, yet she felt as if she'd just been galloping at breakneck speed along the beach. Izzy headed for the staffroom, in need of a cool drink of water before she tackled the next patient, wanting to get her scrambled brain into some sort of order after the adrenaline rush of earlier.

A premature delivery would do that to anyone, Izzy told herself as she grabbed a cup. Except, as a large lazy bubble in the water cooler rose and popped to the surface, she felt as if she were seeing her insides spluttering into life after the longest sleep.

She couldn't have been flirting.

She was in no position to be flirting.

Except, Izzy knew, she had been.

They had been.

The lone figure in the staffroom caught her by surprise and Izzy had begun to back out when she saw who it was. Josh was sitting there, head in hands, his face grey, and Izzy was quite sure she was intruding.

'Don't go on my account,' Josh said. 'I was just heading back. How is she?' he asked.

'Upset,' Izzy admitted. 'I think she was only just getting used to the idea of being pregnant, but...' Her voice trailed off, Josh nodded and stood up and walked out, but before that, even as she spoke, realisation dawned.

Josh hadn't been enquiring how the mother was. Instead he'd been asking about Megan.

CHAPTER THREE

'ARE you sure you don't want me to stay and help clear the board?' Izzy checked as the clock edged towards ten.

'Go home and get some well-earned rest,' Ben said. 'You haven't had the easiest start back.'

'And I thought you'd break me in gently.'

'Not my style,' Ben said. 'You did great, Izzy. Mind you, you look like you've been dragged through a hedge!'

The power dressing had lasted till about three p.m. when she had changed into more familiar scrubs, her mascara was smudged beneath her eyes and her mouth devoid of lipstick.

It had been Chest Pain Central for the rest of the shift and apart from two minutes on the loo, Izzy had not sat down.

'One day,' Izzy said, 'I'm going to manage to stay in my own clothes for an entire shift. I am!' she insisted as Josh joined them. She'd had a good shift. Josh had been lovely—as sharp as a tack, he had been a pleasure to work with, his strong Irish brogue already familiar to Izzy.

'It will never happen!' Josh said. 'I thought the

same—that maybe when I made consultant... I had some nice suits made, didn't I, Ben?'

They had been friends for years, Izzy had found out, had both worked together in London, and as Izzy grinned and wished them both goodnight she was glad now about her decision to return to work.

It *was* good to be back.

The patients didn't care about the doctor's personal life, didn't know the old Izzy, they just accepted her. Any doubts she might have had about the wisdom of coming back at such a fragile time emotionally had soon faded as she had immersed herself in the busy hub of Emergency, stretching her brain instead of being stuck in that awful loop of wandering around her home, thinking.

It was only now, as she stepped out of her professional role, that the smile faded.

She didn't want to go home.

She stared out past the ambulance bay to the staff car park and she felt a bubble of panic. She could call Security to escort her, of course. Given what had happened, who would blame her for not wanting to walk though the car park alone.

It wasn't even dark. It was one of those lovely summer nights in St Piran when the sky never became fully black.

It wasn't just the car park she was afraid of, though, she decided as she turned and headed up the corridor to the stairwell.

She just wasn't ready to go home.

Her fingers hovered over the NICU intercom, wondering what exactly she was doing. Usually she wouldn't have thought twice about this. The old Izzy had often popped up to the wards to check on cases she had seen in Emergency, but her pregnant status made it seem more personal somehow and it wasn't just the baby she had delivered that had drawn her there tonight. Still, despite more than a passing thought about him now as she neared his territory, it wasn't just Diego pulling her there either—it was after ten, the late staff would long since have gone.

There was a very private answer she was seeking tonight.

It *was* more personal because she was pregnant, Izzy admitted to herself. She wasn't just here to see how the baby was doing, rather to see her reaction to it, to see if the little scrap she had delivered that morning might somehow evoke in her some feeling for the babe she was carrying.

She was being ridiculous, Izzy told herself, as if a trip to the NICU would put her mind at ease.

Turning on her heel, Izzy decided against visiting.

She'd ring the NICU tomorrow and find out how he was doing.

'Hey!' Having made up her mind and turned go, Izzy jumped slightly as the doors opened and she was greeted by the sound of Diego's voice.

Even before she turned and saw him, even though it was just one syllable he'd uttered, she knew that it was him and she felt her cheeks colour up, wondering what reason she could give as to why she was there.

'You're here to see your delivery?' He wasn't really looking at her; instead he was turning on his phone and checking the messages that pinged in.

'If that's okay...' She was incredibly nervous around

him, flustered even, her words coming out too fast as she offered too much of an explanation. 'I often chase up interesting cases. I know it's a bit late, so I decided to ring tomorrow...'

'Day and night are much the same in there,' he said. 'It won't be a problem.'

'I'll just ring tomorrow. I'm sure they're busy'

She'd changed her mind before she'd seen him, yet Diego wouldn't hear it.

'One moment,' he said. 'I'll take you in. Let me just answer this.'

She didn't want him to take her in.

She glanced at the ID badge he now had around his neck.

Diego Ramirez was so not what she needed now.

Still, he was too engrossed in his phone to read her body language, Izzy thought. His *bag* was a large brown leather satchel, which he wore over his shoulder, and on *anyone* else it would have looked, well, stupid, but it just set him aside from the others.

God, what was it about him?

Diego didn't need to look at Izzy to read her. He could *feel* her tense energy, knew she was nervous, and he knew enough to know that a pregnant woman who had delivered a prem baby would, perhaps, have a few questions or need a little reassurance.

Any of his staff could provide that, Diego said to himself as he checked his message from Sally.

The term 'girlfriend' for Sally, would be stretching it, but she *was* gorgeous and she was sitting outside his flat in a car right this minute, texting to see when he'd be home.

He loved women.

He loved curves on women.

He loved confident women

He loved lots of uninhibited, straightforward sex—
and it was right there waiting at his door.

Busy at work—txt u tomoz x

Not regretfully enough he hit 'send', but he did wonder
what on earth he was doing. Why, instead of heading
for home, he was swiping his ID card to gain entry into
the area and walking this slinky-malinky long-legs, who
was as jumpy as a cat, through his unit?

'Wash your hands,' Diego prompted, following his
own instructions and soaping up his hands and rather
large forearms for an inordinate amount of time. 'It is
a strict rule here,' he explained, 'and one I enforce, no
matter the urgency. And,' he chided as Izzy turned off
the handle with her elbow, 'I also ask that staff take an
extra moment more than is deemed necessary.'

Oh.

Chastised and not liking it a bit, Izzy turned the tap
on again and recommenced the rather long ritual.

'I do know how to wash my hands.'

He didn't answer.

'I don't have to be told.'

He turned and looked at her rigid profile.

'Yes, Doctor, you do.' He turned off the tap and
pulled out a wad of paper towels. 'Doctors are the worst
culprits.'

She rolled her eyes and he just laughed.

'By the way,' Diego said. 'I'm not.'

It was Izzy who didn't answer now, just pursed her
lips a touch as she dried her own hands, refusing to
give him the satisfaction of asking what the hell he was

talking about. Instead she followed him through NICU, past the endless incubators, most with their own staff member working quietly on the occupant.

It was incredibly noisy—Izzy remembered that from her paediatric rotation, but she'd been such a confident young thing then, curious more than nervous. Now it seemed that every bleep, every noise made her jump.

'Here he is. Toby is his name.' Diego looked down into the incubator then spoke with the nurse who was looking after the infant Izzy had, just that afternoon, delivered. Yet when he glanced over at the rather brittle doctor he found himself momentarily distracted, watching Izzy frown down at the tiny infant, then watching as her huge eyes darted around the large ward, then back to the baby.

'He's doing well,' Diego explained, 'though it is minute by minute at the moment—he's extremely premature, but Megan has done a thorough maturation assessment and thinks he's more like twenty-four weeks.'

'That's good news,' Izzy said, only Diego didn't look particularly convinced. 'Well, it's good that she delivered in hospital,' Izzy said, 'even if she was in the wrong department.' She stared at the baby and as she felt her own kicking she willed herself, begged herself to feel something, this surge of connection to her own babe that she knew she should feel.

'Do you get attached?' Izzy asked, and Diego shook his head.

'Too dangerous here. It's the parents who get to me if anything.'

She'd seen enough. The baby was tiny and fragile and she hoped and prayed he would be okay, but the bells weren't ringing for her, the clouds weren't parting. There was no sudden flood of emotion, other than she suddenly felt like crying, but only because of her lack of feeling for her own baby she carried. 'Well, thank you very much.' She gave a tight smile. 'As I said, I just thought I'd pop in on my way home.'

'I'll walk with you,' Diego offered.

'There no need.' Izzy said, but he ignored her and fell into step beside her. She really wished he wouldn't, she just wanted out of the stifling place, away from the machines and equipment, away from babies, away from the endless guilt...

'How far along are you?'

'Sorry?'

'How many weeks pregnant?'

She was momentarily sideswiped by his boldness and also glad for the normality of his question. It was the question everyone *hadn't* asked today—the bump that everyone, bar Jess, seemed to studiously avoid mentioning.

'Twenty-eight weeks,' Izzy said. 'Well, almost,' she continued, but she had lost her audience. Diego had stopped walking and she turned her head to where he stood.

'Here.'

Izzy frowned.

'Over here.' Diego beckoned her over and after a slight hesitation she followed him, coming to a stop at an incubator where a tiny baby lay. Tiny, but comparatively much larger than the little boy she had delivered that afternoon. 'This little one is almost twenty-nine weeks, aren't you, *bebé*?' Diego crooned, then pumped some alcohol rub into his hands. 'You're awake...'

'I thought you said you didn't get attached!' Izzy grinned and so too did the nurse looking after the little girl.

'If that's Diego detached,' joked the nurse, as Diego stroked her little cheek and chatted on in Spanish, 'then we're all dying to see him in love.'

'She's *exceptionally* cute,' Diego said. 'She was a twenty-four-weeker too, though girls are tougher than boys. She's a real fighter…' His voice seemed to fade out then, though Izzy was sort of aware that he was still talking, except she didn't really have room in her head to process anything else other than the baby she was looking at.

This was what was inside her now.

This was what had bought her up to the NICU to-night—a need for some sort of connection to the baby growing inside her. And Diego had led her to it.

Her little eyes were open, her hands stretching, her face scrunching up, her legs kicking, and Izzy watched, transfixed, as the nurse fed her, holding up a syringe of milk and letting gravity work as the syringe emptied through the tube into the infant's stomach as Diego gave her a teat to suck on so she would equate the full feeling with suckling.

'She's perfect,' Izzy said.

'She's doing well,' Diego said. 'We're all really pleased with her.' He glanced at Izzy. 'I imagine it's hard to take in.'

'Very,' Izzy admitted.

'Come on,' he said, when she had stood and looked for a moment or two longer. 'You should be home and resting after they day you've had.' They walked to-gether more easily now, Izzy stopping at the vending machine and trying to choose between chocolate and chocolate.

'You'll spoil your dinner.'

'This is dinner!' Izzy said, and then grimaced, re-membering who she was talking to. 'I mean, I'll have something sensible when I get home…'

He just laughed.

'Don't beat yourself up over a bar of chocolate!' Diego said. 'You need lots of calories now, to fatten that baby up.' He could see the effort it took for her just to sustain that smile. 'And you need to relax; they pick up on things.'

'I do relax.'

'Good.'

He fished in his satchel and pulled out a brown bag. 'Here, Brianna forgot to take them.'

'What are they?' For a moment she thought they were sweets. 'Tomatoes?'

'Cherry tomatoes.'

'Miniature cherry tomatoes,' Izzy said peering into the bag. 'Mini-miniature cherry tomatoes.'

'Keep them in the bag and the green ones will redden. I grow them,' Diego said, then corrected himself. 'I grew them.' He frowned. 'Grow or grew? Sometimes I choose the wrong word.'

They were outside now, heading for the car park..

Izzy thought for a moment and it was so nice to think about something so mundane. 'Grow *or* grew. You grow them and you grew these.'

'Thank you, teacher!'

He was rewarded by her first genuine smile and she looked at him again. 'So what's this about your job title?' Izzy remembered a conversation from Resus.

'The powers that be are revising our titles and job descriptions. Two meetings, eight memos and guess what they came up with?' He nudged her as they walked. 'Guess.'

'I can't.'

'Modern Matron!' She could hear someone laughing and realised with a jolt it was her. Not a false laugh but a real laugh, and then he made her laugh some more. 'I said, "Not without a dress!" And I promise I will wear one; if that is the title they give me. Can you imagine when my family rings me at work.' He glanced at her. 'Surgeons, all of them. I'm the *oveja negra*, the black sheep.'

'I like black sheep,' Izzy said, and then wished she hadn't, except it had honestly just slipped out.

They were at her car now and instead of saying goodnight, Izzy lingered. He was sexy and gorgeous but he was also wise and kind and, despite herself, somehow she trusted him, trusted him with more than she had trusted anyone in a very long time.

'You said that babies can pick up on things…' Izzy swallowed. 'Do you believe that?'

'It's proven,' Diego said.

'So if you're stressed or not happy…'

'They know.'

'And if you're not sure…' She wanted him to jump in, but he didn't, he just continued to lean on her car. She should just get in it. Surely she should just drive off rather than admit what she didn't dare to. 'I mean, do you think they could know if you don't…?' She couldn't say it, but Diego did.

'If you don't want them?'

'Shh!' Izzy scolded, appalled at his choice of words.

'Why?' There was a lazy smile on his face that was absolutely out of place with the seriousness of her admission. 'It can't understand your words—they're not *that* clever.'

'Even so!' She was annoyed now, but he just carried on smiling. 'You don't say things like that.'

'Not to an over-protective mum!'

Oh!

She'd never thought of it like that, never thought that her refusal to voice her thoughts, her refusal to even let herself properly *think* them might, in fact, show that she did have feelings for the life inside.

It was her darkest fear.

Of the many things that kept her brain racing through sleepless nights, this was the one that she dreaded exploring most—that her feelings for her baby's father might somehow translate to her baby.

That love might not grow.

'You're not the only woman to be unsure she's ready,' Diego said. 'And lots of mothers-to-be are stressed and unhappy, but I'm sure you're not stressed and unhappy *all* the time.' His smile faded when she didn't agree and they stood for a quiet moment.

'What if I am?'

He was silent for a while, unsure why a woman so beautiful, so vibrant, so competent would be so unhappy, but it wasn't his business and for a dangerous moment Diego wished it was. So instead he smiled. 'You can fake it.'

'Fake it?'

'Fake it!' Diego nodded, that gorgeous smile in full

flood now. 'As I said, they're not *that* clever. Twice a day, fake happiness, say all the things you think you should be saying, dance around the house, go for a walk on the beach, swim. I do each morning, whether I feel like it or not.'

He so didn't get it, but, then, how could he?

'Thanks for the suggestions.' She gave him her best bright smile and pulled out her keys.

'Goodnight, then.'

'Where are you parked?'

'I'm not. I live over there.' He pointed in the direction of the beach. 'I walk to work.'

'You didn't have to escort me.'

'I enjoyed it,' he said. 'Anyway, you shouldn't be walking through car parks on your own at night.'

He really didn't get it, Izzy realised.

He was possibly the only person in the hospital who didn't know her past, or he'd never have said what he just had.

She turned on the engine and as she slid into reverse he knocked on her car window and, irritated now, she wound it down.

'Sing in the shower!' He said. 'Twice a day.'

'Sure' Izzy rolled her eyes. Like *that* was going to help.

'And by the way ,' he said as she was about to close her window, 'I'm not!'

Izzy pulled on her handbrake and let the engine idle and she looked at those lips and those eyes and that smile and she realised exactly why she was annoyed— was she flirting?

Did twenty-eight weeks pregnant, struggling mentally

to just survive, recently widowed women ever even begin
to think about flirting?

No.

Because had she thought about it she would never
have wound down that window some more.

'Not what?' Izzy asked the question she had refused
to ask earlier, her cheeks just a little pink.

'I'm not a frustrated doctor,' Diego said, 'as many of
your peers seem to think every male nurse is.'

'Glad to hear it,' Izzy said, and took off the handbrake, the car moving slowly beside him.

'And I'm not the other cliché either!' he called, and
her cheeks were on fire, yet for the first time in the
longest time she was grinning. Not forcing a smile, no,
she was, from ear to ear, grinning.

No, there was absolutely no chance that Diego
Ramirez was gay!

'I'd already worked that out!' Izzy called as she
pushed up her window. 'Night, Diego!'

'It went well, Mum!' Izzy buttered some toast as she
spoke to her mother and added some ginger marmalade.
'Though it was strange being back *after...*' Izzy stopped,
because her mother didn't like talking about *before*, so
instead she chatted some more, told her mum about
Toby, but her mum didn't take the lead and made no
mention of Izzy's pregnancy.

'So you had a good day?' her mother checked as Izzy
idly opened the brown paper bag and took out a handful
of tiny tomatoes. They tasted fantastic, little squirts of
summer popping on her tongue, helping Izzy to inject
some enthusiasm into her voice.

'Marvellous,' Izzy said, smiling at the choice of word and remembering Diego's smile.

It was actually a relief to hang up.

She was so damn tired of putting others at ease.

So *exhausted* wearing the many different Izzy masks...

Doctor Izzy.

To add to Daughter Izzy.

Domestic Abuse Victim Izzy.

Grieving Izzy.

Mother-to-be Izzy.

Coping Izzy.

She juggled each ball, accepted another as it was tossed in, and sometimes, *sometimes* she'd like to drop the lot, except she knew she wouldn't.

Couldn't.

She could remember her mother's horror when she had for a moment dropped the coping pretence and chopped off her hair. Izzy could still see the pain in her mother's eyes and simply wouldn't put her through it any more.

Oh, but she wanted to, Izzy thought, running her bath and undressing, catching sight of herself in the mirror, her blonde hair way-too-short, her figure too thin for such a pregnant woman.

How she'd love to ring her mum back—ask her to come over, to *take* over.

Except she knew she couldn't.

Wouldn't.

Since that night, there had been a huge wedge between them and Izzy truly didn't know how to fix it. She just hoped that one day it would be fixed, that maybe when the baby came things would improve. Except her mother could hardly bring herself to talk about the impending arrival.

Damn Henry Bailey!

Whoosh!

The anger that Jess had told her was completely normal, was a 'good sign', in fact, came rushing in then and, yes, she should do as Jess said perhaps, and write pages and pages in her journal, or shout, or cry, or read the passage in her self-help book on anger.

Except she was too tired for Henry tonight.

Too fed up to deal with her so-called healthy anger.

Too bone weary to shout or cry.

She wanted a night off!

So she lit six candles instead, the relaxing ones apparently, and lay there and waited for them to work, except they didn't.

She *had* to relax.

It was important for the baby!

Oh, and it would be so easy to cry now, but instead she sat up and pulled the plug out, and then she had another idea, or rather she decided to try out Diego's idea.

She'd fake it.

Cramming the plug back in the hole, she topped up with hot water and feeling stupid, feeling beyond stupid, she lay back as the hot water poured over her toes and she sang the happiest song she could think of.

A stupid happy song.

And then another.

Then she sang a love song, at the top of her voice at midnight, in her smart townhouse.

And she was used to the neighbours banging on the walls during one of her and Henry's fights, so it didn't really faze her when they did just that. Instead she sang louder.

Izzy just lay there in the bath, faking being happy, till her baby was kicking and she was grinning—and even if, for now, she had to fake it, thanks to a male nurse who wasn't a frustrated doctor and certainly wasn't the other cliché, by the time her fingers and toes were all shrivelled up, Izzy wasn't actually sure if she was faking it.

For a second there, if she didn't analyse it too much, if she just said it as it was…

Well, she could have almost passed as happy!

CHAPTER FOUR

DIEGO was not in the best of moods.

Not that anyone would really know.

Though laid back in character, he was always firm in the running of his unit. His babies came first and though friendly and open in communication, he kept a slight distance from his staff that was almost indefinable.

Oh, he chatted. They knew he loved to swim in the Cornish sea, that he came from an affluent long line of doctors in Madrid, they even knew that he was somewhat estranged from his family due to his career choice, for Diego would roll his eyes if any of them rang him at work. His staff knew too about his rather pacy love life—the dark-eyed, good-looking Spaniard was never short of a date but, much to many a St Piran's female staff member's disgust, he never dated anyone from work.

No, the stunning women who occasionally dropped in, waiting for him to finish his shift, or called him on the phone, had nothing to do with hospitals—not public ones anyway. Their hospital stays tended to be in private clinics for little *procedures* to enhance their already polished looks.

There was just this certain aloofness to Diego—an

independent thinker, he never engaged in gossip or mixed his private life with his work.

So no one knew that, despite his zealous attention to detail with his precious charges that day, there was a part of Diego that was unusually distracted.

Cross with himself even.

Okay, his relations with women veered more towards sexual than emotional, and if his moral code appeared loose to some, it actually came with strict guidelines—it was always exclusive. And, a man of honour, he knew it was wrong to suddenly be taking his lunches in the canteen instead of on the ward and looking out for that fragile beauty who was clearly taken.

Wrong, so very wrong to have been thinking of her late, *very late*, into the night.

But why *was* she so stressed and unhappy?

If she were his partner, he'd make damn sure…

Diego blew out a breath, blocked that line of thought and carried on typing up the complicated handover sheet, filling in the updates on his charges, now that Rita the ward clerk had updated the admissions and discharges and changes of cots. It was Monday and there was always a lot to be updated. It was a job he loathed, but he did it quicker and more accurately than anyone else and it was a good way of keeping current with all the patients, even if he couldn't be hands on with them all. So Diego spent a long time on the sheet—speaking with each staff member in turn, checking up on each baby in his care. The NICU handover sheet was a lesson in excellence.

'I'm still trying to chase up some details for Baby Geller,' Rita informed him as Diego typed in the three-days-old latest treatment regime. 'Maternity hasn't sent over forms.'

'He came via Emergency.' Diego didn't look up. 'After you left on Friday.'

'That's right—the emergency obstetric page that went out.' Rita went through his paperwork. 'Do you know the delivering doctor? I need to go to Maternity and get some forms then I can send it all down and he can fill it in.'

'She.' Diego tried to keep his deep voice nonchalant. 'Izzy Bailey, and I think I've got some of the forms in my office. I can take them down.'

'Is she back?' Rita sounded shocked. 'After all that's happened you'd think she'd have stayed off till after the baby. Mind you, the insurance aren't paying up, I've heard. They're dragging their feet, saying it might be suicide—as if! No doubt the poor thing *has* to work.'

Diego hated gossip and Rita was an expert in it. Nearing retirement, she had been there for ever and made everyone's business her own. Rita's latest favourite topic was Megan the paediatrician, who she watched like a hawk, or Brianna Flannigan, the most private of nurses, but today Rita clearly had another interest. Normally Diego would have carried on working or told her to be quiet, but curiosity had the better of him and, not proud of himself, Diego prolonged the unsavoury conversation.

'Suicide?' Diego turned around. 'Are you talking about Izzy's husband?'

'Henry Bailey!' Rita nodded. 'It wasn't suicide, of course; he just drove off in a blind rage. She'd left him, but he turned up at work, waited for her in the car park...' She flushed a little, perhaps aware that she was being terribly indiscreet and that Diego was normally the one to halt her. 'I'm not speaking out of turn; it was all over the newspapers and all over the CCTV, though of course it would have been before you arrived in St Piran's.'

No, it wasn't his proudest morning, because once the handover sheet was complete, Diego headed for his office and closed the door. Feeling as if he was prying but wanting to know all the same, it didn't take long to find out everything Rita had told him and more. Oh, he would never abuse his position and look up personal information, but it was there for everyone, splashed all over the internet, and as he read it he felt his stomach churn in unease for all she had been through.

Pregnant, trying to leave an abusive marriage, real estate agent Henry Bailey had beaten his wife in the darkened hospital car park. Rita was right, the whole, shocking incident had been captured on CCTV and images of footage and the details were spelt out in the press.

He felt sick.

Reading it, he felt physically sick and also strangely proud.

Her first day back.

Mierda! He cursed himself as he remembered his throw-away comment about the car park. He replayed the conversation they had had over and over and wished he could start with her again.

His door knocked and he quickly clicked away from the page he was viewing, before calling whoever it was to come in, but he felt a rare blush on his cheeks as the woman herself stood before him. Diego actually felt as if he'd been caught snooping as Izzy let herself in, a wide smile on her face, and he wondered how on earth she managed it.

She had leggings on again and a bright red dress with bright red lipstick and, Diego noticed, bright red cheeks as he just continued to stare up at her.

'You need me to sign off on the delivery?' It was Izzy who broke the silence; Diego was momentarily lost for words. 'Your ward clerk just rang…'

'We would have sent them down to you.'

'Oh!' Izzy blushed a shade darker as she lied just a little. 'I thought it sounded urgent.'

'I should have some forms…' He was unusually flustered as he rummaged through his desk. 'Or I'll ring Maternity. Here…' Diego found them and was pathetically grateful when the door knocked and one of his team stood there. with a screaming baby with a familiar request.

'Would you mind?'

'Not at all.' He washed his hands, *thoroughly*, then took the screaming baby and plonked it face down on his forearm, its little head at his elbow, and he rocked it easily as he spoke.

'Genevieve!' he introduced. 'Goes home this week, please God! I do not envy her parents.'

Well, Genevieve looked as if she'd happily stay with Diego for ever! The tears had stopped and she was already almost asleep as he bounced away.

'If you want to get started on the forms I'll just go and get the details you'll need.' He paused at the door. 'I was just about to get a drink…'

'Not for me, thanks,' Izzy said, and then changed her mind. 'Actually, water would be great.'

'Would you mind…?' It was his turn to say it and he

gestured to the baby. Izzy went to put out her hands and then laughed.

'Joking!' she said, then went over to his sink and *thoroughly* washed hers. 'Am I clean enough for you?'

Oh, God, there was an answer there!

And they just both stood there, looking a bit stunned.

Izzy flaming red, Diego biting down on his tongue rather than tell her he'd prefer her dirty.

And thank God for Miss Genevieve or he might just have kissed her face off!

Diego got them both water.

Well, he couldn't do much with two polystyrene cups and tap water but he did go to the ice dispenser and then had a little chat with himself in his head as he walked back to his office.

What the hell was wrong with him?

He hardly knew her, she was pregnant, and she obviously had *major* issues.

Why was he acting like a twelve-year-old walking past the underwear department in a department store? Nervous, jumpy, embarrassed, hell, he couldn't actually fancy her, and even if he did, normally that didn't pose a problem—he fancied loads of women.

This, though, felt different.

Maybe he felt sorry for her? Diego wondered as he balanced a file under his arm and two cups in one big hand and opened his office door.

But, no, he'd been thinking about her long before Rita had told him what had happened.

Then she looked up from the form she was filling in and smiled, and Diego was tempted to turn round and walk out.

He more than fancied her.

Not liked, not felt sorry for, no. As he washed his hands and took Genevieve from her and sat down behind his desk it wasn't sympathy that was causing this rather awkward reaction.

Diego was used to women.

Beautiful women.

Ordinary women.

Postnatal women.

Pregnant women were regular visitors to his unit—often he walked a mum-to-be around his unit, telling her what to expect once her baby was born.

He was more than used to women, yet not one, not one single one, had ever had this effect on him.

'How is Toby doing?' Izzy looked up from the forms and Diego made a wobbly gesture with one hand.

'Can I have a peek?' Izzy signed off her name and then reached for her water. 'I'm done.'

'Sure,' Diego said. 'I'll put this one down and take you over—we've moved him.'

Genevieve was sleeping now, and Izzy walked with him to the nursery. It was a far more relaxed atmosphere there.

There were about eight babies, all in clear cribs and dressed in their own clothes, the parents more relaxed and, Izzy noticed, everyone had a smile when Diego walked in and put Genevieve back in her cot.

He was certainly popular, Izzy thought as they head back out to the busy main floor of NICU.

'You need to—'

'Wash my hands,' Izzy interrupted, 'I know.'

'Actually…' Diego gave a small wince. 'Your perfume is very strong. Perhaps you could…'

'I'm not wearing perfume,' Izzy said as she soaped up her hands, 'and you're hardly one to talk, I can smell your cologne from here!'

'I don't wear cologne for work.'

'Oh.' Izzy glanced over. 'Then what...?' She didn't finish, she just turned back to the taps and concentrated really hard on rinsing off the soap.

She could smell him.

If she breathed in now she could taste him—she'd even commented to Megan on his cologne, but Megan had said... Izzy swallowed as she recalled the flip conversation. Megan hadn't even noticed it...

She could smell him and Diego could smell her and they'd just told each other so.

There was no witty comeback from that.

It was the *most* awkward five minutes of her life.

Okay, not *the most* awkward—the last few months had brought many of them. Rather it was the most pleasantly cringe-making, confusingly awkward five minutes of her life.

She peered at Baby Geller and asked after his mother, Nicola. She tried to remember that breathing was a normal bodily function as the nurse who was looking after the babe asked Diego to hold him for a moment while she changed the bedding. The sight of the tiny baby nestled in his strong arms, resting against his broad chest, was just such a contrast between tenderness and masculinity that it had Izzy almost dizzy with the blizzard of emotions it evoked.

'I'd better get back.' Her mouth felt as if was made of rubber—even a simple sentence was difficult.

She managed a smile and then she turned and walked briskly out of the department. Only once she was safely out did she lean against the wall and close her eyes, breathing as if she'd run up the emergency exit steps. Shocked almost because never in her wildest dreams had she considered this, even ventured the possibility that she might be attracted to someone.

She was so raw, so scared, so just dealing with functioning, let alone coping, that men weren't even on a distant horizon yet.

And yet...

She'd never been so strongly attracted to someone.

Never.

Even in the early days with Henry, before he'd shown his true colours, she hadn't felt like this. Oh, she had loved him, had been so deeply in love she'd been sure of it—only it had felt nothing like this attraction.

An attraction that was animal almost.

She *could* smell the delicious fragrance of him.

Right now, on her skin in her hair, she leant against the wall and dragged in the air, and still his fragrance lingered in her nostrils.

'Izzy!' Her eyes opened to the concerned voice of Jess. 'Are you okay?'

'I'm fine!' She smiled. 'I was just in NICU, and it's so hot in there...' God, she felt like she'd been caught smoking by the headmistress, as if Jess could see the little plumes of smoke coming from behind her back. She tried to carry on as if her world hadn't just upended itself. Jess would hardly be thrilled to hear what was going through her patient's mind now.

It was impossible that it was even going through her mind now.

There wasn't room in her life, in her heart, in her head

for even one single extra emotion, let alone six feet two of made-in-Spain testosterone.

'How are you finding it?' Jess asked as they walked in step back to the emergency department, and then Jess gave a kind smile, 'I'm just making conversation…'

'I know.' Izzy grinned and forced herself back to a safer conversation than the one she was having with herself. 'Actually, it's been really nice. It's good having something else to think about.'

Only she wasn't just talking about work.

CHAPTER FIVE

'THE nurses are all tied up and I've got to dash over to the children's ward,' Megan said into the phone. 'I'll ask Izzy.'

'Ask Izzy what?'

She'd been back a full week now.

It was late.

She was tired.

And the patient she was dealing with wasn't exactly helping Izzy's mood.

'I've got a patient on NICU,' Megan explained. 'A new admission. His mum's bipolar and Diego wants some sedation for her. The baby was an emergency transfer so there's no local GP and her medications are all at home. She's getting really agitated, and really it sounds as if she just needs a good night's sleep and then her husband can bring in her meds in the morning. Diego wants her seen straight away, though. Is there any chance? I'd do it but I've *got* to go up to the ward.'

'You'll have to speak to Josh or one of the nurses,' Izzy was unusually terse. 'I'm about to suture someone and then I'm going home.'

She was aware of the rise of Megan's eyebrow. Normally Izzy was accommodating, but Diego's name seemed to be popping up in her day all too often—and her thoughts were turning to him too, rather more than Izzy was comfortable with.

Still it wasn't just a sexy neonatal nurse that had caused Izzy's terse reaction. Just as Jess had predicted, there would be patients that would touch a very raw nerve with Izzy, and even though she had assured Jess she would have no trouble dealing with them, Evelyn Harris *had* hit a nerve.

In her early forties she had presented having tripped over the cat and cut her head on the edge of the coffee table. Vivienne, the student nurse, had had a quiet word with Izzy before she had examined her, telling her that she had noticed some other bruises on her arms when she had checked her blood pressure and, sure enough when Izzy had *checked* the blood pressure again, she had seen the new fingertip bruises, but had chosen not to comment.

'You're going to need a few stitches!' Izzy had said instead. 'How's the cat?'

The relief in the room at Izzy's small joke had been palpable, Evelyn had laughed and John Harris had said the cat would be in the naughty corner, or some other light-hearted thing, and Izzy had smiled back.

Had let him think, as he no doubt did, that she was stupid.

'Vivienne?' Izzy called out to a student nurse. 'Could you set up the minor theatre?' She smiled at Mrs Harris. 'I'll take you over and I'll be in with you in a moment.'

'I'll stay with you,' Mr Harris reassured his wife, and then explained why to Dumb Doctor Izzy. 'She doesn't like needles.'

'Sorry!' Izzy breezed. 'We can only have the patient.'
She gave a very nice smile. 'We shan't be long, at least
I hope not. You're my last patient for the night…' She
chatted away, not letting the husband get a word in, acted
dizzy and vague and rushed, as if getting home was the
only thing on her mind, telling them both to take a seat
outside minor ops. Then she headed for the annexe,
checked who the on-call social worker was for the night
and was just considering her options when Megan had
asked the favour. With her emotions already bubbling
to the surface, the thought of seeing Diego was the last
thing she needed.

There was something about him that got under her
skin, though in a nice way, and Izzy, right now, just
wasn't comfortable with nice.

Wasn't used to nice.

And was nowhere near ready for it either.

As Izzy came into the minor theatre, Vivienne was
just bringing Evelyn through and Mr Harris's voice came
through the open door as his wife stepped inside.

'I'm right outside, darling,' he said, only Izzy could
hear his clear warning.

'Lie down here, Evelyn,' Izzy said, then headed over
to the small bench in the corner and turned on the radio.
'Let's have some music to distract you.' She washed
her hands and pulled on some gloves and then gently
gave the wound a clean before injecting in some local
anaesthetic. 'I'm fine on my own, Vivienne,' Izzy said.
'It's pretty busy out there.'

'I'm to cut for you,' came the response, but Izzy could
cut her own stitches and wanted to be alone with Evelyn,
except Vivienne wouldn't budge. 'Beth told me to get
into Theatre as much as I could.'

'Could you get me some 3-0 catgut?' Izzy said, knowing they had run out but checking the wound as if that was the thread she needed. 'There's none here, but I think there should be some in the store cupboard.'

'There isn't any,' Vivienne said. 'I did the stock order with Beth this afternoon.'

Vivienne needed a crash course on taking a hint, but Izzy didn't have time right now. Evelyn only needed a couple of stitches and Mr Harris would no doubt start to get impatient soon, so Izzy dragged the stool over with her foot and given the time constraints realised she would have to be more direct than she would normally choose.

'Evelyn,' Izzy said, 'is there anything you want to tell me?'

'Nothing.'

'I know,' Izzy said gently. 'I know that you didn't just trip…' She watched her patient's nervous lick of her dry lips, her eyes anxiously dart to the theatre door. 'He can't hear,' Izzy said. 'That's why I put the radio on. You can talk to me.'

'Can you just do your job and suture me?' Evelyn bristled. 'I tripped! Okay?'

'There's a bruise on the opposite cheek, finger marks on your arms. I can sort out help…'

'Really?' The single word was so loaded with sarcasm, just so scornful and filled with dark energy that Izzy let out a breath before she spoke next.

'I can ring the social worker. There are shelters…'

'I've a seventeen-year-old son.' Evelyn's lip curled in bitter response. 'The shelters won't let me bring him with me. Did you know that?' she challenged, and Izzy shook her head.

'So what do you suggest, Doctor? That I leave him with him?'

'No, of course not, but if I get someone to speak with you, they could go through your options. I can speak to the police. You don't have to go back tonight.'

'You're not helping, Doctor,' Evelyn said. 'In fact, you could very well be making my life a whole lot worse.'

The stitches took no time, and Izzy knew that dragging it out and keeping Evelyn's husband waiting would only make things worse for her patient, but as Vivienne snipped the last thread Izzy had one more go.

'Is there anyone you can talk to? A friend perhaps…'

'You really don't get it, do you?'

Except Izzy did.

'I don't have *friends*! At least, none of my choosing.'

Evelyn struck a dignified pose as she swung her legs down from the gurney and Izzy recognised the glare in her eyes only too well, because she had shot out that look many times before if anyone had dared so much as to assume that her life was less than perfect.

'Do I need to sign anything?' Evelyn asked.

'No.' Izzy shook her head. 'If you…' She looked at Evelyn and her voice trailed off. Evelyn's decision to stay wasn't going to change, not till her son's future was taken care of. Izzy just hoped to God she'd survive that year. 'When was your last tetanus?'

'I had one…' Evelyn swung her bag over her shoulder '…six weeks ago.'

I'll bet she did, Izzy thought as she stood there, clearing the trolley. She could see her hands shaking as she disposed of the sharps and as Evelyn left Theatre, Izzy had to bite on her lip as the young nurse's disbelieving voice filled the still room.

'Straight back to him…' Her voice was incredulous. 'Why doesn't she just lea—' And then Vivienne's voice abruptly halted as perhaps she remembered who she was talking to and what had had happened the night Izzy had tried to *just* leave.

'She has her reasons,' Izzy said. 'And, frankly, if that's your attitude, she's hardly likely to share them with you.'

'I'm sorry, Izzy.'

And she could have left it there, but Izzy chose not to. Vivienne was thinking of a career in Emergency and, well, it was time she faced a few home truths.

'You're a nurse,' Izzy said, and her voice wobbled with long-held-in emotion, 'not the bloody jury. Remember that when you're dealing with patients in Emergency.'

Her shift was nearly over and all she wanted was out, so she left the messy trolley and was tempted to just go to the lockers and get out of there. She was angry and close to tears and there was Evelyn walking out of the department, her husband's arm around her. Then he stopped and fished his phone from his jacket and took a call, and Evelyn patiently waited then she turned and for a second. For just a teeny second their eyes locked and and it was the secret handshake, the password, the club, and Evelyn's expression changed as she realised her doctor was a fully paid up member…

'Mrs Harris…' Izzy scribbled down her mobile number on a head injury information chart and walked briskly over. 'Sorry.' Izzy gave a busy shrug. 'I forgot to give you this. Here's your head injury instructions, have a read through…'

'Thank you.'

'And watch out for that cat!' Izzy added, then gave a vague smile at Evelyn and one to her husband before they walked off into the night. Izzy's heart was thumping, not sure what she had just done and not sure what she would even do if Evelyn did call.

She just wanted to do something.

'Izzy!'

That Spanish voice was too nice for her mood right now.

'Can I ask a favour?' Diego gave her a smile as he poked his head out of a cubicle, but she didn't return it.

'I'm about to go off duty.'

'I was off duty forty minutes ago and I'm back on in the morning.' Diego wasn't quite so nice now. One of his mums was about to tip into trouble, the mother of one his precious babies no less. He had spent two hours dealing with red tape, trying to get hold of her GP to fax a prescription, to no avail, or to get a doctor on NICU to see Maria, but of course she wasn't actually a patient at the hospital.

Yet!

Maria was growing more agitated by the minute and no one seemed to give a damn. 'I have a woman who gave birth four days ago, following twenty-four hours of labour. Her child has multiple anomalies, she has hardly slept since her baby was born and she and her husband have driven one hundred miles today as there was no room for them in the helicopter.' Oh, he told her, even if it was Izzy, he told her, even as she opened her mouth to say that she'd see the patient, still he told her, because Diego knew Izzy was far better than that. 'Now she can't settle and is doing her best not to go into meltdown. Can I get a doctor to prescribe me some sedation?'

'I'm sorry, okay?' Izzy's apology was instant and genuine—she had never been one to dash off at the end of her shift, but Evelyn had unsettled her, not to mention Diego. She was having great trouble keeping her mask from slipping, but it wasn't the patients' fault. 'Of course I'll see her.'

Maria was agitated and pacing and the very last thing she needed was endless questions and an examination, and Izzy could see that. Diego had given her a good brief and on gentle questioning Izzy found out what medications the patient was on.

'If I could just get some sleep,' Maria pleaded, and Izzy nodded.

'I'll be back in just a moment.'

She was and so too was a nurse from the neonatal unit to relieve Diego.

'Take two tablets now,' Izzy said, and gave the hand-over nurse the rest of the bottle. 'She can have two more at two a.m., but don't wake her if she's resting. Will someone be able to check her?'

'Absolutely,' Diego said. 'Maria's staying in the parents' wing, but I'll get my staff to pop in and see her through the night.'

'I'm sure,' Izzy said to her patient, 'that once you've had a decent rest you'll be feeling a lot better. I'm on in the morning,' Izzy added, writing some notes. 'If Maria doesn't settle,' Izzy added to the nurse, 'she'll need to come back down to us.'

It was straightforward and simple and as the nurse took Maria back up to the ward, Diego thanked her.

'I'm sorry if I came on strong.'

'Not at all,' Izzy said. 'She needed to be seen. It's just been a…' She stopped talking; he didn't need to hear about her difficult shift, so she gave him a brief smile and walked on.

Except Diego was going off duty too.

'How's faking it going?' Had he fallen into step beside her that morning, or even an hour ago, Izzy would have managed a laugh and a witty retort, but even a smile seemed like hard work right now, so she just hitched her bag up higher and walked more briskly through the sliding doors and into the ambulance forecourt. But Diego's legs were longer than hers, and he kept up easily.

'Izzy, I was wondering….'

'Do you mind?' She put up her hand to stop him talking, gave an incredulous shake of her head. What was it with people today that they couldn't take a hint if she stood there and semaphored them? 'I just want…' Oh, God, she was going to cry.

Not here.

Not now.

She hadn't yet cried.

Oh, there had been *some* tears, but Izzy had been too scared to really cry, to break down, because if she did, maybe she wouldn't stop.

Scared that if she showed her agony to others they would run when they saw the real her, and scared to do it alone because it was so big, this black, ever-moving shape that had no clear edges, that grew and shrank and transformed.

But she couldn't outrun that black cloud tonight.

She was trying not to cry, trying to breathe and trying to walk away from him to get to her car, as she had tried to that awful night.

No, there was no getting away from it.

Her hands were shaking so much she dropped her keys and it took all her strength not to sink to her knees and break down right there. Instead she got into the car, sat gripping the wheel, holding it in and begging it to pass, but it held her a moment longer, pinning her down. She sat in her car and she was tired, so tired and angry and ashamed and sad…

Sad.

Sad was bigger than angry, bigger than tired, bigger than her.

It was in every cell and it multiplied. It was the membrane of every cell and the nucleus within, it spread and it grew and it consumed and she couldn't escape it any longer. As she doubled over she could feel her baby kick inside and it was so far from the dream, so removed from anything she had envisaged when she had walked down that aisle, that the only word was sad.

She didn't even jump when the passenger door opened and Diego slid into the passenger seat.

'Can't you just leave me alone?'

Diego thought about it for a moment then gave an honest answer. 'It would seem not.'

'You know, don't you?' Izzy said, because everyone else did and so he surely must.

'A little,' Diego admitted. 'I didn't at first, but that morning, when you came to my office, I'd just found out.'

'I thought you were a bit awkward.'

Maybe for a second, Diego thought, but he'd been awkward for another reason that morning, but now wasn't really the time to tell her.

'I've done something stupid…' Izzy said. 'Just then,

when you asked me to see Maria.' He sat patiently, waiting for her to explain. 'I had a woman, I think her husband beats her—actually, I don't think, I know. She wouldn't let me help her. I can see now that I rushed in, but I didn't want her to go home to him. I knew what he'd be like when they got home, you could just tell he was annoyed that she was even at the hospital, even though he'd put her there. Anyway, she wouldn't let me get a social worker or the police....' She turned and saw the flash of worry on his face. 'I didn't confront him or anything, he's none the wiser that I know.'

'You can't help her if she doesn't want it.'

'I gave her my phone number.' Izzy waited for his reaction, waited for him to tell her not to get involved, that she had been foolish, but instead he thought for a long moment before commenting.

'I think,' he said slowly, 'that your phone number would be a very nice thing to have.' She blinked. 'And I'm not flirting,' Diego said, and she actually gave a small smile. 'Other times I flirt, but not then. Did *you* talk to anyone?'

'No,' Izzy admitted. 'Megan, we're friends,' she explained, 'asked me what was wrong once, and I remember then that I nearly told her. God—' regret wrapped her words '—I wish I had. I was on my way to my mum's when it happened—I was going to tell her. Henry and I had had a massive row that morning. I knew I was pregnant, that I had to get out of the marriage. I told him I was leaving, I still wasn't sure how, but I came to work, scraped through the shift and afterwards I was going to land on my parents' doorstep...' she gave a shrug '...or Megan's. All I knew was that I wasn't going home.'

'What if someone had given you a phone number?'

Diego asked. 'If you had known that that person knew what it was like…'

'I'd have rung them,' Izzy said. 'Not straight away perhaps.' Then she nodded, confirmed to herself that she hadn't done a stupid thing. 'What do I say if she rings?'

'What would you have wanted someone to say to you?'

'I don't know,' Izzy admitted. 'Just to listen…'

She'd answered her own question and Izzy leant back on the seat and closed her eyes for a moment, actually glad that he had got into the car, glad that he hadn't left her alone, glad that he was there.

And she didn't want to think about it any more so instead she turned to him.

'I forgive you.'

'*Cómo?*' Diego frowned. 'Forgive me for what?'

'Having a satchel.' She watched as a smile spread across his face and she smiled too. 'I never thought I could,' Izzy said, seriously joking, 'but I do.'

'Leave my satchel alone,' Diego said, and he saw something then, her humour, a glimpse of the real Izzy that would soon be unearthed, because she would come out of this, Diego was sure of that. She would grow and she would rise and she would become more of the woman he was glimpsing now.

He knew.

And he knew if he stayed another minute he'd kiss her.

'I'd better go,' Diego said, because he really thought he'd better.

'I'll drive you.'

'No, because then I would have to ask you in.'

'Would that be so bad?' Izzy asked, because it felt as if he was kissing her, she could see his mouth and almost taste it on hers. Sitting in the car, she didn't want him to get out and she didn't want to drive on. She wanted to stay in this moment, but Diego was moving them along.

'If you come in, I might not want you to leave...' It was big and it was unexpected and the last thing either had planned for, yet, ready or not, it was happening. 'We need to think.'

He climbed out of her car and Izzy sat there. Without him beside her logic seeped in.

It was way too soon.

It was impossibly way too soon.

And yet, had he chosen to, he could have kissed her.

CHAPTER SIX

QUÉ diablos estás haciendo?

As Diego pushed through the waves, over and over he asked himself what on earth he was doing.

On leaving Izzy, he'd gone home to find Sally in the car outside his flat, with a bottle of wine and a dazzling smile, but instead of asking her in, he'd sent her on her way. The words 'It's been good, but...' had hung in the air, as had the sound of her tears, but it had been the only outcome to their relationship, Diego had realised as he'd let himself into his flat.

It *had* been good.

Sencillo, Diego's favourite word—straightforward, uncomplicated. Sally had been all those things and everything Diego had thought he wanted in a relationship. Only his life had suddenly become a touch more complicated.

He needed to think and he couldn't do that with Sally. Wouldn't do that to Sally and also he needed to be very sure himself.

Walking out of the water towards the beach, he wasn't sure if he was even pleased that Izzy had taken his advice, for there she was, walking along the beach, her face flushing when she saw him.

'I thought you were on an early...'

'I'm on a management day, so I don't have to be in till nine,' Diego explained, then he teased, 'Why? Were you trying to avoid me?'

'Of course not!' Izzy lied.

'It's good to see you out.'

'It's good to be out,' Izzy admitted. 'I used to walk on the beach each morning. I don't know why I stopped.'

'You've had a lot to deal with.'

Which she had, but Izzy hadn't walked since her marriage, another little thing she'd given up in an attempt to please Henry, but she didn't say anything.

'Do you want company?'

And she looked into dark eyes that were squinting against the morning sun, his black hair dripping, unshaven, wet, and his toned body, way smoother than a name like Ramirez suggested, and she didn't know what she wanted because, here was the thing, she'd spent the whole night in turmoil, telling herself she was being ridiculous, that it was impossible, that she should be sorting out herself instead of getting involved with someone.

She didn't actually have to tell herself. The books said the same too, even Jess.

But here, on the beach, when she should be thinking alone, it was his company her heart required. Here in the lovely fresh start of morning it just seemed natural for them to talk.

They walked along the beach, admiring the rugged Cornish coastline. Despite the warmth of summer, the wind was up, making the beach the coolest place as the breeze skimmed off the ocean and stung her cheeks, and it was a relief to talk about him.

'This beach is one of the reasons I choose to settle in St Piran. I love the beach.'

'What about Madrid? Do you miss it?'

'The nearest beach is Valencia. Over a hundred miles away...' Perhaps he realised he was being evasive. 'Sometimes I miss it. I have been away two years now...' She glanced at him when his voice trailed off.

'Go on.'

'My family and I were rowing—we did not part on good terms,' Diego admitted. 'We get on a bit better now. I talk to my mother often on the telephone, but for a while there was no contact.'

He left it there, for now. But there was something about the ocean. It was so vast and endless that it made honesty easier, problems mere specks, which was perhaps why they found themselves there so often over the next few days. They would walk and talk and try to put on hold the chemistry between them and instead work on their history. They sat in the shallows, just enough for the cool water to wash around their ankles and up their calves, and they talked. It was absolutely, for Izzy, the best part of her day and she hoped Diego felt the same.

'I told you it was expected that I would study medicine? It did not go down well when I chose to study nursing instead. Padre said it was women's work...'

'Not any more.'

'He ridiculed it, my brothers too. I also studied *partero*, I'm a midwife too,' Diego explained. 'My mother said she understood, but she would prefer I study medicine to keep my father happy.' He gave a wry smile. 'That was the rule growing up and it is still the rule now—keeping him happy. Getting good grades, melting into the background, anything to keep him happy. I wish she had the guts to leave him.' He looked over at Izzy. 'I admire you for leaving.'

'I didn't have children,' Izzy said. 'And it was still a hard decision. Don't judge her for staying, Diego. What made you want to do nursing?'

'My elder sister had a baby when I was eighteen. He was very premature and my sister was ill afterwards. I used to sit with him and I watched the nurses. They were so skilled, so much more hands on than the doctors, and I knew it was what I wanted to do. Fernando was very sick—I was there night and day for ten days. My sister had a hysterectomy and was very sick too…' There was a long silence. 'She was at another hospital so she didn't get over to see him—she was too ill.' Diego suddenly grimaced. 'I shouldn't be telling you this…'

'I'm not that precious.' Izzy squeezed his hand.

'He died at ten days old. It was tough. In those ten days I really did love him and even now sometimes my sister asks for details about him and I am glad that I can give them to her.'

'What sort of details?'

'He loved to have his feet stroked and he loved to be sing to.' He gave a slight frown and Izzy just sat silent rather than correct his grammar. 'My sister had always sung to him while she was pregnant and I taped her singing and played the songs.'

'It must be hard,' Izzy said. 'Your work must bring it all back…'

'No.' His response surprised her. 'It has certainly made me a better nurse. I know, as much as I can know, how helpless and scared the parents feel. How you constantly watch the monitors and become an armchair expert, but never, not even once, have I come close to the feelings I had for Fernando with a patient. I suppose I detach, of course there are stories and babies that touch you more than others, but you could not do this job and care so deeply at that level.'

And she looked at him and couldn't see how his parents could be anything but proud. She had seen his work at first hand, the way his colleagues and all the parents respected him. There had been an almost audible sigh of relief that Diego had been around when Toby had been born and she told him that.

'There is a managerial position at my father's hospital—I am thinking of applying for it. Of course, it has not gone down well. He says it would be an embarrassment to the Ramirez name if I take it.'

They were only just getting to know each other, but still her breath caught at the impossibility of it all, of anything happening between them, and she tried to keep the needy note from her voice when she asked a question.

'Why would you go back?' Izzy asked, 'After all that, if they don't respect what you do...'

'I respect what I do now,' Diego said. 'That is the difference. I would like to go back and be proud.'

He would go back.

They were sitting in the sand at the water's edge. Izzy's shorts were soaking, the water rushing in then dragging back out, as if taking all the debris of the past away. But the tide returned and bought with it fresh problems and Izzy told herself to slow down, to not even think about it, that his decisions didn't affect her. They were friends, that was all—they hadn't so much as kissed.

Except Diego discounted that theory before it had even properly formed.

She could feel his face near her cheek and knew if she turned her head their lips would meet.

It was six a.m. and the clearest her head would be all day, but she turned to him, to the sweet, confusing relief of his mouth. He tasted like a blast of morning, with the promise of night. It was a kiss that was tender on the outside—a mesh of lips, a slow, measured greeting, but there was raw promise beneath the surface, his tongue sliding in, offering a heady taste of more, and Izzy wanted more. She liked the press of him, the weight of him that pressed her body back to the sand. There was the tranquillity of escape she found as his kiss deepened and his hand moved naturally, sliding around her waist to caress her, and then even before Diego paused, Izzy's lips were still.

She rested her head on his shoulder a moment to steady herself, the weight of her baby between them.

'I think...' Izzy pulled her head up and made herself look at him '...we should pretend that just didn't happen.'

'It did, though,' Diego pointed out.

'Well, it can't again,' Izzy said, and she hoisted herself to standing. 'Let's just keep it as friends,' Izzy insisted, because that was surely all they could be for now, except her lips were tender from the claim of his kiss as she tried to talk about *other* things, and as they walked back her hand bunched in a fist so she didn't reach out and take his.

They were back at her car, his apartment just a short walk away, and how he wanted to take her up there, to peel off her wet clothes and call in sick, spend the day getting to know her in the way he so badly wanted to.

And friends could kiss goodbye on the cheek, except they had passed that now and any contact between them was dangerous.

He faced her, but that only made him want to kiss her again so Diego looked down and saw the swell of her stomach, her belly button just starting to protrude, and his hand ached to capture it, only his mind wasn't so sure.

'We have a lot to think about,' Diego said, 'or maybe it's better not to think about it, just…' He looked up at her and his face was honest and it scared her, but somehow it made her smile as he offered her a very grown-up slant on words said in playgrounds the world over. 'I don't want to be your friend any more.'

CHAPTER SEVEN

'YOU'RE expected to go, Diego!' Rita was adamant. 'You can't not go to the Penhally Ball.'

They'd been having this conversation all morning. Rita had found out that he wasn't going and it seemed every time he passed her work station, she thought of another reason why he must go.

He'd just come from a family meeting with the parents of Toby Geller, which had been difficult at best, and, really, the last thing Diego cared about was if he was *expected* to attend some charity ball that was being held on Saturday.

'You're going, aren't you, Megan?' Rita looked up and Diego rolled his eyes as Megan gave a thin smile.

'It is expected,' Megan agreed, but from her resigned voice it was clear she wasn't looking forward to it.

'All the units send their senior staff,' Rita said, still talking as she answered the phone.

'Spare me,' Diego said. 'Is it awful?'

'No.' Megan shook her head. 'It's actually a great night…'

'So why the long face?' He was friends with Megan. Well, not 'ring each other up every night and why don't we go for coffee type friends', but certainly they were friendly and Diego couldn't help but notice she was unusually low.

'Just one of those days!' Megan said, which given they had just been in with Toby's parents, could have explained it, except Megan hadn't been her usual self lately. Diego suddenly wondered if it had anything to do with the rumours that were flying around the hospital about Izzy and himself.

Diego hadn't realised just how many people he knew. And Izzy too.

It seemed that everywhere they went, be it a walk on the beach or to a café near his flat, they would bump into someone from work. But it wasn't just the rumour mill causing problems. Izzy was almost nine weeks from her due date now, and despite them both trying to be nothing more than just friends, that kiss had unleashed the attraction between them. It was so palpable, so present, it was killing Diego not to whisk her away from the home she was selling and bring her back to his flat, feed her, nurture her and make love to her. Except in a few weeks' time, Izzy would be a mother, which meant there would be a baby, and that was something way down on his list.

So far down, he hadn't actually thought whether one day he might want one of his own—let alone someone else's.

But he wanted her.

'It's a lovely night.' Rita just wouldn't let up; she was off the phone and back to one of her favourite subjects— prying about Megan. 'All the money raised goes to the Penhally Rape Crisis Centre. Will you be taking anyone, Doctor?'

Ah, but Megan was always one step ahead. 'You

heard the man.' Megan flashed Rita a smile that was false. 'He doesn't want to go.'

'Oh!'

Diego couldn't help but grin as a Rita's eyes momentarily widened as she wondered if she'd stumbled on the news of year, but then she remembered the latest information from her sources. She turned back to the computer and resumed typing. Attempting nonchalance, she tested the seemingly gentle waters. 'It's good to support these things.' Rita tap tapped away, 'Look what happened to our own lovely Izzy. I'd have thought you, Diego, more than anyone, would...' And she stopped, just stopped in mid-sentence, because even if she wasn't looking at him, even if Diego hadn't spoken, the atmosphere was so tense, she just knew he wasn't smiling now. 'We should all do our bit,' Rita attempted, typing faster now, hoping she'd rectified it, and hoping Diego hadn't understood what she had implied.

She was wrong on both counts.

'Me? More? Than? Anyone?' Diego's voice was pure ice as he challenged her—each word separate, each word a question, and Diego looked at Megan, who shook her head in disbelief at Rita's insensitivity. 'What do you mean by that, Rita?'

Still she typed on. 'Well, you're a nice young man, I thought you of all people...' Her face was pink and she licked her lips before carrying on. 'Well, that you'd support such a thing.'

'Do you know why I hate gossip, Megan?' Diego looked at his friend.

'Why?' Megan answered.

'Because the fools that spread it get it wrong. Because

the fools that spread it are so miserable in their own lives they have to find that part in others…' Rita stood up.

'I have to get on.' She picked up some papers, *any* papers, and walked off, but Diego's voice chased her.

'Because though they insist their lives are perfect, gossiping about others ensures that for that moment no one is gossiping about them.'

Rita spun on her heel. 'You can't stop people talking.'

'Ah, but you can,' Diego said, and pointedly turned to Megan, ignoring Rita completely. 'Before you go, I've got two in the nursery that need their drug charts re-written and Genevieve is ready to go home. Her mum wants to thank you.'

It was a relief to talk about work.

For Megan to fill in the drug charts and then to head to the nursery where Genevieve was wearing a hot pink all-in-one with a hot pink hat, and a car seat was waiting to finally, against all the odds, take her home. Diego smiled as Megan picked up the little lady and gave her a cuddle, and he could see the tears in her eyes too because, unlike Diego, Megan did get attached. She gave her heart and soul to her patients, took it personally when a battle was lost. Diego wasn't sure it was a healthy thing for her to do, but today was a good day and those, Diego suddenly realised, were the ones Megan struggled with most.

'We can't thank you enough.' Genevieve's mum was effusive in her gratitude. 'It's because of you that we get to take her home.'

Yes, today was a good day.

'Good job,' Diego said before he headed back to his

charges. 'For a while there I didn't think we'd get to this day with Genevieve. You never gave in, though.'

'I never would,' Megan said, and then she paused and her voice was more pensive than jubilant. 'Be careful, Diego.'

He knew exactly what they were talking about.

'We're just friends,' he said, but he could hear the protest in his heart and Megan could hear it in his voice.

'She's fragile…'

'She's getting stronger,' Diego countered, because he would not label Izzy, because he could feel in his soul all she was going to be.

'Just, please,' Megan said, and it was the most she would say to him, 'handle with care.'

'You're looking well.' Gus smiled as he called Izzy into his surgery.

He was a wonderful GP. He read through her charts and checked her blood pressure, even though the midwife had done the same and told Izzy it was fine.

'How is it?'

'Perfect,' Gus said. 'How have you been feeling?'

'Very well,' Izzy said, and it was the truth. For the first time in her pregnancy it wasn't Henry and the nightmare of her past that consumed her, it was something far nicer.

There had been no repeat of that kiss, but there was an energy and promise in her days now and Izzy knew it was just a matter of time.

'You're eating well?' Gus checked, and though his face never flickered, Izzy was a doctor too and could hear the slight probing nature of his question. Often her antenatal visits seemed more like a friendly catch-up, but today Gus was going through her notes, double-checking everything.

'I'm eating really well.' Which was true. In the very dark weeks after Henry's death, even though eating had been the last thing on her mind, Izzy had made herself eat, for the baby's sake. She had even gone as far as to set a reminder on her mobile, forcing down smoothies or even just a piece of toast. But since she'd been back at work, and of course since she'd met Diego, her appetite had returned—for food, for life. She was laughing, she was happy, she was eating—except her weight, Gus said, was down.

It seemed ironic that when she was eating the most, when she was happiest, she hadn't put on any weight. Gus asked her to lie on the examination bed, and though he was always thorough, today his examination took a little longer than usual.

'You're a bit small,' Gus said, and Izzy lay there staring at the ceiling, because if Gus said she was a bit small, then she *was* small. He ran a Doppler over her stomach and listened for a couple of moments to the baby's heartbeat, which was strong and regular. 'How's the baby's movement?'

'There's lots,' Izzy said, trying to keep her voice light and even.

'That's good.' He was very calm, very unruffled and he helped her sit up and then she joined him at his desk.

'Are you worried?' Izzy asked.

'Not unduly,' Gus said. 'Izzy, you've had unbelievable stress throughout this pregnancy—but you're thirty-one weeks now and this is the time that the baby starts to put on weight, so we really do need to keep a slightly closer eye on you. I was going to schedule an ultrasound for a couple of weeks, but let's bring that forward.' He glanced at his watch. It was six on Friday evening. 'Let's get this done early next week and then…' She was due to start coming to fortnightly visits now, but Gus was nothing if not thorough. 'Let's get the scan and I'll see you again next week.'

'You know that I'm working?' Izzy felt incredibly guilty, but Gus moved to reassure her.

'Lots of my mums work right up till their due date, Izzy. You're doing nothing wrong—for now. I just want you to try and reduce your stress and really make sure you're eating well. You need some extra calories. I'd suggest you add a protein shake to your breakfast.'

'I'm supposed to be going to the Penhally Ball tomorrow…'

Out of the blue Diego had suggested they go together— face the gossip and just get it over and done with, and what better way than at the Penhally Ball, when everyone would be there. They had, Diego had pointed out, absolutely nothing to be ashamed of. To the world they were friends and friends went out! Except Izzy still cared what others might think and almost hoped Gus would shake his head and tell her that the weekend might be better spent resting on the couch with her feet up, thus give her a reason not to go, but Gus seemed delighted. 'That's good—I'm glad you're starting to go out.'

'Shouldn't I be resting?'

'Izzy, I'm not prescribing bed rest—I want you to relax and a social life is a part of that. I just want to keep a closer eye on you.'

'The thing is…' She was testing the water, just

dipping in her toe. She respected Gus, and his reaction mattered. 'Things have been awful, but for the last few weeks, for the first time since I've been pregnant, I haven't had any stress or, rather, much less, and I have been eating better...'

'Well, whatever it is you're doing, keep it up,' Gus said, and Izzy gave a small swallow.

'I'm going to the ball with a friend, Diego.'

'Ramirez.' Izzy frowned as Gus said his surname.

'You know him?'

'There aren't too many Diegos around here. The neonatal nurse?'

And she waited for his shock-horror reaction, for him to tell her she should be concentrating on the baby now, not out dancing with male *friends*, but instead Gus smiled.

'He seems a nice man.'

When Izzy just sat there Gus smiled. 'You deserve nice, Izzy.'

She still didn't know it.

CHAPTER EIGHT

SHE'D cancel.

Izzy could hardly hear the hairdresser's comments as she sat with a black cape around her shoulders, pretending to look as a mirror was flashed behind her head.

'It looks fantastic!'

Well, she would say that, Izzy thought to herself. The hairdresser was hardly going to say, 'It looks awful and what on earth were you thinking, taking a pair of scissors to your locks, you stupid tart?' But as the mirror hovered behind her Izzy actually did look, and for once she agreed with the woman who wielded the scissors.

Okay, maybe fantastic was stretching things a touch, but it had been three months and three trips to this chair since that moment of self-loathing and finally, finally, she didn't look like a five-year-old who had taken the kitchen scissors to the bathroom. The last of her home-made crop had been harvested, the once jagged spikes now softened, shades of blonde and caramel moving when her head did, which it did as Izzy craned her neck for a proper look.

'I've hardly taken anything off at the front or sides, just softened it a touch, but I've taken a fair bit off the back…'

Izzy could have kissed her but instead she left a massive tip, booked in for six weeks' time, skipped out to her car and somehow made it home without incident, despite the constant peeks in the rear-view mirror at her very new 'side fringe'.

And then she remembered.

She was cancelling.

So why was she running a bath and getting undressed?

A tepid bath so it didn't fluff up her hair.

She couldn't do it, couldn't go, just couldn't face it.

So instead of climbing in to the water she wrapped herself in a towel and padded out to the living room.

She had every reason to cancel, Izzy told herself as she picked up the telephone, except there was a voicemail message. It wasn't Diego stuck at work, as she had rather hoped, but the real estate agent with a pathetic offer. 'It's a good offer, you should seriously consider it,' played the message. Henry had been a real estate agent and had practically said those words in his sleep so she deleted it and got back to fretting about Diego. The fact that she was pregnant and had worked all morning, the fact that she wasn't ready for the inevitable stares if she walked into the Penhally Ball with a dashing Spaniard on her arm when she should be home…

Doing what? Izzy asked herself.

Grieving, feeling wretched…

Her introspection was halted by the doorbell. No doubt the postman had been while she was out and it was her neighbour with another box of self-help or baby books that she had ordered on the internet during one of her glum times—a book that at the time she had convinced herself would be the one to show her, tell her, inform her how the hell she was supposed to be feeling...

'Diego?'

It was only five p.m. and he shouldn't be there, the ball didn't start till seven.

There was no reason for him to be there now and, worse, she was only wearing a towel.

'I thought I'd come early.' He leant in the doorway and smiled, and either the baby did a big flip or her stomach curled in on itself. He was in evening wear, except he hadn't shaved, and he looked ravishing, so ravishing she wanted to do just that—ravish him, drop the towel she was clinging to, right here at the front door. 'To save you that phone call.'

'What phone call?' Izzy lowered her head a touch as she let him in, wishing there had been a warning sign on the kitchen scissors to inform her that it would be a full twelve to eighteen months before she could again hide her facial expressions with her hair if she chose to lop it all off. A fringe simply wouldn't suffice. Her whole body was on fire, every pulse leaping at the sight of him.

'The one where you tell me your back is aching, or you're tired or that it was lovely of me to ask, but...'

'I was just about to make it,' Izzy admitted.

'Why?'

'Because it's too soon.'

'For what?'

'For me to be out, for me to be...' She blanched at the unsaid word.

'Happy?' Diego offered. 'Living?'

Neither was quite right. Izzy didn't correct him at first, she just clung to her towel, not to keep him from her but to keep her from him, and she stared at a man who had brought nothing but joy into her life. She wanted more of the same.

'For me to be seeing someone,' Izzy corrected. 'Which I think I am.'

'You are,' he confirmed, and crossed the room. It was a relief to be kissed, to kiss him, to be kissed some more, to kiss back. He was less than subtle, he was devouring her, and any vision that their next kiss would be gentle and tender was far removed from delicious reality. Diego had waited long for another kiss and he was claiming it now, pressing her against the wall as she rejoiced in him, her towel falling. He kicked it away and all she wanted was more, more, more.

He tasted as he had that morning but decisiveness made it better. He smelt as he always had, just more concentrated now, and this close to Diego, this into Diego, she forgot to be scared and hold back.

Izzy just forgot.

She could have climbed up the wall and slid onto him he felt so delicious, but just as her senses faded to oblivion, Diego resurrected one of his.

'Is that a bath?'

Now, this bit she didn't get.

Sense *should* have prevailed.

In her mad dash to turn off the taps, okay, yes it was okay that he followed, but then, *then* she should have shown him the door, should have closed it on him and had a few moments' pause, except she let him help her into the bath and then she remembered to be practical. 'Diego, we can't.'

'I know.' He took off his jacket, hung it on the

doorhandle and then sat on the edge and looked at her, and she couldn't believe how normal it felt.

'We can't,' he confirmed, because of the baby she carried. 'How far along are you again?' He grinned and then rolled his eyes as he did the mental arithmetic, because this thing between them had already been going on for a couple of weeks!

'Poor Diego.' Why was she laughing? Lying in the bath and laughing like she was happy. And the fact that she was made her suddenly serious.

'How can this work—ever?' Izzy asked, because surely it was impossible. 'You're going back to Spain.'

'Nope.' He shook his head. 'I didn't apply.'

'There'll be other jobs though. One day you will go back.' And he couldn't argue with that, so instead she watched as he rolled up his sleeves and two tanned olive hands took a lilac bar of soap and worked it. She could see the bubbles between his fingers, see the moist, slippery sheen of his hands, and her body quivered and begged for them to be on her. As his hands met her shoulders her mind stopped looking for reasons to halt this and her brain stopped begging for logic and all she did was feel—feel his strong fingers on her tense shoulders, feel the knots of tight muscles spasm in momentary protest as this large Spaniard had the nerve to tell them to let go. For months, no, maybe a year, or had it been longer, those muscles had been knotted with the serious job of holding her head up high and now they were being told to let go, to give in, that they could relax, regroup and get ready for the next mountain Izzy was certain that she would surely have to climb. But Diego's hands worked on and convinced her shoulders, if not her mind, to do as the master skilfully commanded, and let go.

Her fringe almost met the water with the relief.

Like popping a balloon she just gave in, just groaned as her tension seeped into the water and then steamed out into the room.

She just couldn't let go for long, though.

'I can't get my hair wet!' She flailed at all his hands were offering, she just couldn't relax and enjoy it in long stages. 'How can this work, Diego?' she asked again.

'*Sencillo*,' Diego said, 'It doesn't have to be complicated. Why not just for now? Why not for as long as we make each other happy?'

'Because in nine weeks I'll be diving into postnatal depression and I won't be making anyone happy!'

She wanted guarantees.

Wanted a little piece of paper stamped with *I won't hurt you* to be handed to her now, except she'd had that once, Izzy realised as she lay there, a big piece of paper called a wedding certificate, and it hadn't counted for a thing.

Before Diego had come along living had been like essential surgery without analgesia.

Why would she deny herself the balm of relief?

And there was a wobble of guilt there, but for him. 'What if I'm using you!' God, she had never been so honest, and certainly not with a man. All her relationships had been Izzy pleasing others, Izzy saying the right thing, and now here she was, ten minutes into a new one and saying the wrong thing, saying truthfully what was on her mind. 'What if I'm using you to get through this?'

And he thought about it for a moment, he actually did, and then he came to his decision.

'Use away!'

'What if I'm avoiding my pain by...?'

'Shut up.' He grinned and leaned over and kissed her a nice lazy kiss. Then he kissed her shoulder and along the slippery wet lines of her neck.

Oh, Diego loved women. He loved curves on women and two of Izzy's were floating on the water, just bobbing there, and his hands moved to her shoulders, because it seemed more polite. But then his hands just moved to where they wanted to be and he caressed them, caressed her. His big, dark hands cupped and soaped her very white, rather large, to Izzy rather ugly breasts, but maybe they weren't so ugly, because from the trip in his breathing and the bob of his tongue on his dark lips, she had the feeling that one tug of his tie and he'd be in the water with her, and there would be two empty seats at the Penhally Charity Ball.

'We can't,' she said again and it was the feeblest of protests, because the stubble of his chin was scratching her breast now, his tongue on her nipple and her fingers in his hair.

'You can,' Diego said, as his hand slid beneath the water.

She never fully forgot about the hell of the past months and years. No matter how good, how happy, how busy she was, no matter what conversation she was holding, it never completely left her mind, but as his hand slid beneath the water and Izzy could feel his fingers at the top of her thighs, ever-present thoughts started to fade. She could feel his hot mouth on her cool shoulder and always, always, always she had thought of pleasing *him*, not Diego, but *him*, and the mute button hit and there was nothing to think of but this, nothing to relish but Diego's tender explorations as she wriggled in his palm.

Her cynical voice gave one last call for order. After all, she didn't come with instructions, and he must do this an awful lot, because his fingers read her so well, but she was kissing his neck and above his white collar, coiling her wet fingers in his dark hair as a heavenly regular pressure beat beneath the water. And suddenly she didn't care if he did this a lot, he was doing it to her, right now, and he could go on doing it for ever, it was so divine. He stroked her back to life, cajoled her hibernating clitoris from its dreamless sleep, and it stretched and peeked out and Izzy was sure this feeling must end, that she'd shift or he'd pause and that the magic would stop, and she didn't want it to.

She couldn't lean back because she didn't want to.

She couldn't reach for the sides of the bath because then she couldn't hold him.

She held his shirt-clad back with wet arms and muffled her face in his neck and beneath the cologne that he was wearing tonight was the true scent of him, the one that every cell in her body had flared for on sight and burnt now with direct contact.

Let go, his fingers insisted. *Let go*, the stubble of his chin told her eyelids as she pressed her face into him. She could hear the lap, lap, lap of the water and the patience yet relentlessness of him and she did as his fingers told her, she didn't know what she said and she didn't know what she did—she just let go. She was almost climbing out of the bath and into his arms, but he held her down and it was so much better than being just friends. And as she opened her eyes he closed his; as he struggled to get through the next nine seconds,

Izzy was wondering how they'd get through the next nine weeks. She wanted more of him.

'We're going to be late.' He was trying to sound normal.

Really, really late, because Izzy now had to sort out her hair and do her make-up *and* show him where the ironing board was so he could iron his shirt dry.

But it was more than worth it.

CHAPTER NINE

SHE had known heads would turn and they did, but what Izzy hadn't expected were the smiles that followed the arches of the eyebrows as they walked in together.

Real smiles, because how could they not?

Izzy had been through so very much and her friends and colleagues had been worried about her, had not known how to react in the face of such raw pain and grief, but tonight she was glowing and it wasn't just from the pregnancy.

'Don't you dare say you're just friends, because I won't believe you.' Megan came over as Diego went to the bar. 'Friends,' Megan said, 'are able to go two minutes without eye contact,' she pointed out as she caught Izzy and Diego share a lingering look from across the room. 'Friends don't light up a room with their energy when they walk in. Friends don't cause every head to turn. Friends, my foot...' Megan laughed.

'Okay, 'Izzy said, and though it was all a bit like a runaway train, she felt exhilarated as she rode it, smiled as she said it: 'We're more than friends.'

'Happy?' Megan checked.

'Very.'

'Then I'm happy for you,' Megan said. Izzy was sure

she would have loved to have said more, but sometimes good friends didn't. Sometimes good friends had to let you make your own success or mistakes and be there for you whatever the outcome. Megan confirmed that with her next words.

'I'm always here.'

'I know that.'

'So how did you manage the night off? I thought you were on.'

'No.' Izzy shook her head, 'I told you, I'm only doing days till the baby's born. I thought you were on call?'

'Richard didn't want to come to the ball, so he's covering for me,' Megan said. 'So who's holding the fort in A and E tonight?'

'Mitch,' Izzy said.

'He's only a resident.'

'Oh, Ben is on call, said he might pop in if he can get away....' And her voice trailed off, because Izzy realised then that Megan hadn't actually been enquiring about her roster, she had been fishing to find out the whereabouts of someone else. And as Megan stood and kissed Izzy on the cheek and headed off into the throng of people, Izzy found a corner of an unexpected jigsaw.

She could see Megan, her usually pale cheeks, suddenly flushed and pink, desperately trying to focus on a conversation, but her green eyes kept flicking over to Josh. It was as if there were an invisible thread between them, a thread that tightened. She watched as Josh worked the room, each greeting, each two-minute conversation seemed to be dragging him on a human Mexican wave towards Megan. The pull was so strong,

Izzy could have sworn she could have reached out and grabbed it.

And then it snapped.

Izzy watched as a blonde woman walked over, all smiles, and kissed Josh possessively on the lips. Izzy saw the wedding band glint on her finger and as Megan's face turned away, Izzy knew Megan had just seen it too.

'Excuse me…' All the colour had drained out of Megan's face and she walked quickly to the ladies. Izzy looked over at Josh who was concentrating on something his wife was saying, but then he caught her eye and Izzy couldn't read his expression, but something told her it was a plea to help.

'Here…' Diego was back with the drinks and it was Izzy's turn to excuse herself, but by the time she got to the ladies Megan was on her way out.

'Hey?' Izzy smiled. 'Are you okay?'

'I'm great!' Megan gave a dazzling smile. 'It's always a good night.'

'Megan?' Izzy caught her friend's arm, but Megan shook it off.

'I must get back out there.'

Oh, she wanted to know what was going on, to help, to fix, to share, only it was clear all Megan wanted to do was to get through this night.

'Sit with us,' Izzy suggested. 'I thought we would be with the emergency guys and girls or NICU, but we left the booking too late and we're with the maternity mob. Come and keep us company.' It was the best she could do for Megan right now and when Megan jumped at the suggestion, Izzy knew she had been right.

There was something going on with Megan and Josh.

Or, Izzy pondered, there had been.

It was actually a good night—the food was wonderful, the company great. Diego was clearly a hit with the maternity team as well, but as the table was cleared and the dancing commenced Izzy was uncomfortable all of a sudden in the hard chair. Stretching her spine, she shifted her weight and she was glad to stretch her legs when Diego asked her to dance.

It was such bliss to be in his arms.

To smell him, to be held by him.

She wished the music would last for ever—that somehow she could freeze this moment of time, where there was no past to run from and no future that could change things. She wished she could dance and dance, just hold this moment and forever feel his breath on her neck and his warm hands on her back, to feel the bulge of her pregnant stomach pressed to his and to remember…

She was dizzy almost remembering a couple of hours earlier.

'Glad you came?' Diego asked.

'Very,' Izzy said, and then pulled back and smiled. 'And more than a little surprised that I did.'

Every day he saw another side to her.

Diego was far from stupid. Of course he had questioned the wisdom of getting involved with someone at such a vulnerable time—fatherhood was not on his agenda. After a lifetime of rules and the stuffy confines of his family, he had sworn it would be years before anyone or anything pinned him down. He was devoted to his work and everything else was just a pleasure, but now, holding her in his arms, life was starting to look a little different.

'Hey.' He'd sensed her distraction. 'What are you watching?'

'What's going on,' she asked, 'with Megan and Josh?'

Diego rolled his eyes. 'Not you too? Rita, my ward clerk, is obsessed with them.'

'Megan's been different lately,' Izzy insisted. 'Surely you've noticed?'

'I've had my mind on other things,' he said, pulling her in a little tighter. 'There's nothing going on,' Diego said assuredly, and glanced at the subjects of their conversation. 'They're not even talking to each other.'

Which was such a male thing to say, but Megan was right, Izzy thought, watching Josh's eyes scan the room as he danced with his wife, watched them locate and capture and hold their target, almost in apology, until Megan tore hers away.

Friends don't share looks like that.

But in that moment all thoughts of Josh and Megan faded, all thoughts of Diego and romance too, because the back pain she had felt while sitting returned, spreading out from her spine like two large hands, stretching around to her stomach and squeezing. It wasn't a pain as such, she'd been having Braxton-Hicks' contractions, but this felt different, tighter. This didn't take her breath, neither did it stop her swaying in the darkness with Diego, but she was more than aware of it and then it was gone and she tried to forget that it had happened. only Diego had been aware of it too.

He had felt her stomach, which was pressed into his, tighten.

He didn't want to be one of those paranoid people. She was just dancing on so he did too, but he was almost more aware of her body than his own. He could feel the slight shift and knew that even though she danced on and held him, her mind was no longer there.

'You okay?'

'Great,' she murmured, hoping and praying that she was. The music played on and Diego suggested that they sit this next one out. Izzy was about to agree, only suddenly the walk back to their table seemed rather long. The music tipped into the next ballad and Izzy leant on him as the next small wave hit, only this time it did make her catch her breath and Diego could pretend no more.

'Izzy?' She heard the question in his voice.

'I don't know,' she admitted. 'Can you get me outside?' she said, still leaning on him, waiting for it to pass. 'In a moment.'

Their exit was discreet. He had a hand round her waist and they didn't stop to get her bag, and as the cool night air hit, Izzy wondered if she was overreacting because now she felt completely normal.

'Izzy.' Discreet as their exit had been, Gus must have noticed because he joined them outside, just as another contraction hit.

'They're not strong,' Izzy said as Gus placed a skilled hand on her abdomen.

'How far apart?' Gus asked, and it was Diego who answered.

'Six, maybe seven minutes.'

'Okay.' Gus wasted no time. 'Let's get you over to the hospital and we can pop you on a monitor. I'll bring the Jeep around.'

'Should we call an ambulance?' Diego asked, but Gus shook his head.

'We'll be quicker in my Jeep and if we have to pull over, I've got everything we need.'

'I'm not having it,' Izzy insisted, only neither Diego nor Gus was convinced.

It was a thirty-minute drive from Penhally. Diego felt a wave of unease as Izzy's hand gripped his tighter and she blew out a long breath. He remembered his time on Maternity and often so often it was a false alarm, the midwives could tell. Izzy kept insisting she was fine, that the contractions weren't that bad, but he could feel her fingers digging into his palms at closer intervals, could see Gus glancing in the rear-view mirror when Izzy held her breath every now and then, and the slight acceleration as Gus drove faster.

His mind was racing, awful scenarios playing out, but Izzy could never have guessed. He stayed strong and supportive beside her, held her increasingly tightening fingers as Gus rang through and warned the hospital of their arrival. A staff member was waiting with a wheelchair as they pulled up at the maternity section.

'It's too soon,' Izzy said as he helped her out of the Jeep.

'You're in the right place,' Diego said, only he could feel his heart hammering in his chest, feel the adrenaline coursing through him as she was whisked off and all he could do was give her details as best as he could to a new night receptionist.

'You're the father?' ahe asked, and his lips tightened as he shook his head, and he felt the relegation.

'I'm a friend,' Diego said. 'Her…' But he didn't know what to follow it up with. It had been just a few short weeks, and he wasn't in the least surprised when he was asked to take a seat in a bland waiting room

He waited, unsure what to do, what his role was—if he even had a role here.

Going over and over the night, stunned at how quickly everything had changed. One minute they had been dancing, laughing—now they were at the hospital.

The logical side of his brain told him that thirty-one weeks' gestation was okay. Over and over he tried to console himself, tried to picture his reaction if he knew a woman was labouring and he was preparing a cot to receive the baby. Yet there was nothing logical about the panic that gripped him when he thought of Izzy's baby being born at thirty-one weeks. Every complication, every possibility played over and over. It was way too soon, and even if everything did go well, Izzy would be in for a hellish ride when she surely didn't deserve it.

They could stop the labour, though. Diego swung between hope and despair. She'd only just started to have contractions…

'Diego.' Gus came in and shook his hand.

'How is she?'

'Scared,' Gus said, and gave him a brief rundown of his findings. 'We've given her steroids to mature the baby's lungs and we're trying to stop the labour or at least slow down the process to give the medication time to take effect.'

'Oh, God…' Guilt washed over him, a guilt he knew was senseless, but guilt all the same. However, Gus was one step ahead of him.

'Nothing Izzy or you did contributed to this, Diego. I've spoken with Izzy at length, this was going to happen. In fact…' he gave Diego a grim smile '…an ultrasound and cord study have just been done. Her placenta is small and the cord very thin. This baby really will do better on the outside, though we'd all like to buy another week or two. I knew the baby was small for dates. Izzy was going to have an ultrasound early next week, but from what I've just seen Izzy's baby really will do better by being born.'

'She's been eating well, taking care of herself.'

'She suffered trauma both physically and emotionally early on in the pregnancy,' Gus said. 'Let's just get her through tonight, but guilt isn't going to help anyone.'

Diego knew that. He'd had the same conversation with more parents than he could remember—the endless search for answers, for reasons, when sometimes Mother Nature worked to her own agenda.

'Does she want to see me?'

Gus nodded. 'She doesn't want to call her family just yet.'

When he saw her, Diego remembered the day he had first met her when she had come to the neonatal ward. Wary, guarded, she sat on the bed, looking almost angry, but he knew she was just scared.

'It's going to be okay,' Diego said, and took her hand, but she pulled it away.

'You don't know that.'

She sat there and she had all her make-up on, her hair immaculate, except she was in a hospital gown with a drip and a monitor strapped to her stomach, and Diego wondered if she did actually want him there at all.

She did.

But how could she ask him to be there for her?

She was scared for her baby, yet she resented it almost.

Nine weeks.

They'd had nine weeks left of being just a couple, which was not long by anyone's standards. Nine weeks to get to know each other properly, to enjoy each other, and now even that nine weeks was being denied to them.

How could she admit how much she wanted him to stay—yet how could she land all this on him?

'I think you should go.'

'Izzy.' Diego kept his voice steady. 'Whatever helps you now is fine by me. I can call your family. I can stay with you, or I can wait outside, or if you would prefer that I leave…'

He wanted to leave, Izzy decided, or he wouldn't have said it. The medication they had given her to slow down the labour made her brain work slower, made her thought process muddy.

'I don't know…' Her teeth were chattering, her admission honest. Gus was back, talking to a midwife and Richard Brooke, the paediatric consultant, who had just entered the room. They were all looking at the printout from the monitor and Izzy wanted five minutes alone with Diego, five minutes to try and work out whether or not he wanted to be there, but she wasn't going to get five minutes with her thoughts for a long while.

'Izzy.' She knew that voice and so did Diego, knew that brusque, professional note so well, because they had both used it themselves when they bore bad tidings. 'The baby is struggling; its heartbeat is irregular…'

'It needs time to let the medication take effect.' Izzy's fuzzy logic didn't work on Gus. He just stood over her, next to Diego, both in suits and looking sombre, and she felt as if she were lying in a coffin. 'We want to do a Caesarean, your baby needs to be born.'

Already the room was filling with more staff. She felt the jerk as the brakes were kicked off the bed, the clang as portable oxygen was lifted onto the bed and even in her drugged state she knew this wasn't your standard Caesarean section, this was an emergency Caesarean.

'Is there time…?' She didn't even bother to finish her sentence. Izzy could hear the deceleration in her baby's heartbeat, and knew there wouldn't be time for an epidural, that she would require a general anaesthetic, and it was the scariest, out-of-control feeling. 'Can you be there, Diego?' Her eyes swung from Diego to Gus. 'Can Diego be in there?'

For a general anaesthetic, partners or relatives weren't allowed to come into the theatre, but the NICU team were regularly in Theatre and after just the briefest pause Richard agreed, but with clarification. 'Just for Izzy.'

'Sure,' Diego agreed, and at that moment he'd have agreed to anything, because the thought of being sent to another waiting room, *knowing* all that could go wrong, was unbearable, but as he helped speed the bed the short distance to Theatre, Diego also knew that if there was a problem with the babe, he wanted to be the one dealing with it. This was no time for arrogance neither was it time for feigned modesty—quite simply Diego knew he was the best.

The theatre sister gave Diego a slightly wide-eyed look as she registered he was holding hands with her emergency admission, whom she recognised too.

'Diego's here with Izzy,' the midwife explained. 'Richard has okayed him to go in.'

'Then you'll need to go and get changed,' came the practical response. 'You can say goodbye to her here.'

And that was it.

Diego knew when he saw her again, she would be under anaesthetic.

Izzy knew it too.

'I'm glad you're here…' She was trying not to cry and her face was smothered with the oxygen mask. 'You'll make sure…'

'Everything is going to be fine.' His voice came out gruffer than he was used to hearing it. He was trying to reassure her, but Diego felt it sounded as if he was telling her off. 'Better than fine,' he said again. His voice still didn't soften, but there wasn't time to correct it. 'Thirty-one-weekers do well.'

'Thirty-two's better.'

'I'll be there,' Diego said. 'And it *is* going to be okay.'

He couldn't give her a kiss, because they were already moving her away.

He turned to Gus, who as her GP would also have to wait outside the operating theatre, and exchanged a look with the worried man. 'Go and get changed, Diego,' Gus said, and his words shocked Diego into action. He changed his clothes in a moment, then put on a hat and made his way through to Theatre.

'Diego!' Hugh, the paediatric anaesthetist greeted him from behind a yellow mask. 'Extremely bradycardic, ready for full resus.'

'Diego's here with the mother.' Brianna was there too, ready to receive the baby, and her unusually pointed tone was clearly telling her colleague to shut the hell up.

The surgeon on duty that night had already started

the incision, and Diego knew the man in question was brilliant at getting a baby out urgently when required, but for Diego the world was in slow motion, the theatre clock hand surely sticking as it moved past each second marker.

'Breech.' The surgeon was calling for more traction. Diego could see the two spindly legs the surgeon held in one hand and for the first time in Theatre he felt nausea, understood now why relatives were kept out and almost wished he had been, because suddenly he appreciated how fathers-to-be must feel.

Except he wasn't the father, Diego told himself as the baby's limp body was manoeuvred out and the head delivered.

This baby wasn't his to love, Diego reminded himself as an extremely floppy baby was dashed across to the resuscitation cot.

He *never* wanted to feel like this again.

He never wanted to stand so helpless, just an observer. It would, for Diego, have been easier to work on her himself, yet he was in no state to.

He could feel his fingertips press into her palms with impatience as Hugh called twice for a drug, and though the team was fantastic, their calm professionalism riled him. Richard was fantastic, but Diego would have preferred Megan. Megan pounced on tiny details faster than anyone Diego had seen.

'She's still bradycardic,' Diego said, when surely they should have commenced massage now.

'Out.' Brianna mouthed the word and jerked her head to the theatre doors, but he hesitated.

'Diego!' Brianna said his name, and Diego stiffened in realisation—this wasn't his call, only it felt like it.

Brianna's brown eyes lifted again to his when Diego would have preferred them to stay on the baby, and he knew he was getting in the way, acting more like a father than a professional, so he left before he was formally asked to.

CHAPTER TEN

'THAT's it, Izzy…' She could hear a male voice she didn't recognise. 'Stay on your back.'

She was under blankets and wanted to roll onto her side, except she couldn't seem to move.

'You're doing fine,' came the unfamiliar voice. 'Stay nice and still.'

'Izzy, it's all okay.'

There was a voice she knew. Strong and deep and accented, and she knew it was Diego, she just didn't know why, and then she opened her eyes and saw his and she remembered.

'You've got a daughter.' His face was inches away. 'She's okay, she's being looked after.'

And then it was fog, followed by pain, followed by drugs, so many drugs she struggled to focus when Diego came back in the afternoon with pictures of her baby.

'She looks like you,' Diego said, but all Izzy could see were tubes.

'Are you working today?'

Diego shook his head. 'No. I just came in to see you.' And he sat down in the chair by her bed and Izzy went to sleep. He flicked through the photos and tried very hard to only see tubes, because this felt uncomfortably familiar, this felt a little like it had with Fernando and he just couldn't go there again.

He certainly wasn't ready to go there again.

There was a very good reason that a normal pregnancy lasted forty weeks, Diego reflected, putting the photos on her locker and heading for home—and it wasn't just for the baby. The parents needed every week of that time to prepare themselves emotionally for the change to their lives.

He wasn't even a parent.

It was Tuesday night and a vicious UTI later before anything resembling normal thought process occurred and a midwife helped her into a chair and along with her mother wheeled her down to the NICU, where, of course, any new mum would want to be if her baby was.

'We take mums down at night all the time,' the midwife explained, when Izzy said the next day would be fine. 'It's no problem.'

Except, privately, frankly, Izzy would have preferred to sleep.

Izzy knew she was a likely candidate for postnatal depression.

As a doctor she was well versed in the subject and the midwives had also gently warned her and given her leaflets to read. Gus too had talked to her—about her difficult labour, the fact she had been separated from her daughter and her difficult past. He'd told her he was there if she needed to talk and he had been open and upfront and told her not to hesitate to reach out sooner rather than later, as had Jess.

She sat in a wheelchair at the entrance to NICU, at

the very spot where she had first flirted with Diego, where the first thawing of her heart had taken place, and it seemed a lifetime ago, not a few short weeks.

And, just as she had felt that day, Izzy was tempted to ask the midwife to turn the chair around, more nervous at meeting her baby than she could ever let on. Diego was on a stint of night duty and she was nervous of him seeing her in her new role too, because his knowing eyes wouldn't miss anything. What if she couldn't summon whatever feelings and emotions it was that new mums summoned?

'I bet you can't wait!' Izzy's mum said as the midwife pressed the intercom and informed the voice on the end of their arrival. Then the doors buzzed and she was let in. Diego came straight over and gave her a very nice smile and they made some introductions. 'Perhaps you could show Izzy's mother the coffee room.' Diego was firm on this as he would be with any of his mothers. If Izzy had stepped in and said she'd prefer her mum to come, then of course it would have happened, but Izzy stayed quiet, very glad of a chance to meet her daughter alone.

'I already know where the coffee room is,' Gwen said, 'and I've already seen the baby.'

'Izzy hasn't.' Diego was straight down the line. 'We can't re-create the delivery room but we try—she needs time alone to greet her baby.'

Which told her.

'You know the rules.' He treated Izzy professionally and she was very glad of it. They went through the hand-washing ritual and he spoke to her as they did so.

'Brianna is looking after her tonight,' Diego said. 'Do you know her?'

'I don't think so.'

'She's great—she was there at the delivery. I'll take you over.'

Nicola, Toby's mother, was there and gave Izzy a sympathetic smile as she was wheeled past, which Izzy returned too late, because she was already there at her baby's cot.

Brianna greeted her, but Izzy was hardly listening. Instead she stared into the cot and there she was—her baby. And months of fear and wondering all hushed for a moment as she saw her, her little red scrunched-up face and huge dark blue eyes that stared right into Izzy's.

Over the last three days Diego had bought her plenty of photos, told her how well she was doing and how beautiful she was, but seeing her in the flesh she was better than beautiful, she was hers.

'We're just giving her a little oxygen,' Brianna explained as Diego was called away. 'Which we will be for a couple more weeks, I'd expect…' She opened the porthole and Izzy needed no invitation. She held her daughter's hand, marvelling that such a tiny hand instinctively curled around her index finger, and Izzy knew there and then that she was in love.

'She looks better than I thought…' Izzy couldn't actually believe just how well she looked. Her mum had been crying when she'd returned the first day from visiting her granddaughter and Richard, the consultant paediatrician, had told her that her baby had got off to a rocky start.

'She struggled for the first forty-eight hours, which we were expecting,' Brianna said calmly, 'but she picked up well.'

Diego had said the same, but she'd been worried he'd

just been reassuring her, but now she was here, now she could see her, all Izzy could feel was relief and this overwhelming surge charging through her veins that she figured felt a lot like love.

'Now, would you like to hold her?' Brianna said to Izzy's surprise. 'She's due for a feed, but she needs it soon, so would you like to give her a cuddle first?'

She very much would.

Brianna brought over a large chair and Izzy sat, exhausted, then got a new surge of energy.

'Open up your pyjama top,' Brianna said

'It's popping open all the time...' Izzy said, staring down at her newly massive breasts that strained the buttons.

'Your skin will keep her warm and it's good for both of you.'

She hadn't expected so much so soon. Her dreams had been filled with tiny floppy babies like ugly skinned rabbits, yet her baby was prettier and healthier than her photos had shown. Brianna was calm and confident and then there she was, wearing just a nappy and hat and resting on her chest, a blanket being wrapped around them both, skin on skin, and Izzy at that moment knew...

She knew, as far as anyone could possibly know, that the doom and gloom and the shadow of PND was not going to darken her door.

She could feel her baby on her skin and it was almost, Izzy was sure, as if all the darkness just fell away from her now, as pure love flooded in.

A white, pure love that was tangible, that was real. All the fears, the doubts, the dark, dark dread faded, because she had never been sure, really, truly sure that love *could* win, that love would come, that it would happen.

But it just did.

Diego witnessed it too.

He had seen many moments like this one, both in NICU and in the delivery room, and it was more something he ticked off his list than felt moved by—especially in NICU, where bonding was more difficult to achieve. Only it wasn't a list with Izzy, because it did move him, so much so that he came over and smiled down as he watched.

It crossed so many lines, because he didn't want to feel it, and also, as Gwen came over, Diego realised he had sent her own mother away.

Yet he was here.

'She's a Ross all over, isn't she?' Gwen said, and Diego saw Izzy's jaw clench as her mother stamped her territory on her granddaughter and told her how it would be. 'There's nothing of him in her.'

Of course, Henry's parents begged to differ when they came two days later to visit.

They had been in France, trying to have a break, after the most traumatic of months, and had cut their holiday short to come in and visit what was left of their son.

It was an agonising visit. Emotions frayed, Henry's mother teary, his father trying to control things, telling Izzy their rights, blaming her at every turn till she could see clearly where Henry had got it from! And, that evening, as soon as they left, Izzy sat on the bed with her fingers pressed into her eyes, trying to hold it together, wondering if now tears would come.

'Bad timing?' Izzy jumped as heard footsteps and

saw Josh, the new consultant, at her door. 'I'll come by another time.'

'I'm fine.' Izzy forced a smile. 'Come in.'

'You're sure?' he checked, and Izzy nodded.

'I'm sorry to mess up the roster.'

'That's the last thing you should be worrying about,' Josh replied, just as any boss would in the circumstances, and it was going to be an awkward visit, Izzy knew that. A guy like Josh didn't really belong in the maternity ward with teary women. 'Ben's on leave, but he rang and told me you'd be stressing about details like that, and could I come up and tell you that you're not to worry about a thing and that if there's anything we can do for you, you're to ask.

'Is there anything,' Josh pushed, 'that we can do for you now?'

'I'm being very well looked after. I'm fine, really, it's just been a difficult evening.' She waited for a thin line from Josh about the baby blues, or something like that, but he just looked at her for a long time before he spoke.

'I'm quite sure this is all very difficult for you,' Josh said.

And he was just so disarmingly nice that Izzy found herself admitting a little more. 'Henry's parents just stopped by. They've gone to see the baby.'

'Henry's your late husband?' Josh checked, and Izzy nodded.

'I'm sure you've heard all the gossip.'

'I don't listen to gossip,' Josh said, 'though Ben did bring me up to date on what happened before you came back to work, just so that I would know to look out for you. You know Ben's not into gossip either, but he felt

I should know—not all of it, I'm sure, but he told me enough that I can see you'd be having a tough time of it.'

His directness surprised her. Instead of sitting stiffly in the chair and making painful small talk, he came over and sat on the bed, took her hand and gave it a squeeze and a bit of that Irish charm, and Izzy could see why he was such a wonderful doctor.

'Henry's parents blame me,' Izzy admitted. 'They thought our marriage was perfect, they think I'm making it all up.'

'They probably want to believe that you're making it all up,' Josh said wisely.

'They were in tears just before, saying what a wonderful father Henry would have been, how a baby would have changed things, would have saved our marriage, if only I hadn't asked him to leave. They don't know what went on behind closed doors.'

'They need to believe that you're lying,' Josh said. 'But you know the truth.'

'A baby wouldn't have changed things.' With his gentle guidance Izzy's voice was finally adamant. 'Babies don't fix a damaged marriage. That was why I had to leave. I can't even begin to imagine us together as parents. A baby should come from love...'

'Do you want me to call Diego for you?' Josh said, but Izzy shook her head.

'He's already been to visit,' Izzy said. 'He's on a night shift tonight. I can't ring him for every little thing.'

'Yes,' a voice said from the doorway, 'you can.' There stood Diego, but only for a moment, and she dropped Josh's hand as he walked over.

'I'll leave you to it.' Josh smiled and stood up. 'Now,

remember, if there's anything we can do, you just pick up that phone. Even if it's just a decent coffee, you've got a whole team behind you twenty-four seven. Just let us know.'

Izzy thanked him, but she sat there blushing as he left and waited till the door was closed.

'Nothing was happening.' Izzy was awash with guilt. 'I was just upset, so he held my hand—'

'Izzy!' Diego interrupted. 'I'm glad Josh was here, I'm glad you had someone to hold your hand.'

Yet she still felt more explanation was needed. 'Henry would have had a fit if he'd—'

'Izzy! I'm not Henry—I don't care how many times I have to say it—I'm nothing like him.'

And he wasn't.

She leant on his broad chest and heard the regular beat of his heart, felt the safe wall of his chest and the wrap of his arms, and if she didn't love her so, it would be so easy to resent her baby—because nine weeks of just them would have been so very nice.

'I'd better go.' Reluctantly he stood up. 'I'll drop by in the morning and let you know what sort of night she had.'

'Tilia,' Izzy said.

'Tilia,' Diego repeated, and a smile spread over his face. 'I like it. What does it mean?'

'It's actually a tree…' Izzy's eyes never left his face, because somehow his reaction was important. 'I'm only telling you this—my mum would freak and I can't have a proper conversation with Henry's parents. It's a lime tree. Henry proposed under this gorgeous old lime tree…' Still he just looked. 'We were happy then.'

'I think it's wonderful,' Diego said. 'And one day,

Izzy, you'll be able to talk about him to Tilia, and tell her about those good times.' He gave her a kiss and headed for work, and Izzy lay back on the pillow and even though he'd said everything right, she still couldn't settle.

She looked at new photos of herself holding Tilia and she didn't see the drips or tubes, she just saw her baby.

And there in one photo was a side view of Diego.

The three of them together, except he wasn't kneeling down with his arms around her.

She couldn't imagine these past weeks without him.

Yet she was too scared to indulge in a glimpse of a future with him.

She kept waiting for the axe to fall—sure, quite sure that something this good could never last.

A midwife took her drip down and turned off the lights but the room was still bright thanks to the full moon bathing St Piran's, and while Izzy couldn't get to sleep, Diego on the other hand would have loved to because between visiting Izzy and working he still hadn't caught up from Tilia's rapid arrival.

It was a busy night that kept him at the nurses' station rather than the shop floor, where Diego preferred to be.

And, worse, from the computer he could hear her crying.

He glanced up and Brianna was checking a drug with another nurse working at the next cot, and Diego could hear Tilia crying. Brianna must have asked the other nurse for an opinion on something, because they were reading through the obs sheet. It was *normal* for babies to cry—he barely even heard it, so why did he stand up and head over?

'Brianna.' He jerked his head to Tilia's cot and he wished he hadn't, knew he was doing something he never would have done previously. If a baby was crying it was breathing was the mantra when matters where pressing. But Brianna didn't seem worried at his snap. Actually, she was more discreet than anyone he had ever met, but he could have sworn he saw her lips suppress a smile.

And as for Josh, well, as tired as he might be, bed was the last thing he wanted.

He'd visited Izzy when really he hadn't had to. Ben had actually asked for him to drop in over the next couple of days, but Josh had convinced himself that it was his duty to go after his shift.

Then, having visited her, he had hung around till someone had made some joke about him not having a home to go to, so eventually he'd headed there, but had stopped at the garage first.

As he pulled up at the smart gated community and the gates opened, Josh checked his pager and knew in his heart of hearts he was hoping against hope for something urgent to call him in.

God, had it really come to this, sitting in his driveway, steeling himself to go inside?

Izzy's words rang in his ears.

'A baby wouldn't have changed things… Babies don't fix a damaged marriage… I can't even begin to imagine us together as parents… A baby should come from love…'

There *had* been love between him and Rebecca.

A different sort of love, though, not the intense,

dangerous love he had once briefly known. That had been a love so consuming that it had bulldozed everything in its path. He closed his eyes and leant back on the headrest and for the first time in years he fully let himself visit that time.

Felt the grief and the agony, but it was too painful to recall so instead he dwelt on the consequences of raw love—a love that ruined lives and could destroy plans, a love that had threatened his rapid ascent in his career.

His and Rebecca's love had been different—safer certainly.

She wanted a successful doctor—*that* he could provide.

They had been good for each other, had wanted the same, at least for a while.

Josh could see her shadow behind the blinds, see her earrings, her jewellery, the skimpy outlines of her nightdress that left nothing to the imagination, and knew what Rebecca wanted from him tonight.

And he also knew that it wasn't about him.

'At least I'll have something to show for four years of marriage…' He recalled the harsh words of their latest row and then watched as she poured herself a drink from the decanter. He felt a stab of sympathy as he realised that Rebecca needed a bit of Dutch courage to go through with tonight.

Maybe he should get a vasectomy without her knowing, but what sort of coward, or husband, did that? Josh reeled at his own thought.

So he checked his pocket for his purchase from the garage, because he couldn't face her tears from another rejection. They hadn't slept together in weeks, not since…

Josh slammed that door in his mind closed, simply refused to go there, and tried very hard not to cloud the issue. In truth his and Rebecca's marriage had been well into injury time long before they had come to St Piran.

He went to pocket the condoms, to have them conveniently to hand, because no doubt Rebecca would ensure they never made it up the stairs and he knew for a fact she'd stopped taking the Pill.

'What the hell am I doing?' he groaned.

Yes, it would be so much easier to go in and make love.

Easier in the short term perhaps to give her the baby Rebecca said she wanted.

But since when had Josh chosen the easy path?

He tossed the condoms back into the glove box, a guarantee of sorts that he wouldn't give in and take the easy way out.

There was a conversation that needed to take place and, no matter how painful, it really was time.

They owed each other that at least.

Taking a breath, he walked up the neat path of his low-maintenance garden, waved to his neighbours, who were sipping wine on their little balcony and watching the world go by.

'Beautiful night, Josh.'

'It's grand, isn't it?' Josh agreed, and turned the key and stepped inside.

To the world, to his neighbours, the dashing doctor was coming home after a hellishly long day to his wonderful smart home and into the loving arms of his beautiful trophy wife.

* * *

It *was* a beautiful night.

The moon was big and round and it just accentuated the chaos as Evelyn Harris surveyed the ruin of her kitchen, plates smashed and broken, her ribs bruised and tender, the taste of blood in her mouth. She heard her husband snoring upstairs in bed.

She picked up the phone and not for the first time wondered about calling Izzy—but would the doctor even remember her? Surely it was too late to ring at this hour, and her son had an exam in the morning and she had lunch with John's boss's wife to get through, so she put down the phone and chose to sleep on the plush leather sofa.

Izzy was right.

Nobody *did* know what went on behind closed doors.

CHAPTER ELEVEN

'SHE's a tough little one.'

Like her mother, Diego thought.

Tilia, though small for dates and premature, was also incredibly active and strong. She had only required a short time on CPAP and was doing well on oxygen.

It really was a case of better out than in—now she could gain weight and as was often the case with babies who had been deprived nutrition *in utero*, Tilia's forehead often creased in concern as if she was constantly worried as to where her next meal was coming from.

'She wants her mum.' Brianna could not get Tilia to settle. 'I might ring Maternity and see if Izzy's still awake, she might get a nice cuddle. Then I'm going to have my coffee break. Could you watch mine for a moment while I call?'

They often rang Maternity, especially when babies were active and if there was a nurse who could bring the mother over—well, the middle of the night was a nice time to sit in rocking chair and bond a little. But when Diego had left Izzy she had been drained and exhausted and she could really use a full night's sleep—not that he was going to say that to Brianna. The gossip was already flying around the hospital since their appearance at the ball—had a certain little lady not put in such an early appearance, they might have been old news now, but given the turn of events and that Diego had been in the labour ward and was up twice day visiting on Maternity, he felt as if all eyes were on them. The scrutiny was just too fierce and strong at such a fragile time.

He was actually more than glad to be on nights, away from Rita's probing, and he had deliberately allocated Brianna to care for Tilia.

Brianna was one of the most private people Diego had met. She said nothing about her private life. She was there to work and work she did, loving and caring for her charges—gossip the last thing she was interested in.

'They've given Izzy a sleeping tablet,' Brianna said when she came back. 'Never mind, little lady, I'll give you a cuddle.'

'You go and have your break,' Diego said. 'I'll sort her.'

He didn't want to be doing this.

Or had he engineered it?

Diego didn't want to examine his feelings. Brianna was long overdue her coffee break, it was as simple as that. So he washed his hands in his usual thorough manner, put on a gown and then unclipped the sides of the incubator.

Often, so very often he did this—soothed a restless baby, or took over care while one of his team took their break.

And tonight it would be far safer to remember that.

He would sit and get this baby settled and perhaps chat with another nurse as he did so, or watch the ward from a chair.

He sat and expertly held Tilia, spoke as he always did to his charges—joking that he would teach her a little Spanish.

Which he did.

Then Chris, another of the nurses on duty that night, came over and asked him to run his eyes over a drug.

Which he did.

And then he felt something he hadn't in more than a decade.

Something he had tried never to feel since Fernando.

He adored his babies, but they weren't *his* to love.

He had loved Fernando, had held him three times in his little life, and it had never come close since.

But holding Tilia, it came close.

Dangerously close.

She wasn't a patient and she wasn't his new girlfriend's baby.

She was Tilia.

Izzy's baby.

But more than that.

He smelt that unmistakable baby smell that surrounded him each day but which he never noticed, he looked into huge eyes that were the same shape as her mother's and she had the same shape mouth. Even her nostrils were the same.

And there, sitting with all the hissing and bleeping and noise that was a busy neonatal unit, Diego, felt a stab of dread.

That he might lose her too.

He looked over to where Toby's mother had come in, restless and unable to sleep, for just one more check on her son, and he knew how she felt—how many times in the night at eighteen he had woken with a sudden shock of fright and rushed to check on Fernando, asking the nurses to check and check again, petrified that they had missed something, but it wasn't that fear that gripped him as he held Tilia.

'You're going to be fine,' Diego said to Tilia in Spanish. 'You're going to be clever and grow healthy and strong...'

Only would he be around to see it?

'And your mother's getting stronger each day too,' Diego went on. 'Just watch her grow too.'

He wanted that for Izzy. He vowed as he sat there, holding her baby while she could not, that he would help Izzy grow, would do everything to encourage her, even if that meant that she grew away from him.

How could he let himself fall in love with this little babe when who knew what her mother might want days, weeks or months from now? When who knew what he might want?

Diego ran a finger down her little cheek.

But how could he not?

Staying in the parents' wing had been the right choice.

It was a precious time, one where she caught up on all she had missed out on, one where there was nothing to focus on other than her baby.

Always Diego was friendly, professional, calm, except for the visits before or after her shift, when he was friendly and calm but he dropped the professional for tender, but there was never any pressure, no demands for her time. Now, as Tilia hit four weeks, the world outside was starting to creep back in and for the first time since her daughter's birth, Izzy truly assessed the situation, wondering, fearing that it was as she had suspected—that her daughter's birth had changed everything for them, that his lack of demands meant a lack of passion.

A soft rap at her door at six-thirty a.m. didn't wake her. She'd been up and fed Tilia and had had her shower, and often Diego popped in at this time if he was on an early shift, bearing two cups of decent coffee and, this morning, two croissants.

'She went the whole night without oxygen.' Izzy beamed.

'We'll be asking her to leave if she carries on like this!' Diego joked, and though Izzy smiled and they chatted easily, when he left a familiar flutter took place in her stomach. Tilia was doing well, really well, and though at first the doctors had warned it could be several weeks before her discharge, just four short weeks on Tilia was defying everyone—putting on weight, managing the occasional bottle, and now a whole night without oxygen and no de-sats. Discharge day would be coming soon, Izzy knew, but if Tilia was ready, Izzy wasn't so sure she was.

Diego was working the floor today. Once a week he left his office and insisted on doing the job he adored. From nine a.m. he was working in Theatre with a multiple birth and a baby with a cardiac defect scheduled for delivery. The unit was expecting a lot of new arrivals, and it fell to him to tell the mother of a thriving thirty-five-weeker that her room would be needed in a couple of days.

He'd stretched it to the limit, of course.

Not just because it was Izzy, not just that she was a doctor at this hospital, but with all she had been through, he would have done his best for any woman in that situation—though he waited till he was working to tell her.

'She won't take it.' Izzy was in the nursery, feeding her daughter, jiggling the teat in Tilia's slack mouth. 'She took the last one really well...'

He tickled her little feet and held his hand over Izzy's and pushed the teat in a bit more firmly, tried to stimulate the baby to suck, but Tilia was having none of it, her little eyelids flickering as she drifted deeper into sleep. Izzy actually laughed as she gave in.

'She's not going to take it.' There was no panic in her voice, Diego noted. Izzy was a pretty amazing mum. Often with doctors or nurses they were more anxious than most new parents and even though he'd expected that from Izzy, she'd surprised him. She revelled in her new motherhood role and was far more relaxed than most.

'They're like teenagers,' Diego said, 'party all night, and sleep all day. That last feed would have exhausted her.'

Chris, one of the nurses, came over and saw the full bottle, and because Tilia was so small and needed her calories, she suggested they tube-feed her, and Izzy went to stand to help.

'Actually, Chris, I need a word with Izzy.'

'Sure.' Chris took Tilia and Izzy sat, frowning just a little, worried what was to come because Diego, when at work, never brought his problems to the shop floor.

'Is she okay?' Her first thought was something had been said on the ward round that morning and he was about to give her bad news.

'She's wonderful,' Diego assured her. 'So wonderful,

in fact, that I need your room for some parents we are getting whose baby will not be doing so well.'

'Oh.'

'I know it seems pretty empty over in the parents' wing at the moment, but I'm getting some transfers from other hospitals today, and I have some mothers in Maternity now needing accommodation too. You don't need to leave today...'

'But it would help?'

'It would,' Diego admitted. Normally they gave more notice, but Izzy had been told last week that if the room was needed, given her close proximity to the hospital and Tilia's improving status, she was top of the list to leave if required. Izzy had been happy with that. Well, till the inevitable happened.

How could she tell Diego that she didn't want to go home?

More than that, she had never wanted to bring her baby back to the home she had shared with Henry.

'Izzy!' Rita was at the nursery door. 'You've got visitors. Mr and Mrs Bailey, Tilia's grandparents...'

He saw her lips tense and then stretch out into a smile and he'd have given anything not to be on duty now, to just be here with her as she faced all this, but Diego knew it would surly only make things worse. So instead he stood, smiled as he would at any other relatives and said to Izzy, 'I'll leave you to it.' Just as he would to any of the mums—except he knew so much more.

'Could I have a word, Doctor?' Mr. Bailey followed him out.

'I'm not a doctor; I'm the nurse unit manager. Is there anything I can help you with?'

Up shot the eyebrows, just as Diego expected. 'I'd

prefer to speak to a doctor,' Mr Bailey said. 'You see, we're not getting enough information from Izzy. She just says that Tilia is doing well and as her grandparents we have a right to know more.'

'Tilia *is* doing well,' Diego said. 'We're very pleased with her progress.'

'I'm not sure if you're aware of the circumstances. Our beloved son passed away and Izzy is doing her level best to keep us out of the picture. Tilia's extremely precious to us and we will not be shut out.'

And at that moment all Diego felt was tired for Izzy.

'I'd really prefer to speak with a doctor.'

Which suited Diego fine. 'I'll just check with Izzy and then I can page—'

'Why would you check with her? I've already told you that she's doing her level best to keep us misinformed. I know she seems quite pleasant, but she's a manipulative—'

'Mr Bailey.' Diego halted him—oh, there were many things, so many things he would have loved to have said, but he was far better than that. 'I will first speak to Tilia's mother. Let's see what she says and then we can take it from there.'

Of course she said yes.

Diego looked over when Richard agreed to speak to them and could see Izzy sitting by Tilia, looking bemused and bewildered, and if he'd done his level best to keep work and his private life separate, right now he didn't care.

'They don't trust me to tell them everything!' Izzy blew her fringe upwards. 'They're annoyed I waited two days to ring them after she was born...'

'They're just scared you'll keep them from seeing her.'

'Well, they're going the right way about it!' Izzy shot back, but Diego shook his head.

'Don't go there, Izzy.'

'I won't!' Izzy said, but she was exasperated. 'They've been in every day, I've dressed her in the outfits they've bought, I text them a photo of her each night. What more do they want?'

'Time,' Diego said. 'And so do we.' He glanced over to make sure no one was in earshot 'Do you want to come to my place tonight?' He saw her swallow. 'I'm closer to the hospital. If it makes the transition easier…'

'Just for tonight,' Izzy said, because she didn't want to foist herself on him, but she couldn't stand to be alone at the house on her first night away from Tilia.

'Sure.'

He got called away then, and Izzy sat there awash with relief, grateful for the reprieve, until it dawned on her.

She was staying the night with Diego.

How the hell could she have overlooked that?

CHAPTER TWELVE

SHE felt incredibly gauche, knocking at his door that evening. 'Where did you disappear to?' he asked as he let her in. 'I wasn't sure if you were coming.'

'I got a taxi and took my stuff home,' Izzy said airily, because she certainly wasn't going to admit she'd spent the afternoon in the bathroom—trying and failing to whip her postnatal body into suitable shape for Diego's eyes. 'By the time I got back for her evening feed, your shift had ended.'

'You've got hospital colour!' Diego smiled as she stood in the lounge. 'I never noticed it on the ward but now you are here in the real world, I can see it.'

There was a distinct lack of mirrors in Diego's flat, so Izzy would just have to take his word for it, but she was quite sure he was right. Apart from an occasional walk around the hospital grounds, a few very brief trips home and one trip out with Megan, she'd been living under fluorescent lighting and breathing hospital air, and no doubt her skin had that sallow tinge that patients often had when they were discharged after a long stay.

'Have a seat out on the balcony,' Diego suggested. 'Get some sun. I'll join you in a minute.'

It *was* good to sit in the evening sun. Izzy could feel

it warming her cheeks and she drank in the delicious view—the moored boats and a few making their way back in. There was no place nicer than St Piran on a rosy summer evening, made nicer when Diego pressed a nice cold glass of champagne in her hand.

'One of the joys of bottle-feeding!' Diego said, because Izzy's milk supply had died out two weeks in.

And then he was back to his kitchen and Izzy could only sit and smile.

He was such a delicious mix.

So male, so sexy, yet there was this side to him that could address, without a hint of a blush or a bat of an eyelid, things that most men knew little about.

'How does it feel to be free?' Diego called from the kitchen as she picked a couple of tomatoes out of the pots that lined his balcony.

'Strange,' Izzy called, but he was already back. 'I keep waiting for my little pager to go off to let me know she needs feeding. I feel guilty, actually.'

'It's good to have a break before you bring her home.'

'Most new mums don't get it.'

'Most new mums have those extra weeks to prepare,' Diego said, arranging some roasted Camembert cheese and breadsticks on the table, which Izzy fell on, scooping up the sticky warm goo with a large piece of bread.

'I've been craving this,' Izzy said. 'How did you know?'

'Tonight, you get everything that has been forbidden to you in pregnancy, well, almost everything. Some things can wait!' Diego said, as Izzy's toes curled in her sandals. His grin was lazy and slow and she hated how he never blushed, hated that her cheeks were surely scarlet. God, she'd forgotten how they sizzled, Izzy thought as he headed back to prepare dinner.

There *were* so many sides to Diego and recently she'd been grateful for the professional side to him and for the care he had shown off duty too, but she was in his territory now, not pregnant, not a patient, not a parent on the unit. Tonight she was just Izzy, whoever Izzy was.

And that night she started to remember.

'You can cook!' Izzy exclaimed as he brought a feast out to her—shellfish, mussels, oysters, prawns and cream cheese wrapped in roast peppers, and all the stuff she'd craved in the last few weeks of her pregnancy.

'Not really. You could train a monkey to cook seafood.' Diego shrugged. 'And the antipasto is from our favourite café...'

She didn't know if it was the champagne or the company, but talking to Diego was always easy so she figured it was the latter. They talked, and as the sky turned to navy they laughed and they talked, and more and more she came back.

Not even Izzy Bailey, but a younger Izzy, an Izzy Ross, who she had stifled and buried and forgotten.

Izzy Ross, who teased and joked and did things like lean back in her seat and put her feet up on his thighs, Izzy Ross, who expected a foot rub and Diego obliged.

But it was Izzy Bailey who was convinced things were all about to change.

'So, what did the real estate agent say?'

'That it's a good offer!' Izzy poked out her tongue. 'It's not, of course, but it's better than the last one, though they want a quick settlement.'

'Which is what you wanted?'

'When I was pregnant and hoping to find somewhere before she was born.' She looked at him. 'In a few days she'll be home,' Izzy said, 'and as well as having a baby home, I'm going to have to pack up a house and find a new one, and I'm going to have to find a babysitter just so we can *date*.' Her voice wobbled. 'We haven't even slept together and we're talking nappies and babysitters...'

He had the audacity to laugh.

'It's not funny, Diego.'

'You're making problems where there are none. Sex is hardly going to be a problem.'

God, he was so relaxed and assured about it, like it was a given it was going to be marvellous.

The icing on the cake.

'Come on.' He stood up.

'Where are we going?'

'The movies and then there's a nice wine bar, they do music till late...'

'I don't want to go to the movies!' Izzy couldn't believe Mr Sensitive could get it so wrong. 'And if you think I've got the energy to be sitting in a wine bar...'

'I thought you wanted us to date!'

'Ha, ha.'

'Izzy, you need time with your baby and that's the priority. I'll slot in, and if it's an issue that we haven't slept together yet, well, we both know it's going to be great.'

'You don't know that.'

'Oh, I do.' Diego grinned. 'I'm looking forward to getting rid of your hang-ups.'

'Can you get rid of them tonight?'

And suddenly he didn't look so assured.

'It's too soon…'

'No,' Izzy said slowly. 'No heavy lifting, no strenuous exercise…'

'Do you want me, Izzy?' He was always direct and now never more so. 'Or do you just want it over?'

'I don't know,' Izzy admitted, and there should have been a big horn to denote she was giving the wrong answer, but she was incapable of dishonesty with him—or rather she didn't want to go down that route, saying the right thing just to keep *him* happy. She wanted the truth with Diego even if it wasn't what he wanted to hear.

'What are you scared of?'

'That I'll disappoint you,' she admitted. 'Because on so many levels I disappointed him.' She snapped her mouth closed. Diego had made it very clear that he didn't compare to Henry, which he didn't, but… She looked over to where he stood, tried to choose words that could explain her insecurities, but there were none that could do them justice. 'Things weren't great in that department,' she settled for, but Diego's frown just deepened. 'I know I was pregnant and so there must have been a relationship…' She swallowed. 'His parents take it as proof that our marriage was healthy, that…' She couldn't explain further and thankfully she didn't have to because Diego spoke.

'It would be nice,' Diego said slowly, 'if babies were only conceived in love…' There was silence that she didn't break as he thought for a moment. 'If there was some sort of…' Again he paused, trying to find the English for a word he hadn't used in his time in the country 'Cósmico, contraception.' It was Izzy who then frowned and she gave a small smile.

'Cosmic.'

'Cosmic contraception,' Diego continued, 'where no experimenting teenagers, no rape victims, no women in a terrible relationship who just go along with it to keep the peace...' His strange logic soothed some of the jagged parts of her mind. She liked his vision and it made her smile. 'Here's a happy couple,' Diego continued, 'said the sperm to the egg. You know it doesn't work like that.'

'People think...'

'People are stupid, then.' Diego would not let her go there, would not let her care what others thought. 'People choose to be ignorant rather than face unpleasant truths. You know what your marriage was like and you don't have to live it again, explaining details to me, to justify why you're pregnant. But I will say this.' For the first time his voice bordered on angry. 'If he expected a great sex life, if he was disappointed by your lack of enthusiasm in that department after the way he treated you, then he was the most stupid of them all.'

And he was so convincing that she was almost... convinced.

Almost.

But still the cloud of doubt hung over her and Diego could see it.

It had never been his intention to sleep with her tonight.

For her to stay was a hope, but sex—hell, wasn't that supposed to be the last thing on her mind?

Wasn't it too soon?

And he liked straightforward, only this was anything but.

But he looked over to where she sat, not in the least

offended that she wanted it over with, another thing to tick off her list as she moved on with her life. And again it wasn't a time for arrogance or feigned modesty. He knew he was good, knew he could make her happy—and wasn't happy part of their deal?

'I'll sleep with you on one condition.'

Why did he always make her smile?

'That you never fake it for me.'

'Or you.'

'Er, Izzy,' he said, and that made her blush and give an embarrassed laugh.

'I mean, don't pretend afterwards that it's okay, just so you don't upset me.'

Diego rolled his eyes, but he was smiling now too. 'The talking doesn't stop when we get to the bedroom. I can do both!'

And he knew then that they could talk about it for ever, but words could only reassure so far. This was so not what he had imagined for tonight. There was something almost clinical about it and yet Diego had so much confidence in her, in them, in all they were going to be, that if this was a hurdle for her, perhaps it was better to jump it.

He pulled her onto his lap, but his kisses weren't working. He could feel her trying, feel her doing her very best to relax, but he wouldn't put her through it. He pulled back his lips, looked into her eyes and feigned a martyred sigh 'Shall we just get this over with?'

She almost wept with relief.

'Please.'

'Ring the hospital.'

Which took away her little excuse to suddenly stop later. Diego was onto her, she realised.

So she rang and, no, Tilia didn't need her to come in.

Oh, God, what was she doing?

She felt as if she was walking into Theatre for surgery as he took her hand and they headed for the bedroom. Izzy half expected him to tell her to get undressed and pop on a gown and that he'd be back in five minutes.

Couldn't it happen more seamlessly?

Couldn't they just have had a kiss on the balcony and somehow ended up naked on his massive bed without the awkward bit in the middle? But that hadn't worked and Izzy realised she would have been faking it because she would know where it would lead, to this, the bit she was dreading, the part that was holding her back from moving on.

God, it was a room built for nothing but a bed. Izzy gulped.

Massive windows, floorboards and one very large, very low bed and not much else, bar a table that doubled as a washing basket.

'Where are your things?' Izzy would rather deal with basics than the bed.

'What things?'

'Alarm clock, books…' Her hands flailed. 'A mirror, a wardrobe…'

'Here's the wardrobe.'

Okay, there it was, hidden in the wall, but apart from that…

'Curtains?' Izzy begged.

'It looks out to the ocean,' Diego said, and to her horror he was stripping off. 'And I don't need an alarm clock—I wake at five.' He was unbuckling his belt, his top already off, stripping off like a professional and chatting about nothing as Izzy stood, champagne in hand, wishing she'd never started this.

'Five?'

'It's hell.' He pushed his denim jeans down past thick thighs as he explained his plight to a distracted audience. 'Even when the clocks change my brain knows and I wake up.'

Oh, God.

He wasn't *erect* erect, but he was erect enough that it was pointing at her—this conversation going on as this thing waggled and danced and she did her best not to look at it, tried to worry about windows and passing ships, but he was completely naked now.

'Are you always this uninhibited?'

'I've been undressing for bed for many years now,' Diego said, and then his voice was serious. 'Let's just start as we mean to go on.'

But would he want to go on afterwards?

'I've changed my mind,' Izzy said, in the hope of delaying the inevitable, so sure was she that when he found out just how hopeless she was, he wouldn't want her or, worse, would feel stuck with her.

'Why don't we just sleep together?' Diego suggested. 'Given it will probably be our one interrupted night for the foreseeable future.'

And though she wanted to turn and flee, he was right, Izzy realised, because as hellish as this was for her, next time there might be more than passing ships to worry about. There might be a baby in the room too!

'I forgot my phone…'

'Your phone?' Izzy said to his departing back, and as he spoke about staff ringing some nights if there was a problem, and he'd rather that… Izzy took the moment to get out of her clothes and under the sheet before he returned.

Just as Diego had expected her to do.

He didn't need his phone, of course.

And he was, in fact, nervous.

Just not for the same reasons as Izzy.

Diego liked sex.

Correction.

Diego *loved* sex.

And he liked relationships too, but short-term ones.

There was nothing short term about Izzy.

As he climbed into bed and turned and faced her, it was the sense of responsibility that unnerved him a touch.

Not just the obvious, not just Izzy and her baby, but a self-imposed responsibility towards Izzy, because in every area of her life she was getting it together, managing it herself, but for this part to be right she needed another, and she had trusted herself to him.

'Better?' Diego asked, and, yes, it was.

Much, much better, not because she was in the dark and under a sheet, just better because she was, for the first time, lying next to him and he was so solid and bulky and just him.

'In a few short weeks,' Diego said into the darkness, 'you'll be ripping your clothes off in the middle of the day and we'll be on the kitchen floor!'

'Your confidence is inspiring.'

'Oh, you will!' Diego said. 'Remember the bath?'

How could she forget?

'That just sort of happened.'

Izzy lived on her nerves.

Diego lived on instinct.

Instinct that told him his parents were wrong, that he'd do better by not following their chosen course for him.

Instinct that had told him over and over again that, despite neat numbers on a chart, a baby was struggling.

And instinct was all very well, but it got in the way sometimes.

Like now, when he knew he should be closing his eyes and trying to sleep, to let her come to him, a little problem arose.

Or rather quite a big problem that crept along the side of her thigh, nudging her like a puppy that wanted to be stroked.

'*Perdón*!' Diego said, and he would have moved away but he heard her sort of laugh and he wasn't a saint. She was right there next to him and naked and warm and he'd had to go and remind them both of that bath.

Yes, it was instinct that drove his lips to her neck, the hand that wasn't under her roaming her body a little and then, for Izzy, instinct overrode nerves.

His lips were soft but firm at the same time, kissing her, breathing onto her skin. Diego, a man who had only ever given, now wanting badly, and from his deep murmurs of approval as his hands slid to her breasts it was her that he wanted.

And she wanted a little more of him too.

She turned and faced him, so she could kiss him properly, not the nervous kiss about where this might lead she had endured on the balcony, but a bolder kiss, knowing where this might lead, in the bedroom.

He tasted of him, his tongue cool and lazy and then suddenly insistent and then back to lazy. He drove her wild with his mouth, because her body was at its own bidding now. Her thighs parted a little and captured him as they kissed, he could feel himself hard but smooth between the tender skin of her thighs, and she wanted him higher, her legs parting, only Diego wasn't rushing.

'I know where you were this afternoon…' His hand was there, exploring where she had shaved. 'Next time I'll do it.' And she felt this bubble of moisture at the very thought as his fingers slipped in and it felt divine.

'Condoms!' Izzy said, common sense prevailing, even if the last thing she wanted was him getting up and heading for the bathroom.

But this was Diego.

He sort of stretched over her and she felt his arm rummage in the dark beneath the bed and come up with the goods.

Oh, God, he was so male, so… She flailed for a word…basic.

It was the only one she could think of and it didn't really suit, but it was the best she could do.

And then he rolled off her and lay on his back and Izzy came up with another word.

Raw.

He didn't slip it on discreetly as he kissed her. No, he lay back and she watched, she actually propped up on her elbow and watched, this shiver inside as he gave himself two slow strokes, two long, slow strokes that had Izzy licking her lips and feeling suddenly contrary. This was something she had wanted over and done with, something she still wanted over and done with, except she was balling her fist not to reach out and touch him.

So she did.

Like warm silk he slid down her palm, the pulse of

him beneath her fingers, and she did it again and it felt so nice that she did it again, till his hand closed around hers and halted her.

'Aren't I doing it right?' said her old fears, and for a moment there was no reply.

'Izzy.' He paused again. 'Any more right and we won't need the condom.'

And then she got her seamless kiss, because that was what he did, he rolled over and kissed her, his tongue, his breath filling her mouth and his body over her and then the nudge of him between her legs.

And she was scared, but she wanted him.

Like hating flying and preparing for take-off, wanting just to get there, except there's a slight delay in departure and cabin crew are bringing round drinks and you taste your first Singapore sling.

Oh, my!

He was slow and tender and, yes, she was ready, and it had little to do with nerves that he had to squeeze inside. Izzy screwed her eyes closed, told herself to breathe as her body stretched to greet him, the slow fill of him more than she could accommodate, except slowly she did.

And then she breathed out as he slid out, right to the tip and she braced herself for him to fill her again, which he did.

And then again and each time she had to remember to breathe.

His elbows held most of his weight, his rough chin was on her cheek and his breath tickled at her ear, and suddenly Izzy remembered where she was and it wasn't happening so easily. She knew she should be a touch more enthusiastic, but she was a mother now and surely sensible, so she made the right noises and lifted her hips and would have settled for his pleasure, except Diego had other ideas.

He smothered her feigned gasps with his mouth and offered her more weight, wrapping his arms around her, kissing her, not harder but deeper, and she remembered his demand that she not fake it. So she lay there and let herself just feel him—lay there as he kissed her eyes and then her cheeks and then she felt the shift in him, the kissing stopping, his heavier weight and the ragged breathing in her ear, and she forgot where she was again, forgot about rather a lot of things, just the delicious feel of him, and the scratch of his jaw and the stirrings of the orgasm he had given her before. Then she found that she *was* making noises now, but of her body's own accord, and as he bucked deep inside her, she did something she would never have envisaged from this night.

'Not yet.'

She was too deep into herself to wonder at the transition to voicing her wants, her real wants, but Diego recognised it and it gave a surge of pleasure that almost tipped him over. He would have waited for this for ever, yet now was struggling to wait another minute, but for Izzy he did.

He could feel her pleasure and it was his.

Both locked in a dance that moved faster than them.

'Not yet!' She was in another place and he could hear her calling and he chased her, he was holding back and driving harder, he could hear her moans, feel the surge in her that was akin to panic, but he knew her body too, could feel her body tight around him, feel her trip and he just knew.

Knew she needed all of him before she could give that bit more.

Her words were futile, Izzy realised, because Diego was moving at a different speed now, reaching for the finish line with a surge of energy that had her breathless.

She could hear her name, feel the unbridled passion and just the sheer strength of him as he thrust inside her. And she stopped trying then, stopped trying to chase or catch him, she just felt the moment.

Felt him over her, in her and his arms behind her, she could hear her name, taste his skin, and then it was his name she heard her voice calling, his name said in a tone she didn't recognise, then a shout of surprise as she let go.

Her thighs were shaking and her hips pushing up against his, her hands digging into his back, and deep inside she trembled as Diego pulsed into her.

And most delicious of all, it didn't matter that she was a teeny bit late for the party, she was there, she had made it, her late entrance dazzling, because he got to feel every beat of it as he delivered those last emptying strokes and instinct had served him well.

As he felt her crash and burn beneath him, as he tried to get his head out of white light and back to the dark, he knew he had just met the real Izzy.

'Tell me again,' Diego said, when he could get the words out, 'what exactly your hang-ups are.'

CHAPTER THIRTEEN

'SHE'S fine!' a night nurse greeted her as Izzy dashed in at seven a.m.

She'd given Diego a fifteen-minute head start so they didn't arrive together and it seemed to take ages for the intercom to answer when she buzzed, because the staff were all in handover.

Izzy felt guilty with pleasure and was sure there must be a penance to pay for having such a wonderful night, except Tilia was fine—completely adorable and wide awake. Chris, her nurse for the day, informed Izzy when she came out of handover that Tilia might even be ready for her first bath.

Izzy was glad to have Chris beside her, encouraging her.

Tilia seemed so small and slippery and she wouldn't stop crying.

'I thought they liked their bath,' Izzy said.

'Just rock her a little.'

Which Izzy did, and Tilia's cries softened.

Her tufts of hair were shampooed and by the time Izzy had dried and dressed her, it was all sticking up and Izzy thought her heart would burst as she sat in the rocking chair and held her.

'How soon do you think?' Izzy asked the perpetual question.

'When she's taking all her feeds and just a bit bigger,' Chris said. 'She's doing so well. I know you're impatient to get her home, but she still needs top-ups and a little one like this...' She took an exhausted Tilia from Izzy and popped her in her cot then put the saturation probe on her, checked her obs and popped a little hat on. 'Even a bath wears them out. Why don't you go down to the canteen and get some breakfast?' Chris suggested, rightly guessing that Izzy hadn't eaten.

'Good idea,' Izzy agreed. 'I'll go and see if Nicola wants to come down with me.'

'Actually,' Chris said gently, 'maybe it's best if you leave Nicola for now.'

'Oh!' Izzy waited for more information, only she wasn't a doctor on duty here and there was no information forthcoming. 'I'll be at the canteen, then,' Izzy said. 'I've got my pager.'

She walked through the unit, her eyes drawn to Toby's cot. There was Nicola and her husband, and Diego was sitting with them. His face was more serious than she had ever seen it and Izzy felt sick as Megan came into the unit and instead of waving to Izzy just gave a very brief nod and headed over to them.

It was the longest morning.

Tilia awoke at eleven but wouldn't take her bottle and Izzy came close to crying, except she shook her head when Chris passed her a box of tissues.

'You are allowed to cry.'

But it seemed so petty. Tilia was thriving, okay, a little slower than Izzy would like, but she was getting bigger and stronger every day and, anyway, Izzy knew, there was a lot more to cry over than that—and now just wasn't the time to.

'Hey, where's Chris?' Diego gave her a tired smile as he came in later to get an update.

'Two minutes,' Chris called from the sinks, where she was helping another mum with a bath.

'How are you?' Diego asked.

'Good.'

'Tilia?'

'Misbehaving—she won't take her feeds.'

'She had a bath, though,' Diego said, but she could tell he was distracted and who could blame him?

'How's Toby?'

'He's not good,' Diego said. 'I know you helped deliver him.' He was walking a fine line. 'We can talk another time.'

'Sure.'

'Two more minutes!' Chris called again.

'I'm going to be working late tonight.' His voice was low. 'I can give you a key if you want…'

'I might go home tonight,' Izzy said, hoping he wouldn't take up her offer of an out. 'I'm really tired and you're working…'

Except he took it. 'Sure.'

And then Chris was walking over, ready to bring Diego up to date with her charges, and Izzy didn't see him again apart from the back of his shoulders for the rest of the day.

And that night, when she sat at home, she told herself she was being ridiculous—he was working late, he had every reason to be sombre, and she had been the one to say she'd prefer to go home, but, just as a mother could often pin-point the moment their child became sick long before the doctors were concerned even when the child itself said it was well, Izzy could sense change.

Even as she tried to leave the past where it belonged, she could sense a shift, could sense a black cloud forming, and it had hovered over Diego today.

'Neonatal Unit—Diego speaking.'

'It's me.' Izzy hadn't really expected him to answer the phone. It was edging towards ten p.m., which meant he had done a double shift. 'I was just ringing to check up on Tilia.'

'She's had a good night so far, I think,' Diego said. 'I'll just have a word with the nurse who's looking after her.' And she sat there and held her breath as he did what all the nursing staff did when a mother rang at night to check on their baby. She could even hear his voice in the background and Izzy held her breath as he came to the phone. 'She's settled and she's taken her bottle. You can relax, she's having a good night.'

'Thank you.'

He said goodnight, he was lovely and kind, but he was Nurse Unit Manager and that was all.

Something had changed.

Izzy just knew it.

The phone rang again and Izzy pounced on it, sure it was Diego, only it wasn't, and she frowned at the vaguely familiar voice. 'I'm sorry to trouble you. It's just that you gave me your number. You're the only one who seemed to understand it's not as simple as just leaving...'

'Evelyn?'

'I can't go on like this.'

'Evelyn.' Izzy kept her voice calmer than she felt. 'Where are you now?'

'I'm at home. He's at the pub...' Even if she wanted

to dwell on Diego or Tilia, or to just go to bed, Izzy
pushed it aside and listened. So badly she wanted to
tell Evelyn to get out, to just pack her bags and go, but
Izzy remembered how she had rushed it last time, knew
that it was good Evelyn was taking this small step, so,
instead of jumping in and fixing, Izzy bit her tongue
and just listened, learning fast that sometimes it was
the best you could do.

'Are you okay?' Izzy was quite sure Megan wasn't.
She had come and sat with her in the canteen and Izzy
could tell she'd been crying, but, then, so had a lot of
people.

Toby had passed away last night and both Diego and
Megan, Izzy had heard from another mother, had stayed
till the end.

'I've been better,' Megan admitted. 'All I put that
baby through and the parents too—and for what?'

'Don't,' Izzy said, because they'd had these conversations before. Megan set impossible standards for herself, wanted to save each and every baby, and took it
right to her heart when nature chose otherwise. 'Look
at Genevieve!' Izzy said.

'I know.' Megan blew out a breath. 'This really got
to me, though, and Diego—he doesn't normally get
upset, but I guess finding out his dad's so sick...' Her
voice trailed off, realising she was being indiscreet. 'I
shouldn't have said that.'

'I'm not going to tell him.' Izzy felt her throat tighten.
It was such a tightrope—they were all friends, all colleagues, all different things to each other. 'What's wrong
with him?'

Megan screwed her eyes closed. 'Izzy, please don't.'

'Just because I've had a baby it doesn't mean my

brain's softened. Nobody would tell me anything about Toby, forgetting the fact I delivered him, and now I'm not supposed to be told Diego's father's sick. I knew there was something wrong last night.'

'He probably doesn't want to worry you.'

'Well, I am worried,' Izzy said. 'Is it bad?'

Reluctantly Megan nodded but no more information was forthcoming and Izzy sat quietly for a moment with her thoughts. 'I've had an offer on the house,' Izzy said, 'but they want a quick settlement. Thirty days.'

'Ouch!' Megan said. 'Will you be able to find somewhere?'

'Probably.'

'What about your mum's?' Megan managed a smile at Izzy's reaction. 'Okay, bad idea.'

'I think I should be concentrating on Tilia, not trying to find somewhere to live.'

'There's always Diego's,' Megan teased, adding when she saw Izzy close her eyes, 'I was joking—I know it's way too soon to even be thinking—'

'But I do,' Izzy admitted, and Megan's eyes widened.

'You hardly know each other.'

'I know that.' Izzy nodded. 'I can't stand being in the house, but I think it's best for now…' She was trying to be practical, logical, sensible. 'I don't want to force any decisions on us.' She looked at her friend. 'I'm trying to hold onto my heart here. I'm trying to just be in the now with him, but practically the day I met him I was knocked sideways. I felt it, this connection, this chemistry.' She looked at Megan, who was frowning. 'Sounds crazy, doesn't it?'

'No.' Megan swallowed and then her voice was urgent. 'Don't sell your house.' Megan, who normally was happy to sit and just listen, was practically hopping in her seat to give advice. 'Izzy, Diego's lovely and everything…' She was struggling to give the right advice, tempted to tell Izzy to turn tail and run because she'd felt that way once too and look where it had left her. Love had swept in for Megan and left a trail of devastation that all these years on she was still struggling to come to terms with—pain so real that she still woke some nights in tears, still lived with the consequences and would till the day she left the earth. 'Be careful, Izzy,' Megan said, even if wasn't the advice Izzy wanted. 'Maybe you should have some time on your own. At least, don't rush into anything with Diego—you've got Tilia to think of. Diego's father's sick, he could just up and go to Spain…' And then Megan stopped herself, saw Izzy's stunned expression and realised she had been too harsh, realised perhaps she was talking more about herself than her friend.

'Izzy, don't listen to me,' Megan begged. 'Who am I to give advice? I haven't been in a relationship in ages, I'm married to my career.' Megan swallowed. 'And I don't have a child. I'm the last person to tell you what you should be doing. Maybe speak to Jess…' She was close to tears and feeling wretched. The last thing Megan had wanted to do was project her own bitterness onto Izzy, especially at such a vulnerable time, but the last few weeks had been hell for Megan—sheer hell. Since Josh had come to work at St Piran's she was struggling to even think straight. 'Maybe you should talk to Jess,' Megan said again as her pager went off, summoning her to the children's ward. She gave her friend's hand a squeeze. 'You'll make the right choice.' She turned to leave, but there he was, right there in front of her.

'Megan…' Josh said. 'Did you get my message?'

She went to walk on, but Josh was insistent.

'Megan, we need to talk—there are things we need to discuss.' He caught her wrist and Megan looked at his hand around hers, their first physical contact in years, and she couldn't stand it because it was there, the chemistry, the reaction, her skin leaping at the memory of him, and it terrified her—it truly terrified her. She shook him off.

'There's nothing to discuss,' Megan said.

'There's plenty,' Josh insisted, and she felt herself waver, because there *was* so much to discuss but, worse, she knew that he felt her waver, knew they were still in sync. 'Not here,' Josh said, because heads in the corridor were turning.

Megan grappled for control of her mind, held onto the pain he had caused as if it were a liferaft, because if she forgot for a moment she would sink back into his charm.

And she remembered more, enough for a sneer to curl her lips.

Then she let herself remember just a little bit more, enough to force harsh words from her lips.

'Where, then, Josh?' Megan spat. 'Where should we meet?' She watched as he ran a tongue over his lips, knew then he hadn't thought this out, perhaps hadn't expected her to agree. 'There's a nice restaurant on the foreshore,' she sneered. 'Oh, but we might be seen!' she jeered. 'How about Penhally, or is that too close? Maybe you could pop over to mine…' She was blind with rage now, shaking just to stop herself from shouting. 'You're married, Josh, so, no, we can't meet. You're a married man.' If she said it again, maybe if she said it enough times, she would come to accept it. 'Which means there is absolutely nothing to discuss.'

And she remembered some more then, not all of it, because that would be too cruel to herself, but Megan remembered just enough of what she had been through to make the only sensible choice—to turn on her heel and walk quickly away.

She wasn't upset that he hadn't told her about his father.

In truth, Izzy knew he hadn't had a chance. Her dad had been over the last two nights trying to get the spare room ready for Tilia, who had, after twelve hours of not taking a drop from the bottle, awoken from her slumber and had taken her feeds like a dream. Now on the eve of her discharge, they were scrambling to find two minutes alone.

She was sitting in the nursery, feeding Tilia her bottle, Brianna was on her break and Diego was doing Tilia's obs.

'Do you want me to come over tonight?' Diego offered. 'Help you get everything ready for tomorrow?'

'My mum's coming,' Izzy said, but right now she didn't care about her mother's reaction. 'I could cancel, tell her why perhaps…about us.'

'I think…' she sensed his reluctance '…you should wait till Tilia is no longer a patient.'

He was right, of course he was right, but though there were a million and one reasons they hadn't had any time together, Megan's words had hit home. Izzy was sure, quite sure, that Diego was pulling back—he looked terrible. Well, still absolutely gorgeous, except there were black rings under his eyes and he was more unshaven than usual and there was just this air to him that his world was heavy. And Izzy was quite sure she was a part of his problem. 'Her obs are good.' He checked Tilia's chart. 'She's put on more weight.' And then he suggested that while Tilia was sleeping she watch a video in the parents' room, but apnoea was the last thing Izzy wanted to deal with right now, she was having enough trouble remembering to breathe herself.

'I'm going to go home now.' She looked down at her sleeping daughter, because it was easier than looking at him with tears in her eyes. She didn't want to push or question, because she didn't want to sound needy—but, hell, she felt needy.

They had made love and suddenly everything had changed.

'I'd better make sure everything's ready for the big day. I'll see you in the morning,' Izzy said, and watched him swallow. 'You can wave her off...'

'I've got a meeting tomorrow morning,' Diego said, and she couldn't mask her disappointment. She wasn't asking him to take her baby home with him, or to out them to her family, just for him to be there, even if all he could manage was professional on the day she took her daughter home, she wanted that at least.

'Can you reschedule?' She hated to nag but hated it more that he shook his head.

'I really can't.'

'There's a call for you, Diego.' Rita came over.

'Thanks.'

'The travel agent,' Rita added, and Diego wasn't sure if she'd done it deliberately, but Rita must have felt her back burning as she walked off, with the blistering look Diego gave her.

'My father,' Diego said eventually, but he could barely look her in the eyes. 'He's sick. Very sick,' he added. 'I wanted to speak to you properly—I need to go back.'

Izzy nodded and held Tilia just a little bit tighter, felt her warm weight, and it was actually Tilia who gave her strength. 'Of course you do.'

'Diego!' She could hear shouts for his attention, hear

the summons of the emergency bell, and for now the travel agent would be forgotten, but only for now. His real future was just being placed temporarily on hold.

Izzy sat there and held her baby, her world, her family, and she was sure, quite sure, that she was about to lose Diego to his.

'Thank you.' Izzy said it a hundred times or more.

To Richard, to Chris, to Rita, to all the staff that popped in to say goodbye and wish her and Tilia well, but the people that mattered most weren't there. Megan, Brianna and Diego had a 'meeting'. And though the NICU was used to babies going home, Izzy wasn't used to taking one home and wished they could have been there for this moment.

'She looks such a big girl.' Gwen was the doting grandmother now and her father carried the car seat with Tilia inside. Finally she was out of the neonatal unit and taking her baby home.

'You know I'm happy to stay over. Between your mother and I, you don't have to be on your own for a few weeks….'

Except she wanted to be alone.

Or not quite alone.

There was the one she wanted to share this moment walking towards her now, with Brianna and Megan at his side, and with a stab of realisation at her own selfishness Izzy realised just how important their 'meeting' had been.

Diego was in a suit and he'd discarded the tie, but Izzy knew it had been a black one. Megan was in dark grey and Brianna too.

'Hey! Looks who's going home.' Brianna snapped to happy, fussed and cooed over Tilia, and Megan gave her friend a hug, but it was more than a little awkward, almost a relief when Megan had to dash off.

Had to dash off.

Megan actually thought she might vomit.

She felt like this each and every time she had to attend one of her precious patients' funerals, but today had been worse. With Josh back in her life Megan was having enough trouble holding things together, but when even Diego had struggled through a hymn, when the one who never got too involved held the song sheet and she could see his hand shaking, this morning had been the worst of them all.

Bar one.

'Megan!' Josh caught her arm as she tried to dash past him, his face the last she needed to see now. He took in her clothes and pale cheeks, her lips so white she looked as if she might faint at any moment. 'I'm sorry...'

'Sorry?' She was close to ballistic as she shot the word out and Josh blinked.

'You've clearly just been to a funeral...'

'Perk of the job,' Megan spat. 'I get to go to lots. I get to stand there and relive it over and over.'

'Is Megan okay?' Izzy watched from a distance as her friend ran up the corridor.

'It's been a tough morning,' Diego said. 'I'll talk to her later. You concentrate on you for now—enjoy taking Tilia home.'

'Thanks for everything,' Gwen said. 'Everyone's been marvellous.' And Izzy caught Diego's eyes and they shared a teeny private smile at her mother's choice of words.

'Thank you,' she said, and because she had hugged Brianna and Megan, she got to hug him, and then he had to go and so did Izzy, but she wished, how she wished, it was him taking them home.

CHAPTER FOURTEEN

HER parents adored Tilia.

It was, of course, a relief, but it came with a down side.

Instead of Gwen bossing and taking over and whizzing round the house doing the little jobs that were rapidly turning into big jobs, the doting grandparents sat on the sofa, cooing over their granddaughter, occasionally rising to make a drink or lunch, then it was back to admiring their granddaughter. Then when Tilia fell asleep Gwen shooed Izzy off for a sleep of her own as she headed for the door, keen to get out of the way before Henry's parents arrived, because Tilia's two sets of grandparents in the same room wasn't going to happen for a while yet.

'You're supposed to sleep when the baby does,' was Gwen's less than helpful advice.

Except Izzy couldn't.

She lay in her bed and stared at her daughter—wished her homecoming could somehow have been different, wished for so many things for her, and for herself too. Unable to settle, Izzy headed downstairs, made herself a coffee and rather listlessly flicked through her neglected post as she waited for the kettle to boil.

And it came with no ceremony no warning.

What she'd expected Izzy didn't really know. The envelope looked like any of the others from the insurance company and she just assumed there was something else they were requesting that she send. She briefly skimmed the letter, intending to read it properly later, but it wasn't a request for more information.

Instead, it was closure.

No relief washed over her. She read the letter again and stared at the cheque, and she didn't know how she felt, except it was starting to look a lot like angry. Angry at Henry for what he had done to her life, for the money that couldn't fix this, for her daughter who was without a father and for all that Izzy would have to tell her one day.

Izzy had never felt so alone.

The only person she wanted now was Diego.

Except how could she foist more of her drama on him? And, anyway, he would soon be back in Spain.

Lonely was a place she had better start to get used to.

Though she was beyond tired, when Henry's parents arrived she made them coffee and put out cake and tried small talk as Tilia slept on. In the end, Izzy gave in and brought her daughter down. She watched her mother-in-law's lips disappear when Izzy said, no, Tilia wasn't due for a feed yet and, no, she didn't need a bath.

'I'll do it,' Mrs Bailey fussed. 'You won't have to do a thing.'

'She's asleep,' Izzy pointed out, 'and a bath exhausts her.' And exhausted was all she felt when, clearly disappointed with the social skills of a tiny baby, Henry's parents left.

The house that had been so tidy looked like a bomb

site; there were coffee cups and plates all over the kitchen and Izzy went to load the dishwasher but realised that she had to empty if first and right now that task seemed too big.

There were bottles to be made up, once she had sterilised them, washing to be put on—eight hours home and Izzy, who had felt so confident, who had wished for this moment, when finally she was home alone with her daughter, wanted to go back to the safety of the nursery.

She could hear Tilia waking up at completely the wrong moment, because long held-back tears were coming to the fore.

She didn't want an insurance payout, she didn't want to raise her baby alone. She wanted to have met Diego when she was who she had once been, except this was who she was now.

A mother.

Which meant even when her own heart was bleeding, she had to somehow put her grief on hold and pick up her screaming baby at the same time the phone rang and the doorbell went and she remembered that it was bin night tonight.

'She's fine,' Izzy said down the phone through gritted teeth to her mother and, holding a phone and her baby, somehow answered the front door, and there, out of his suit and in his white nursing uniform, was Diego, carrying a tray with two coffees, which he quickly put down and took from Izzy a screaming, red-faced Tilia. 'She's due for a feed,' Izzy said to Gwen. 'Babies are supposed to cry.' As she reassured her mother, Izzy glanced at Diego. She so hadn't wanted him to catch her like this. He was gorgeous amidst the chaos and started to make up bottles with his free hand far more skilfully than she could with two. The last time he had been here, her house had been spotless, ready at any given second for the real estate agent to warn her he was bringing someone round. Her intention, if Diego ever came over, had been to have Tilia asleep and the house looking fantastic. Oh, and for her to be looking pretty good too—just to show him that a baby didn't have to change things!

By the time she had hung up the phone to her mother, Diego was cooling a bottle under the tap and though pleased to see him, Izzy could hardly stand what was about to come next. She tried to make a little joke, tried to lighten the tense mood, tried to tell him in one line how she knew and understood that everything must now change.

'If you've come for torrid sex…' Izzy smiled as he came in '…you've come to the wrong house!'

'I couldn't even manage a slow one!' For the first time in days Diego grinned. 'All I want to do is sleep.'

'The perfect guy.'

She wasn't joking.

She so wasn't joking.

'I wore my uniform in case you had visitors.' He was changing Tilia's nappy. 'I was going to say it was a house call!' He smiled down at Tilia. 'Do you think they'd have believed me?'

'I have no idea,' Izzy admitted.

'It's a good idea…' Diego seemed to ponder it for a moment. 'It's always hard when you leave NICU.'

'I would have been fine…' Izzy said, and then she paused and then she told them what she couldn't face telling her own parents yet, what she dreaded telling

Henry's. 'The insurance paid.' She was so glad he didn't comment. 'The mortgage and everything,' Izzy elaborated, and Diego knew this was the very last thing she needed to deal with today. 'I just wanted to bring her home,' Izzy said. 'I just wanted one day where I can pretend it's normal for her.'

'Here.' He took the letter and folded it, threw it in the kitchen drawer as if it was a shopping list. 'Think about it later.'

But it was already there and she told Diego that and he just stood there, let her rant and rave for a while and then told her an impossible truth.

'You need to forgive him, Izzy.'

'Forgive him?' Diego was supposed to be on her side, Diego was supposed to be as angry with Henry as she was, yet he steadfastly refused to go there.

'For your daughter's sake.' Diego stood firm. 'Don't you think he'd rather be here?' Diego demanded. 'Don't you think he'd rather be here today, bringing his daughter home from the hospital, enjoying this moment? Without forgiveness you won't get peace.'

'And you know all about it, do you?'

Diego didn't answer. Instead he sat on the sofa, put his feet up on the coffee table and fed Tilia as Izzy sat there, refusing to believe it was that simple to move on.

'He's looking after her.' Diego fed Tilia her bottle. 'Maybe this is the only way he could look after you both.' He looked down at Tilia. 'You need to forgive him for this little girl's sake.' He handed her baby to her. 'You need to be able to speak to her about her father without bitterness in your voice, because you don't want her to grow up feeling it.'

'It's so hard, though.' She knew he was right, but it was *so* hard.

'Then keep working on it.' Diego was resolute. 'Fake it,' he said, 'like I told you that first day, and eventually it might even be real.'

He made it sound doable. He knelt beside her as she cradled Tilia and she couldn't imagine these past weeks without him, or rather she could and how very different they would have been!

He turned things around. His calm reason, his humour, he himself allowed rapid healing. He made her stronger, made her get there sooner, so much sooner and so much stronger that as she sat in the silence and nursed her baby, Izzy knew she could face it, could do it alone if she had to.

Thanks to Diego.

She changed Tilia, put her back into her cot and stood as she watched her daughter sleeping, and the strength of his arms around her made her able to say it.

'Your father loves you, Tilia. He's looking after you.'

And then she did what she had never done and certainly didn't want to on the day she bought her baby home. She sobbed and she cried and Tilia slept right through it, and Diego lay on the bed with her and with his help she got through another bit she had dreaded.

'You should sleep when the baby does,' Diego said, only he didn't leave her to it. Instead he took off his uniform and climbed into bed beside her. Maybe he didn't have the heart to dump her on the day her baby came home, and maybe she should just be grateful for the reprieve, but Izzy was fast realising it was better to face things and so, in the semi-dark room with his arms

around her she did the next bit she was dreading and
asked him about his father.

'He had a seizure. They did an MRI and he has a brain
tumour—they're operating next Thursday. Izzy, I don't
want to leave now, but I really feel I should go home and
see him before the operation. It's just for a few days.'

'Of course you have to see him. He's your father.'
And then she took a breath and made herself say it.
'Have they asked you to move home?'

There was a long silence.

'My mother asked if I could take some time and come
home for a while. If he survives the surgery it will be a
long rehabilitation. He won't be operating again—they
expect some paralysis.' She felt the tension build in him.
'I've said I can't. The truth is, I won't. The way my father
treated me, the names he called me, the taunts even now.
He still goads me because I choose to nurse.' He shook
his head. 'I want time with you...'

And it was the answer she wanted. It just wasn't the
right one.

'You need to resolve things, Diego.'

'Flights are cheap, I can come and go. Don't worry
about it, Izzy. I've been trying not to burden you with
it.'

'Talk to me,' Izzy said, because she wanted more of
him than he was giving.

'Okay.' He told her the truth. 'How are we supposed
to get to know each other if I am in Spain? How are
we supposed to make each other happy, if you are here
and I am there? There's taking it slowly and then there's
a place where you take it so slowly you stop.' And so
then did Diego. 'We can't do this tonight. Let's not

worry about it now and just try and enjoy the rest of tonight—having Tilia home…'

There was no hope of pretending a baby didn't change things because there wasn't even a crackle of sexual tension in the air. She slept like a log and actually so did Diego. And how nice it was to have her own modern matron to get up at midnight and again at four and bring her Tilia's bottle and then to put her back in her crib and to sleep again.

Diego was asleep and he rolled into Izzy, his large, warm body cradling, spooning into hers, and it was the nicest place she had ever known in her life—Tilia sleeping safely, Diego beside her, peace in her heart about Henry, summer rain rattling the windows. She had everything here in this room, only she wanted still more.

She just didn't quite know what.

Izzy found out what woke Diego at five as the most basic alarm clock stirred and she lay with him in this lovely silent place, just before waking, and Izzy closed her eyes and felt the lazy roam of his body, the natural wander of his hands before he awakened, and it wasn't sleep she wanted but him, so she pushed herself a little into him, loving the feel of a half-asleep Diego, a man following his instinctive want and her want calling him. Sex, Izzy learnt, could be peaceful and healing. She was warm and he slipped in and filled her, he was wrapped around her and deep within her, with no words needed because the air tasted of them.

She could never have imagined such peace, even as he drove in deeper, even as she throbbed in orgasm. All she wanted was peace and this every morning and the only person who could give her that was him.

'*Mierda*!' His curse woke her up an hour later, and was completely merited as it was the first time in his life he'd overslept. She drifted back to sleep as Diego dived under the shower and Izzy suddenly let out a curse of her own a few minutes later as she heard the garbage truck thumping down the street. She had to quickly find a dressing gown and race to get the bins out, then she took two coffees back to bed.

'Your razor's blunt.' He grinned as he came out of the shower and then he looked at her. 'Why is your hair wet?'

'I forgot to put the bins out last night.'

'Did you catch them?' Diego asked, and the conversation was normal and Diego looked so much better than he had last night. More than that, Izzy felt better too. 'I'll get it from everyone this morning—at least I'm only on till one,' Diego said as he hauled on his clothes.

'You'll only be a few minutes late.' Izzy grimaced as she looked at the clock, only Diego wasn't worried about the time. He drank the coffee she had made, glanced in at Tilia who was starting to stir and then went down stairs and came back with a bottle in a jug and his satchel, which looked curiously sexy over his shoulder. He mimicked nosy Rita. '*You look tired, Diego. Did you not get much sleep, Diego?* And then...' he rolled his eyes '...she'll subtly talk about the Dark Ages, when she brought her baby home from the hospital! You wait,' Diego said, and drained his coffee. 'I guarantee it.'

He didn't need to.

As he kissed her and left, Izzy lay there and tried to wrap her head around what had happened. Somehow, despite everything, last night, Tilia's first night home, *had* been wonderful, but more than that, Izzy realised, she didn't need Diego's guarantees—she was starting to find her own.

CHAPTER FIFTEEN

'THANKS for seeing me.'

She was back again, only this time she wanted to be there.

And Izzy didn't insist on the office, it was nice to just walk around the hospital grounds and not try to convince Jess everything was perfect. In fact, she rather hoped Jess would convince her that she was going out of her mind.

That she was mad, that it was absolutely ridiculous to be even considering going to Spain.

Izzy wanted logic and reason to preside, for Jess to tell her to wait twelve months, for her to tell her she was rushing in, for her to warn her to be careful.

Only when she spilled it all out, Jess didn't do that.

'I let Henry consume me,' Izzy said. 'In the end, I hardly saw my family and friends.'

'Is Diego anything like Henry?'

'No,' Izzy said. 'But as you said, people suggest you wait twelve months before making any major life decisions…'

'I offered you a theory,' Jess said, 'but as you pointed out yourself, we don't all have the requisite twelve months to lick our wounds and heal. Life keeps coming at us, bad things, good things, wonderful things…'

'So you don't think I'm crazy to be considering going to Spain.'

'I'd think you were crazy if you were going with no consideration.' Izzy's face tightened in frustration at Jess's refusal to commit.

'Even my friends are warning me to be careful!' Izzy said, still reeling from Megan's warning. 'Megan was so...' She tried to find the right words. 'I've never seen her so upset.'

'And then she apologised,' Jess pointed out. 'Izzy, in medicine we are used to coming up with solutions.' Izzy frowned and then Jess corrected herself. 'As a doctor you are used to coming up with an answer, finding the best course of treatment, perhaps telling the patient what needs to be done. My job is different,' Jess explained. 'Of course I would love to rush in at times, but I have to ask myself, would that really help? The best I can do is allow you to explore your options—which,' she added, 'you're doing.'

'This morning,' Izzy explained, 'it was normal.' She looked at Jess. 'We could have been anywhere in the world and it wouldn't have mattered. Diego says that he doesn't want to burden me with his stuff...'

'Is it a burden?' Jess asked.

'No,' Izzy admitted. 'It's harder not knowing how he's feeling.' And Jess *was* so easy to talk to that Izzy admitted something else on her mind. 'Shouldn't I just know?' Izzy asked. 'If it's so right, what I am doing here?'

'You're looking out for you,' Jess said. 'Which shows how far you've come.' Jess gave her a smile. 'For many years, Izzy, you've had your inner voice turned off. You told yourself and others that everything was okay, when, in fact, it was far from it. Can I suggest your inner voice is coming back?'

Izzy nodded.

'You might need a little help recognising it at times, but it's there, if only you listen.'

Jess was right.

So right that there was somewhere else Izzy needed to be.

'I need to talk to Diego. I need to tell him just how much he means to me.' She stalled for a second, wondered how she could be so absolutely honest with someone if it was going to freak him out, that his girlfriend of a few weeks would drop everything and follow him to Spain with a baby in tow. 'How?'

'Maybe ring him, ask him to come over tonight.'

But she didn't mean that. 'He's at my house now,' Izzy said. 'Watching Tilia.'

'Can I ask where he thinks you are?'

'Oh, I told him I was seeing you.' Jess watched Izzy's slow reaction as her own words registered with herself. Her casual words sinking in. She had, on ringing Jess, asked Diego if he'd mind watching Tilia for an hour or so. He hadn't probed, hadn't asked why. Diego had come straight over from his half-day shift, had just accepted that this was where she wanted to be, that this was what she needed now.

'Not many people who come into my office can say that,' Jess said. 'Izzy, I think it's wonderful that you're going to talk with Diego and be honest, but can I suggest when you are telling him how you feel that you also listen? He might surprise you with what he has to say.'

* * *

'Shh!' Diego put a finger up to his lips as Izzy burst in the house. She'd practised her speech, gathering strength all the way home, and had swept into her house, ready to blurt it all out, but as she'd entered the living room Diego, lying on the sofa with Tilia on his shoulder, had halted her. 'She's nearly asleep.'

Izzy could tell from her little red face that it had been a noisy hour. There were bottles and soothers and half the contents of the nappy bag all strewn around the sofa and they sat quietly, Diego chatting low and soft in Spanish, till finally, *finally* Tilia gave in and Diego gingerly stood, taking her to her cot. Izzy had to sit, tapping her toes in nervousness, as she waited for Diego. She listened to the intercom and heard Tilia, on being laid in the cot, protest for a few minutes at being out of his arms.

Who could blame her?

'Diego.' Izzy's voice was firm when he came into the room, because if she didn't tell him now, she might never do so.

'One moment…' He flashed that lovely smile. 'I *must* eat, and make a phone call.' He picked up his phone and headed to the kitchen. 'My mother rang. I told her I would call her back as soon as I got Tilia to sleep.' He rolled his eyes, clearly not relishing the prospect.

'How is she?'

'The same,' Diego said, and he was chatting easily, slicing up bread and tomatoes as Izzy talked on.

'She wants you to come to Spain, doesn't she?'

'And as I told her, I am coming.'

She could hear him keeping his voice light, but she could see the dark smudges under his eyes, almost feel the burden he was carrying alone, and her speech went out of the window because Izzy realised it wasn't about whether she'd follow him or not—it wasn't about her, this was about Diego.

'I can understand her being upset. She knows that you need to spend some time with your father,' Izzy said. 'Not just a quick visit.'

'I have a job, I have a life here.'

'And your family is there,' Izzy said, and she watched his tongue roll in his cheek.

'Do you want pepper?' was his response, and then he changed the subject. 'I was right about Rita. All morning she spoke about bringing her daughter home from the hospital, her daughter bringing her daughter home from the hospital…' Izzy would be sneezing till next year with the amount of pepper he was shaking! 'Then she started about how the place was quiet without Tilia, how she'd love to know how she was getting on.' He looked at Izzy, a guilty smile on his face. 'Do you know what I did?'

Izzy shook her head. She didn't want to hear about Rita, she wanted to sort out their own situation, but he did make her smile and he did make her laugh, he did make her happy, then she frowned as he continued, because in all of this he made her happy.

'She was at lunch when I left and I got a piece of A4 paper and wrote *Gone Fishing* and stuck it on her computer.'

And she could have laughed, could have just stayed happy, but Izzy was realising that wasn't quite what she wanted.

'You told me I needed to forgive Henry,' Izzy said. 'And it's the best thing I've done. You need to make peace with your father and if it means going to Spain, then that's what it means. This is something you need to sort out and I'll be okay with whatever you decide.' She took a deep breath and made herself say it. 'Whatever *we* decide.' And she was so, so wary of making demands on him, of foisting herself and her baby and all her problems onto a man who she had so recently met, so she offered a word, *we* instead of *you*, and she held that deep breath and wondered if he'd even notice.

He did.

'There's nothing to decide. We don't have to discuss it. I'm so angry with him, Izzy. Part of me doesn't even want to go for a few days, and still he goads—women's work...' He shook his head. 'You don't need this now.'

'But I do,' Izzy said. 'Because I'm a lot stronger than you think. I'm certainly stronger than I was even a few weeks ago, even since yesterday. You can tell me about things like Toby and that you've just got a call that your father is sick and how difficult that must be for you, how hard it was to get through Toby's funeral with your father so ill... We chose the wrong words, Diego—that we will last for as long as we make each other happy. Well, that's not real life. How about we will last as long as we make the world better for each other than it would be without?'

'Better?'

'Better.' Izzy nodded. 'Because I'd have got through all this and I'd have been fine, but it's been better with you. The same way you'll get through your father's illness and whatever lies ahead...'

It was a new contract, a different agreement, and Diego checked the small print.

'What do *you* want, Izzy?' Diego asked.

And she screwed her eyes closed and made herself say it.

'You,' Izzy admitted. 'And I'm sorry if it's too soon and too much and too everything, but that's how I feel.'

'Where do *you* want to be?' She peeled her eyes open just a little bit and he wasn't running out of the door and collapsing under the pressure of her honest admission—he was just standing there, smiling.

'With you,' Izzy said, and then made herself elaborate. 'And if that means going to Spain, I will. As soon as she's big enough...'

'Tilia comes first.' Diego stood firm. 'Always in this, she must come first.' And he sounded like a father and then she found out, he felt like a father. 'Always people tell me that my job will get tougher when I am a father—it annoys me, because I was there for Fernando. Always I tell them they don't know what they are talking about.' He looked right at her. 'They were right. Toby's funeral was awful, for all the reasons they are all awful, only it wasn't that my father was sick that upset me, it was how I felt about Tilia. She was a patient on my ward and I had to work, to look after her instead of be there for her...' He closed his eyes in frustration. 'Do you know what I want, Izzy?' She shook her head. 'Today, when Rita was going on, I wanted to take out my phone and show her a photo of Tilia, and I want to tell my mother when she calls and she thinks it is a baby crying at work that I am not at work—I am with my family.' She caught her breath. 'I want you and Tilia as my family.'

And good families tried to sort things out, even when the phone rang during important conversations. Diego let it continue to ring.

'Then tell her,' Izzy said.

'Tell her?' Diego checked, and Izzy nodded. 'You're sure?'

'Very,' Izzy said. 'We don't have to hide anything, we can tell people and it's up to them what they think.'

'We know,' Diego said, because they did.

It was time for the world to know the truth they had just confirmed. He pressed redial and put it on speaker and then took a deep breath as his mother answered. *'Qué pasa?'* He tipped into Spanish, chatting away to his mother, and she heard the words *bebé* and Tilia and *novia,* which Izzy knew meant girlfriend, and he occasionally rolled his eyes as his mother's voice got louder, but Diego never matched it, talking in his deep, even voice as *madre* got a little more demanding. And Izzy guessed when he used the word *prematuro* and his mother became more insistent that he was telling her it wasn't so easy—that his *familia* couldn't just pack up and come, and she stood there in wonder because he was talking to them about her, that she too was his family.

'Te quiero.'

He ended the most difficult call with *I love you* and when Señora Ramirez huffed, Diego grinned and said it again. *'Te quiero.'*

'Te quiero, Diego,' his mother admitted finally.

'Better?' Izzy asked, and after a moment he nodded. 'I said that I will be there for the operation and I have said I will come out again just as soon as I can…'

'What did she say about us?'

'That it's too fast, too soon—even though I lied.' Diego gave a bit of a sheepish grin. 'I hope you don't mind but we've been together a few months, not a few weeks.'

And then he kissed her and that made it better too.

His kiss made things better—they didn't fix, they didn't solve anything, they just made it all so much nicer.

'*Te amo*,' Diego said. 'It means I love you.'

'I thought it was *Te quiero*,' Izzy said, and she smiled because there was a lot to suddenly get used to and, oh, yes, a new language to learn too!

'*Te quiero*, what I said to my mother, does mean I love you,' Diego explained, 'but it's a different I love you. *Te amo* I save for you.' Then he kissed her again, made the world just that bit better till it was Izzy's turn to admit it.

'*Te amo*.' She spoke her first two words in Spanish to the only person who would ever hear them, to the man she had loved from the moment she had met him, to the man who, it turned out, felt the same.

And now they were a family.

EPILOGUE

YOU can't do it for her.

You can't change the world.

She might go back...

Diego didn't say any of those words and Izzy would love him for ever for it.

There was a trust fund for Tilia and when she was old enough and deciding her options, Izzy could tell her that her father was still supporting her.

And there was the house to fall back on as well.

A house Izzy had wanted to get rid of, a house she had hated, but now she could remember the good times there too.

And perhaps she could just sell. There were some gorgeous cottages along the coast she had considered but, as Diego had pointed out, his apartment had brilliant views and they could babyproof the balcony.

Diego was Daddy, or Papà.

They didn't ram it down anyone's throats, and certainly not to Henry's parents, but behind closed doors, when it was just they three, no one really knew that this very new couple were an established family.

And, no, Izzy couldn't change the world.

But she could help when someone wanted to change theirs.

'The washing machine jumps,' Izzy explained. 'If you put in too many towels, you'll find it halfway across the kitchen.'

'Thank you.' Evelyn stood in the hall, her face bruised and swollen, leaning on her son for support. 'We won't stay for long…'

'Stay for as long as you need,' Izzy said, and she meant it. 'Get your son through his exams, take your time…'

Many phone conversations, and a couple of sessions Izzy had arranged for Evelyn with a counsellor who specialised in these things had all helped Evelyn in her decision to take those first steps to empowerment. And on the eve of Izzy heading back to Spain, she realised why she'd chosen to keep the house.

'How long are you away for?' Evelyn asked.

'A couple of months this time around,' Izzy said. 'We're back and forth a bit. Diego's father hasn't been too well, but he's improving.' She glanced at her watch. 'I really have to go.'

And she knew, she just knew as she handed Evelyn the keys, that in six months or a year those keys would go to someone else who needed them—and Izzy wished she had a thousand keys, or a hundred thousand keys, except she didn't. She had one set and she would do her level best to use them wisely.

'How is she?' Diego asked, as Izzy climbed into the car, and looked over at four-month-old Tilia, who was sleeping in the back.

'She's going to be fine,' Izzy said. 'She just doesn't know it yet.' She looked at Diego, his face surly as it always was as they were about to head for his home. He loved St Piran but, despite it all, he loved his family too and so, after a lot of toing and froing, they were heading for a few months in Madrid. Diego had a temporary position at his father's old hospital and Izzy, well, she wanted to practise her Spanish.

'It'll be fine.' Izzy grinned. 'Your dad's being lovely now.'

'Yes, there's nothing like a brain tumour to help you get your priorities straight in life. At least he's stopped saying I'm gay.'

That still made her laugh.

She looked at the love of her life, at a man who hadn't stuck by her—no, instead he had pushed her.

Pushed her to be the best, the happiest she could be.

To go out, to make friends, to work, to laugh, to love, to heal, and she was ticking every box.

He put a smile on her face every day and watching him scowl as Heathrow approached, and later, watching him haul the luggage off the conveyor belt when they landed in Madrid and Diego braced himself for another round of facing his demons, Izzy was more than happy to put a smile on his.

'I'd help, but I shouldn't be lifting.'

'I can manage.'

There was the stroller and another of their suitcases whizzing past but Diego missed them and turned round, that frown on his face he got when he didn't quite get what she was saying.

'Tell him he's going to be a grandfather,' Izzy said. 'That should keep him happy.'

'A grandfather *again*,' Diego said, because at every turn, with everyone, Tilia was his, and Izzy knew a new baby wouldn't change that fact.

She knew.

'What took us so long?' Diego pulled her and Tilia into his arms, and kissed Izzy thoroughly right there in the airport, but this was Spain so no one batted an eyelid.

Six months from meeting and now two babies between them—and Izzy defied anyone to say it was way too soon.

They'd been waiting for each other all their lives.

2 FREE BOOKS
AND A SURPRISE GIFT

We would like to take this opportunity to thank you for reading this Mills & Boon® book by offering you the chance to take TWO more specially selected books from the Medical™ series absolutely FREE! We're also making this offer to introduce you to the benefits of the Mills & Boon® Book Club™—

- **FREE home delivery**
- **FREE gifts and competitions**
- **FREE monthly Newsletter**
- **Exclusive Mills & Boon Book Club offers**
- **Books available before they're in the shops**

Accepting these FREE books and gift places you under no obligation to buy, you may cancel at any time, even after receiving your free books. Simply complete your details below and return the entire page to the address below. You don't even need a stamp!

YES Please send me 2 free Medical books and a surprise gift. I understand that unless you hear from me, I will receive 5 superb new stories every month including two 2-in-1 books priced at £5.30 each and a single book priced at £3.30, postage and packing free. I am under no obligation to purchase any books and may cancel my subscription at any time. The free books and gift will be mine to keep in any case.

Ms/Mrs/Miss/Mr _____ Initials _____

_____

Surname _____

Address _____

_____

_____ Postcode _____

E-mail _____

Send this whole page to: Mills & Boon Book Club, Free Book Offer, FREEPOST NAT 10298, Richmond, TW9 1BR